ROBERTA KRAY
THE DEBT

sphere

SPHERE

First published in Great Britain by Constable in 2006
Paperback published by Robinson in 2006
This edition published in 2019 by Sphere

3 5 7 9 10 8 6 4 2

Copyright © Roberta Kray 2006

The moral right of the author has been asserted.

*All characters and events in this publication, other than those
clearly in the public domain, are fictitious and any resemblance
to real persons, living or dead, is purely coincidental.*

All rights reserved.
No part of this publication may be reproduced, stored in a
retrieval system, or transmitted, in any form or by any means, without
the prior permission in writing of the publisher, nor be otherwise circulated
in any form of binding or cover other than that in which it is published
and without a similar condition including this condition being
imposed on the subsequent purchaser.

A CIP catalogue record for this book
is available from the British Library.

ISBN 978-0-7515-5980-4

Typeset in Garamond by M Rules
Printed and bound in Great Britain by
Clays Ltd, Elcograf S.p.A.

Papers used by Sphere are from well-managed forests
and other responsible sources.

MIX
Paper from
responsible sources
FSC® C104740

Sphere
An imprint of
Little, Brown Book Group
Carmelite House
50 Victoria Embankment
London EC4Y 0DZ

An Hachette UK Company
www.hachette.co.uk

www.littlebrown.co.uk

Through her marriage to Reggie Kray, Roberta Kray has a unique and authentic insight into London's East End. Roberta met Reggie in early 1996 and they married the following year; they were together until Reggie's death in 2000. Roberta is the author of many previous bestsellers including *No Mercy, Dangerous Promises, Exposed* and *Survivor*.

Also by Roberta Kray

The Pact
The Lost
Strong Women
The Villain's Daughter
Broken Home
Nothing But Trouble
Bad Girl
Streetwise
Dangerous Promises
Exposed
Survivor
Deceived

Non-fiction
Reg Kray: A Man Apart

*For Reg, who had so many
stories left to tell . . .*

*And with thanks to Karen Alexander,
Janelle Posey and John Ledgard for
their friendship and support*

Prologue

Johnny

So I'm smiling at the plump florid man who's sitting across the table. It's always a pleasure to see old friends. Time passes slowly inside, the hours dictated not by revolutions of the earth but by an unchanging routine, each week identical to the last, each year a groundhog repetition of the one before. So I'm staring intently, drinking in every detail; I'm making the most of this most welcome of visits. How long has it been since we last met? It must be over eighteen years.

I've still not decided how exactly I should kill him.

'How's the family then? Dee's okay, I hope? And those boys of yours? They must be all grown up by now.'

'Fine, fine,' the stout man replies too quickly.

Perhaps a look of sly amusement creeps into my eyes but I'm careful to keep the voice genial. 'Glad to hear it. You're looking well too.'

This, of course, is a lie. That Jim Buckley wishes he had never stepped across the threshold is patently clear. His red face has taken on a deeper shade of mauve and under his arms two widening stains of sweat expose his guilt. Never one to waste an opportunity, I press home the advantage. 'So what do you say, mate? We're only talking a couple of months. Shouldn't put you out too much.' I leave a friendly pause before dropping the bombshell. 'And don't forget – you owe me big time.'

The implicit threat has the desired effect. As Buckley's bowels cramp into dread, his distended stomach flinches against the table. I know what he's thinking: *Shit, this has been a mistake, a terrible shitting mistake.* Of course he realized the moment he opened the envelope and saw the visiting order that he should stay away. No point tempting providence. But then he couldn't live with the uncertainty either. He had to know if he was in the frame.

The word when it emerges is barely audible. 'What?'

I grant him a few more seconds of undiluted terror before starting to laugh. 'All those drinks, mate, all those free meals at the club. I reckon you owe me some hospitality.'

Jim's left leg is dancing a nervous jig, his heel beating a brisk staccato rhythm against the floor. I can read him like a book. He can't work out if I know. Do I? Don't I? His mind's spinning round like a waltzer, getting dizzier by the second. He's starting to feel sick. But then logic kicks in and everything gradually slows. He considers that if I knew the truth he'd be dead by now, history, sleeping soundly with the little fishes. So as he's still alive that must surely mean . . . His mouth stumbles eagerly towards a smile of relief.

'Yeah,' he eventually croaks.

And who am I to disillusion him?

'Of course it goes without saying, I'll see you both right.' I glance around the hall, gesturing for him to move closer as I lower my voice to a conspiratorial whisper. 'It's all still there – you know what I mean. I just need somewhere to stay when I come out, somewhere private, somewhere I can keep my head down until ...'

I pause as Buckley's scared piggy eyes slowly brighten into greed.

The seconds tick by.

Fear battles unsuccessfully with avarice. 'How much?' he eventually murmurs.

'Five k.' I force my mouth into a curl. I'm close enough now to smell his stinking breath, close enough to wrap my fingers round his neck – but there's time enough for that. Inching back a fraction, I remove the temptation. 'In return for some privacy, right? I don't want the world and his dog to know where I am.'

Now Buckley's not the sharpest knife in the drawer but he's not completely stupid either. He shifts uneasily in his seat, a frown slowly puckering his forehead while he considers this unexpected proposition.

I sit back casually and fold my arms. I can sense his caution, can almost see it too, dripping like treacle through his treacherous mind. Silently, I wait. And believe me, if there's one skill Johnny Frank possesses it's patience. Never rush a sure bet. It takes a while, two minutes, maybe three, and I don't say a word but finally he produces the questions I've been anticipating.

'But why me? Why us? There must be—'

I have to fight to suppress the grin. 'Look,' I interrupt quickly, shifting forward and placing a firm hand reassuringly over his, 'I know we've had our differences but that's all behind us now, isn't it? It's in the past. I need someone I can trust, someone I can rely on. Everything's changed out there. I need some time, a bit of space while I make the . . . arrangements.'

How often have I rehearsed this glib disingenuous response? On at least a thousand occasions, cursing, raving, pacing my cell with my brains in the balance. Now my right hand curls tightly into a fist. *Fuck him*. It takes an effort to keep my voice steady but I do – I have to.

'It's okay, I'll understand if you . . . if you can't, that's fine. No hard feelings.' I give a swift dismissive shrug. 'Forget it.'

From the expression on his face it's clear there's nothing Buckley wants more than to forget the past – that dreadful place he's consigned to history. Nothing, perhaps, except for good hard cash. And the honeyed scent of money is wafting sweetly through the air. Things haven't been going so well lately. He could make some lousy excuse and leave but he won't. I know he won't. He's made the mental calculations and thinks he's got control.

Like a predatory snake he flicks out his tongue, moistening his lips. 'A couple of months?' he repeats tentatively.

I nod. 'Ten weeks max.' Aware my face is under scrutiny, I keep its expression benign. I even smile again. Now there's a genuine pleasure in the gesture, in the satisfaction of a job well done. The bastard's about to take the bait. There's no going back. This is the beginning of the end.

He grunts. 'I'll think about it.'

'Sure – but don't take too long. I'm out in a fortnight.'

Jim's eyes dart around the room, unsure as to where to settle. His head is saying yes, of course it is, there's all that lovely brass up for grabs, but his instinct is still whispering caution. And now he's thinking – what? He's thinking we were never mates, *never*, associates at best. He's trying to justify what he did, realigning the past and twisting wrong back into right. I was always out of his league, smarter, richer – and a fuck sight more successful. Flash, that's what he thinks I was, a smug self-satisfied git. And I can't argue with that. I had everything he wanted. I *was* everything he wanted. And he knows the only thing we ever had in common was … well, that's something he'd rather not dwell on; carnal knowledge of his wife is hardly the basis of an enduring friendship. Although he certainly got his own back. Eighteen years and counting.

Which is a reason and a half for him to just walk away.

But then there's the money.

His red face crunches into indecision. 'Give me a couple of days. I'll talk it over with Dee.'

As if outmanoeuvred by a master of negotiation, I shrug and say: 'Okay, make it ten but that's my final offer. Take it or leave it.'

He's shocked. His eyebrows hit the roof. Ten? Fuck, that's hardly a sum to be sneered at, not for a few weeks' bed and board. I must be desperate. And if I'm offering ten then how much more can he get his hands on? Oh, he remembers the job all right: Hatton Garden, late eighties – a haul of diamonds, and not just any chunks of ice but the rare and famous pink ones too. And those sweet babies are very much in fashion ...

Buckley's eyes gleam suddenly bright. This is an offer he can't refuse. As if he's doing *me* a favour, he sighs and says: 'Okay. It shouldn't be a problem.'

I quickly nod before he can change his mind again. 'Thanks. I appreciate it.'

We shake hands.

The bastard's palms are clammy. Surreptitiously, I reach down and wipe my fingers along my thighs. There's no such thing as something for nothing. Buckley should have learned that by now, but some people never learn – they go on making the same stupid mistakes over and over again.

Thank fucking Christ.

Chapter One

Simone

Now you don't just wake up one morning and find yourself inadvertently married to a gambling, womanizing, convicted fraudster – well, not unless you're a thirty-two-year-old accountant who's had her eyes firmly closed for the past five years. So okay, I'll put my hands up and say I've been a fool but that doesn't mean I haven't tried to make it work. And I doubt if Marc's the worst spouse in the world even if his CV does read like an illustrative extract from *The Smart Woman's Guide to Husbands to Avoid*.

No, I'm sure there are deadlier partners out there. He has his good points: he's generous, kind and indisputably sexy. On his good days he can even totter some way down the path towards love. But I guess the bottom line – and there's really no getting away from it – is that Marc Buckley's an out-and-out cheat.

So it's hardly a marriage made in heaven although I guess if nothing else it's been an education, a useful lesson in the triumph of adversity over hope. And I'll know not to make the same mistake again.

I'm almost home now, walking up the gravel drive, approaching the house. Despite the less-than-happy reflections on my personal life I'm actually smiling, for the snow has started to fall again, drifting down in muffling clouds and transforming all suburbia into a sparkling paradise of white. My feet may be cold but it's impossible to be downhearted in the light of so much beauty.

That is, until I step inside.

In the hallway I pause, senses alert, before carefully closing the door behind me. Such caution isn't strictly necessary for above the rumpus of my in-laws, locked once again in gladiatorial combat, my entrance will be neither heard nor cared about. As I climb the stairs the snow tumbles from my coat leaving a clear but rapidly melting trail of evidence.

Their voices penetrate even to the third floor, Dee's fierce and strident, Jim's equally booming but more defensive.

'I don't fucking want him here!'

'Well, you go and fucking tell him then!'

This is a battle that's been raging on and off for the last couple of weeks, a fight that's already diminished the china and has now progressed to sturdier projectiles. Whether any territory has been conceded is impossible to judge.

My money, as always, is on Dee.

With a sigh I open the door to the self-contained flat at the top of the house. In an attempt to block out the noise, the TV is turned up extra loud. Marc is lounging on the sofa, feet on the coffee table, watching – or at least pretending to watch – the evening news. His eyes are actually focused on an indeterminate point somewhere to the right of the box. A thin stream of smoke rises from his cigarette. On the screen the aftermath of yet another but more distant war is being played out, full-volume death and desolation spilling straight into our living room.

He glances up as if surprised to see me. 'Hi, love. Are those two still at it?'

'Full on.'

'Shit. Why can't they just ignore each other like any normal married couple?'

Like *us*, he means, as if non-communication is some higher art form, an ideal state to be aspired to. I try not to snarl. And as he clearly isn't going to wear out his legs by leaping up and welcoming me home with a beneficial cup of tea, I go to the kitchen and switch on the kettle myself. While I wait for it to boil I lean against the doorjamb and ask: 'So who exactly is this Johnny guy?'

Marc stubs out his cigarette and instantly lights another. 'If you're making a brew, I wouldn't mind a refill.'

Normally I'd tell him to get up off his arse and make it himself but tonight, desperate to know more about what's going on downstairs, I choose the road of least resistance. 'Okay.' Sometimes I feel more like a mother than a wife, attempting to squeeze out through constant repetition, bribery or corruption one tiny piece of information from a recalcitrant infant. I ask again, casually: 'So what about this guy?'

He shrugs. 'Just some geezer they used to know. Johnny something. *Frank*, that's it. Johnny Frank. Dad's invited him to stay. He's been away for a few years.'

'Away as in abroad or away as in *inside*?'

He gives me one of his thin-skinned sensitive looks. 'What does it matter?'

'It doesn't,' I answer patiently. 'I was just wondering. Only there's major hostilities going on downstairs and he seems to be at the centre of it all.'

It's always hard to tell which way he'll jump. Marc's moods come and go. Sometimes he'll close up tight as a clam and like some Trappist monk take a convenient vow of silence. But this evening, perhaps as sick as I am of his parents' constant rowing, he decides to share his knowledge. Leaning his head against the back of the sofa he declares: 'He's been in the nick – for the past eighteen years.' My mouth falls open. 'What?' He nods. And in case that announcement might not have shocked me sufficiently, he adds dramatically: 'For murder.'

My instant reaction is one of horror. I'm hardly surprised Dee is throwing saucepans. 'What do you mean, *murder*? What *kind* of murder?' As if killing can be neatly categorized, from bad, to very bad, to disgustingly evil – the question sounds ridiculous even as I ask it. Perhaps I've been reading too many tabloids.

'Dunno,' he replies, as unconcerned about this apparent piece of minutia as he is about most things. 'Don't worry about it. Some villain. Roy Foster. It was years ago.'

I'm partly mollified, although I'm not sure I should be.

But at least it's not a child or a woman. 'And he's coming to stay here?'

'Not if Mum gets her way.'

'And if she doesn't?'

Marc shrugs again. 'Well, he's done his time. What's the problem?'

The problem is that it's hard enough living with a man you want to leave without his volatile parents, his psychotic brother, and now a convicted killer joining the scenario. If I still had a sense of humour, I'd laugh.

Marc, perhaps tired of the Question and Answer routine, is already putting on his jacket. 'Skip that tea, I've got to get to the club.'

And although I hate myself for doing it, despise myself for sounding like some suspicious nagging wife, I look at the clock and say: 'But it's only six thirty.'

'Exactly,' he replies briskly, 'if I don't go now, I won't get anything done. You know what the noise is like in that place – especially on a Saturday.' Then he softens and smiles. 'Hey, why don't you come along later? We could have a drink, grab something to eat.'

But he knows I hate the club. Jim's rather dismal lap-dancing establishment, situated on the rim of London's East End, is named, somewhat ironically, The Palace. Now, I'm pretty easy-going – each to their own and all that – but my idea of a good night out bears no relation to sitting in a smoky dungeon and watching ten sleekly oiled half-naked girls shake their butts at a crowd of sweaty and erectile men. Apart from which, my breasts just can't take the competition.

'Tempting as that offer is, I think I'll give it a miss.'

He grins, leans down and bestows a perfunctory kiss. 'Okay, love. Have a good evening. See you later.'

Then the door has closed and he's gone. Dressed in his suit and a new white shirt, he's prinked and pressed and closely shaved. It inevitably crosses my mind that he could be going to meet another woman, some twenty-something Tara or Tanya who will run her fingers, without judgement, through those tousled curls and gaze adoringly into his innocent blue eyes. And what is even more unsettling than this prospect is the fact that I don't really care; it's only my pride rather than my heart I'm trying to protect now.

Which isn't to say I don't care about Marc. I do. Between us there's still a tiny nugget left, a hard firm cyst of benign love and loyalty. It would be so much easier if we could just cut that part away.

I turn and step into the kitchen. Tea for one, then. And two minutes later I'm standing aimlessly by the window, sipping from the mug and gazing down into the garden. For God's sake, what am I doing? It's Saturday night! The weekend! And while the rest of the population is preparing for a riotous night out on the town all I need is a pair of fluffy slippers and a marginal shift in attitude to slip effortlessly into my dotage.

How did it come to this?

I'm not old. I'm only thirty-two. I can still walk and smile and dance. My auburn hair still shines and I've got a full set of teeth. On a good day I can even string a sentence together. Most of my mental processes, if not entirely intact, are in adequate condition and my body – although showing hints of betrayal – has not really yet embarked on that gravitational journey south. Even my wrinkles are slight enough to pass for laughter lines.

I don't have to sit around and watch TV. I don't have to vegetate. I could go out and party. I could paint the town as brightly red as anyone else. I could ring some friends and meet them for a drink ... except, well, to be quite honest we're currently a bit low on the friendship front.

If Katie was around it would be different, but my long-standing pal has sensibly decamped to Australia for the season of goodwill. I miss her.

'Why don't you come?' she'd asked a couple of months ago, spreading out the brochure in all its Technicolor luxury. 'The hotel's right on the beach. Sun, sea and buckets of wine – nothing but glorious self-indulgence. What do you reckon?'

I reckoned it would be pretty damn fine but with Marc only recently out of prison it hardly seemed feasible.

'Well, you can bring him along too!' she exclaimed, although the unspoken addendum of *if you really have to* hovered in the air between us. Because it's a fact that Katie doesn't like my husband much and it's not just to do with his financial indiscretions. Long before his sticky fingers brought him to the attention of the justice system, she had identified an even more fatal flaw in the character of Marc Buckley – he was not the faithful sort.

Not that she ever put it quite that bluntly. Smiling comments such as, 'That man's too handsome for his own good' or 'He's incredibly charming, isn't he?' were slipped almost as asides into our premarital conversations. Her implied criticisms were shrouded so carefully in compliments that, more often than not, they flew straight over my head. Or maybe, having balanced those rose-tinted glasses firmly on my nose, I was just loath to admit to chronic myopia.

But Katie was right. She clearly saw what I was blindly incapable of. However, she's never been smug about it since, never gloated once or reminded me of how stupid I was. Neither has she pushed or encouraged me to leave him, although she has let me know in her own subtle fashion that should I ever choose to go down that road then she will, as always, be there for me.

Sadly the jaunt to Australia, although alluring, was never feasible. For one, although I have some meagre savings, I'm not exactly rolling in money. And for two, having already lost their son to a couple of festive periods at Her Majesty's pleasure (he served eighteen months of his three-year sentence), Dee and Jim wouldn't be overjoyed at the prospect of forgoing yet another family Christmas. And who could blame them? It would have been selfish to even suggest it.

So I didn't.

And so while Katie is lounging on the beach, topping up her tan – I check my watch trying to recall the time difference – I'm wondering what other acquaintance I might contact to reestablish my credentials as a social human being. Slowly I flick through our address book, studying the pages with at first an eager and then a progressively despondent eye as each name is considered, thought about and then dismissed.

Of course it was different the first time Marc was convicted; then it was only a minor fraud, and he was so thoroughly repentant and so utterly convincing that even the judge was impressed. He wore his remorse as elegantly as his Savile Row suit. He claimed an aberration, a moment of weakness, depression, confusion, extenuating circumstances. He hung his head in stylish shame.

Six months, that's all he'd got. He was lucky.

Then friends had rallied round, giving him the benefit of the doubt. *Everyone makes mistakes*, they said softly. They were supportive and forgiving, overflowing with the milk of human kindness. They wrote him letters, sent him gifts, and invited me round for warming dinners and words of reassurance. Secretly, although they tried not to show it, they were fascinated by this vicarious brush with criminality and under the cover of sympathetic understanding probed for details of prison visits and life inside.

'So is the food really that bad?' they asked, wide-eyed, tucking into their Dover sole with renewed appetite.

'Does he have to share a cell?' They shuddered. 'Lord, just imagine, you could find yourself bunking up with—'

'What are the screws like? What about the other cons?'

They'd all watched *Bad Girls* and the occasional more brutal episodes of *Oz*. And having garnered the idiom, they'd strangely started to spill it back as if such talk might somehow make me feel more at ease.

'Are you allowed to touch or do you have to sit behind one of those barrier things? Are you allowed to kiss?'

'So Simone, how's he bearing up?'

My answer to the last question was always the same – a resigned, despondent shrug. 'Well, you know . . .' Although the truth was that he was bearing up just fine, as completely unfazed by this sudden change in circumstances as he was by everything else. Like a chameleon Marc had the ability to merge effortlessly into any environment.

But that wasn't what they wanted to hear. Not that they were nasty or cruel, it wasn't that, but in order to justify their faith in him – decent upright citizens as they were – they had to believe he possessed a degree of remorse from which some minor suffering necessarily ensued.

And who was I to disillusion them?

When Marc was released they welcomed him back with open arms and through their help and references he quickly got a new job. We moved across to the other side of the city and for the next eighteen months life almost returned to normal. With his talent and charm he skipped rapidly up the corporate ladder and by the time he reoffended even *I'd* started to believe that his lapse might have been an unfortunate blip in what might still prove to be a reasonably honest future.

Which only goes to show how wrong you can be.

His next digression was not so easily dismissed. Marc's smooth-talking spiel fell on deaf ears as the judge passed sentence with a smile of dry self-satisfaction. Three years for a £90,000 fraud. I was still in shock as they took him down. We'd both been earning good salaries so what he'd done with all the extra cash was anyone's guess – although I suspect there may be a bookie out there who, after his extra-long vacation, could cast some light on the mystery.

And just as Marc's luck finally ran out so too did that milk of human kindness. If it flowed at all it was only in small sour drops of tainted disapproval. Forgiveness had its limits. What had been perceived initially as a slip had suddenly turned into a disreputable habit and now there was no sympathy, no commiseration and no comfort.

'Simone. Hi.' A long uncomfortable pause. 'It's good to hear from you. How are you?'

'I'm fine. I was just—'

'Oh, that's great. It's great. Er, look, can I ring you back? I'd love to talk but this isn't a very good time. We've got people here for dinner and ...'

My calls, taken at first with a stammering embarrassment, eventually went unanswered. There was only silence. I quickly got the message. I was the woman who was married to a thief. I was guilty by association.

His fall, *our* fall, from grace was absolute.

If it hadn't been for that terrible silence, I might have left him too. I mean, I could hardly comprehend that he'd done it again. I wanted to slap him, to scream and shout and shake him to his bones. *Why? Why have you done this?* It left me so bewildered, so wretched I could hardly bear to meet his gaze.

What was wrong with him? What was wrong with me that I hadn't even realized what was going on?

I wanted to hurt him back – but he'd already got his punishment. And to kick a man when he's down, much as I was tempted, goes against the grain.

I couldn't do it.

I think he was surprised, even touched, by the fact I

chose to stand firm. Loyalty, along with fidelity, has always been an alien concept to him. It shouldn't have been, his mother was staunch enough, but he could never entirely believe in her ideals. He knew how badly he'd betrayed me but as to whether he understood that my decision to stay was based partly on a negative – a blatant refusal to join the conservative and condemnatory ranks of his thin-lipped associates – is another matter altogether. It's something that we never have discussed and never will.

'Thank you,' he murmured, the first time I visited that dreary depressing place. He took my hand and held it. And for one crazy moment, as we gazed across the table in a facsimile of married love, it even seemed possible that we might find a way forward. Hadn't we been through so much? Survived so much? Surrounded by the ebb and flow of tumultuous emotions, of so many expressions of hope or despair, we smiled uncertainly and clung on to what we knew.

'I'll never do it again, Sims,' he whispered, using his pet name for me. He squeezed my hand tighter and gazed into my eyes. 'I promise. I swear.'

But even as he spoke I was sure he was lying.

'I believe you,' I said.

But I didn't. For all his remonstrations, for all his sad and sweet remorse, all he really meant was that next time – and of course there would always be a next time – he didn't intend to get caught.

Because Marc is a thief. There's no denying it. He can't resist temptation. But his thefts aren't to do with acquisitiveness – or at least not directly. That isn't at the heart of all this mess. He's not driven by a desire to be rich, to drive a red Ferrari, to wallow in a million crisp new notes. I understand that now. His frauds are a means to an end and the end isn't the money – it's the reckless excitement of taking a risk, of going against the odds. It's the kick of the ultimate gamble. He can't resist the thrill of taking a chance, of doing something that he shouldn't, of deliberately crossing that dangerous and forbidden line. It's not money he wants to play with – it's his life.

Which isn't an excuse, far from it. It's only a reason.

But it's why he'll never stop.

And it's why I have to leave.

I take a hot shower, get dressed again in sweat pants and T-shirt, and create a gourmet meal of scrambled eggs on toast. I put my feet on the table and watch some banal television. It's after eight by the time I realize we're running out of milk. Since Marc went out I've switched to instant coffee and have been revving up my nerves ever since.

When I turn off the TV there's no sound coming from the ground floor. In fact the lack of noise is eerily disturbing. Cautiously, I open the door. Nothing. I wait a while. Maybe it's just a lull, a temporary break in hostilities but no, even two minutes later, everything's calm. Whether this unusual peace signifies an armistice or a slaughter is impossible to tell – but faced with the choice of a dry breakfast or a walk through the killing fields, I decide to take my chances and trek downstairs.

The light in the kitchen is still on and Dee glances up as I peer tentatively round the corner.

'It's okay, love. It's safe.' She smiles wryly as she beckons me in. Dee's in good condition for her age, a well-preserved fifty-three, but tonight the bright neon strips don't do her any favours; her face looks grey and tired, and the slight bags under her eyes are exaggerated.

'Are you all right?'

Patting her ash blonde hair with one perfectly manicured hand, she gestures towards the cupboard with the other. 'Grab a glass,' she insists, 'and help me finish this. I don't want a hangover in the morning.'

There's a half-empty bottle on the table.

I do as she says. Not having any pressing appointments, I may as well. The wine's cold and pleasantly crisp. As I sip it I ask: 'Has Jim gone to The Palace?'

'God knows,' she replies shortly.

So, sensibly, I don't pursue the subject. Instead I shift the conversation into more neutral waters. 'We had a good day at the shop, sold over twenty Christmas wreaths. And a guy came in from those solicitors down the road – Langley's, is it? – asking for a quote for regular displays. I said you'd get back to him. Oh, and that wedding's been confirmed for the fifth of January, Sally Chambers, at St James's.'

But even this news doesn't seem to lift her spirits. 'Weddings and funerals,' she mutters a little thickly, making me wonder if this is the first bottle she's opened, 'weddings and bloody funerals.' She fumbles with a cigarette, eventually lights it, and sucks in deeply. When she exhales it's with a long exhausted sigh. 'Sorry, love,' she says, reaching over to pat my hand.

She seems deep in thought so I don't break the silence with any more unwanted information about the day's trade. The florist shop named, unsurprisingly, Dee's is where I work now. Although I trained as an accountant, my position with Charlton & Castle was compromised by having a convicted fraudster as a husband. People are funny about these things. In the end I went before I was pushed, and for the past twenty months have been absorbed into the fragrant world of roses, of orchids and lilies, of pink and blue hyacinths. I only meant to stay a few weeks but there is something so seductive, not to mention soothing, about the double-fronted shop on the High Street that I have never moved on. In fact it is safe to say that there is nowhere I am happier.

'Well, that's good,' she adds, almost as if she's been reading my mind. Then I realize she's referring to my earlier comments although I'm not sure how much she actually heard. She takes another gulp of wine and unsteadily refills her glass.

'Are you all right?' I ask again. 'Has something happened? Come on, Dee, talk to me.' It's rare to see her like this. Usually so bright and feisty, she's not the type to sink into introspection. When I look closer I see that her eyes, the same distinctive blue as Marc's, are liquid and red-rimmed.

'Can you believe it?' she replies, shaking her head. 'Everything he put us through and that bloody fool still invites him here.' She makes another assault on her glass before opening her arms in a drunken gesture. Rather more loudly than necessary and in a mimicking tone she shouts: 'Hey old friend, come on in, our home is yours. Happy Christmas and welcome to our life.'

The old friend I presume is Johnny Frank. I ask with more than a hint of anxiety: 'But he's not coming, is he? Can't you just say no?'

'What do you think I've been trying to do?' This time her tone is a little snappy but as if she instantly regrets it she lays her hand over mine again. 'It's not that easy, love.'

And it suddenly occurs to me with equal amounts of alarm and astonishment that Dee has already lost the battle. At some earlier point in the evening, perhaps for the first time ever, she has raised the white flag and surrendered.

I take a moment to catch my breath. Such defeats are unheard of in the Buckley household.

'I suppose not,' I eventually agree, although only because it feels like the right and conciliatory thing to say. And also, if I'm being truthful, because I want to find out more. 'Is he really that bad?'

She smiles and looks at me sadly. It's a kind but impatient look, the sort adults usually reserve for children or for those of a diminished mental capacity. Although on the surface indulgent, underneath it screams: *You can't understand*.

'I told him,' she says, a fact that has been quite self-evident over recent days, 'I told him I didn't want him here. Never! But did he listen?' She makes a huffing sound in the back of her throat. 'I told him—'

'So why did Jim ask?' I persist, quickly interrupting what might become a lengthy ramble.

She lifts her shoulders in a gesture of resignation. 'He didn't,' she says, contradicting her earlier statement.

Now I'm confused. 'So why—'

This time it's her turn to interrupt. 'He invited himself.' Dee frowns into her glass. Then she opens her mouth again and laughs; it's a harsh barking sound that bears no relation to humour. 'And no one argues with Johnny Frank.'

Not knowing Johnny Frank, or even wanting to, I can't reasonably respond to this opinion. Which isn't to say that Dee's words don't make my blood run cold. And somewhere, in the distant regions of my mind, I'm still trying to decipher her *everything he put us through* comment, a phrase that begs a hundred questions and bears slim relation to Marc's dismissive description of 'just some geezer they used to know'.

Now I'm no lawyer but I recognize conflicting testimonies when I hear them. So either Marc is prevaricating, not entirely impossible if past experience is anything to go by, or he's as much in the dark as I am. But whatever the truth, there's still some family history here – and it's not of the pleasant or cuddly variety.

I'm staring into the middle distance, trying to make sense of it all, when Dee stands up and wanders over to the fridge. Her steps, although not exactly in pace, are still far from staggering as she retrieves another chilled bottle of wine and with the skill of a sommelier opens it with a few twists of her wrist.

So much for not wanting a hangover.

'Here,' she says, sloshing a generous measure into my glass.

'Thanks.' And although I've theoretically given up, I

also accept a cigarette. There's a time and a place for heroic denial. Suspecting there are things, probably unpalatable things, that I will need to face I'm keen to gather all the crutches I can.

For a while we smoke and drink in silence. Five years ago this interaction would have been unthinkable. When I first met and married Marc there was nothing but suspicion between us: like two territorial cats we slowly circled each other, hissing gently. For me, Dee was one of those almost obsolete matriarchs, a protector not just of her son but of a thousand other arcane East End principles of love and loyalty – and for her I was just some stuck-up ambitious prissy bitch who came from the other side of the tracks. It's taken us a while to cross the boundaries.

Perhaps the real turning point came not after Marc's first conviction but after his second. I think she was as stunned as I was by what he'd done. And equally shocked that I didn't pack my bags and leave. During that terrible period, often sharing the twice-monthly two-hour prison visits, our strained relationship gradually slipped into something less hostile. What was the point in arguing? With so much else to rail against – the long queues, the smug officers and the inevitably humiliating searches – we no longer had the will to fight each other as well.

Not that we're exactly best friends now; I doubt if anyone could meet the exacting standards she demands of any woman fortunate enough to marry her firstborn. But we rub along and on the whole our relationship is pretty equable.

'So what would *you* do?' Dee asks, breaking suddenly into my reverie. This time her expression is different, almost pleading, as if I might actually be able to offer some useful advice.

I'm startled. It's so out of character for her to ask for anyone's opinion, least of all mine, that I suspect she must feel seriously out of her depth. But how can I help? I haven't got a clue as to what this nightmare is about. All I know is that there's something nasty lurking in the woodpile. Speaking my thoughts out loud I mutter: 'How did this ... how did Jim ... how did ...' No, this is useless. Taking a long drink and then a deep breath, I demand more forcefully: 'So who exactly *is* this Johnny Frank?'

I'm not sure whether it's the directness of the question or just the booze that momentarily sends her reeling. Whatever the reason, Dee jumps back as if she's been hit. Her chair scrapes a few inches across the floor. Then as quickly she recovers and finds the way forward to her glass. She takes a few fast gulps, before she looks at me again. 'You want to know about Johnny?' she asks.

I nod encouragingly.

She gives me that smile again, the one that reminds me of how much I'll never understand. 'Well, then I'll tell you.' Although she doesn't immediately, pausing perhaps for effect or just for a chance to gather her thoughts.

I take temporary refuge in a study of the table. It's a nice piece of furniture, wide and long and scored with generations of use. Oak, I think, although I'm not entirely sure.

When she eventually speaks it's with a low hiss. 'He's

scum. Johnny Frank is scum. He's a no-good, low-life, murdering bastard.'

And there's not much you can say to that. So I don't even bother trying.

Chapter Two

Johnny

Last night I burned all Sarah's letters.

I didn't read them again. Why should I? I put them in the basin, set them alight, and watched the pages slowly turn to ashes. Then I doused them with water and shoved the sodden remains down the bog. A fitting and symbolic end to an era.

And I could claim I don't regret it, but I do. It might have been a necessary action, the only way to move forward, but a part of me still wants to go back and put my hand down that fucking U-bend and drag them out again.

Sarah.

The road is slipping past and I'm staring intently through the windscreen, trying to block out Jim's incessant manic chatter and wondering, ridiculously, if I might see her again. What if I catch a glimpse of that seductive swaying walk, if by chance she suddenly appears, if she raises those hazel eyes and ...

But what the hell am I talking about? She doesn't even live here any more. She's long gone. It's been over ten agonizing years since we ...

Shit, that was an awful day.

I can still remember what she was wearing. Black. Of course it was black. A demure black sweater and matching skirt, black tights and black shoes. Sarah always had a sense of occasion.

And this was some fucking funeral.

'I'm sorry, Johnny.'

And I knew what she was going to say. I knew what she was going to do. The moment of doom, like some bloody meteorite, was hurtling towards me.

'I'm so sorry,' she whispered again.

I wanted to scream at her to shut up. *Please. Please.*

She tried to take my hand but I pulled away. I couldn't bear for her to touch me, for this to be the last time she touched me. The room was beginning to turn, to slide in and out of focus. I bit down hard on my tongue to stop myself from speaking. Blood seeped into my mouth. But that was better than talking. A man has his dignity and I wasn't going to beg.

That she had finally chosen to leave was no great shock. Perhaps the greater surprise was that she stayed so long. For six long years she held on to the dream but faced with another ten, another twelve, another fuck knows how many – well, what kind of love can survive that?

A better person might have spared her the pain of trying to find out. A decent man might have set her free.

But I have never professed, or aspired, to be either.

And if Buckley would just stop talking for a minute, just close his babbling guilty mouth, I might be able to concentrate on what brought us to that point in the first place. Why does he imagine I have any interest in his tedious commentary on the motorways of outer London? Glaring out of the window I try to nullify his voice before I'm tempted to silence it for ever.

But maybe, as hard as I am trying to remember, he is trying to forget.

It all started with the Hatton Garden job, the perfect robbery. Eighteen years ago. Four of us – Dixie, Roy Foster, the driver Eddie Tate, and me. In and out in fifteen minutes, a bloody good result and one to be proud of. A decent haul of gems and jewellery and the split was more than lucrative.

Then three or four days later, Foster comes knocking at the office door of the club, drunk as a skunk and screaming like a banshee. Claimed we'd ripped him off. Where was the rest of his share? Dixie trying to quieten him down while we pulled him inside, away from the punters. Foster's skinny weasel face pink and twisted, his hand flourishing the newspaper, slapping it down against the desk over and over. *Where is it? Where is it? You fucking thieving bastards!* Accusing us of cheating him.

Well, you can't have it, can you? A man's got his reputation to consider. So no, I'm not denying I gave him a slap, just hard enough to bring him to his senses, to rattle those sodden brains of his back into some semblance of sobriety.

And then out the other door to the top of the stone stairwell that led down to the rear fire exit. Escorted off the premises as they say. Or at least that was the intention. But he was too far gone to be sensible about it, grabbing my jacket, struggling, twisting, almost spitting in my face. It was only a push, a push to get his grasping grubby fingers away from me. And before I know it he's rolling down those steps like some fucking sack of spuds, rolling and rolling . . .

Shit, I can still hear the crack as his skull hit the concrete wall. And the silence that came after.

Anyone else might have survived with a few cuts and bruises, a mild concussion, but not Foster. No, that fucker had to go and get his head caved in. He always was a malignant little bastard.

So there we are with a corpse on our hands – and what jury's going to believe that this was accidental? At the very best I'm looking at a manslaughter charge. So getting rid seems like the smartest option, dumping him somewhere over the river, and hoping it will look like he took a drunken tumble. Which isn't so far off the truth.

And we might have got away with it if someone hadn't witnessed the event, and if that someone hadn't been Jim Buckley, and if I hadn't slept with Jim Buckley's fucking whore of a wife, and if he couldn't wait to get his fucking revenge. So there you go. Truth and consequences.

Before we know it the Old Bill are crawling all over and it's not so easy to explain why you've got a corpse curled up in the boot of your car. And it's only a few quick easy steps from there to the Old Bailey and from there to a life sentence . . . and the rest, as they say, is history.

It took me a while to find out *who*. Almost a decade.

Because I didn't know Buckley was in The Palace that night. I hadn't seen him on my usual rounds and hadn't expected to. Since the whole Dee business we hadn't exactly been on speaking terms, but of course it was typical he'd be lurking in the shadows somewhere, licking his wounds, and waiting for some cowardly way to get his own back. Shit, he must have gone down on his knees and praised the Lord.

I can't recall who mentioned his name. Another villain, some loser passing through the system who was worried perhaps that I might accuse *him*. Running through the list of everyone he'd seen that evening, like a roll call of possible suspects. And suddenly there he was, Mr James fucking Buckley, and it didn't take a genius to put two and two together.

I sneak a sideways glance at his fleshy profile, at his multiple chins and reddened bulbous nose. That face has haunted my dreams. Has he lost any sleep over what he's done? Has he ever regretted, even for a moment, that he picked up that phone and dialled away my life? If he had the chance would he do the same again?

'It probably looks a bit different, huh?' he's asking. 'The streets and all.' And when I don't reply, as if he's frightened of the silence, he frowns and starts to chatter on again.

And I'm back to thinking of Sarah. Imagining her walking along the road. Imagining one more day, one more night with her.

But Sarah's gone. She's in the past. The bastard who's sitting beside me was responsible for that. He made a choice and I paid the price.

And now he's going to pay too.

Chapter Three

Simone

It's Monday, a few days before Christmas, and the shop is busy. I'm trying not to think about the impending arrival of our guest; the truth is that he worries me too much. Not that I'm afraid in the physical sense – I don't expect him to be roaming the house with a bloodied axe – but I feel he may be dangerous in a far more subtle way.

Dee is still on tenterhooks, short-tempered and quick to take offence. Although she hasn't mentioned our chat and I haven't raised the subject either, I suspect she wishes it had never taken place. Today, she came in for a couple of hours and disappeared at noon.

Marc is unforthcoming about what might or might not have happened in the past. When I told him about the conversation he simply looked blank but as this is an expression he has carefully cultivated, and which is almost second nature, I'm still in the dark as to how much he actually knows.

'Don't you think it's odd?' I asked. 'You know what your mother's like. She doesn't usually get fazed by anything – or anyone. I've never seen her like that before. She looked . . .' I hesitated to use the word frightened, it seemed too strong a description. ' . . . She looked *anxious*.'

He gave one of his shrugs. 'She's just stressed out about the shop and Christmas and everything. It's a busy time of year. Don't fret about it.'

Although if I didn't, I'm not sure who would. Sometimes Marc is so laid back only a cattle prod could galvanize him into action. 'Has your dad mentioned anything?'

'About Mum?'

'About *him*.'

He heard the irritation in my voice and scowled. 'God, Simone, I don't see why you're getting so worked up about this. He's not Jack the Ripper! Relax. Everything will be fine.'

But I couldn't stop pacing the room. 'I just don't understand how your parents ever got involved with him. I mean isn't he . . . wasn't he . . . some kind of gangster?'

This time he laughed out loud. 'Didn't I ever mention the Buckley *connections*? Oh, very shady. The criminal fraternity shakes in its boots every time the name's mentioned.' He took a moment to appreciate his own joke before throwing an arm along the back of the sofa and tilting his head. 'Why don't you sit down? You're making me dizzy.'

'Don't look at me then!'

'How's that possible when you're so adorable?' He leaned forward, grabbed my arm and pulled me down beside him. 'Come here, wife! I need you.'

I took a moment to gaze into his face, at those magnificent blue eyes, at the Roman nose, and the cleft in his chin I had once loved so much. The face of a hero, of a movie star. Which only goes to prove how deceptive looks can be. We embraced in that familiar and comforting way. Not passionately. Not with fiery red-hot flames. But easily and tenderly.

However, even as his mouth closed over mine it crossed my mind, and this is how paranoia starts, that he might only be doing it to shut me up.

But that's not something I want to think about either. So now I'm trying to concentrate on the job in hand, trying to stay focused while I organize the next day's deliveries and fulfil the seemingly endless requests for bouquets. There's plenty of passing trade today, mainly from men with guilty demeanours, men perhaps who misbehaved at the office Christmas party, had a drink too many, an indiscreet fumble or worse, and now have a lot of making up to do. On the whole they choose red roses, an unimaginative but suitably expensive gesture.

Kerry Anne brings me a mug of tea and hovers while I smooth the cellophane of yet another splashy offering. In a final flourish I wrap a length of baby pink ribbon around the base, twisting it easily into a perfect bow. *Voila!* Twenty months ago my bows were limp and uninspired but practice makes perfect and now they positively clamour for congratulation.

The man, in his mid-forties, pays by cash and tentatively picks up the arrangement. While he waits for his change he awkwardly holds the flowers away from him. *They won't bite!* I want to say but wisely hold my tongue.

As he's opening the door, Kerry Anne leans forward and whispers: 'I bet they're for his mistress.'

I glance at her, my eyebrows raised in a question mark.

'Cash,' she explains, 'so it won't show up on his credit card statement. I bet his wife goes through it with a fine-tooth comb.'

She's probably right. But I know she isn't standing here just to pass on her nineteen years' worth of accumulated wisdom on the perfidy of the male sex. It's twenty past five and she's hoping I'll let her leave early. She's got a party to go to. Or a date to get dressed up for. Whereas all I've got to look forward to is ... but I don't want to finish that thought.

He's arriving today.

'You can go if you like,' I say, putting her out of her misery.

'Are you sure?' she replies, acting all wide-eyed and innocent as if the idea hadn't even occurred to her.

I like Kerry Anne, she's hard-working and sweet-tempered, but sometimes her tendency to believe she can twist me round her little finger is trying. Or am I being over-sensitive? Perhaps most girls her age are equally patronizing to any woman over thirty.

'Yeah, it's fine.' And I give her a smile to show that I mean it. 'You get off, I can manage on my own.'

Unexpectedly, instead of dashing for her coat she lingers for a while longer, pretending to tidy the ribbons but actually just moving them aimlessly around the counter. She has something else on her mind but can't quite bring herself to say the words.

She worries on her bottom lip, chewing off the lipstick, before

finally finding the courage to speak.

'Is Marc picking you up tonight?'

There's an attempt at casualness but she doesn't even get close. Her voice emerges with a mouse-like squeak. Kerry Anne has a crush the size of Mount Everest on my husband, a tormenting all-consuming passion that sends her cheeks into a blaze of scarlet every time he comes into the shop.

Recalling similar unrequited loves of my teenage years, I feel a wave of pity. For I'm in no doubt at all that her passion will never be reciprocated. This, of course, is not through any notion of fidelity on Marc's part but because, with her short stature, plump build, mousy hair and freckles, she is simply not his type.

However, he does nothing to discourage her attentions. In fact the very opposite. Not willing to shun the egotistical pleasure of being worshipped, he revels in her gauche adoration, throwing her small compliments like scraps to a hungry puppy.

It's kind of sad to watch.

'No, not tonight,' I say kindly, setting her free to leave with no regrets.

She smiles and blushes simultaneously, her hopeless infatuation battling with her conscience, for Kerry Anne is fond of me and her love for my husband makes her feel guilty. Quickly, she goes through to the back to retrieve her coat and bag, and seconds later after a hasty 'See you then!' she's whirled through the shop and out through the exit.

'Have a nice time,' I call out but I'm talking to the air.

Which leaves me alone with my thoughts again.

Fortunately there's a steady but not too demanding flow of customers over the next forty minutes, most of them buying bundles of brightly berried holly or optimistic sprigs of mistletoe. The red poinsettias, of which I'm not enamoured, are also popular, maybe as last-minute presents for almost-forgotten elderly aunts. The wrapping and serving keeps me busy until the clock reaches six, when I bring in the outside containers and close up.

I take my time, not really wanting to go home. Not yet.

I don't want to leave my haven. I don't want to go and meet the man who has only today got out of prison, the man who disturbs the unflappable Dee, the man who I suspect is bringing a bucketload of trouble to the Buckley household.

It's as I'm cashing up that I recall again the brown paper parcel in Dee's kitchen. After we'd said our goodnights it was several minutes before I realized I'd forgotten the milk. When I went back down the light was off and there was no sign of her. I took a pint from the well-stocked fridge and was turning to go when I spotted the package sitting on a shelf alongside the jars of tea and coffee. I might have ignored it if one corner hadn't been torn open and there inside, clear to see, were several large bundles of used twenty-pound notes. Money from the club perhaps, waiting to be banked – but surely that would be in the safe? And why was it so neatly wrapped?

No, this was something else.

Cautiously, glancing first over my shoulder to make sure I was alone, I stood on my toes and investigated more closely. I drew a quick breath. At a rough estimate there was about five thousand there. What was it doing left carelessly on the kitchen shelf? I examined the outside of the parcel. Across the middle, scrawled in large block capitals, was the name Jim Buckley and in the top right-hand corner the instruction, 'By hand.'

A delivery then. Some kind of payment. But what for? And who from?

Only one name sprang to mind.

But maybe I was jumping to conclusions. Although, on the other hand, the arrival of a large sum of money closely followed by the arrival of Mr Frank was surely a coincidence too far.

I place the day's takings in the safe, a healthy sum that should please even the disgruntled Dee. Then I put on my coat, set the alarm and lock the door. Outside the temperature seems to have dropped another five degrees. I consider waiting for a bus but seeing the snarled-up traffic decide my chances of freezing to death will be slightly reduced by walking.

Briskly I set off in the direction of home. By now an icy rain is falling and the snow beneath my feet has dissolved to a grey unpleasant slush. I think while I walk, wondering about the money again. There could be other reasons. A loan? Some dodgy deal? Drugs? No, not drugs. Although I've never been naive enough to presume that Jim is whiter than white, he'd never get involved in drugs. Not after all Carl's problems.

Which brings me back, full circle, to Johnny Frank.

I'd like to delay my return as long as possible but the cold propels me forward and I cover the distance in a respectable twenty-five minutes. Very quietly I open the front door, hoping to slip inside, dash up the stairs and grab a hot shower before the inevitable and unwelcome introductions. But I'm barely on the second step before Jim has stumbled from the living room and shouted loud enough for everyone to hear: 'Simone, love! Come in. Come in.'

Damn!

'Er, Jim, look – I'm soaked,' I reply, dripping the evidence on to the hall carpet. 'I was just going to . . .'

But with the insistent determination of the drunk, he takes a few steps forward and grabs my arm. His warm whisky breath assails my face. 'Come and meet Johnny!'

And so, feeling like the lamb to the slaughter, I'm dragged into the midst of the smoky gathering. I'm not sure how long the party has been going on although the scattering of empty bottles and full ashtrays would suggest more than a few hours. The room has that careless feel, as if inhibitions, along with all formalities, have long been shed.

With Jim still firmly attached to my elbow, I acknowledge the presence of Dee, Marc, his younger brother Carl and Carl's girlfriend Melanie, before my gaze finally and uneasily comes to rest on the infamous stranger. He looks up and courteously rises from his chair to greet me.

I've only a few seconds to absorb some fleeting

impressions. He's tall, that's the first thing I notice, almost the same height as Marc – but leaner and older. On the wrong side of fifty and resigned to it. Grey. His hair is grey. His eyes are grey too. Even his lips, tight and thin, hold a hint of dull silver. His pale face is almost ascetic, the cheekbones sharp as razor blades. There's nothing especially ugly or handsome about him; he occupies that neutral middle ground, that ambiguous position that can slip one way or another, dependent perhaps only on a look or a smile.

So this is Johnny Frank.

So this is the *no-good, low-life, murdering bastard*.

'This is Marc's wife, Simone,' Jim slurs, releasing my arm in time for me to shake the outstretched hand. 'Marc's wife,' he repeats as if my identity is entirely reliant on my connection to his son.

'Pleased to meet you,' I say, attempting a smile as his long cool fingers close firmly around mine. My heartbeat quickens a little. It's not every day you get to meet a killer.

'I'm pleased to meet you too, Simone,' he replies.

I bristle at the deliberate repetition of my name, an affectation he probably believes to be charming but which I only find irritating. His voice though is surprisingly easy on the ear, soft and lilting, the accent holding hints of Scottish origins.

'How are you?' I ask a little stupidly, saying the first thing that comes into my head. Are there rules of etiquette for addressing a man who has just served eighteen years in prison?

He smiles back. 'Very well, thank you.'

For a few seconds following this mundane exchange there is silence in the room. Whether this is down to a faux pas on my part or just a general fascination with every word and action of our guest is hard to ascertain. Whatever the cause everyone suddenly stands up and congregates around us. A glass of wine is thrust into my hand and responsibility for small talk effectively removed.

'So, do you remember . . .'

'Hey, whatever happened to . . .'

The next five minutes dissolve into a blur of muddled chat and reminiscence. I stand there, grinning inanely and sipping the wine. The rain is seeping down my back. I shift from foot to foot, cold and wet and uncomfortable. All I want to do is get away. I glance at Marc – but he's too busy staring at Johnny. *Everyone's* looking at Johnny. Even Dee seems to be disguising her enmity. Although there's still a slight brittleness, she's standing close to him, laughing and joking, her hand reaching out for his arm, her honeyed friendly words a far cry from her accusations a few nights before.

What's going on?

I hover for a while longer before depositing my glass on a table and slipping quietly out of the room. No one seems to notice. Upstairs, I strip off my clothes and take a long hot shower. I raise my face to the water and close my eyes. I try not to brood on what is going on downstairs – but of course that is all I can do. I soap my skin and try to scrub it away. I turn the radio on loud. I try to forget it. I can't. Even as I wrap the towel around me, as I get dressed again in faded jeans and T-shirt, it's still firmly ingrained on my mind.

And there's a stone in my stomach, a feeling of dread that I just can't shake.

I would like to stay where I am, to huddle in front of the TV – it's been a long hard day and my legs are aching – but know I have to do my social duty. This is Jim and Dee's house and I must show due respect to their guest.

As I re-enter the room I find that seats have been resumed and I perch on the sofa next to Marc. I don't choose this place because it's next to my husband but because it's the furthest spot from the two people I least want to talk to – Johnny and Carl.

They are occupying adjacent armchairs by the window overlooking the garden, and I see Johnny's eyes rise from time to time to glance at what is currently a bleak and sodden landscape. Only the bank of cyclamen under the old beech tree provides a flash of colour. Perhaps it's these tiny flowers that continuously draw his gaze or maybe it's the sheer novelty of having any kind of view at all. If he is thrilled, however, he doesn't show it. His grey face has an almost expressionless quality. Even when he smiles, as he's doing now, it goes no further than his mouth, his eyes retaining their icy coldness.

It would be a bad idea, I think, to get on the wrong side of Johnny Frank.

Carl is regaling him with some tale of a friend in Parkhurst. 'Terry Randall, you know, George Randall's son, lives on the Roman Road. You must have heard of George?'

He shakes his head. 'Sorry.'

But as if he must eventually be impressed by this rather weak link to the world of criminality, Carl persists: 'Well, Terry went down for a blag three years ago. That bank job on Old Street. We used to knock around together ...'

And Carl is *determined* to impress. Like a more desperate version of Kerry Anne, but without any of her endearing qualities, he's almost licking Johnny's boots. His eyes are excitedly bright although whether this is from the thrill of having a real-life villain in the house, an effect of the alcohol, or the result of some other uplifting substance is impossible to tell. As if he's got ants in his pants he's squirming from side to side and talking incessantly.

I wonder if Johnny is even listening.

I don't like Carl. And by that I don't mean that I mildly dislike him. No, it's much stronger than that. He induces a feeling that borders on revulsion. Part of it may be down to what his ex-wife Gena has told me but truth is I felt the same way from the moment I met him.

Marc's brother is twenty-six, nine years younger than my husband, and although of equal height and build and with the same blue eyes, that's pretty much where the similarity ends. Carl's hair is straight, the colour of barley, and his lips are like Jim's, wide and fleshy. Some might call his mouth sensual but I see only petulance in its pout. He's conceited and selfish. Which isn't to say he can't be charming because, like Marc, he can enchant the most perceptive of people, but beneath the surface lies a streak of sadistic cruelty. He was the kind of child, I imagine, who tortured kittens.

Which is probably why he's so attracted to Johnny, a man

who has crossed the line into that darker place, the place that as yet is just the subject of Carl's dreams.

My thoughts are interrupted by Dee squeezing on to the sofa and giving me a brief, if drunken, interrogation on the day's events. 'So how did it go, sweetheart? Did that delivery arrive from Murphy's? Did the wreaths for the Parker funeral go out okay?'

But she's only going through the motions, not even pretending to listen to the answers. Even as I reply she's already looking round the room, searching for something more, waiting to spot an empty glass to top up so she can pour herself a fresh one too.

I'm going easy on the booze, still sipping my first drink. I've got work tomorrow and the heady scent of flowers doesn't mix well with a throbbing head and a gut turning somersaults.

As quickly as she arrived, Dee takes off again, flitting over to sit beside Melanie. I know little of Carl's latest acquisition apart from the obvious, that she's a dumb but rather striking blonde – with terrible taste in men. But I can hardly talk. Marc isn't exactly the catch of the century. And as I've barely exchanged more than half a dozen words with her, there's perhaps just a touch of the green-eyed monster in my judgement, for there's no denying that with her slim waist and bounteous cleavage she comes close to the male ideal of Barbie-doll perfection.

I resolve to put aside my first impressions and to make the effort, when I'm feeling less tired, to be nicer. Truth is, I really miss Gena – especially at times like these. As the two outsiders we formed an alliance that saw us through the worst. Together, we could laugh our way through anything. Well, at least until Carl ...

I don't blame her for leaving.

As if she has died, Gena's name is rarely mentioned now. And if some reference has to be made, for divorce proceedings are still slowly stumbling through their endless machinations, Dee only ever calls her The Bitch. Never, however, deliberately within my hearing, for despite my preference for a quiet life this is a subject over which we have almost come to blows. Across the kitchen, we have narrowed our eyes and glared at each other. And raised our voices. And moved close enough to smell each other's angry breath.

'Don't *ever* call her that again,' I demand.

'It's my poor son who's the victim,' she screeches back.

'Oh, right, and it's your *poor* son who ... '

And things might have gone further, much further, if Jim hadn't crucially interposed his bulk between us and cried: 'Stop it! Stop it!'

But all that was over six months ago.

Dee's loyalty to Carl is understandable but her refusal to nudge even vaguely towards the truth is harder to accept. I'm willing to respect her maternal love but can never collude in her crazily misplaced contempt and accusations.

The only victim in this unholy mess is Gena. And she's got the scars to prove it.

But back to the present. Jim is now strolling round the room, loudly proclaiming the death of the East End in a muddled diatribe involving Asians, Oswald Mosley, and the betrayal of the government. No one appears to be paying attention but that doesn't deter him. Although he long ago moved out of the area and into the leafy suburbs of Essex, Jim retains a sentimental picture of the slum he once fought so hard to escape from.

'Ah, for fuck's sake,' Carl eventually exclaims, 'don't start all that rubbish again! Diphtheria, outside bogs, bloody starvation – what was so great about all that?'

Jim retorts: 'You don't know what you're fucking talking about.'

And Melanie, hoping perhaps to divert from this magical family exchange or just completely oblivious to it, pipes up in her little-girl voice: 'Carl darling, you couldn't get me another drinky, could you?'

Which has the effect, at least, of temporarily silencing everyone.

I glance surreptitiously at my watch. Hopefully, with my duty done, I can make my escape before too long. Before everything turns sour. For even without the added bonus of Johnny Frank's ominous presence, I hate these family gatherings. All too often they descend into futile bickering and recriminations. Already the atmosphere is starting to shift, the earlier good-hearted tipsiness slipping into harder-edged inebriation.

Wearily, I lean my head against Marc's shoulder. I've seen it all a thousand times before. Are they a dysfunctional family? I have no idea. My own experience of family life is pretty limited and I guess I have seen both better and worse examples.

Glancing up as Melanie repeats her request I accidentally catch Johnny's eye. For the first time I see a glimmer of humour in his expression although I can't decide whether this is genuine amusement or something bordering on hysteria. Of all the places in the world, why on earth has he chosen to come here? Perhaps I should do a bit of digging.

Accordingly, I ask: 'So, do you have any family, Johnny?'

He continues to look straight at me, holding my gaze as if it's a sign of weakness to look away first. That odd, rather chilly smile, is hovering on his lips again.

'No,' he eventually replies. 'Of course I did, but ... ' He lets the sentence dissolve into a shrug.

'Ah, I'm sorry.' I'm the first to lower my eyes. Curiosity got the better of me and perhaps it was an indiscreet enquiry. Eighteen years inside probably depletes the relations somewhat.

'And you?' he asks surprisingly, as if the Buckleys don't count.

A difficult question to answer as I don't wish to offend anyone. In fact I have only a few distant cousins I neither see nor hear from. No mother or father or siblings. So I say diplomatically, if a little cheesily: 'I guess this is my family now.'

Which provokes a thin and possibly pitying smile from Mr Frank. 'I see.'

And I realize with a shock that in less than an hour he's already started to unravel my precarious position within this house. He *knows* about Marc, about me. He *knows* that I intend to leave. I give myself a mental shake. No, he can't.

That's ridiculous. I'm reading more into his look than is actually there. It's just my guilty conscience playing tricks.

But something else peculiar gradually sinks into my consciousness. I wonder why I didn't notice it before. Unlike all the others, Johnny isn't drunk. In fact – and I'm sure he would appreciate the simile – he's as sober as a judge. On the table beside him sits an untouched glass of whisky. Although *he's* the one with most reason to celebrate, he's chosen to forgo the pleasure of the bottle.

Why is that?

I'm about to say, *You're not drinking, Johnny*, when, glancing slowly up from the glass, I meet his gaze again and instantly think better of it. His frown is not exactly threatening but it isn't friendly either. Promptly, I close my mouth.

He sits back in his chair, relaxes, and with his long thin fingers steepled on his chest stares out of the window. There's an unnatural stillness about him, like the calm before the storm.

And that unpleasant word springs into my mind again – *murderer*.

Chapter Four

Johnny

So this is the house that Jim built. And off my bloody back I might add, because if I hadn't gone down when I did he'd never have been able to buy The Palace at such a discount. And that's what made his fortune. Of course it was a decent place then, not the squalid dump he's turned it into. I built that club up with my own sweat and tears and that bastard reaped the rewards. Although, in one of those fitting twists of fate, he's managed to squander most of the profits. He never did have the brains for business.

Yes, it's a nice house. Very clean. Very comfortable. Good security too – just to make me feel at home – with a hi-tech alarm system, electric gates and a nice high wall. You don't want just anyone wandering in. I've been given a double bedroom on the second floor with en suite bathroom and a view over the garden. There's food on the table and a regular laundry service. It's almost as good as a hotel. I'm sure I'll enjoy my stay.

Dee welcomed me with a peck on the cheek. 'Johnny, darling! How lovely to see you again.'

Almost casual, as if I'd been on holiday for a few weeks rather than banged up for the last eighteen years. She stank of booze. Dutch courage, I imagine. If there's one thing she must have hoped for it was to have me disappear – permanently.

'You haven't changed a bit,' I replied. Which I'm sure is true. At least on the inside. On the outside, well, she's not wearing badly for fifty-three but she's hardly the sex kitten she was.

And she knows it.

She flashed me a look, trying to keep the rage out of her eyes. That's what happens with women. They start off loving and end up hating. And it's always in direct proportion. The more they love the more they hate, as if there's some natural balance to be preserved.

But I'll get round her. I always could. A few weeks together, a few trips down memory lane, and she'll be eating out of my hand. Somewhere deep down, in that dank dark place she doesn't want to visit, lie the roots of her old feelings.

No need to rush it though.

First there's the rest of the family to investigate: strengths, weaknesses, motivation. It's the detail that matters, the accumulation of data. Watch and listen. *Know your enemy.* Fortunately, there was a welcoming committee so I could get started straight away. The Buckley clan had gathered to pay homage to the prison freak.

'Take a seat, Johnny. No, that chair's more comfortable, the one by the window.'

'Have a drink. Scotch okay?'

'Are you hungry?'

And Jim was still burbling away as if he could vanquish his demons by talking over them. 'All those years. It's a disgrace, Johnny, a fucking disgrace. There was no need for it, no need at all. Haven't I always said: It was a travesty of justice.'

Although he was still finding it hard to look me in the eye.

And the sons. Shit, they were a shock. Kids when I went inside and now both grown men. Makes me feel bloody old. Lucky enough to inherit Dee's physical genes but as to their characters it's too soon to say. I suspect there's weakness there, a less fortunate legacy from Jim. The older one's already done two stretches for fraud. The younger one, Carl, was all over me like a rash; yes, he's going to be useful.

From time to time I sneaked a glance at the luscious Melanie. She's got the face of an angel and the body of a whore, all wide-eyed innocence, jutting tits and wriggling arse – a living breathing fantasy. Best not to get distracted but I could look, couldn't I? And she knew I was looking. She fluttered her lashes, threw back her long blonde hair and offered me the occasional provocative smile. A few sweet crumbs for the starving man.

God, this house, these people; they still seem unreal. Like an actor on a stage, I'm going through the motions, speaking my lines, and following a plot that was written years ago. Should I be excited, thrilled? Isn't that how you're supposed to feel when your dreams are coming true? I wouldn't know. Bitterness has hollowed me out and left me empty of all but the most base of emotions.

I may have taken three hours to begin mentally undressing Melanie but it took Jim even longer to find the courage to begin his surreptitious examination of me. His piggy eyes cautiously scanned my face. I knew what he was searching for. The damage. Because there's always damage. You just have to know where to look for it. For some long-term cons it shows on the outside, a blatant physical fading. In others it's more insidious, a slow internal destruction like some fucking creeping cancer. How long does it take? Fifteen years? Twenty? And then there's no going back. It's in the bones, in the flesh. It's final. And what is lost is irretrievable.

So Jim was right to be hopeful.

But too drunk and too stupid to find what he was seeking.

Tongues had started to loosen as the alcohol kicked in. For which I was grateful. All that conversation was a strain. I'm hardly attuned to the niceties of social interaction. Easier to sit back, to watch and to listen. One thing's clear as crystal though, there's tension in the Buckley family – and only a part of it is down to me. The cracks are already there. Just add a little gunpowder to the mix and . . .

But it doesn't do to get over-confident. I realized that when she asked about my family. Simone, the one with the long legs and the cool supercilious gaze, had suspicion in her eyes. And what she was really asking was: *What the hell are you doing here?* She doesn't trust me. She doesn't like me either. But then I get the impression she doesn't like anyone that much so I'll try not to take it too personally.

She had the good grace to look vaguely abashed when I laid on the guilt trip: What a poor guy am I, no family to turn to and just out of prison. It threw her but she wasn't fooled for long. She was watching me as closely as I was watching everyone else. And she picked up on the fact I wasn't drinking.

I wonder what she sees when she looks at me: just a killer perhaps, just an undesirable con sitting quietly in a chair, a user, a loser, a leech come to take advantage of the Buckley hospitality? No, she's smarter than that. I could have read her once, known exactly what she was thinking, but I've lost the touch. I've spent too many years apart from women. Their more serious looks are like a foreign language now, confusing and mysterious.

But then it was time for us all to raise our glasses and drink another toast to the liberty of Johnny Frank.

Chink, chink.

'Congratulations!'

'Here's to the future!'

And if nothing else, I could drink to that.

Chapter Five

Simone

It's Christmas Eve and the good news is that I've seen hardly anything of Johnny since he arrived. He's been keeping himself to himself. To the best of my knowledge he hasn't even gone out – well, at least no further than the garden, which he regularly prowls like a cat establishing its territory.

The bad news is that Carl, after a few days' absence, has returned to the fold. Home from work, late in the afternoon, I come through the door to find his cases stacked untidily in the hall.

'Hi,' he says, emerging from the kitchen with a cigarette in one hand and a beer in the other. 'Glad to have me back?'

'Thrilled,' I reply with a sinking heart.

'I thought you might be.'

I don't stop to chat. Our dislike is mutual and our attempts to disguise it border on the negligible. He suspects, quite rightly, that Gena has talked, that she has told me things he doesn't want anyone to know. Like how he gets his kicks, for example, about how he likes to *hurt*. And with Christmas so close it's pretty hard to forget what I witnessed last year.

It still makes my stomach turn over.

Walking quickly enough to get away, but not so fast as to let him think he's intimidated me, I've just reached the first-floor landing when he calls up: 'Johnny's been asking about you.'

Which stops me dead in my tracks.

'Don't you want to know why?'

The question leaves me with the choice of submitting to a fearful curiosity – and facing Carl's smug self-satisfied expression – or just ignoring him. After a brief struggle I choose the latter. He's probably lying anyway. Why would Johnny have any interest in me?

'Suit yourself.'

His mocking laughter follows me up the stairs.

As I step inside the flat, Marc's emerging from the bathroom, a towel wrapped around his waist. In an uncharacteristically romantic gesture, he's booked a table for two at Luigi's for this evening. It's either a sign of a guilty conscience or some kind of recompense for having to endure another Christmas with the Buckleys. Maybe a combination of both.

'Hi, love.'

He comes over and gives me a kiss. Over the past few days, he's been more attentive than usual but quieter too, as if he's got something on his mind. There's worry in his eyes and the frown lines on his forehead have become a permanent fixture. Instead of moving away he wraps his arms gently around me and pulls me closer.

'I've missed you.'

Like a child seeking comfort, he buries his face in my hair and sighs. I can smell the lemony scent of the soap on his warm damp skin and feel the steady beating of his heart. Stroking his back, I murmur those sounds that are not so much words as primitive whisperings of reassurance. At times like these, when he seems more vulnerable than arrogant, I can remember why I fell in love. Aside from the fact he was the sexiest man I'd ever met, his occasional flashes of a tender, almost desperate need rocked my heart.

Will I ever make sense of him?

For a second, as he lifts his head, I think he's about to tell me something, to confide, perhaps even to take my face in his hands and kiss me again – but the moment is broken by a loud crash from downstairs. Startled, we jump apart.

Carl's vicious tones rise through two floors of plaster and cement. 'I know your fucking game and I'm not going to stand around while—'

'You think you can just walk back in here with your pile-of-crap lies, upsetting your mother and—'

'*Me* upsetting her! Shit, that's a joke. You're the one who's—'

'I'm the one who hasn't done anything except fucking feed you and clothe you and put a roof over your fucking head for the last twenty-six years. Not that I've ever got any thanks for it. Not that I've ever got—'

Another loud crash reverberates through the house.

'And don't even—'

'And don't even think about telling me what to fucking do!'

It's all vaguely reminiscent of every other Buckley argument. The characters might change, the dialogue vary slightly, but the song remains the same – rage runs through this family like a seam of poisonous lead. Only Marc refuses to participate, channelling his frustrations in a different but perhaps no less destructive direction.

Before I can find out exactly what Jim is being accused of, Marc strides over to the radio, stabs at the start button and turns up the volume. A stream of heavy rock shakes the room. We both flinch. It's not the kind of music either of us likes but I guess it's the lesser of two evils and has the effect of drowning out the more dramatic downstairs acoustics.

To be heard, I have to raise my voice. 'So what's all that about?'

But he only shrugs, turning away. 'Nothing. Let's get out of here.' Glancing at his watch he notes with a grimace that we're still a few hours adrift from dinner. 'We can get a drink first. I wouldn't mind trying that new bar on the High Street.'

'Okay, but . . .'

But already it's too late. Conversation over. He's disappeared into the bedroom to get dressed. That rare moment of intimacy has dissolved as rapidly as it arrived. I go to the bathroom to take a shower and, quickly stripping off my clothes, step frowning under the hot spray. If we could talk more often our relationship mightn't be so fragile – but we can't, and there's no point dwelling on it. Instead, I find myself wondering what Carl was accusing Jim of, not to mention what he meant earlier about Johnny. He's only been back five minutes and already the house is in turmoil.

Has Johnny been listening to this latest example of familial love and togetherness? He's in the room directly underneath so unless he's wearing earplugs he couldn't fail to overhear. I still can't figure out why he's chosen to come here, just as I still haven't figured out what he did that was so terrible all those years ago, the episode for which Dee has clearly never forgiven him. I'm pretty sure it's not to do with the killing. It's something that happened before that. And if there's so much bad feeling, why in God's name has he decided to plant himself right back in the middle of it? If he's not searching for company then what exactly is he looking for?

But they're the kind of questions guaranteed to destroy your peace of mind.

By the time we arrive at Indigo, Marc has sufficiently recovered his humour to crack a smile or two. Public appearances always cheer him up and tonight he's looking particularly stunning. Dressed in a dark blue tailored suit and a shirt that matches his eyes, he's the most elegant man in the bar; heads, both male and female, turn as he flows gracefully through the room. In his wake he leaves a flutter of undisguised admiration.

Even after we have sat down, greedy glances continue to seek him out. Although he appears oblivious, neither acknowledging nor returning the looks, the attention, as if by a process of osmosis, seems to sink into his subconscious producing a kind of radiance, a glow from within. Perhaps it is only at moments like this that Marc is truly content: a distant object of desire, with nothing more required of him.

And yet he isn't vain. There's a streak of arrogance to be sure, an over-developed self-confidence that has brought him to his knees on more than one occasion, but it is less to do with conceit than with some deeper need, a yearning for respect or approbation. Where he has so patently failed in other areas of his life, here, in the arena of physical beauty, he can reign supreme.

We order cold beers and sip them for a while in silence. I don't press him to talk. If he has something to tell me he will do it when he's good and ready. In the meantime I entertain myself by staring down a predatory vamp or two; it's a skill I've had plenty of practice in and have now honed to a bitchy perfection.

When he does eventually speak, he surprises me. Leaning across the table, he lowers his voice. 'Sims, could I ask you something?' He pauses for a second as if he's not sure whether to go on and then takes a deep breath. 'I know this is going to sound crazy but do you think Dad could be having an affair?'

I'm so astounded I laugh out loud – but seeing his expression quickly stifle it. 'Jim? God, whatever makes you say that? I've never even seen him look at another woman.' Which is true. Despite its volatility, his marriage to Dee has always seemed rooted in solid ground, as secure and eternal as a grand old oak.

The frown deepens on his forehead. 'Well, okay, maybe not an affair then but . . . I don't know . . . some sort of mid-life crisis? You don't think he's been behaving strangely?'

When it comes to the Buckleys I'm not sure what constitutes 'strangely' but I shake my head anyway. 'A bit on edge perhaps but . . .'

'I mean, you say he never looks at other women but haven't you noticed the way he stares at Melanie?'

'Oh, come on – that's different. *All* men gawp at Melanie,' I insist, 'unless they're gay. She's pretty hard to ignore. But that doesn't mean he'd ever do anything or *want* to do anything about it. Not your dad. He's not the type.'

Marc takes another sip of his beer. 'It's not just her. There's another girl at the club. Aimee, she's a dancer there. A redhead. He's been paying her a lot of attention, you know, like *too* much attention. He's always hanging round. Every time I look over my shoulder he's got his face in her tits.'

I can't resist a grin, his words conjuring up a picture that is not only bizarre but completely at odds with what I know about Jim. Somehow I just can't see him as an ageing Lothario or a lascivious lech. I've always had the impression that it's money rather than sex that rocks Jim's boat. But then I'm hardly the best judge of character.

'Is that what the row was about this afternoon?'

He nods. 'I didn't say a word to anyone, but Melanie knows the girl. I mean, they work together, don't they? Aimee must have talked to her, and she's told Carl, and now he's gone off at the deep end accusing Dad of . . . well, of having some kind of relationship.'

I didn't realize that Melanie worked in the club but then that's probably nobody's fault but my own. I haven't exactly taken an interest in her.

'And of course he's denying it,' Marc continues, 'but then he would, wouldn't he?'

I make an effort to keep my eyebrows in place, sensing that now is neither the time nor the place to air my own grievances in that department. 'Have you any idea what Aimee actually said? Maybe Melanie got it wrong or Carl's exaggerating. You know what he's like, any excuse to have a go at your dad. They don't exactly get on, do they?'

'Okay, that's possible – but I've still seen what I've seen.'

'That's hardly evidence. And surely he talks to all the girls. It doesn't have to mean there's anything going on. In fact, if there was, wouldn't he be more likely to avoid her when you were there?' I'm not sure why I'm defending him so hard. Maybe it's partly down to Carl being such a stirrer but I suspect it's mainly because if good old steady Jim is being unfaithful then it doesn't hold out much hope for the fidelity of the rest of the male population.

'I guess.' He gives an elegant shrug of his shoulders. 'But what's that saying – no smoke without fire? And Mum's really upset. This has knocked her for six.'

I wonder sometimes at the gross hypocrisy of my husband. If she's been knocked for six then I'm definitely into the thirties. But clearly in his mind there is no correlation between his father's far-from-proven adultery and his own frequent and damaging affairs.

'Surely Dee doesn't believe it? She can't. She knows your

dad better than anyone. I mean, God, he wouldn't *dare* – and especially not in public.'

Sighing, Marc replies: 'And two months ago he wouldn't have dared invite Johnny Frank to stay.'

Which is incontrovertibly true. And which, for the first time, plants a tiny seed of doubt in my mind. Jim has never been renowned for his backbone but it's certainly the case that Dee has been losing more battles than she's been winning over recent weeks. But still I retort: 'I heard he rather invited himself.'

'Dad didn't have to agree. He could have said no.'

'I thought you didn't mind about Johnny being here?'

'I don't,' he snaps back, 'that's not the point.' Then, just as Dee had done less than a week ago, he quickly places a hand on my arm and says, 'Sorry.' He raises his worried blue eyes and looks at me. The corners of his mouth have turned down, his forehead creasing again into a series of deep and anxious furrows. For the first time since we walked in, he has forgotten about his audience. 'I'm sorry, Sims. You're right. There's probably nothing going on but . . .'

'There's something else, isn't there?'

He doesn't answer straight away. Retrieving a pack of cigarettes from his pocket, he takes one out, rolls it between his fingers and lifts it slowly to his mouth. Then he flicks open his silver lighter and puts a flame to it. Even this simple act is perfectly choreographed, a work of art in itself. Eventually he says: 'There's a problem with The Palace. It's losing money and Dad doesn't seem to care. I've shown him the books but he's not interested. He just keeps on saying not to worry, he's got it sorted – but he hasn't got a damn thing sorted.'

Now it's my turn to look bewildered. 'But I thought the club made a good profit.'

'It used to. Not any more. There's too much competition, other clubs opening every five minutes, and it's not exactly the classiest joint in the world, is it? It needs an overhaul, new decor, new ideas, a bit of investment, but he won't even discuss it.'

I'm not sure if any lap-dancing establishment could be described as classy but then I've always presumed that the sleazy aspect was part of their appeal. Then again, I guess there's sleazy and there's downright squalid and The Palace doesn't have to work too hard to fit comfortably into the latter category.

I find myself pondering on that money again, on that wad of cash stashed carelessly on the shelf, and wonder if I should mention it. The problem is that if I do then I'll also have to explain what I was doing rooting around his parents' kitchen in the middle of the night – and I doubt if my natural curiosity will serve as any kind of adequate defence.

Instead I ask: 'What about Dee? Surely *she's* not going to let things fall apart? Have you discussed it with her?'

'She's got enough on her mind. I can't stress her out with this on top of everything else. I will have to tell her but I'm going to wait until after Christmas. Perhaps he'll have come to his senses by then.' He blows out a thin stream of smoke. 'Do you see what I mean though, Sims? I'm worried. He's not behaving normally. He's not behaving like . . . well, like Dad.'

Now I'm starting to worry too. Jim has always been, if

64

nothing else, a good husband and provider. It's inconceivable that he'd just stand back and watch his livelihood disappear. But then five minutes ago it would have seemed inconceivable that he'd have the hots for an amply bosomed redhead called Aimee. That's if it's true. And I'm also fretting, in a purely selfish way, about another aspect of this possible decline and fall – if The Palace goes under Marc will lose his job, and if he does that then how will he ever get back on his feet again? And if he doesn't get back on his feet, get his life back together, then how can I possibly think about leaving?

I can almost hear Katie's voice saying: *He's not your responsibility.*

Marc peers at me, frowning, and asks, 'Sims? What do you think?'

I shake my brain back to the subject under discussion. 'He has been drinking a lot,' I comment. 'In fact, now I come to think of it, he's been a bit moody too, quieter than usual. Well, apart from this afternoon. Perhaps he *is* worried about the club but just can't face up to it – I mean, he's been running that place for years. Maybe he's in some sort of denial.' I shift a straying lock of hair back behind my ear. 'I still don't believe he's having a fling though.'

'That's what Johnny says.'

I look up, startled. 'What? You've talked to Johnny about this?' When it comes to Buckley business I'm used to being the last to know about anything but now it appears I'm even lower in the pecking order than our houseguest. 'Why on earth did you—'

'Not me,' he interrupts. 'Mum.'

I'm even more astounded. 'Your *mother*? But why would she ... she can't stand him ... she didn't even want him to stay.'

Marc gives one of those dismissive waves of his hand as if he's swatting a fly. 'Oh, you know what she's like. She never was very good at holding grudges.'

Try telling that to Gena, I think. 'So, what, they're suddenly the best of friends now?'

He pulls a face as if I'm accusing Dee of some nefarious activity. 'They've always been friends. They just had a sort of ... misunderstanding.'

I look at him and shake my head. Yes, some sort of *no-good, low-life, murdering bastard* misunderstanding. Not the kind of thing you usually manage to overcome in a few days. But then the mysteries of the Buckleys are many and profound and it's doubtful that even a ten-year scrutiny, never mind my meagre five, could begin to scrape the surface. I want to find out more about this new and unexpected alliance but decide to leave it until later. The contents of a bottle of wine will do more to loosen his tongue than any blatant interrogation.

'Well, I guess that's good,' I state in a conciliatory tone.

He looks faintly surprised at this sudden reversal, my attitude towards Johnny having previously being made quite clear to him, but rewards me with a heart-warming smile. 'Sure,' he agrees, 'it's better that we all get on.'

Before I can be tempted to stray back on to the fascinating subject of Mr Frank and Mrs Buckley, I quickly change the subject. 'Do you want to stay for another or shall we make a move?'

He looks at his watch. 'Yeah, let's go. I don't think much of this place, do you? They must have bribed the reviewer.'

I've been so involved in the conversation I haven't really taken a proper look round. Marc, on the other hand, without ever having appeared to give it a second glance, has clearly made a detailed examination. I do a quick survey; it's all violet walls and chrome fittings, a bright and shiny retro creation that I might have found mildly amusing a decade ago but which only gives me a creeping sense of déjà vu now. The music, a relentless hip-hop, has been turned up a notch since we came in and the clientele have a highly strung anticipatory air about them, maybe because it's Christmas Eve but more likely thanks to an excess of hormones and cocaine.

'Mm,' I murmur. 'I see what you mean.'

He grins. 'We must be getting old, Sims.'

'Speak for yourself, buster.' I grab my coat and bag and we head outside.

It's started to drizzle again but as the restaurant is less than a couple of blocks away we decide to brave the elements and walk. It's not cold enough for snow, all hopes of a white Christmas remaining only in the hearts of eternal optimists. There is some small consolation, however, in the illuminations strung across the High Street; as the rain falls the drops catch briefly in the light, sparkling like a thousand tiny diamonds.

Marc takes my hand as we negotiate the road, dodging the cars and zigzagging through the last-minute shoppers and early celebrants. Much as I try, it's impossible to be unmoved by the festive atmosphere, by that curious childlike thrill that seeps uninvited into my bones. A shiver of delight wriggles down my spine. And although I shouldn't, although it's certainly a mistake, I like the warm safe feeling of his fingers wrapped around mine. I like that feeling of *belonging*. It'll all end in tears, my head whispers, but my mouth ignores the threat and curls rebelliously into a smile.

As the rain starts thrashing down against the pavement, we run the last two hundred yards and arrive slightly breathless at our destination. Laughing, we dash inside and grin at each other like a pair of kids. Luigi's is busy as ever, filled with its usual supply of well-heeled appreciative diners. A buzz of conversation fills the room whilst in the background some vaguely classical piece of music struggles to be recognized.

Marc provides our name and we're efficiently propelled between the potted palms to a table by the window. The marble floor, white walls and gilt accessories remind me of a rather too exuberant bathroom but hey, I'm not complaining; the surroundings may be sterile but the food is always excellent.

We order two dry martinis and settle down to examine the menu.

I've barely begun to scan its delights when Marc leans forward as if I've asked a question and says: 'Actually, I was just thinking about what I was doing this time last year.' He puts his elbows on the table, his chin in his hands, and expels a long and weary sigh. 'It feels like a lifetime ago.'

'You don't have to worry about that. It's behind you now.'

He shakes his head. 'I really fucked up.'

'It's over,' I respond softly. 'There's no point dwelling on it. It's the future that . . . '

But as he raises those beautiful if doleful cobalt eyes, I get the disturbing impression that the future doesn't hold any more promise for him than the past. It's a sad but incontrovertible fact that our closeness is in inverse proportion to the happiness of our circumstances. When everything is going well, Marc inevitably withdraws, and it's only when the coin is flipped, when trouble looms, that we're able to form any kind of bond again, to temporarily re-establish a close connection.

If he only needs me when he's in trouble, does that make me a bad-time girl?

Before I can think of an answer to this *Sex and the City*-type conundrum the waiter has arrived. He's small and dark with a slim waist and pencil-thin moustache. Although probably in his mid-forties, he seems almost ageless, exuding the practised civility of a man who has learned to balance the trials and tribulations of his job with the benefits of its tips. Suavely he delivers our drinks, smiles courteously and produces his notepad.

'Good evening, sir, madam. Welcome to Luigi's. May I take your order?' His accent, although ostensibly Mediterranean, has a distinctly Cockney twang.

I plump for the tarragon chicken, a simple but delicious speciality of the house. Marc orders a steak, studies the wine list and eventually opts for a bottle of champagne.

As I glance up at the extravagance, he grins and says: 'Why not? It's Christmas after all.'

The waiter scribbles his instructions, nods and glides professionally away. I'm still following his progress through the room, wondering at his effortless speed and agility as he negotiates the tables, palms and assorted members of the public and staff, when Marc starts speaking again.

'You know, he's not as bad as you think.'

I look at him, confused, my thoughts still focused on the disappearing figure. 'I'm sorry?'

'*Johnny*,' he elucidates. 'Will you stop watching that man's butt and concentrate for a moment.'

'I was not—' I begin indignantly.

But he's laughing again. 'Jeez, I can't take you anywhere, woman. As I was saying, Johnny's actually okay. And you know, I feel pretty sorry for him; it can't be easy coming out after all these years, trying to start again, trying to pick up the pieces. I met a few guys like him, lifers coming to the end of their sentence and they were all . . . ' He pauses and shrugs. ' . . . kind of *empty* somehow.'

It seems a shame to have to talk about Johnny when the evening, especially since we left the bar, has been on such an upward curve. I feel as though Marc has brought our brief escapist interlude to an end. Which is crazy as I was the one who intended to press him for more information – and here it is, being handed to me on a plate.

'It's not that I dislike him, exactly,' I reply disingenuously. 'I mean, we don't really know him, do we? We've barely seen him since he arrived and it's pretty hard to form an opinion on a couple of hours' acquaintance.' It's a fact that since our initial meeting I've only passed him once or twice on the stairs and we've exchanged no more than half a dozen words – but a sneaking suspicion is creeping into my mind: *I might not have spent any time with him but as for Marc . . .*

He doesn't answer immediately. Then, as if anticipating the logical progression of my thoughts, he downs the last of his martini and explains: 'I've probably seen a bit more of him than that. It didn't seem right to leave him on his own. And with you and Mum out all day, and with Dad behaving like he is . . . well, we've had a few chats and he's okay, Sims, he really is. It's tough for him. You should give him a chance.'

A chance to do what, I wonder? I don't trust Johnny Frank, not an inch. Since his name was first mentioned there's been nothing but grief in the house. Not that it was ever exactly the Garden of Eden, more like Regent's Park zoo, but the strife has increased five-fold since he arrived.

'I can't believe he survived it,' Marc continues, 'all those years. Can you imagine what that's like?'

I'm about to retort: *No, I can't – but he did kill someone*, when a shadow passes over his face and I suddenly realize this conversation is maybe as much about him as it is about Johnny, a reminder of where his own life has gone so terribly wrong. And I wonder if I've taken Marc's insouciance too much at face value, whether his imprisonment was ever as painless as he affected.

Anyway, whatever the ins and outs, it seems wrong to spoil a perfectly good dinner with bad feeling so I keep my suspicions to myself. 'Okay, I'll be nice to him.'

Marc smiles. 'Oh, and Sims, if you could . . . well, not

mention it to anyone that Johnny's staying with us, I'm sure he'd appreciate it. He wants a bit of time to himself, you know, to get readjusted, to get used to being on the out again.'

'Who would I tell?' I reply lightly. 'I can't think of anyone who'd be interested.'

But my levity hides a greater concern. This desire to remain hidden bothers me, along with all those cosy little chats everyone seems to be having. First Dee, now Marc, and I'm certain Carl hasn't wasted a single opportunity to bask in the glow of his gangster hero. Come to think of it, I even saw Jim walking in the garden with him the other evening. For a man who claims to want some space, some time to think, he's been keeping pretty busy. There must be a small queue forming outside his door.

Perhaps I should make an appointment.

Another issue pops suddenly into my mind. I recall what Carl said earlier, his goading little comment as I came in from work. I balance my chin on my elbow and ask casually: 'Marc, has Johnny said anything to you about *me*?'

'About you?' he replies. 'Why on earth should he say anything about you?'

There's an irritating incredulity to his tone as if my existence could barely hope to register on the Richter scale of Johnny Frank's consciousness. Or maybe I'm just being oversensitive.

'Oh, it's nothing.' I shake my head. 'Just something Carl mentioned. He said Johnny had … it doesn't matter. Forget it.'

Marc ponders for a moment and then, just as I think the subject is closed, he says: 'God, yeah, I remember. Sorry. He must have meant about his wife.'

'Gena?'

'No, *Johnny's* wife.'

I look at him, surprised. 'I didn't know he had one. Why isn't she ...'

'No, he hasn't, not any more. But that was it, the other day he was saying you reminded him of her a bit.'

I feel a tightening in my stomach. Tentatively, anticipating that I'm about to hear something I'd really rather not, I ask: 'So what happened to her?'

'Oh, she died, years ago. A car accident, I think. Just after they separated. Shit, that really must have done his head in, her asking for a divorce on top of everything else. You can tell he was mad about her. He didn't want to let her go.' Marc shook his head. 'Losing someone like that – God, it drives you crazy when you're inside.'

I feel an unwelcome shiver shimmy down my spine. How crazy exactly? Crazy enough to ... no, this is just my imagination working overtime, my dislike of him twisting a terrible tragedy into some ill-founded suspicion. An accident is an accident. There's no reason at all to believe he had anything to do with it. You don't kill the person you love. You have to be ... well, *crazy* to do a thing like that.

The waiter has arrived with the food and champagne.

But somehow I don't feel quite so hungry as I did.

Chapter Six

Johnny

I'm not expecting anyone when the knock comes on the door. Shit. Talk about bad timing.

I raise a finger to my lips, nod towards the bathroom, and my companion scurries inside with a grimace. Then I quickly cross the floor, open the door and smile.

'Dee! What a lovely surprise! I thought you and Jim had gone out.'

I try to look flattered that she has deigned to climb the stairs yet again to spend a few precious moments in my company. It's become a habit over the last couple of evenings and one I should have anticipated. Over-confidence has made me careless.

'Oh, only to the Swan. I can't stand round chatting to his cronies all night.' Then, perhaps picking up a hint of distance in my tone, she narrows her eyes and adds suspiciously: 'I'm sorry, love, am I disturbing you?'

'No, of course not. Come in, come in.'

As I stand aside to let her enter, the pungent scent of her perfume wafts unpleasantly into my nostrils. She's dressed in a short red skirt and white T-shirt, looking more like a poor impression of a teenage US cheerleader than a fifty-three-year-old wife and mother. All she needs is a pair of pom-poms. It takes an effort to keep my mouth curled in the right direction but I'm used to going that extra mile. When it comes to effort I'm the expert – after all, it takes determination to wade your way through eighteen years of fucking nothing.

'Let me get you a drink.'

'I can't stay long.' She smiles faintly. 'Well, go on, just a small one then.'

While I do the honours, she drifts around the room as if she's never seen it before, as if it isn't *her* room, in *her* house, as if she hasn't put the sheets on the bed or the flowers in the vase. I hold my breath as she passes the bathroom, hoping she won't decide to pop inside and check if the plumbing is still working efficiently. But thankfully she proceeds to the window and stares down into the blackness of the garden.

'Maybe you were right,' she says eventually, 'about Jim . . .'

Good, so it's still on her mind, although that's hardly surprising after Carl's outstanding performance this afternoon. I try not to snigger at the recollection, the best piece of entertainment I've had for quite a while. 'Of course I was,' I insist solemnly, pressing the glass into her hand. 'Cheers! I mean, it's not his style, is it? Other men, yeah, they might be tempted by some chit of a girl with it all hanging out, but not Jim. He's got more sense – and more taste.'

'If I imagined for one second—' she begins.

'Don't,' I insist, 'don't even think about it. Whatever Carl saw, or whatever he *thought* he saw, I'm sure it was all completely innocent.'

'What do you mean?' she snaps back, rising to the bait. 'Carl didn't say he saw anything. What did he see? He only said the girls were talking, that some of them were claiming that Jim and that Aimee slut were ... What's he said to you?' Her lips have drawn into a tight straight line. 'What's he told you?'

I raise my hands in a gesture of submission. 'Nothing, I swear. Calm down. That's what I meant – what Carl *heard*. Nothing else. It's just malicious gossip. Forget it.'

But she can't. She peers at me, broodingly, over the rim of her glass. She doesn't trust me but then she doesn't trust Jim either.

'Oh, come on,' I urge. 'Jim isn't going to risk everything he's got for a roll in the hay with some brainless little slapper.'

'Unlike you,' she retorts, pretending to joke although her eyes are deadly serious. The laugh that emerges from her crimson mouth is harsh and bitter.

I've wondered how long it would take her to get around to this. She's been leading up to it from the moment I arrived. And the question I've spent the last eighteen years trying to answer rises to the fore again: *Why the fuck did I ever get involved with her?* There are some decisions you make, some bloody stupid decisions, that you end up regretting for the rest of your life, and my fling with Dee, long ago as it was, comes right at the top of the list. Why, why, why? But even before I've finished asking, I already know the answer – because I thought with my cock instead of my brain, because I didn't have the sense to keep it in my trousers, because if it was there for the taking I'd never say no.

'It's not the same. You were hardly a ...' But I think it best not to finish that sentence. 'There's been a lot of water under the bridge since then. It's history. We're over all that stuff now, aren't we? Dee?'

I throw her one of my more irresistible smiles.

She doesn't seem overly impressed.

Instead, she knocks the rest of her drink back in one, goes over to the table, picks up the bottle and sloshes another large measure into her glass. The smell of gin wafts through the room. 'Do you know what I've always wondered? Why you told him. I could never figure that one out. Why *did* you?'

I raise my face to look straight into those hard blue resentful eyes.

Because you were a reckless bitch who was ruining my life. Because you wouldn't leave me alone. Because you mistook a few quick fucks in the afternoon for a lifetime of commitment. Because you made sure Sarah knew about it.

'I didn't tell him anything,' I reply smoothly. 'At least, nothing he didn't already know. It was common knowledge, sweetheart. There wasn't any point in lying about it.'

She makes a sarcastic kind of tsk sound in the back of her throat. 'But you were always so good at lying, a bloody expert. You could have thought of something. What happened? You have a sudden attack of conscience? I mean, God, Johnny, you almost wrecked my marriage.'

That's what I love about women, the way they're able to rewrite the truth to suit themselves. What is it – some kind of selective memory process, a cut and paste option that allows them to delete any unpalatable facts? She's conveniently forgotten that *she* was the one who made all the running, who was panting for it, who had her knickers off before the office door was even halfway closed. She didn't give two fucks about her precious marriage then or when, horror of horrors, she started mapping out our future together.

'I didn't tell him,' I repeat insistently. 'He already *knew*.'

Although I'd made damn sure he was told. Of course I did. All of it. Just as she had made sure that Sarah was apprised of every sordid detail – almost blowing *my* marriage apart in the process. Well, an eye for an eye. You can't say fairer than that.

'Huh,' she mumbles derisively through another slurp of gin.

If Jim had been any kind of a man, he'd have taken the opportunity to floor me, to give me a damn good kicking. I wouldn't have fought back. I wouldn't even have tried. Well, only enough to protect myself. No, I'd have just been glad, fucking glad that it was over, even if it was at the expense of a battered face and a few bruised ribs. But the cowardly bastard couldn't even do that. He just lowered his eyes and walked away. And waited ... and waited ... until he got the chance of an even greater retribution.

It's time to take the offensive. 'Look, I'm sorry. I didn't realize you were so ... Perhaps it's not a good idea for me to stay here. I'd never have agreed if I thought you were still—'

'Oh, don't flatter yourself,' she interrupts. 'You think I

really give a damn about you, about any of that?' She ejects another of her humourless laughs.

I skip the landmine of trying to answer. Whatever I say will be wrong. Silence is often the most judicious of replies. Best just to stare at the floor, dodge the trip wires and try to look chastened.

She pulls a face and starts roaming round the room again. While she paces, she drinks, pouring the gin down her throat like it's going out of fashion. 'I was only asking,' she says. 'No harm in that, is there?'

I shake my head.

Shit, if she keeps going like this, drinking like this, it's only a matter of time before her bladder leads her to the bathroom. And then ...

The next time she passes, I take hold of her arm. 'Can't you stand still for a minute?'

She shrugs me off but doesn't move too far away.

'We're okay, aren't we? Dee?'

She gazes bitterly into my face and for a second I think she might spit at me. She'll never get over the fact I chose Sarah over her. Even after all these years it's still eating away, a festering resentment that refuses to heal. I can almost see her reason vying with her rage, the rational thought of the money, of the diamonds, battling against her more irrational emotions. 'Why shouldn't we be?'

'You tell me.'

She sinks on to a corner of the bed. 'And what's that supposed to mean?'

'It means that this isn't going to work if there's bad blood between us. If you want me to go, I will. I don't want to stay where I'm not welcome.'

Her expression instantly changes. 'Who said you weren't welcome?' She turns and looks up at me. Either the booze has hit a button and sent her hurtling into some nostalgic rose-tinted version of the past or she's decided on a different game plan. 'I never said that.' She stretches out her legs, extends a hand and pats the edge of the bed. 'Why don't you sit down?'

I look into her eyes, still granite hard, and force a smile. 'Sure.'

'You know, Johnny, we were pretty good together once.'

'Pretty good,' I agree in a placatory tone.

'So . . .' she says, tilting her head in a way she maybe imagines to be seductive.

But two can play games. I take a few lascivious steps forward before suddenly stopping and turning towards the door.

'What was . . .'

'What?'

'Didn't you . . . I thought I heard . . . isn't that Jim?'

She leaps up from the bed, taking a moment to recover herself. 'What if it is?' she asks defensively. 'There's no reason why I shouldn't be here.'

'Well no, of course not, not under normal circumstances but . . .' I lower my voice. 'You know, he might be a bit . . .' I glance down at the bed. 'It might seem a bit . . .'

'Oh, don't be ridiculous,' she snorts, 'and anyway, as if *he's* got any right to . . .'

But she still follows me towards the door. With an air of

subterfuge, I open it carefully, peer along the empty hallway and usher her out.

She pauses and then leans back as if she might kiss me. Her breath smells of gin and peppermint. 'Johnny—'

I take a step back. 'You'd better go,' I insist. 'I'll see you tomorrow.'

'Christmas Day,' she says, as if it might have slipped my mind.

I stand for a minute, listening to her footsteps descending the stairs. Then when I'm sure, absolutely sure, that she's gone I retreat to the chair by the bed, sit down and drop half a glass of whisky down my throat.

Fuck.

The door to the bathroom slowly opens.

'Jeez, man, it's freezing in here. Haven't you ever heard of central heating? I didn't dare turn on the radiator in case it hissed or something. God, I thought she'd never go.'

She's wearing a denim skirt, even shorter than Dee's, and an even tinier top. A ruby stone glitters in her flat naked midriff. In her hand she's carrying a pair of strappy red sandals.

'Well, if you don't wear any clothes, what the hell do you expect? And keep your voice down.'

'Ah,' she says, padding over to the table and pouring herself a stiff drink, 'you're not going to go all father-figure on me, are you?'

Which reminds me of Dixie and which in turn reminds me that it's against the rules to lust after your dead best friend's daughter, even if she does send the blood pumping through your veins. I try to keep my gaze focused purely on the area above her neck. 'It's the middle of winter. You want to catch pneumonia?'

She pulls a face, raising her eyes to the ceiling. 'Stop stressing, you'll give yourself a heart attack. You need to loosen up a bit.' Dropping down on the edge of the bed, she leans over to fasten her sandals, giving me an eyeful of cleavage in the process.

I glance at my watch. 'Where's Carl?'

'He's gone to see a mate. It's only nine o'clock, he won't be back for hours.'

I may have agreed to the plan but I still don't feel easy about her contrived relationship with the younger Buckley son. It takes fuck-all stretch of the imagination to understand how she captured his interest – but how far will she have to go, how far has she already gone, to keep it?

'Boy, has Dee still got the hots for *you*,' she grins, straightening up. 'She almost had you by the short and curlies. Another few minutes and you'd have been a goner. You'd better take care of that virtue of yours.'

'I'll try.'

She throws me one of those female *as if* kind of looks before abandoning the advice and changing the subject. 'I paid Aimee. You want her to carry on or should I tell her to lay off for a while?'

'When does the club open again?'

'Next Thursday.'

I think about it. 'Let's see how it goes. I'll let you know.'

She grins widely. 'God, she was good. You should have

seen her, Johnny, all over him like he was bloody Tom Cruise. Jim didn't know what had hit him; the poor sod thought Christmas had come early.' She gives a giggle but then remembering the purpose of the exercise grows suddenly more serious. 'You think Dee believes it?'

'She isn't sure. But it's planted a seed and . . .'

'And now all we have to do is watch it grow,' she adds wickedly.

I glance at my watch again. 'Look, you'd better make a move. It's late. I don't want you getting caught here.'

She gets up, lifting her long fair hair and flicking it over her shoulders. It's another of those gestures that women often do and something else I've almost forgotten.

'Okay. I'll see you tomorrow.' She throws me a kiss. 'Sleep tight.'

'And Mel,' I demand as she advances towards the door, 'watch your back.' Not for the first time I'm having qualms about her being involved although, as she's always insisting, it's as much her battle as it is mine.

'Don't worry,' she laughs, 'I can take care of myself. I *am* Ray Dixon's daughter.'

But as Dixie was stabbed to death fifteen years ago that's hardly reassuring.

Chapter Seven

Simone

It's gone twelve before we head downstairs. Without overtly saying it, we've been putting off the moment for as long as we can, lingering over breakfast, taking our time over the opening of our presents, making endless cups of coffee, and using any excuse to delay the inevitable.

But the moment of reckoning has finally arrived.

It's Christmas Day at the Buckleys'.

And as we enter the living room, there's definitely an atmosphere, a frosty chill that could freeze the toes off an Eskimo. Jim lurches out of his chair, grabs my arms to steady himself and plants a damp kiss on my cheek. 'Simone! Merry Christmas, Merry Christmas!' He's been at the whisky and I can smell the sour stench of his breath.

'Oh, for God's sake, leave the poor girl alone.'

The voice is hard and accusatory. Glancing over his shoulder I catch Dee looking daggers. Suspecting perhaps some sexual slant to this clumsy embrace, she's staring almost as hard at me as she is at him. I gently push him away. 'Happy Christmas,' I announce jovially to the rest of the gathering. It emerges more heartily than I intended.

An audible, if subdued, return of festive greetings drifts back. My stomach takes a dive. It's clear we've just walked in on yet another simmering Buckley row. The air seethes and bubbles with unspoken accusations. And I inwardly swear this will be the last occasion I ever go through this. What is it with families? If this is normal behaviour then I thank the Lord I've been spared. Oh, for Australia, for those long golden beaches! This time next year . . .

Marc has already bagged the space on the oversized sofa beside Melanie, Carl and Dee, leaving only the chair beside Jim – not a good idea – or the one by the window beside Johnny. Reluctantly, I opt for the latter, wondering if it's just my imagination or if Mr Frank has a more-than-normally-smug expression on his face today. And for a man who's just got out of prison, he's remarkably well dressed, attired in a well-cut dark suit, white shirt and charcoal tie: Mr Grey at his sartorial best. I've chosen to wear my blue jeans and although I've paired them with an expensive red cashmere jumper I feel positively downmarket in comparison.

'Happy Christmas,' he repeats softly as I sit down.

I nod, forcing a smile. Hoping to discourage any further exchanges of seasonal goodwill, I pretend to gaze out of the window but the rain-speckled glass obscures the view across the garden and instead I find myself looking, with almost ludicrous concentration, at a six-inch square of opaque smudge.

In the meantime, Marc has started to chatter away. Either immune to the atmosphere or valiantly trying to overcome it, he's embarked on a long and amusing story about Luigi's. It has the effect, at least, of breaking through the ice and temporarily diverting everyone's attention.

Or *almost* everyone's.

As I turn, it's to find Johnny staring blatantly at my chest.

'That's very pretty,' he says.

I glare back at him. 'Pardon me?'

A thin curl touches the edge of his lips. 'Your locket,' he explains. 'It's very charming. Was it a present?'

I could swear the level of his gaze was a good three inches lower but I lift my fingers automatically to touch the silver locket with its two tiny diamonds. It *is* pretty, possibly the loveliest gift that Marc has ever bought me, but there's something in Johnny's tone, in his voice, that suggests this is more than a passing compliment. Yet, when I look into his eyes, I have never met a colder, more assessing gaze.

'Yes,' I reply shortly.

I glance around, but there seems no immediate escape from this unwelcome attention. Dee and Carl are listening to Marc, Melanie is preening, and Jim, filling his glass again, is pursuing his ongoing love affair with the bottle.

Undeterred by my lack of enthusiasm, Johnny continues: 'It suits you. Do you like jewellery?' Then he gives a low laugh. 'Of course you do. All women *love* jewellery. It's in the genes. And especially diamonds.'

Now maybe it's only the fact that Johnny unnerves me, that I'm a touch on edge, but I get the distinct impression that the ensuing silence is not a natural break in the conversation. All heads are suddenly turned towards us. There's a feeling of suspense as if breath is being held, as if a pause button has been depressed. The only sound in the room comes from the television, a faint chorus of carols heralding the eternal joy of Christmas Day.

It's disconcerting to find yourself in the spotlight for no discernible reason. I smile uneasily, glancing from face to face. I'm about to go on the offensive, to ask what's wrong, when as quickly as it arrived, the moment passes, action is resumed, and talk begins again. I look back at Johnny. His grey eyes are still impassive but his mouth breaks slowly into a thin knowing smile. And now I experience the opposite, but equally disturbing, sensation of being completely in the dark.

Just to add to this feeling of disquiet, Dee jumps up abruptly and declares: 'Well, the dinner's not going to make itself.' Sounding flustered, she makes hastily for the door.

Glad of an excuse to escape, I rise as well. 'Let me give you a hand.'

I'm not usually so enthusiastic when it comes to domestic chores but I would rather peel five thousand potatoes than remain another second in Mr Frank's company. He makes the hairs on the back of my neck stand on end.

Dee seems unenthusiastic about the offer. Either she is trying to avoid me or, just as likely, is aware of my lack of culinary skills. 'It's all right, Simone. You stay and have a drink. I can manage. There's only—'

'No, no. I'm sure there's something I can do,' I insist,

breezing past her to the kitchen. Although once I get there it becomes immediately clear that there is in fact very little to do. Dee has obviously been slaving away since dawn and multiple saucepans, already filled with prepared vegetables, sit waiting on the hob. I feel a flash of guilt that we've been lazing around upstairs all morning.

'I only need to baste the turkey,' she explains, putting on the gloves and opening the oven door. She's got that snappy irritable edge to her voice again. 'Why don't you go and make yourself comfortable.'

'Mm, that smells good,' I reply, blatantly ignoring her suggestion. And it's true that a delicious aroma is pervading the air. It's been a while since breakfast and I peek in at the browning turkey hoping that this year, unlike last, we might actually get to eat it. As she spoons over the juices, I wonder what I can do to make myself useful and thus justify my continued absence from the living room. Noticing a small heap of dirty pots sitting beside the sink I leap on them with a previously unknown alacrity. 'I might as well get these out of the way.'

But no sooner have I started to run the water than Dee foils my masterful plan by saying: 'Oh, just dump those in the dishwasher.' She closes the oven door, wipes her brow and checks her watch. 'Another half-hour should do it.'

I'm about to resign myself to a further thirty minutes of agonizing small talk when, glory of glories, Melanie appears at the door with an opened bottle of red wine in one hand and three glasses balanced precariously in the other. 'I thought the workers could do with some refreshment,' she announces brightly. I instantly revise my bad opinion of her.

'Lovely,' I reply, sitting down at the table. 'That's a great idea.'

Even Dee seems marginally cheered by the interruption, pulling out a chair and almost cracking a smile.

Melanie does the honours, generously filling the glasses and then passing round a pack of cigarettes. Breaking my resolution yet again, I accept one. Well, there's no reason to fight it; resolutions are for New Year's Eve and not for any time before.

'Happy Christmas!' we toast simultaneously.

For the next fifteen minutes, there's an amiable flow of chatter about presents given and received, a showing off of watches, lockets and bracelets, followed by a few nightmare recollections of past inappropriate gifts of exotic lingerie. With the contents of the bottle rapidly disappearing, there's an inversely proportionate rise in laughter. Whatever happened earlier begins to fade and waver round the edges, its sharpness gradually dissolving into something less defined.

Did I imagine that peculiar silence?

'Just look at us,' Melanie comments with her childlike giggle, 'we're all in the kitchen while they're talking football and waiting for their dinner. How 1950s is that?'

I smile back at her. 'So much for progress.'

Lifting her baby blue eyes, she stridently proclaims: 'Oh, men are no good! If there's one thing I've learned it's that if you want anything doing, do it yourself.' She tilts her head, throws back her long blonde hair, and smiles at Dee. 'No offence to Carl, of course.'

'None taken,' she says, rising to her feet to prod the potatoes and sprouts.

As soon as she's out of earshot Melanie grins, leans forward and whispers conspiratorially: 'I suppose Marc's the same?'

'He has his moments.'

'But you get on pretty well, don't you?'

And suddenly, despite the effect of the wine, I feel a resurgent need for caution. As innocent as she appears, I can't quite bring myself to trust her. It's as if she's angling for something. 'What do you mean?' I ask disingenuously, keeping my tone light.

She looks at me and laughs, showing her pearly white teeth. 'Oh, I didn't mean anything. I'm sure Marc's the perfect husband.'

'Well, I doubt if any man qualifies for *that* particular status.'

She's about to continue with the cross-examination when the timer on the oven stridently erupts into a more than welcome ring.

It's impossible to say exactly how or when the trouble started. At first everything went smoothly. We gathered round the large dining table, resplendent in its starched green linen cloth, and took our places: Jim at the head, Dee to his left, then Marc, and myself, Johnny opposite me, and Melanie and Carl to his left. This was possibly the first mistake. Had Carl been seated anywhere but next to his father it might never have happened, but despite Dee's clearly stated invitation that Johnny should take the chair beside Jim, he ambled down to the other end of the table and said, 'No, no, this is fine.'

'But I thought if you sat—'

'Gosh, Dee, this all looks *so* beautiful,' Melanie enthused squeakily, interrupting her objection and thus giving Johnny the opportunity to slide into his chosen place. 'Where did you get those plates? They're absolutely *gorgeous*.'

Personally, I'd have preferred it if Dee had got her way but apart from tipping up his chair and forcibly ejecting him there didn't seem much I could do. With his napkin already untwisted and placed over his knee, territory had been irretrievably established.

I couldn't understand why he'd been so adamant in his choice of position. Why didn't he simply take the place that had been allocated? Maybe he liked the idea of the extra space, some elbow room to his right; maybe after prison he preferred not to feel crowded. But although this reason seemed entirely logical I couldn't quite believe it. I'd already formed the opinion, rightly or wrongly, that almost everything Johnny did had an ulterior motive.

'Don't you think, Simone?'

I glanced up at the sound of my name. 'Sorry?'

Johnny, disconcertingly aware that I hadn't been paying attention, explained: 'Melanie was just asking whether you thought women were more predisposed towards loyalty than men?'

I stared from him to her, amazed. God, in the light of recent events this was the last thing we should be discussing. Had the girl got no tact? And *he* wasn't any better. I replied: 'No, not especially,' and then rapidly changing tack said, 'But hey, Melanie, I've been meaning to ask, where did you get that *fabulous* dress?' Not the most skilful of subject changes but the best I could manage at short notice.

Carl, in his usual charming manner, couldn't resist a jibe. 'There's women for you. All they ever think about is clothes.'

'You can talk, honey,' Melanie retorted, 'you spend longer in front of the mirror than I do.' Then as she embarked on a long story about the garment and its designer origins, all I had to do was sit back and nod.

I stole a quick glance round the table. The atmosphere was less chilly than earlier and although there wasn't exactly a heat wave in progress the temperature had risen to a few degrees above freezing.

Jim carved the turkey and the food was distributed, praised and heartily consumed. The conversation flowed, along with the wine, and for a while, as the six white candles flickered in the half-light and the crystal glasses sparkled, all was perfect harmony. Had a passer-by chanced to wander off the road, scale the wall and come to press his face against the window, he would have thought himself witnessing a touching Christmas scene of mutual love and affection.

And then it all kicked off.

Looking back, I couldn't say who started it. There had been one comment, seemingly innocuous, and another. Then a question, a retort, a jibe. The first voice I really registered was Jim's.

'If you've got something to say, why don't you just say it?'

Carl put his elbows on the table and glared at him. '*You* know what I mean. Why don't you just come clean, be fucking honest for once.'

'That's rich coming from you.'

Dee, her cheeks flushed pink, interjected: 'Stop it! Both of you. Can't we have one day when ...'

But already it was too late. I gritted my teeth and waited for the worst. Like a runaway train the wheels had been set in motion and nothing was going to stop it now.

'At least I'm not a fucking cheat. We all know what you did with that slut.'

In the ensuing silence, the only sound was the faint wheezy hissing of Jim's breath. Inches apart, they held each other's gaze, two prize bulls waiting to charge. Beyond the table the room had grown much darker and their faces, contorted by anger, were thrown into fiendish relief by the stuttering candlelight.

God, this was going to end in disaster.

'You fucking shit,' Jim almost spat.

'What's the matter, Dad? Not man enough to admit it?' Daring him, challenging, taunting.

Melanie laid a restraining hand on Carl's arm. 'Hey, honey!'

He almost slapped her away and she withdrew with the hurt expression of a child who has been unfairly punished. I felt sorry for her. If there's one thing I've learned it's never to interfere in a Buckley row.

Carl continued to goad. 'Come on. If you're man enough to do it, then you're man enough to—'

'Stop it!' Dee insisted again, more loudly and forcibly than before. 'I've had enough. Do you hear me? This stops *right now*.'

And she might have had some small chance of putting on the brakes if Marc hadn't chosen that moment to stand up, hurl his fork down with a clatter, and walk out of the room without a word. A few seconds later the front door closed with an almighty slam. I couldn't blame him for taking off but he could have had the decency to wait for me; it was a bit late now to try and follow in his wake.

Dee turned to Jim. 'You see what you've done?'

'*Me?*' he snarled, with what could be claimed to be righteous indignation. 'I'm not the one who started this.'

I considered excusing myself and escaping upstairs but then on second thoughts decided that might only exacerbate the situation. There was still a slim chance that Dee might be able to regain control. Sadly, the futility of this hope soon became apparent as, rather than smothering the flames, she proceeded to pour petrol on them instead.

'Oh, that's right,' she barked, 'nothing's ever *your* fault, is it?'

'Did I say that?'

Her eyes flashed. 'You don't have to. It's not what you say, it's what you *do*. I mean, what do you expect, hanging round those girls every night with your tongue hanging out like some sex-starved puppy? Haven't you got any dignity?' And then, just to rub salt in the wound, she added: 'You're old enough to be their bloody grandfather.'

'Jesus,' he murmured, shaking his head.

But at least he let it rest there, turning away to pour himself another glass of wine. And that might have been the end of it if Dee hadn't persisted.

'Don't you bloody dare ignore me!'

At which Carl sniggered and the rage reappeared in Jim's eyes. As if steadying his nerves he took a long drink, replenished his glass, and prepared for round two.

'That wouldn't be easy with you screaming in my ear.'

Carl took the opportunity to stick his oar in again. 'Oh yes, I'm sure you'd prefer it if she just kept quiet. That would suit you right down to the fucking ground.'

Jim slowly turned his gaze on him. 'Shut your mouth. This has fuck all to do with you.' His voice had the low and forcibly restrained quality of a man about to break.

Regretting that I hadn't taken the opportunity to do a runner, I wondered if there was any possibility of distracting them. An explosion was clearly imminent and although I knew there was nothing I could do to prevent it, my brain still embarked on a ludicrous series of diversions. Perhaps I could launch myself out of the window, faint or start to scream. All I had to do was open my mouth and—

'That's right,' Dee said, 'have a go at him. That's you all over, isn't it? Forget about taking responsibility for your own actions and just blame someone else.'

Jim stared silently back at her.

His silence was more worrying than his words. Glancing up, I caught Melanie's eye and we exchanged a look of alarm. Johnny was staring down at his plate. His face was pale and grey and serious. If I hadn't been so preoccupied, I might almost have felt sorry for him.

'What, cat got your tongue?' Dee took a sip of wine and glared. 'Or are you feeling too guilty to answer?'

Jim gave a brief humourless laugh. 'What have I got to feel guilty about?'

'You need to ask that?'

'Yeah, right,' Carl echoed, 'you need to ask that?'

'I've told you before,' Jim said, losing his cool and grasping him by the shoulder, 'this has *nothing* to do with you.'

Dee leaned over the table and grabbed his hand. 'Leave him alone,' she screeched.

He twisted away. 'Get off.'

'You get off.'

There was an ungainly scuffle, an undignified scrabbling and slapping of arms and wrists. Like a playground fight, it rapidly descended into a series of juvenile taunts and retorts. It wasn't just embarrassing to watch but to listen to as well. Reaching the end of my tether, I finally snapped and said as firmly and calmly as I could: 'What the *hell* are you doing?'

I'd like to claim that the silence that followed was thoughtful, maybe even shocked, but in fact it served only as a brief respite. As I opened my mouth to continue the highly reasoned protest their maddened faces turned as one to glare at me and, recalling my own excellent advice about never getting involved, I wisely shut it again.

Before the dust had even begun to settle, they'd resumed their positions and were at it again. Defeated, I raised my shoulders in a shrug. What was the point of even trying? Mediation clearly wasn't my forte. I could do balances, accounts and VAT. I could add up and subtract. But I *couldn't* do the Buckleys.

As if I hadn't ever spoken, Dee said to Jim: 'How do you think it makes me feel, hearing all that stuff?'

'It's not down to me. It's not my fucking fault if you listen to gossip. You don't have to believe it.'

She gave a mocking laugh. 'I'm your *wife*, for Christ's sake.'

His face dissolved into a scowl. Assaulting his liver with yet another glass of wine, he muttered through red-stained lips, 'When it suits you.'

'And what's that supposed to mean?'

'You know what it means,' Jim said, staring intently down at the table. His hands, lying on the cloth, curled tighter and tighter until the knuckles showed white.

'No,' she insisted, her teeth bared in anger, 'why don't you tell me? Why don't you tell everyone? Come on, we're all waiting.'

'He hasn't got the guts,' Carl goaded, sitting back and folding his arms.

And all my instincts told me to go, to leave right then, to sprint as fast as I could towards the closest available exit, but my arms and legs were heavy as lead. I'd hit that point where the train was hurtling down and I was completely paralysed.

Jim slowly raised his head and stared at her. I could tell he hadn't quite made up his mind, that the retort hovering on his lips might still remain unspoken. It wasn't too late. His fingers flexed and stretched as if they alone could reach a compromise. Caution battled with his mounting rage but was inevitably vanquished. His voice when he spoke was soft and controlled but filled with bitterness. 'Isn't there a saying about people in glass houses ...'

The silence that followed was absolute. It took me a second to grasp the inference; God, was he claiming that... but there wasn't any time for further speculation. Dee suddenly slammed her glass down. It smashed against a plate and shattered, the fragments falling amongst the sprouts and gravy. Like tiny jewels they glistened in the candlelight. Then in one fast jerky movement she scraped back her chair, stood up, and stormed out of the room.

For a few seconds no one spoke. No one moved. Then Carl turned, grinning, to his father and said: 'You happy now?'

I watched Jim rise carefully from his chair, his face puffed and scarlet. Unsteady on his feet he lurched and tipped forward, grasping the edge of the table for support, before finally finding the strength to straighten up. From the corner of his mouth a bead of spittle escaped and dribbled down his chin. A noise, something guttural, more animal than human, emanated from his throat. He swayed a little, glaring down at his son. There was no doubt of what he'd *like* to do – his intention was clear enough for Carl to flinch and shift back out of reach – but from some distant quarter of his drunken brain he managed to dredge up enough restraint to turn his back and walk away.

Carl courageously waited until he was clear of the room before sweeping aside his plate. 'Fucking bastard.' Then appealing to Johnny Frank and Melanie, he said: 'You see what he's like? You see what the fucker's like?' He didn't bother addressing me. There was no point scattering grain on stony ground.

'Don't get upset, honey,' Melanie replied. As if she'd been

blind and deaf to everything that had preceded, she lifted her baby blue eyes and naively insisted: 'It wasn't *your* fault.'

'You see what he's like?' he repeated, with all the imagination of the tedious drunk. This time his attention was entirely concentrated on Johnny. Having harvested one fruitful response, he was eager for the next.

But Johnny's grey eyes were impassive, only his brows lifting a fraction. He was either in a state of shock or utterly indifferent. With the light from the candles throwing dark shadows across his face any subtler indications of his emotions, if indeed there were any, remained shrouded. But eventually he sighed and said softly: 'Perhaps you should see how your mother is.'

In his current frame of mind, I was certain Carl would blow a fuse but surprisingly he smiled and, as if God had spoken, replied respectfully: 'Yeah, I'm sorry, mate. You're right.' He gently pushed back his chair, stood up, and as docile as a lamb gambolled off in search of Dee.

Watching open-mouthed, I heard Melanie ask: 'Do you think I should follow him?'

No, I would have replied, but as I glanced back I was faintly aware of Johnny giving a slight, almost imperceptible, nod of his head. Before I could voice an opinion she had slipped from her seat and disappeared through the door.

And then there were two.

The combatants have scattered and all that remains is the distant sound of their angry footsteps. Johnny has removed his jacket and tie, rolled up his sleeves, and for the last thirty minutes we've been clearing the table, sweeping up the broken glass, and washing and drying the dishes. Unsure of what may or may not be dishwasher-proof – and unwilling to take the risk of increasing Dee's unhappiness – we've reverted to the old-fashioned method of cleaning everything by hand. Although I'm still less than comfortable in his company there is at least the consolation that he's very nicely house-trained and, as circumstances have forced us together, I decide to take the opportunity to do a little probing.

'You must be starting to wonder why you came here,' I say with all the subtlety of a Grand Inquisitor. 'It's not exactly peaceful, is it?'

Refusing to be drawn, he shrugs while he carefully wipes down the draining board. 'I've been worse places,' he replies. Which is unarguably true.

'They're not always this bad but then I don't need to tell *you* that. You've known them for a lot longer than me. You must have been close friends back then. I mean, I'm sure you still are but it must have been a pretty special friendship for you to want to stay here when you . . . ' I let the sentence peter out, my avid curiosity dampened by a sudden spring of tact. This resurgence of good manners is less to do with any sensitivity as regards his emotions than with the possibility of scuppering my own investigation; in what must be his first free Christmas Day in a considerable number of years, it's hardly diplomatic – or endearing – to remind him of the past.

But surprisingly he smiles, folds his arms across his chest, and says: 'When I came out of *jail*? It's okay, you're allowed to mention it. I promise not to faint.' A red and white striped tea towel hangs from his hand. 'And please don't worry about hurting my feelings – I really don't have any.'

I force a laugh, unsure as to the seriousness of this statement. Although I can readily believe it for there's a cold efficiency about everything Johnny does, a lack of warmth that may be integral to his nature or perhaps simply a result of where he has been for the best part of the last two decades. Either way, I think it wise not to loiter on the subject and embark instead on a ramble about Christmas past.

'Still, I suppose it's an improvement on last year. We didn't even make it to dinner then; not a single sprout passed our lips. Carl had an unholy row with Gena – that's his wife, well ex-wife, almost – and World War Three broke out. Now that was a fight, a real battle and a half, there wasn't exactly blood on the walls but ...' Turning away, I lift the plates off the table and start to stack them in the cupboards. 'We were eating cold turkey for the rest of the week.'

What I don't mention (can't mention) is how I fled upstairs and, desperate for some fresh air, opened a window and leaned out. Looking down, I saw them standing together on the grass. At first I thought they were making up, his arms wound tightly around her body, the two of them entwined against the hedge. It was only as I started to squeeze my way back through the window that I heard a sound more fearful than amorous and saw his palm move swiftly over her mouth.

His other hand lingered by her bare shoulder and in the dim light I recognized the tiny, brilliant gleam of a cigarette.

It was over before I could react, an act of vicious malice perpetrated with speed and purpose. Her scream was stifled by his hand, mine by the shock of what I had witnessed. And then suddenly she had struggled free and was gone, running down the drive towards the car. He watched her for a moment and then went inside, whistling softly.

'Simone? *Simone?*'

I come back to the present to find my hands poised mid-air, still holding a pile of plates, and Johnny staring intently at me. 'Sorry,' I murmur, 'I was just . . .' Quickly, I shake my head, trying to chase the image from my mind.

'You look like you saw a ghost.'

'Something like that.' Feeling flustered, I shove the plates in the cupboard and search around for another job but everything is spick and span, all the surfaces shining and all the crockery, cutlery, pans and glasses in their rightful place.

'What you need is some fresh air,' he insists. 'Come on, let's take a walk.'

'No, really, I'm . . .'

But before I can finish the objection he's opened the back door, passed me a raincoat from the porch, and ushered me outside. I wonder if anyone *ever* argues with him. I imagine he was the type of villain who never had to ask twice – or even think about raising his voice. He has a quiet air of authority that borders on the menacing.

Of course there are people I would far rather take an evening stroll with than a convicted killer but beggars can't be choosers and, after the claustrophobia of the house, it's a relief simply to be in the open space of the garden. Dusk has fallen and soon it will be dark. The last of the light filters greyly through the naked branches of the trees and for a while we walk in silence, our feet crunching on the gravel path. As the scent of wet grass drifts up on the breeze, I begin to see the attraction of Johnny's endless perambulations for there's an unexpected sense of restfulness and peace in this suburban plot of land.

However, unwilling to allow our silence to become *too* companionable, and recalling my earlier intention to do some detective work, I assume my policeman's helmet and ask: 'So what do you think Jim meant? You know, what he said to Dee?'

He gives me a sideways glance and does that little upward motion with his eyebrows again. 'I'd have thought that was fairly obvious.'

Slightly riled by his patronizing tone, I retort, 'The accusation may have been clear but what I was *trying* to ask was if you thought there was any truth in it.'

'Why, do you think it's impossible that she's having an affair?' He runs his fingers through his hair, chasing out the drizzle that has started to fall. That familiar thin smile quivers on his lips again. 'Too old perhaps? Too faithful? Too set in her ways?'

I get the distinct feeling he's amusing himself at my expense. Which irritates me even more. 'Did I say that?'

'Isn't that what you meant?'

'How could you possibly know what I meant?'

Which leaves us at a temporary stand-off, or at least I think it does, until we round the path by the pond and he says quietly: 'Perhaps he wasn't talking about now. Perhaps he was referring to something that happened in the past.'

I hate myself for reacting like a gossipy housewife but the words have flown out of my mouth before I can stop them. 'What? You mean Dee ...?'

'It's only a suggestion.' He gazes down at the sluggish water before slowly lifting his eyes. 'For the sake of debate,' he adds, with what might almost be called mischief.

And instantly I know. I know that *he* knows and that he isn't going to tell. Damn him! Although I'm tempted, oh so tempted, to pursue this fascinating line of enquiry, I'm also certain that it will be a waste of time. He has said as much as he is going to say and no matter how hard I push, I'll only succeed in strengthening his resolve to hold his tongue. Unwilling to give him the satisfaction, I merely nod and attempt, perhaps not very successfully, to appear indifferent.

My subsequent muteness seems to amuse him as much as my questions. Walking slowly around the rim of the pond, he gives a small laugh as he reaches out with the tip of his shoe and disturbs the brown and littered surface.

'Do you think there are fish in here?'

'Not unless they're masochists,' I reply, staring down into the murky depths.

He crouches down by the bank, finds a long stick, and like a schoolboy searching for tadpoles begins to root around the weeds. His expression is so intense, so concentrated that I feel an almost perverse curiosity about him. I wonder who he is, who he *really* is, how he's spent the last eighteen years, how he's survived them and, more to the point, what he's intending to do next.

The rain, falling a little harder, pocks the surface of the water and after three empty crisp packets, a bobbing dented can and a shoal of rotting leaves have been driven from the bank, he slowly rises to his feet again. 'You could be right.'

'I usually am,' I respond, joking.

Pulling himself to his full height, a good six inches over me, he draws back his shoulders, turns and says unexpectedly: 'You don't like me much, do you, Simone?'

I couldn't have felt more alarmed if he'd drawn a torch from his pocket and shone the beam in my eyes. My intake of breath is embarrassingly audible. In a few merciless minutes, I've somehow managed to pass from being arch-prosecutor to a thoroughly discomfited defendant. His gaze meets mine and the challenge is irrefutable. For a while I'm not sure what to do and then, taking refuge in that very British middle-class response of ignoring anything embarrassing or difficult, I duly gather my resources and pretend that nothing has happened.

'It's going to pour down,' I say, cupping a hand to capture the rapidly increasing raindrops. 'We'd better head back.'

But as I turn a rumble of thunder rolls ominously overhead and he takes hold of my elbow and says: 'No, we'll get soaked. The shed's closer.' A flash of lightning illuminates the sky and the rain starts to pound, harder and firmer, thrashing down on to the grass and turning the ground beneath our feet to mud. There's no time for argument. Sloshing through puddles we run the five yards, mount the shallow steps to the covered wooden veranda, and take shelter.

'Lovely,' I murmur, gazing out. Inwardly, my mind is still reeling, marginally from how Dee might react to his reference to her beloved summerhouse as a 'shed', but mainly from his direct and provocative question. I'm glad of the protection of the deepening dusk. At least he can't see the flush that burns brightly on my cheeks. I'm quite sure that he senses it though, that he can feel the discomfort oozing from my bones, just as I am equally and alarmingly sure that he is pleased to have inflicted it.

Johnny glances at me sideways through the gloom. Worried that he may be about to resurrect his unnerving interest in my bad opinion, I ask quickly: 'So, what are your plans for the future? There must be lots of things you want to do.'

His smile reappears at my clumsy attempt at distraction. 'What do *you* think I should do?'

'Whatever you like.' I'm tempted to add that he's had plenty of time to think about it. 'I really don't know you well enough to say.'

He gives a low unpleasant laugh. 'But well enough to know that you don't like me.'

Oh Lord, so we're back to that again! I shuffle from foot to foot, hoping the rain will ease, but as if in heavenly denial another fork of lightning splices the sky and the thunder, almost overhead now, crashes loudly around us. Flinching, I draw back a little and pull my coat closer. Then, deciding that what can't be dismissed must inevitably be faced, I take a deep breath and ask with a stridence I don't feel: 'What does it matter what I think of you?'

He pauses for a second, his grey unblinking eyes fixed intently on my mine. Refusing to be intimidated, I stare straight back. A tiny muscle twitches at the corner of his mouth but whether this is down to irritation or humour is impossible to discern.

'It doesn't,' he replies eventually, 'I'm just curious. When someone feels such a clear aversion, I can't help wondering why. Is it my appearance, something I've said, something I've *done*?' He emphasizes the last word as if to remind me of his history. 'You can see my dilemma. If I don't know what's wrong, I can hardly begin to change it.'

In direct contrast to the weather, an unexpected dryness has infiltrated the veranda. I find myself staring at his long thin fingers draped across the rail. 'Why should you want to? I don't imagine you're the type to care much for other people's opinions – good or bad.' I throw him my most challenging smile but like a gift attached to elastic it bounces instantly back.

'Perhaps not,' he responds slyly, 'but when all's said and done, it's nice to have the choice.'

And now I'm assailed by a secondary, even more disturbing, sensation that that I'm being drawn down a path I should avoid, that I'm being led along a route that leads directly into Johnny Frank's manipulative universe. Somewhere, in the back of my mind, I'm receiving the idea that it was him who started the Buckley argument. All it took was a word here, a word there, and Jim and Carl were at each other's throats.

He moves a few inches closer. 'But never mind,' he

continues, 'I won't ask you to explain. I can see it makes you uncomfortable. You've made your judgement and I doubt there's anything I can do to change it.' He expels a long weary sigh. 'I'll just have to live with the disappointment.'

I hold my tongue. In the circumstances, it seems the safest thing to do.

'Although women have been known to change their minds,' he adds, ruminatively. He throws me a mocking glance before shifting forward and leaning his elbows on the rail. Then, looking over his shoulder he grins again. 'There's no need to look so worried, sweetheart. I'm not propositioning you.'

I'm not sure what makes me finally snap: his arrogance, his presumption? Whatever, I feel the red mist rise.

'Well then, *I'll* just have to live with the disappointment,' I angrily retort, and deciding that a soaking is better than his company I stomp down the steps and into the pouring rain.

Chapter Eight

Johnny

There's more than one way to kill a man. First you have to offer him his dream, let him get within grasp of it, let him touch it and smell it – before snatching it away.

Jim's sitting on the sofa, sniffing the air like an overweight pug. It's the second of January and he's had twenty-four hours to think about my latest proposition. The scent of money's in his nostrils but he's trying hard to fake indifference, to pretend a pleasant chat is all he's after on this damp and chilly afternoon. It's been a bad week for Mr Buckley: Dee is still seething, Carl remains hostile and Marc is avoiding him. What he needs is a coup, something spectacular to restore his dignity. What he needs is a hat and a bloody big rabbit to pull out of it.

And I'm offering him both.

'Okay,' I agree, as if instead of sitting quietly he's been busy providing a persuasive argument, 'so I *will* need some back-up, some help in creating a diversion. I'm not denying it. The minute I walk out that gate, as soon as I make a move to pick up the ... merchandise ... Tate and his cronies will be crawling all over me. Not to mention any other bastard who fancies his chances. So fine, we can make a deal – but I won't go higher than twenty per cent.' Burying my hands deep in my pockets, I lower my voice and glance around for imaginary spies behind the furniture. 'That's a bloody good offer and you know it.'

If he's been doing his homework – and I'm sure he has – he'll have the figures neatly stored in that greedy little brain of his. Pink diamonds frequently reach extravagant prices in the international auction rooms. And we're talking thousands of dollars per carat here if the colour and weight and clarity are right. Not that we'd be able to sell them on the open market but ... well, there are always private buyers for any desirable object.

Jim expels a nervous rush of breath. 'Why don't you do a deal with Tate? Get him off your back?'

'Why should I? He's a piece of shit.'

He nods. 'But he thinks you owe him.'

'I owe him nothing,' I hiss, 'nothing at all. He was paid, fair and square, eighteen years ago. If I start doling out second helpings, there'll be a fucking queue winding round the block.'

It's come as no surprise to discover that Eddie Tate, our last-choice lousy driver from the Hatton Garden job, is already hanging round, haunting the street outside the house and hoping for a lucky break. Like Jim, he's got pound signs dancing in front of his eyes. It didn't take him long to find out where I was. Good news travels fast. In fact a damn sight faster than we travelled that night, eighteen years ago, easing back into the London traffic like a party of nervous geriatrics. It would have been quicker to catch a bus. I can still remember Dixie leaning forward and screaming: *Move, you fucker, move!* And now, like some cockroach crawling out of the woodwork, Tate's back again hoping . . . hoping what? That I might be stupid enough to lead him straight to the end of the rainbow?

Still, it's useful that he's here. It gives me the perfect excuse to sit tight while I lay those extra sticks of dynamite. Going on the offensive I ask: 'And how the fuck did he find out where I was?'

'Not me,' he whines plaintively, shaking his head. 'I've not said.'

I give him a long interrogative stare before eventually bestowing my gracious benefit-of-the-doubt smile. 'I'm sure you haven't, Jim.'

Truth is, I didn't expect to have to dangle the lure of the diamonds quite so early on. I thought I'd have a month's grace at least but last night he began enquiring about the rest of the money. He hated to ask, didn't want to put any pressure on me, but would he be able to have it soon? Pressing obligations and all that. He's already had five grand but he's eager to see the rest – worried, probably, that I'll get my act together and do a bunk in the middle of the night. Then there'll be no more cash, no ice, no nothing.

So I didn't have any choice, not having the other five, but to raise the stakes. It was what he wanted anyway, what he was hoping for: a share in the big bonanza. Of course, I pretended to be unhappy, dragged my feet for a good hour or two and only gave in after a convincing show of reluctance.

Now, naturally, he wants to rush straight out and get them. Like a fat kid staring through the window of a sweet shop, he can't wait to fill his face. So it's good that Eddie Tate's impeding any hasty action. It gives me the extra time I need to burrow deep inside the Buckleys and feed that ever-present rot.

'So have you talked to Dee about it?'

Jim mumbles an incoherent response.

'Still mad at you, huh?' I give him one of those man-to-man sympathetic glances. But I know it isn't Dee that's really worrying him. She'll jump at the opportunity of a fresh start, of a new life out on the Spanish Costa – luxury villa, limitless sunshine, new cars, expensive clothes. No, what's still nagging at Jim, although he'll never admit it, is that he's about to commit a crime.

Now Jim could always talk the talk but when it came to anything more you wouldn't see his heels for dust. Sure, he'd hide the occasional firearm, launder a little iffy cash, even turn a blind eye to a spot of illegal gambling on the premises – but that was his limit. Although he encouraged the villains, the hard men, the gangsters, to frequent his tiny East End bar, it was only to bask in the thrill of it. He was always an onlooker, never a participant.

So what he's getting involved in here is handling stolen property – but not just any stolen property. Those rare pink diamonds have passed into the archives of criminal mythology. Hidden for nearly two decades they've acquired an almost religious significance, a Holy Grail of sparkling carbon. And he knows what that means: if we're caught he may have to face a sizeable stretch inside. He's the same age as me, fifty-four, and he doesn't fancy spending his remaining years at Her Majesty's pleasure.

I can't help smiling. The very idea gives me a nice warm feeling in the pit of my gut.

But it isn't going to happen. And Jim isn't going to get his grubby little fingers on one single perfect pink-blushed diamond. Still, he can hope . . . and the bigger the hope, the greater the disappointment.

I light a cigarette but keep silent, letting him advance towards his own irreversible decision. He's in the process of doing what he has always done – justifying the unjustifiable. In this case, he's saying to himself that the gems were taken so long ago that they can barely be classified as 'stolen' any longer, more *missing* than stolen, and that all he will be doing is reclaiming something that was lost. He will keep saying it, over and over, until he eventually believes it to be true.

Once I'm convinced he's at least halfway towards this resolution, I resume the conversation. Picking up where I'd left, referring to Dee, I say despairingly: 'Women! You never know what they're thinking, do you?'

Jim gives a shrug of resigned agreement.

Although I know exactly what Dee was thinking when she came to my room yet again last night, her blouse opened a button too far, her eyes sly, her speech slightly slurred.

'Johnny! You didn't come down to dinner this evening. I was worried about you.'

It's not as though she really desires me, not any more, only that she's got a point to prove – that she's still attractive, that she *could* have me if she snapped her fingers. And there's no harm in pretending that she might be right. There's no harm in playing along. Especially if it gets me what I want.

'Best to be cautious,' I've been busy advising her, 'especially when it comes to money. Best to keep an eye on things. Not that I believe any of this Aimee stuff but . . .'

Now, Dee's built for suspicion; it courses through her veins like blood. And the more she suspects, the more she thinks she has good reason. It's a self-perpetuating cycle and one I'm more than happy to exploit.

So all's well on that front.

Turning back to Jim, I ask softly, 'So have we got a deal?' I'm suddenly sick of his company, eager to be free.

'How long will it take? How long before we can—'

I produce a noise from the back of my throat, an exaggerated sound of irritation. 'How long's a piece of string? It'll take as long as it takes. A month, maybe two. What's the rush? You'll need some time to prepare, to get the club sold – and the rest.'

I see uncertainty rise like a wave into his gaze.

'No loose ends,' I insist. 'I'd have thought that was pretty obvious.'

He grunts, not liking my tone. But then there isn't much he *does* like about me. Just to rub salt in the wound I add nastily, 'Perhaps you need to talk to Dee about it.'

Jim flinches. He knows what I'm implying – that she's the one in charge, that she's the one who makes all the decisions. And no man likes to be accused of being under the thumb. Even if it's true, perhaps *especially* if it's true. His face turns pink and then scarlet. Hate flashes in his eyes. He bares his teeth for a second before recovering his senses, before hiding them behind an impassive smile. Even he's not so stupid as to cross me at such an important time. No, he'll store away his resentment like he's always done, saving it up for a rainy day.

I shift a little closer, invading his space. 'So is that a yes? Do we have a deal?'

Jim stares back. My tobacco breath's in his face and he's trying not to grimace. The words of the last few minutes are still firing down on him; like tiny arrows they're piercing the skin of his pride. He wants to punch my lights out, but he won't even try. In Jim's greedy little world there are greater priorities than dignity – and he knows he'll never get a better offer for as long as he lives.

'So it's a deal?'

Eventually he nods. He can't actually bring his mouth to utter the word, can't trust himself to speak, but the rest of his body's busy doing the talking. He even puts out his hand to shake mine. I see it there, suspended, too large and white, too fleshy, too dirty . . . stretched out . . . waiting.

I have to force myself to take it.

Quickly, briefly.

Then he's gone, thank God, mumbling some excuse about the club. I'd like to fuck off too but I can't – not until he's left the building, not until he's out of reach. I'm too afraid of my rage. It's taken every ounce of self-control to stop myself from ... I don't even want to think about what I might do, *could* do, if I lost control. It's in my head, twenty-four hours a day – that angry vicious voice screaming for revenge. It's eating away at me.

So I sit on the sofa, confined to base, while I wait for him to leave the house. It's safer this way. I stare at the walls, at the chintzy curtains, at the cabinets filled with flowery china plates, and try not to go insane.

It's over fifteen minutes before I finally hear his footsteps in the hall, before the front door opens and slams shut. Walking quickly upstairs, I'm into my room and stripping off my clothes before Jim's even reached his car. I head straight for the bathroom and turn on the hot water. I fall into the shower, sloughing off the feel of him. I scrub and scrub until my flesh turns pink. I can sense his presence on my skin and under my fingernails, ingrained as coal dust, dark and filthy. I brush my teeth until my gums bleed. There's a sour taste in my mouth that never goes away.

Slowly, I dry myself, wrapping a towel around my waist. When I look in the mirror I hardly recognize my reflection. The more I stare the stranger I become. Someone else's face, someone else's hair. I've never been handsome, only younger. Now age has invaded, creating lines and hollows. My cheekbones rail against my skin, too sharp, too protuberant. Where did he go, that other man whose flesh was hard and firm, that man who looked towards the future as a place to be lived and not just to be survived?

Time. I know all about the passing of time. I can break it

into weeks and days, hours and minutes; I can divide it into memories, split it into expectations. I've sliced it thinly and examined it under a microscope. Inside, there is no worse enemy than time. Like a long empty tunnel it stretches ahead, the nothingness, the barrenness, the cold eternal walk. It turns men inwards, against themselves; they curl and diminish, corrode and crumble away. There's something else too, equally terrible but never spoken of – the vicarious excitement that whispers through the prison wings, the watching, the listening, the silent, almost grateful witnessing of *other* people's suffering. There but for the grace of God …

It's just after six when I make my way downstairs again. Like an over-eager puppy, Carl jumps up as soon as he sees me, loping across the room as if he's going to lick my hand. I recoil from him, disgusted.

At that very moment Simone comes through the front door and stops, key in hand, to stare at us. She has seen the flinching and it confuses her. She looks briefly from me to Carl and then back, two tiny vertical creases appearing on her forehead. Her hair is damp from the rain and one small strand has slipped free to fall across her cheek. She nods in her peculiarly neutral way, not even bothering to smile, before walking quickly up the stairs.

I turn to Carl and see his blue eyes, accusing and doleful in equal measures, as if I haven't just shunned him but landed a good hard kick in the process. The truth is, I don't like anyone too close. It makes me uneasy. It makes me want to lash out. And Carl is as bad as his mother, always crowding me, always in my face. However, I force myself to slap his shoulder in a comradely fashion. 'How are you doing, mate? It's good to see you.'

Instantly he brightens. 'You want a beer?'

I follow him into the kitchen where he opens the fridge and takes out a couple of bottles. He snaps off the caps and hands me one. I'm sure he'd rather stay inside where it's warm and dry but I can't stand the enclosed space. I need to be outside, breathing the fresh air, even if it has started to rain again. Perhaps because it's started to rain again – I like the cool feel of it against my face. I like the cold chill that seeps through my blood, cleaning and sterilizing, keeping me free from Buckley infection.

Darkness has fallen but I could walk this garden in my sleep now. I know all its nooks and crannies, where the paving stones are broken, where the ground slants up or suddenly dips down, where the gnarled roots lie hidden in its wilder part. Anyway, it's not pitch black; the light from the kitchen floods gently across the grass and, at the further end, the distant street lamps cast a faint orange glow.

I let him make the conversation, pretending to pay attention. I nod and grunt while my eyes sweep the shadows. He likes me to talk about the past, to tell him how The Palace used to be, to recite the stories of my life. What he really wants to hear about – but cannot quite bring himself to ask yet – is the killing of Roy Foster. He wants to know the gruesome details. He wants to see the picture and hear the noises. He wants to know what it's like, what it *feels* like, to commit murder.

Carl Buckley revolts me almost as much as his father. But

I need him. I need to have him on side. So I go along with his endless requests for information. I feed his fascination with a mixture of old anecdotes, myths, facts and lies. I play down the sordid angles and exaggerate the glamour. Disguised as a plush red carpet, I roll out the shoddy path that led me to the here and now.

Tonight, I have a new story for him.

He's heard about the diamonds of course. Everyone in this house has – except perhaps for Simone. He's heard about Hatton Garden, about the perfect robbery, about how Dixie and I got arrested over Foster before the pink ice could be sold on. But he hasn't heard the details. And he hasn't heard about the offer I've made to Jim.

So I tell him a little about the job, distorting the truth and jazzing up the thrills, watching his eyes widen as the tale unfolds. Oh, he loves this stuff! He wants to be a part of it, inside it. He wants to feel the rush. He wants to be cool, to be a renegade, a gangster. Not that I ever was. A criminal, yes, but never a gangster. There's a difference. But Carl doesn't realize that. He believes what he wants to believe. And that suits me just fine.

After I've finished I throw him a look. 'So what do you think?'

'Yeah, man,' he says, 'amazing. One hell of a job.'

I frown. 'I wasn't referring to that.'

Carl frowns back. 'Right.' He glances at the ground and then into the far distance, suddenly afraid of making a fool of himself.

I let a few seconds of silence pass between us. The only

sound is the soft steady tread of our shoes against the path. He isn't sure what to say next. Of course he isn't. He hasn't got a clue what I'm talking about. I look aside so he can't see my smile, the parting of my lips, the slow smirk of satisfaction.

Timing, that's what it's all about.

As we reach the pond, I think about the last time I stopped here – Christmas Day with Simone. She's barely spoken to me since. She's said good morning, of course, always polite, but her eyes are cold and challenging. What colour are they? Not brown exactly. Lighter. Hazel? Like Sarah's. She narrows them when we meet on the stairs, looks at me and forces a smile – no, not exactly a smile, more a polite widening of her lips. Her contempt rolls like a wave. I want to grab her arm, to touch her, to claim: 'You don't know me, you can't judge me.' But I don't. I let her pass. I smile and let her pass.

I turn and say quietly to Carl: 'I meant about the offer I made your father.'

Now he's got a decision to make, and he's got to make it quickly. Does he admit his ignorance or feign the knowledge that he craves? He scuffs the toes of his trainers against the chipped stones that line the bank. His eyes flash, hot and angry. Searching for an answer, he gazes briefly into the distance again. Curiosity gradually overwhelms any sense of pride or caution. 'What was that?' he asks, trying to sound casual, his head still turned away.

'He hasn't told you?' I sound surprised. 'Oh, perhaps I shouldn't have mentioned it. Maybe he didn't want—'

'To let me know?' Carl interrupts, almost spitting the question out. He drives one hand deep into his pocket while he uses the other to draw the bottle to his mouth. 'That bastard never tells me anything.'

'I'm sure he's just been thinking things over.'

Carl kicks a few pebbles into the water. His mouth has formed a straight thin line. 'What offer?' he asks sulkily.

It takes an effort but I lay my hand firmly on his shoulder, like a father standing with his son. 'The diamonds, of course – without some help, how do you think I'm going to get them back?'

Instantly his face changes. Christ, he can't believe his luck. Now he's in the big league; he's working with Johnny Frank. And he can't stop talking about it, asking questions, making crazy suggestions. For these few minutes he's forgotten about Jim's failure to inform him but later he'll remember and he won't be happy. He won't be happy at all.

'Good to have you on board,' I murmur. As we're walking back towards the house, I wipe my fingers carefully down my jeans.

Chapter Nine

Simone

It's a relief to be back at work, to be out of the house. There's an atmosphere there. I can't exactly put my finger on it: the rows are still going on – when do they ever stop? – but there's something else too, a kind of restrained excitement mingled with a furtive whispering. Marc tells me I'm imagining things. Which make me all the more certain that I'm not.

Just to make matters worse, every time I turn around Johnny's there, on the landing, on the stairs, as I'm coming through the door. He's like a permanent shadow. And he's got this way of staring as if he's taking in every detail, as if he's saving it all up to use as evidence against me. I can't stand the man. I don't ever want to be alone with him again.

No, it's better in the shop even if we are suffering from the post-Christmas lull. It's only the dead keeping us occupied at the moment, January's cold weather claiming its seasonal tally. The table in the back room is strewn with the remnants of white lilies and chrysanthemums. I take my time over these wreaths, carefully arranging the blooms, sympathetic to the finality of the gesture but struck too by a creeping awareness of my own mortality. What am I doing? Life is passing me by and I still haven't made any definite plans.

Dee came in earlier but has since left us to it. There's no point in the three of us being here and her mind's not exactly on the job. She's been the same since Johnny arrived, tetchy one moment and effervescent the next. I saw her coming out of his room last night, a little dishevelled, a little the worse for wear, and there was something about the way she glanced cautiously along the landing that made me wonder if . . . but no, that's just crazy, she wouldn't, she couldn't possibly. *Jim's* supposed to be the partner with the straying hands. And come on – Johnny? How could anyone consider touching, never mind sleeping with, that cold grey creature . . .

But I didn't mention what I'd seen to Marc. Why not?

I must be scowling because Kerry Anne suddenly asks, 'Hey, what's the matter?'

'Nothing.'

'Have you had a row with Marc?' There's as much hope as curiosity in the question. Perhaps we'll get a divorce and she can step into the breach.

'Of course not,' I reply. And her face instantly falls. It's a slightly different face to before Christmas, more subtly made-up and curtained with a freshly cut-and-coloured bob of fine blonde hair. Although she will never be a Melanie she has the softer, more innocent look of a plump and affectionate cherub. 'What makes you ask that?'

Kerry Anne shrugs. 'Nothing,' she replies in an echo of

my own response. Her mouth aims for a smile but purses instead into a tiny Cupid's bow of disappointment.

I spend most of the afternoon searching for things to do. The shop has never been so clean; swept, mopped, polished and dusted, every surface gleams. It has rarely been so empty either. I sort and re-sort the flowers, creating ever more alluring displays for the forecourt. Surely something must attract a customer – the delicate arrangement of pink and white roses, the lilac-blue sprays of iris, the velvety rows of winter pansies?

It's almost four when the man wanders in off the street. It's been so quiet he has my undivided attention. I watch as he meanders through the shop, glancing to left and right, before proceeding slowly to the counter. He's a small sullen-faced male, over fifty, skinny and pale. His skin has the colour and texture of old parchment. A pair of bright red ears, chilled by the wind, stick incongruously out from the side of his head. As his cunning eyes skim the flowers I know – even before he reaches me – that he hasn't come to buy anything.

He slows to a stop, plants his legs apart and folds his arms. It's an intimidating stance despite his stature. There's a ring on his little finger, an ugly gold sovereign that looks too heavy for his hand. I stare at it. He stares at me. 'Simone?' he asks in a thin reedy voice.

I raise my eyes as he says my name. I jump too. I can't help it. Who is he? How does he know my name? There's something dark about him, something malevolent.

'Simone Buckley?'

He has the officious tone of a low-level bureaucrat, of a man who wants more power than he has. But he's not that and he's not a copper either – no cop is this badly dressed. Five years ago I would have just said *yes* – but I've changed since then. I've learned the advantages of silence. And I've also learned how to recognize a villain when I see one. Admitting to nothing, I merely make a small upward shift of my eyebrows.

The corners of his mouth turn down. He shifts his feet and grunts. It's clear I've annoyed him, that his scenario hasn't gone to plan, but he can always fall back on that ancient art of the well-worn threat. 'It doesn't matter,' he sneers, 'I know who you are.'

We glare at each other across the counter.

'Okay,' he says bitterly. 'If that's how you want to play it.'

I don't want to play anything. What the hell is going on? Is this something to do with Marc, with one of his crimes, with one of his frauds? I glance over my shoulder, glad that Kerry Anne is around but equally relieved that she's out of the way, employed in her usual fifteen-minute routine of making a basic cup of coffee.

'I've got a message,' he drawls, lowering his voice into Hollywood gangster mode. 'For Mr Frank.' He pulls an envelope from his pocket and throws it down in front of me.

Suddenly it all becomes clear. Johnny! God, I should have guessed. My breath rushes out in a gush of relief.

'Make sure he gets it.'

But even as I begin to reach out, thankful this is not

personal, I remember the promise I made on Christmas Eve. No one is supposed to know where Johnny Frank is living. Quickly I withdraw my hand. 'Who?'

'Best if you just do as you're told, sweetheart.'

Sweetheart?

But before I can think of a suitable retort he's swaggered out of the shop.

'Who was that?' Kerry Anne asks, making me jump again.

I wonder how long she's been there, how much she's heard. 'No one,' I reply, slipping the envelope into the pocket of my apron. Turning, I take the mug of coffee from her. 'Just some bloke trying to find Bishop Street.'

She looks at me, wide-eyed and unconvinced. 'You've gone all white, Simone. Did he ...?' But unsure as to what perversity he might be guilty of, she leaves the question hanging.

Lord, the last thing I need now is an interrogation from Kerry Anne. In fact the sooner I get out of here the better. 'You know what?' I reply, with what I hope sounds like brisk indifference. 'I think we should call it a day and shut up early. It's dead in here.'

'But won't Dee—'

'Don't worry about Dee. I'll sort it with her later.'

And Kerry Anne, smiling now and forgetting all about the scruffy stranger, rushes to bring in the displays.

Soon I'm out of the door and heading down the High Street. Typically, there's a bus pulling in across the road. I skilfully jaywalk through the traffic, getting honked at by irate drivers, but still find myself stranded on the island in the middle. Despondently I watch as the bus disappears into the distance. Damn and blast!

I'm too angry to wait around for the next one. I need to get home now and confront Johnny Frank. Whatever's going on, I don't want to be a part of it. As soon as a taxi appears I flag it down and spend the rest of the journey quietly seething in the back seat. I knew he was trouble – but whatever he's involved in, he's not using me as his message-taker.

I take out some of my frustration on the gravel as I stomp up the drive. I haven't really thought about what I'm going to say; the rage is welling inside me like a volcano about to blow. How dare he? How *dare* he try and drag me into his grubby little world! I've had enough of crime and criminals to last me a lifetime.

I slam the door shut and storm into the kitchen. It was a good guess. He's sitting there, Mr I'm-so-cool-and-collected, having a cup of coffee with Dee. I get the impression she isn't too pleased to see me – that I've interrupted a cosy tête-à-tête – but her feelings are the last thing on my mind. He smiles faintly. 'Simone.'

Just hearing him speak my name inflames my anger. Resisting the urge to slap his smug grey face, I throw the envelope down on the table. 'I'm not the bloody messenger. Tell your mates to use the post in future.'

If Johnny's surprised by my tone he doesn't show it. He slowly looks down at the envelope and then back up. Even that simple gesture reminds me of his creepy friend.

Only Dee gives a tiny flinch, her eyes narrowing as she

stares at me. Then she glances pointedly at her watch. It's barely four thirty and the shop usually stays open until six. I mentally dare her to say something – one snide comment and I'll tell her where to shove her job. And her flat. And come to that, her lying cheating son too. I've had enough of the whole damn lot of them.

But wisely she holds her tongue.

As we watch, Johnny slides a finger under the flap and tears the letter open. He removes the single sheet of paper, scans it quickly and throws it back down. 'Eddie Tate,' he says, glancing at Dee.

'What does *he* want?'

Johnny shrugs. 'What do you think?'

As if she's warning him not to say too much, her gaze swivels briefly in my direction. It's a gesture guaranteed to infuriate me even more. Lies, secrets, and more bloody lies. That's all this family consists of.

Suddenly he laughs. It was about the worst thing he could have done. 'I'm glad you find it funny,' I snarl, feeling the blood rush into my cheeks. How enraging can any one man be?

'Look,' he says, lifting his hands in a supplicatory fashion, 'I'm sorry if he frightened you but—'

'He didn't *frighten* me,' I almost shout back, conveniently dismissing those slim shivers of dread. In front of him, I'm not about to admit to any form of weakness. 'He made presumptions. He *presumed* I knew you. He knew my name. He seemed to think it was okay to use me as his personal postman.' I take another deep breath. 'Well, it isn't okay. Is that clear? I don't appreciate attempts at intimidation from ageing low-life bits of flotsam.'

I'm about to turn tail and dramatically reverse my entrance, when Johnny says, 'Perfectly. As I said before, I'm sorry. Before you jump to any more conclusions, why don't you sit down and let me explain?'

He gestures towards a chair.

I raise my eyes to the ceiling. Why does everyone keep assuming I'll do whatever they ask? As if I want to listen to his feeble excuses, never mind spend a second more than I need to in his company. 'No thanks.'

And I would have left there and then if Dee hadn't stuck her oar in. 'I'm sure Simone's got things she needs to do.'

What?

It's the sight of her sour and disapproving mouth, as much as her words, that makes me instantly change my mind. I've been bossed around enough today. And if something's going on, and I'm damn sure it is, then maybe I should try to find out what.

'You've got five minutes,' I announce, plonking myself down with the minimum of grace.

Dee says to him, 'Are you sure—'

'Don't you have to pick up Jim?' he says.

Now Dee's not the type to be summarily dismissed so it's pretty shocking, after a pregnant pause, to see her rise slowly from the table. It's clear she isn't happy but she isn't going to argue with him either. She nods, saving the full force of her antagonistic glare for me.

'Well, I'll see you both later,' she says icily.

Johnny sits, waiting patiently, until the bitter clicking of her stilettos is abruptly terminated by the slamming of the door.

'Thanks for that,' I snap. 'Today's just getting better and better.'

He picks up a skinny prison roll-up and lights it. 'You don't care what Dee thinks,' he replies, exhaling the smoke through his nose. 'You don't care what anyone thinks.' His mouth almost smiles. 'You're like me.'

Like him? A small laugh barks to the surface. If that's the truth I may as well hang myself right now. 'Oh yeah, and how do you figure that out?'

He leans back in his chair and stares. Does he know how uncomfortable it makes me feel? God, of course he does. Try not to look bothered. Meet his eyes. Don't let him stare you down. But what he says next throws me into a much more precarious zone.

'You're only here because it's safe and convenient.'

My heart does that flip-adrenaline thing, boom boom, and the blood reddens my cheeks again. I know he's referring to those matters I don't want to think about: Marc, the flat, the job. My life, in fact. And for a moment, like on the day I first met him, he's looking right inside me as if I'm made of glass.

'So you see,' he continues slyly, 'we're not so very different.'

There's a bad taste in my mouth. Bile. My stomach makes a grumbling nervous noise and I shift in my seat to try and cover it up. It's not the only thing I want to hide. My voice, when it emerges, has more than a hint of a croak. I clear my throat and start again. 'I don't think so.'

'Why? Because I killed a man?'

My face burns hot and then cold. What the hell am I doing here? I should have gone upstairs when I had the chance; I only stayed to spite Dee, to temporarily shake off the Buckley shackles. Now I'm back in the one place I never wanted to be again – alone with Johnny Frank.

Ignoring the question, I say: 'I thought you wanted to explain about your low-life scummy friend.'

'Well, you've got it wrong,' he says bluntly.

It's not the only thing I've got wrong. I shouldn't even be listening to him. I'm about to open my mouth, to interrupt, to prevent any more of his unpleasant and unwanted opinions, when he starts to talk again.

'Eddie Tate isn't a friend. Far from it. He's just someone that I used to ... associate with.'

His voice drifts as if from a distance. It takes a moment for its content to register in my consciousness. We've moved on. He's no longer talking about me, about us. *Pull yourself together, girl.*

'Right,' I eventually murmur, relief merging with the sharper remnants of alarm. Too warm for comfort, I shrug off my coat and drape it over the back of the chair. It gives me a good excuse not to look at him.

'I'm trying to make a new start,' he continues, 'to put the past behind me. I don't want shit like Eddie Tate around.'

'So what does *he* want?' I retort, echoing Dee's earlier question. Relief has made me strident. 'And why can't he use the phone like any normal person?'

'Because I won't take his calls,' he replies.

'But what does he want?' I ask again, this time deliberately meeting his gaze.

Johnny produces one of his indifferent shrugs. 'The usual. The same thing rats like Eddie Tate always want.' Laying his forearms flat on the table, he sighs. 'To pull you down into the same stinking sewer that he lives in. To make your life as miserable and meaningless as his.'

'He's a villain,' I say, stating the obvious.

'Like me,' he retorts softly.

I stare into his flat grey eyes – there's no hint of emotion – but don't reply.

'He shouldn't have approached you. I'll make sure it doesn't happen again.'

I drop my gaze and examine the table. I suddenly feel tired and empty, drained by the exhaustion that so often follows anger. I feel faintly foolish too as if I've overreacted to an incident that was really no big deal. Dee will think I've lost my marbles. Still, she's never had that high an opinion of me. I guess it's yet another thing to add to her list. I'm still thinking about that when the full impact of what he has said hits me like a thunderbolt. *I'll make sure it doesn't happen again*. My head jolts up and the words, accusing and fearful, are out before I can stop them. 'What do you mean?'

A small frown settles on his forehead but then instantly clears. He shakes his head, amusement quivering the corners of his mouth. 'Oh, Simone,' he says, 'for an intelligent woman you have some very serious prejudices. What do you think I mean? That I'll solve the problem the old-fashioned way, down a dead-end alley on a dark and moonless night?'

'No,' I lie.

He takes a drag of his cigarette. 'Although that might not be such a bad idea.'

This time I don't take the bait. 'I was only asking.' Now I sound petulant, like a teenager. Johnny certainly doesn't bring out the best in my nature.

'Never mind,' he grins, 'you'll be rid of me before too long.'

'Are you leaving?' I ask, with perhaps a touch too much enthusiasm.

He laughs as if I've made a witty comment. 'You're the ones planning a new life in Spain.'

Now it's my turn to laugh. 'Yeah, right.'

'Oh, sorry,' he replies quickly, 'I thought with Jim and Dee selling up ... and from what Marc said – well, I was under the impression you were intending to join them.'

'Selling up?' I repeat, stupidly. *What Marc said?* 'What are you talking about?'

He assumes a bemused expression before focusing his blank grey eyes on me again. Then his lips slide into a grimace and I hear a sharp intake of breath. 'Ah, I'm sorry. Perhaps I shouldn't have said anything. I thought ... I'm sure they meant to – *mean* to ...' Then, with an embarrassed smile, he adds: 'I'm sure nothing's been decided yet.'

'You've got it wrong,' I insist, 'you must have misunderstood.' But even as I speak I know I'm clutching at straws. For God's sake, this is madness. They can't just make plans to sell up and move abroad without mentioning the fact. I want to go on denying it, telling him he's mistaken, but the seeds of doubt are beginning to sprout. Is this what all the whispering has been about, the odd atmosphere, the silences when I walk into a room?

'What did he tell you?' I ask abruptly. 'What did Marc say?'

Hearing the frustration in my voice, he raises his hands in a gesture of submission. 'Hey, maybe I got it wrong. I don't want to cause any trouble.'

But there's a sly look on his face and I suddenly know, contrary to his protestation, that trouble is exactly what he wants. Johnny Frank is doing what he always does best – stirring the pot.

There's a sick feeling in the pit of my stomach as I climb the stairs. Why I should be even mildly surprised by this latest turn of events, I have no idea. It's hardly the first time Marc has kept a secret. Did I really think he'd changed?

Wearily, I push open the door to the flat. As if I've exhausted my supply of anger, I feel only a dull despairing ache. Marc is standing by the window. He turns but his smile slowly fades as he sees my expression. 'What's the matter, babe?'

'When were you planning on telling me?'

He frowns, adding a delicate shake of his head. 'What?'

I throw my coat and bag over a chair. 'Just for once, can we skip the *I don't know what you're talking about* routine and move on? Or is that too much to ask?'

His frown deepens while, in a gesture of assumed indifference, he leans casually back against the ledge. 'If you'd tell me what—'

'I mean our new life on the sunny Costa. I mean your plans for a brave new world. I mean Jim and Dee selling their businesses, selling this house. When exactly were you planning on telling me about it all?'

Marc's good but not quite good enough. I've caught him off guard and there's a moment of hesitation, a short guilty pause, before he gathers his defences and comes back on the attack. 'Oh, that. Who have you been talking to? Mum?'

'No, I got the glad tidings from Johnny.'

'Johnny,' he repeats, smiling again now, nodding and then raising his eyes to the ceiling. There's suddenly a look of relief on his face. 'You know what he's like, Sims.'

It takes an effort to keep my voice calm. 'No, I don't know what he's like – and I don't want to. All I do know is that he seems to have a damn sight more information than I have.'

'Look,' Marc replies, sliding into the voice that irritates me the most, the soft over-patient tone of an adult talking to a child. He must have picked it up from Dee. 'There aren't any plans, not any *definite* ones. I swear. It's only an idea and a vague one at that. Come on, sit down and I'll make you a cuppa. You look done in. Bad day at work?'

But I don't sit down. I carry on standing with my hands on my hips, waiting. This time I'm not going to be deflected by his storm-in-a-teacup routine. I've heard it all too often before. 'Johnny seemed to think that it was more than a vague idea. In fact, he seemed to think it was pretty cut and dried.'

Flopping down on the sofa, Marc expels one of his languorous sighs. 'Well, Johnny knows fuck all.'

'More than me, it would appear.'

He shook his head slowly. 'Look, Sims, I'm not denying that they've mentioned it, Mum and Dad I mean. They're getting on, thinking about retirement, and it's a dream, isn't it – selling up and moving to Spain. But nothing's been decided.

You think I wouldn't have told you if it had?'

'So why is Johnny—'

'I guess he's just heard them talking and jumped to conclusions.'

But I'm still not convinced. Something smells and I'm certain he's lying. Hadn't Johnny claimed that Marc had talked to him about the move too? 'I thought you said The Palace wasn't doing well? How can they afford to retire?'

'All the more reason to flog it – before the rot really begins to show.' Before the rot can't be covered up, I think. Before Marc isn't able to work his magic on the books any more. 'They might still get a decent price at the moment,' he continues, 'but in a few months, well . . . who can say?' He leans back and puts his hands behind his head. 'To be honest, I think it may be the right thing to do. And you know, Sims, perhaps a fresh start would do us all a favour.'

Now we're finally getting somewhere. 'So you want to go too?'

He shrugs. 'Why not? It's worth considering. There's nothing for us here. I'll never get another decent job, you know I won't – not in this country. What have we got to keep us?' He glances towards the window and grins. 'Apart from the bloody rain.'

A more apt question might have been *What have we got to keep us together?* It's clear that Marc has made his mind up, that the vague idea has already passed from possibility into the firmer realm of probability. I wonder how many conversations he's had with Jim and Dee, not to mention Johnny, about this glittering new future.

'It sounds like you've already decided.'

'Don't be like that,' he says, assuming his hurt little-boy-lost expression. 'I haven't decided anything yet. How could I without you? All I'm asking is that you give it some thought. It's not the worst prospect in the world.'

But I know from past experience that the dream would as quickly turn into a nightmare. How long would it take before Marc returned to his former ways, before a sultry señorita caught his eye or an opportunity too good to miss came within his grasp? And I don't intend to be a prison widow – especially in a foreign country. No way. I've seen too much of that grey-faced army of disappointed women, all clinging to a future that will never come, to know I'm not prepared to join their ranks. I'm making the break. I am. I will.

'Sure,' I reply disingenuously. 'I'll think about it.'

He gives me that smile, the beautiful smile that once upon a time would have instantly broken my resolve. But I'm older now – and wiser. If I've been waiting for an opportunity to make the break it's just been handed to me on a plate. I should be glad but in truth I feel only an overwhelming sense of grief.

Quickly, I turn away before my emotions reach my face. I

don't want him to guess what I'm planning to do. Entering the kitchen, I switch on the kettle and then, eager to change the subject, I glance over my shoulder and ask, 'Have you ever heard of a guy called Eddie Tate?'

His reaction isn't what I expect. 'What about him?' he replies too quickly, and there's an edge to his voice, a curious mix of fear and irritation.

Surprised, I step back into the room and stare. Alarm bells are going off in my head. 'You know him, don't you?'

He shrugs. 'I've seen him around, that's all. He's been trying to contact Johnny but he doesn't want anything to do with him. Some creep from his past.'

But it doesn't wash. There's something false about his glib response. 'Why didn't you tell me?' I seem to be asking that question a lot this afternoon.

Marc shrugs. 'There's nothing to tell. Like I said, just some creep. It's no big deal.'

'Well, it's a big deal to me,' I insist, 'especially when he comes to the shop and starts hassling me.'

Now his eyes suddenly narrow and he moves quickly forward. 'What's he been saying?'

I'd like to think this was Marc being protective, concerned about my welfare, but I know him far too well for that. This is about something else entirely, another secret he doesn't want me to share. Turning the tables, I ask: 'What do you think?'

'Don't play games, Simone. I'm not in the mood.' Then, as if belatedly aware of his snappy confrontational tone, he forces his mouth into a rueful smile. 'I'm just worried about you, love, that's all. If this guy's been hassling you, if he's been giving you trouble, then—'

'Nothing I couldn't deal with,' I interrupt.

His eyes search mine, trying to assess what I might or might not have learned from my brief encounter with Mr Tate. I see the indecision in his gaze. He can't decide how far to pursue it. In the end he settles on a bland enquiry. 'So what did he want?'

I wait a moment, watching him. Perhaps I should be grateful for this reminder of how devious Marc can be but somehow it only adds to my feelings of despair. I mimic his shrug.

'Like you said, nothing much. He was just trying to make contact with Johnny.'

The relief in his eyes shines as brightly as a beacon. 'Some people can't let go of the past.'

'No,' I agree, determined not to be one of them.

Chapter Ten

Johnny

If looks could kill, I'd be a dead man by now. Simone stared daggers at me this morning, brushing past on the staircase, her eyes burning into mine. No flicker of a smile, not even a murmured greeting. I could have said *Don't shoot the messenger* but she didn't seem in the mood for witty repartee.

It's been a couple of days since we had our little chat.

I was still watching her from the window, her steps brisk but her head bent despondently down, as she disappeared around the curve in the drive. And okay, maybe I was feeling a bit smug – why shouldn't I? Now the diamonds had entered the equation, everything was going to plan, the Buckleys circling each other like a pack of hungry tigers. I couldn't have hoped for a happier outcome. The others had been easy to manipulate, Jim and Dee, Marc and Carl – all with their own blatant weaknesses – but Simone was the real icing on the cake. Pissing *her* off was really worth the effort.

A few more weeks, maybe a month, and I'd have Jim exactly where I wanted – estranged from his family, destitute, fucked up, a broken man. Then it would be time to . . .

They say pride comes before a fall but nothing had prepared me for what was coming next. When I turned it was to find Carl at my shoulder.

'What are you watching that bitch for?'

'You don't like her,' I replied, stating the obvious.

'She's a bitch,' he repeated. 'She's the worst thing that ever happened to Marc.'

I raised a non-committal eyebrow. 'Nice pair of pins though.'

'If you like that kind of thing,' he snorted, as if the admiration of a pair of long shapely legs fell into the category of sexual deviance. Then, more forward than usual, he added, 'Don't even think about it. She's colder than a fucking Eskimo. You haven't got a chance.'

'Who says I want one?'

He grinned, his damp smile more obnoxious than usual. 'Because you haven't stopped staring at her since the day you arrived.'

Now he was taking liberties, stepping over the boundaries. I didn't like it. I didn't like it one little bit. 'Meaning?' I asked, directing my icy gaze directly into his eyes. You let shits like Carl get away with it once and there's no knowing where it may lead.

Instantly he withdrew. Taking a step back, stumbling on the stair, he read my face and raised his hands in a gesture of submission. 'Nothing, man,' he retorted quickly.

'Sorry. Hey, no offence. All I meant is that she's not worth the effort.'

Having made my point, I nodded. 'Okay.' It was meant as a dismissal, as a signal that he should just sod off and leave me alone, but instead his mouth slid slowly and unexpectedly into a wide ingratiating smile.

'Have you heard about Eddie?'

At first I thought he was just changing the subject, trying to wriggle his way out of a tight spot. I shook my head but humoured him. 'Something I should know about?'

He gave me a sly look. 'Only if you want to pay your respects.'

I'd turned away to glance out of the window again. My head must have spun back faster than a whipcord. 'What?'

'It seems he met with . . . an *accident*.'

'You're kidding?'

He grinned inanely. 'Shame, huh? Should we send a bunch of flowers?'

Shit. Dead. I shook my head. Perhaps I shouldn't have been surprised; Eddie had a habit of annoying people. He always was a double-crossing, good-for-nothing louse. But just when I wanted him alive, when just for once his stubborn crass stupidity was doing me a favour, his time had finally run out. Forcing a smile, I said: 'Well, that's a fucking stroke of luck.'

I was almost down the stairs, trying to think, trying to hide my frustration, when his next words pierced me like a stab in the back.

'Who said luck had anything to do with it?'

My hand tightened and froze around the banister.

'Now there's nothing stopping us,' Carl announced triumphantly. 'We've got a clear run, Johnny. We can pick up the ice whenever we want.'

I turned slowly to look over my shoulder. His eyes were shining almost as brightly as the gems he craved so much. He was staring straight at me, his face gleaming, almost manic, a fine sheen of perspiration covering his forehead and cheeks.

Fuck. What had he done?

The answer blossomed in my gut like deadly nightshade.

'It was you,' I said softly, a statement not a question. He didn't know me well enough to hear the rage behind the words. He thought I was pleased. Shit, the little fucker even thought I was impressed. He jogged down the last few steps like some snotty kid about to receive a lollipop.

We were only inches apart when I made my move. I timed it to perfection. He was younger than me, taller and fitter, but I had something he didn't – the element of surprise.

Bewilderment flashed across his face as I hurled him back against the wall, my forearm tight against his windpipe. 'What the fuck have you done?' He only struggled for a second, his body sensing the futility before it properly registered in his tiny brain. Carl tried to speak, strangulated grunts of protest emerging from his throat until I slapped him hard across the face. A stripe flared red across his cheek. 'Tell me! Tell me, you shit!' I loosened my hold, just enough to let him start breathing again, and then quickly raised my knee. With a satisfying crunch it made contact with his balls. As he slid slowly down the wall, his sharp intake of breath was swiftly followed by a long howl.

'Shut it!' I yelled, trying to drag him upright. It was pointless. His body was a dead weight. I let him fall with a slam against the polished wooden boards. I could have killed him. I could have finished him there and then. I wanted to. He'd just screwed up *everything*. In my mind I could already hear the sirens screaming through the streets, those bloody pigs coming back to have another bite of the cherry. This time I wouldn't see daylight again. Carl fucking Buckley was truly his father's son.

'You want to see me back inside?' I could hear my own voice, an octave too high. 'Is that what you want? Is that what this is all about?'

Gagging, he spewed up a stream of thin green slime. He moaned into the floor, doubled up, his hands still cradling his most precious assets. As well they might. God alone knew where his brains were hidden but they certainly weren't in his head. Eddie Tate was dead, stone cold dead, and if Carl had left a trace, one single tiny clue, I'd be hung out to dry as an accessory.

'Well?'

'No,' he eventually managed to splutter. Even the expulsion of that one syllable made his face crease up. But at least he could talk. And that's all I needed to hear.

'Speak to me,' I said, grabbing him around his collar. 'I haven't got all day. Tell me. Tell me fucking everything or I'll break your fucking neck.'

It had the desired effect.

His head shifted round. 'I thought ... I thought ...' His expression dissolved into pain again. It took a while before he managed to complete the sentence. 'I thought it would help.' He looked up pleadingly, his scared resentful eyes searching mine 'Honest, Johnny, honest. That's all.'

'Help?' I echoed, almost spitting in his face. 'How the fuck does killing Eddie Tate help *me*? You want the pigs swarming round like a plague of bloody locusts? You think that's smart? You think that's keeping a low profile? Do you?' I smashed my fist against the wall, just above his head. I only meant it as a warning but angrily mistimed the blow, punching too hard and smashing my knuckles against the plaster. Which only made me madder. God almighty, could anything get worse?

But of course it could. It always did. It's one of those laws, like the eternal and indisputable rules of physics. It grew ten, a hundred, a thousand times worse as he reluctantly came clean. His confession, although concise, wasn't short on gory detail. As he stumbled through his story, tentative at first but slowly gaining in confidence, I had to fight to stop myself from gagging too. He'd gone after Eddie Tate, tormented and tortured him, before finally bludgeoning him to death. And it was clear, horribly clear, that Carl had taken pleasure in every single second of his victim's agonizing demise.

'I did it for you,' he whined pathetically, 'for *us*.'

Shit, I wasn't just dealing with a killer. Carl was a fully fledged psychopath.

I lowered my head and stared into his wild blue eyes. Behind them lay an ocean of blankness. It took an effort to hold the gaze. My bones were shaking, every nerve trembling with rage. 'There is no *us*. There never was and never will be.'

'Johnny!' he shouted as I walked away.

I resisted the urge to go back and kick him.

I should have seen it. I should have realized. But I was too busy concentrating on the petty stuff to see the bigger picture. If I'd thought... if I'd thought... for God's sake, how could I have been so fucking blind?

Melanie's hunched on the edge of the bed, her eyes glazed with disbelief. With her chin resting on her knees, she looks tiny, more like a child than a woman. She whispers, 'Are you sure?'

Even from across the room I can see her shivers. She'd bargained for all sorts of things – for deceit, for manipulation, for the satisfaction of revenge... but not for this. I slop a large measure of brandy into a glass and hand it to her. 'Here, drink this.'

She sips it like medicine, her face screwing up at the taste.

I'm trying to stay calm, to at least pretend I'm in control, but it's an effort. I get the feeling that one wrong word and she'll shatter as surely as the glass she's holding.

'It's better if you go, Mel. You should leave today.'

There's a tremor in her voice now. 'What if he guesses?'

I know what she's thinking, that he'll kill her too if he suspects she's running out on him. 'He won't, I promise. And anyway, I'll keep him busy until you're well gone. Have you got much at the flat?'

She shakes her head.

'Good.' It isn't really a flat, only a studio room that she rented for the purpose, a convenient 'home' for her to escape to. It's barely twenty minutes away, less than five if she takes a cab. And I want her in that taxi as soon as possible, away from here and any possible danger. I don't think she'll panic – she's tougher than that – but shock can have a strange effect. I speak slowly and carefully, making sure she understands.

'You go back and pick up your stuff but don't rush, okay? You've got plenty of time. Don't leave anything lying around – no addresses or contact numbers for friends.' I pause for a second and wait for her to nod. 'And if he rings, if Carl rings, then answer the phone. Don't avoid him. I don't imagine he will – he's got enough on his mind but ... well, if he does, just try and keep it natural. Keep it cool. Tell him you're out, that you're shopping, with a mate, anything. Tell him you'll meet him at the club tonight. Keep it friendly. I know it won't be easy but he's got no reason to suspect that you've heard about ...' I take a deep breath. 'So don't give him one, okay?'

I pause again. This time it's as much for my benefit as hers. I'm still thinking on my feet, unprepared for this emergency and cursing myself; I should have had a contingency plan, a fallback position, but what I actually have is bloody fuck all. There's no one I trust enough to ring and ask for help. What else should I tell her to do?

Melanie waits, still sipping the brandy like an obedient patient. I want to be able to take care of her, to give her protection, but all I can offer are these lousy bits of advice. Why the hell did I ever let her get involved? Dixie's baby, his treasure, his pride and joy. If he's looking down on me now it must be with stone cold hatred.

The words, when I finally manage to utter them, feel like the final betrayal. 'Where will you go?'

'It's okay,' she says gently. 'Don't worry. I'll sort something out. I'll go up north. I've got friends, good ones.'

Which makes her ten thousand times richer than me and also makes me feel ten thousand times more useless. I pour myself a double measure and sit down. 'People you can trust?'

'Hey, I'm not your responsibility,' she replies, lifting her head. She sounds a little stronger now, not quite so frightened. 'What do you think? That I can't take care of myself?'

But it's as much bravado as anything else. I put my head in my hands and stare at the floor. 'Of course not.' Her words make me want to weep. We may have walked the same road together, talking, planning, even laughing about the revenge we intended to wreak – but now it's not so sweet. Now it's gone as sour as sour can be. I've let her down, let Dixie down. I've fucked up good and proper.

'Ring a cab,' I say, glancing at my watch. And when she doesn't move, doesn't respond, I urge: 'Come on!' I've still got one ear tuned to the outside world, to the open window, to the possible sound of a car pulling in across the gravel. I don't think Carl will return in a hurry but there's no point taking any chances.

She picks up on my anxiety, her voice rising: 'You think he might come back?'

I quickly shake my head. 'No. No, not for a while.' I'm pretty sure where he's gone, to the same place he'll always run – straight to his mother. Crying on her shoulder like a pathetic adolescent. And neither of them will head back here before they have to. Not until they've talked it out and carefully rearranged the truth. They'll give me a wide berth, a few hours yet to recover from my temper.

Mel rises slowly to her feet. 'What about you?' 'Make the call,' I insist. 'I won't be far behind. A few days – tonight. I don't know yet. Soon. I'll ring you soon, I promise.'

She looks at me searchingly, hesitates, and then reaches for her phone. She dials and waits. The exchange is over in a moment.

'How long?' I ask.

'Ten minutes.'

'Good, that's good.' I rub my hands impatiently along my thighs, willing time to pass quickly. The sooner she's away from here the better. Standing up, I go to the window and stare out. Truth is that it's easier than looking at her. Because when I do, all I see are Dixie's blue accusing eyes gazing back. In my mind I'm having a conversation with him, although it's not really a conversation – it's just me saying 'sorry' over and over again.

If it wasn't for me, he'd still be around. If I hadn't pushed Foster … if Dixie hadn't tried to help me get shot of the body … if … shit, he'd never have gone to jail or got in that stupid fucking row and …

I hear the chink as Melanie puts down her glass on the table by the bed. 'Don't go all regretful on me,' she says, 'you never meant it to turn out like this. Neither of us did.'

But I didn't have to let her get involved. When she first came to visit, I should have kept my mouth shut about Jim, about what he'd done. I should have kept my sordid little secret to myself.

When I don't reply she waits for a while, sighs, and then walks over and takes my elbow. 'Johnny?'

Now I don't have any choice but to look at her.

'Come with me,' she pleads, 'please.' She squeezes my arm. 'You've no reason to stay here any more. What's the point? We can *both* be gone before he comes back.'

And I can't say I'm not tempted. In fact, for one mad glorious moment, it seems like a bloody good idea. Why not? Cut my losses and leave. Forget about it all. We could be miles away before they even noticed. We could catch a train, go up north . . .

She tugs on my arm. 'Johnny?'

But it isn't that simple. Nothing ever is. God knows what Carl and Dee will do if they come back to find me gone. Panic, for starters. No, it's too big a risk. I have to stay here, at least for this evening. I have to talk to them; I have to find out what they're thinking, what they're planning to do next. I have to stop them from doing anything too reckless.

I look at my watch. 'You should go.' It's only been three minutes but it feels a lot longer. 'It might be there, the cab, it might be waiting by the gates.'

She loosens her fingers, reluctantly releasing me. 'Make

sure you ring. And Johnny ... take care, okay?' She stands on her toes and kisses my cheek.

'I will,' I murmur hoarsely, 'I promise. You too.' My voice sounds like it's been dragged across sandpaper. I'm sure I should say something else, something reassuring, but what?

The door has already opened and closed. There's only silence left.

She's gone.

I spend the next few hours in an agony of waiting. Four, five cups of coffee until I'm wired up, on edge, and my heart is pumping like some fucking steam piston. And all the time I'm wondering if I should just pack my stuff and scoot, get the hell out of here before the flashing lights arrive.

But I don't. First I need to know what I'm up against, whether I'll have to be looking over my shoulder for the rest of my life. I was too angry earlier to take in all the details. I need to know what kind of chaos Carl has left behind.

It's almost eight before they get back. He crawls into the kitchen like a dog with its tail between its legs. Dee follows quickly behind like his aggressive owner, her eyes sharp and wild, ready for a row. And I'd give her one too if I didn't already know that Melanie was safe, at least a hundred miles away.

She strides across the room and glares at me. 'So?'

'So?' I repeat.

'So look at him,' she says, leaning forward with a growl. She grabs his bruised face by the chin and turns it towards me. 'What the hell do you think you're doing? How dare you!'

Carl squirms in her grasp.

I shrug. 'He deserved it. And he's lucky he didn't get worse. Your fucking murdering son could put me back behind bars.'

'What he did,' she snaps back shrilly, 'was an accident. An *accident*. He didn't mean ... He was only trying to help. He only wanted to warn Tate off.'

'Well, he did that all right.'

'You lay one finger on him ever again and I'll—'

'You'll what?' I offer her a mocking smile. 'Kill me?'

She opens her mouth but slowly closes it again. As if everything that's happened is finally catching up, she slumps down on a chair and stares at me. But the fight's gone. Drained by exhaustion, her face is stricken, her eyes two dark hollows. Fumbling for a cigarette she tries to light it with a shaking hand.

I lean forward with my own lighter. She mumbles, 'Thanks.'

In that moment I almost feel sorry for her. Maybe she wonders what she did to deserve two such distinguished sons, one a fraudster, the other a killer. Not the greatest tribute to her mothering skills.

'It was an accident,' she repeats softly, as though if she says it often enough it might become the truth. She raises her eyes, tearful now. 'He didn't mean it. You should understand that, Johnny. You of all people.' Almost pleading, like she wants me to agree with her.

I lift my shoulders a little, not saying yes or no. This was as accidental as an axe in the head but who am I to shatter what remains of her fragile illusions? She hasn't got much left to hold on to.

'What will we do?' she moans.

I'm not sure if it's a rhetorical question, if she's asking me or herself or maybe even God, but as He's unlikely to answer I take on the burden. 'That depends.' I pause to light a cigarette of my own, inhaling deeply. When I glance up, Carl's still hovering near his mother's shoulder. 'For fuck's sake. Will you sit down!'

He flinches and slides into a chair on the other side of the table. Wisely he's kept his trap shut but now his eyes shift uneasily. I can see the hate in them, and the contempt. He'll never forgive me for what I did to him but then, shit, I doubt I'll lose much sleep over it.

'It depends,' I start again, 'on what kind of bloody stinking mess your son has left behind. Apart from a corpse, that is.' I see a shiver but don't pull back. There's no room for subtlety here. 'We need to talk about what happened last night – go over the details, everything.' I pause. 'Does Jim know about it?'

She gives a tiny almost imperceptible nod.

I wonder why he hasn't put in an appearance but perhaps it's not that surprising. He's probably holed up in the club with a bottle of Scotch for company. He hasn't got Dee's strength. 'Anyone else?'

She nods again. 'Marc.'

Fuck. Three more people to worry about. 'So Simone knows too.' At this rate they may as well have taken out a full-page advertisement in the local paper.

But she shakes her head. 'No, not Simone. Of course not. Marc won't tell her. No one will.'

'Lucky girl. Seems she's the last to know most things round here. Still, at least she might rest easy tonight. She'll probably be the only one.'

Dee throws me a suspicious glance, not sure if I'm accusing her of something. 'It's a family matter,' she says, almost haughtily, as if she's referring to who'll inherit Aunt Maud's china rather than a mutilated body lying on a mortuary slab.

I force a laugh. 'It's that all right.' And I offer up a silent prayer of thanks, that for all the misfortunes of my life I wasn't born into this particular family. 'So, shall we get on? It's getting late.'

Dee glances nervously at Carl. She clears her throat, twice, but when she starts to speak there's still a croak in it. 'Last night he came to The Palace, Eddie I mean. He came to see you.'

I raise an enquiring eyebrow.

'Carl rang him. He told him you were there, that you wanted to talk.'

'What the—'

She smartly interrupts. 'It was my idea, Johnny, not his. I thought if we could find a way to warn him off, to get him off our backs, then . . . but it wasn't supposed to . . . Not like this. Things got out of control.' Dee hears the cynical hiss of my breath. She gives me an anxious glance and quickly carries on. 'No one saw him there. I'm sure. It was late, dark, and he came round the side; he parked his car round the side.'

'You can't be sure of anything,' I retort. 'All it takes is one drunken punter pissing into the wind and ...' But there's not much point in looking for problems when we've already got a bucketful. I give a dismissive wave of my hand. 'Go on.'

'We went down to the basement, to one of those rooms, you know, the ones that are usually used for storage. I got him a drink, said you wouldn't be long.' Dee swallows hard. 'And then ... I ... I left him with ...'

We turn simultaneously to look at Carl. He hunches lower in his seat. Eventually, reluctantly, he raises his eyes to meet ours. 'What?' he asks defensively, his mouth assuming that familiar pout. He's acting like we're his parents, like we're discussing some minor infraction, a football through a window or a petty theft, rather than a full-blown fucking murder.

'He didn't mean it,' Dee insists again. 'He only meant to frighten him.'

And I imagine he did that all right. Poor old Eddie must have been shitting himself. He didn't have a clue what he was walking into. He thought it was *me* he was coming to meet — Johnny Frank, his old associate — not some bloody psychopath. Hell, Carl gives me the shudders so God knows what he did to Tate.

Except I do know — at least as much as Carl has told me. And I don't need or want to hear the details again.

Dee, perhaps of a similar mind, scrapes back her chair and stands up. 'I need a drink.' She stumbles to the cupboard and retrieves a bottle of gin. There's silence while she gets three glasses and puts them on the table. She fills her own, pushes the bottle aside, and leaves us to help ourselves.

Carl pours himself a generous measure.

I stare at the bottle. I should leave it alone. I want a clear head, space to think, but this is all too much to take in sober. I need something to take the edge off, to numb the reality. And I'm not just talking about Eddie's fate here, gruesome as it was, but more essentially my own. This is *my* fucking future in the balance.

Dee saves me the trouble of making a decision. Leaning forward, she picks up the bottle and quarter-fills my glass. 'Here,' she says, sliding it across the table. For a moment her eyes meet mine but I swiftly look away. I don't want to acknowledge what I've seen in them – fear and pain and desperation. I know she's counting on the past, on history, on some long-dead sense of loyalty, to allow Carl – her son – the benefit of the doubt. She wants me to believe what she believes.

But I can't do that.

I can only spare her the details. I take a drink. A large one. 'So, what happened after—'

Dee doesn't let me finish. Although I was intending to skim over the grotesqueries, she presumes I mean after she left. 'Carl tried to reason with him,' she says. 'He did. He really tried. But Eddie wouldn't listen. He flipped. He went completely crazy, shouting and screaming. He said he deserved a share of the diamonds, that you owed him, that you owed him big time. What was Carl supposed to do?' There's a rising edge of hysteria to her tone. 'There were people upstairs – anyone could have heard. He panicked. He hit him.'

I nod. 'Okay.'

She falters, falls back in the chair and stares at me. 'He didn't, he didn't mean to ...'

'I know. It's okay.' I try to sound calm, reassuring. It's not actually okay at all. Far from it. Hers is a vastly different story to the one that Carl disclosed but I'm not about to challenge it. I don't want to watch her fall apart. How her version tallies with what she saw – a man who had clearly been beaten to death – is a matter for her own conscience. I can see why she doesn't want to face it; I find it pretty hard to think about myself. What kind of a match would Eddie have been for Carl? Older, smaller, lighter – he wouldn't have stood a fucking chance. And there wasn't any need for that other stuff, for the torture, for the burns, for the ... No, he only did that for the thrill of it.

A heavy silence falls across the room.

'What about his phone?' I ask. Practicalities are easier to deal with than emotions. I don't understand much about this mobile phone shit but I do know that if Carl rang him it's likely to be traceable.

She gazes absently into the distance. 'We got rid of it.'

Well, that's a start. Thank God for small mercies. Although it wasn't the only item they conveniently got rid of – and that's something else we've got to address. But maybe we should begin with the easier stuff. 'So what about the room, your clothes, they must have been ...'

Dee knows what I'm about to say next and doesn't want to

hear it. *Blood*. There must have been blood all over the place. She reaches for her glass, for the sanctuary of alcohol. She sweeps a hand through her hair. 'I burned all our clothes. We cleaned up. There wasn't . . . it wasn't that bad.'

I sigh. You can scrub to your heart's content and you'll never make it truly clean. There'll always be a stain, a mark, some indisputable spot of evidence. 'But—'

'But no one knows he was there. They won't come looking. Why should they?' She grabs my arm, her nails digging into my skin.

I glance at Carl but he refuses to look up. He's happy to hide behind his mother's skirts. 'Maybe not,' I agree. Then, thinking aloud on a less optimistic note, 'Unless Eddie told someone. He might have done. He might have wanted his back covered.' I feel Dee's desperate gaze on me again. 'But . . . well, knowing Eddie he wouldn't want anyone to suspect what he was up to.'

Dee nods furiously. 'He wouldn't, would he?' She slowly releases her grasp on my arm and the frown on her forehead softens a little. 'He'd keep it to himself. He wouldn't take the chance of someone else muscling in.'

I force a small reassuring smile. 'Yeah, that's probably true.' For Dee's sake, although it isn't easy, I'm trying not to be too negative. I have to keep her hopeful. If she falls apart then the others will tumble like a pack of cards. But I have to move things on. Cautiously I prompt, 'And then you . . .'

Her lips tighten into a grimace. 'We waited until the club closed and then we . . . we wrapped him in a blanket and got him in the back seat of his car.'

'Just the two of you? Wasn't Jim there?'

She kind of half shakes her head. 'He was but ... but he came down to the basement and when he saw him, you know, he just couldn't ...'

So the cowardly shit had left his wife to clear up.

'And Marc had gone home. He didn't know anything about it, not then, and I didn't want to call him. I thought Simone might get curious.'

They must have struggled, just the two of them. Eddie wasn't a big man but he would still have been, quite literally, a dead weight. And I know how that feels, not to mention the heart-thumping dread of discovery, the fuck-awful fear that churns up your guts and turns your legs to lead. No, it can't have been easy. But then Dee's determination, for all her faults, has never been a matter for debate. Once she's set her mind to something (as I've discovered to my cost) it would take a bloody army to prevent her going through with it.

So now The Palace has seen two deaths. Who says lightning never strikes twice? Although maybe there have been others. Maybe there's a veritable host of ghosts stumbling round those dusty corridors.

Dee stubs out her cigarette and instantly lights another. We're approaching the final stages of this unsavoury recital. 'Carl took his, Eddie's, car and I followed in mine. We drove around for a while. We ... we weren't sure where to go.'

I could see that might be a problem. It's not the kind of information you can check out in the Yellow Pages.

'After twenty minutes or so we ended up in Dalston

Lane, took a left and then ... I don't remember the name of the road.' She glances at Carl but he shrugs indifferently. 'It was quiet anyway, and dark. There weren't any lights on in the houses. Carl parked the car – then he got into mine and we left.'

There's a long silence.

Dee sighs, perhaps out of weariness or perhaps simply out of relief that the telling is finally over. She takes a moment and then raises her eyes to look at me again. What can I say? It seems pretty slipshod but then I'm hardly an expert at disposing of bodies.

So I ask the obvious: 'What about prints? What about—'

For the first time the little bastard deigns to opens his mouth. As if it's a matter of personal pride, an attack on his professionalism, he says, 'I was wearing gloves, man. I didn't leave any prints.'

It's a good thing Dee's here. Just the sound of his smug careless voice makes me want to explode. I can feel the rage growing inside me, the almost irresistible temptation to continue where we left off this morning. She senses my shift forward and quickly intervenes.

'We were careful,' she says, laying a restraining hand on my arm.

She's bringing that word *we* into it again, deflecting the focus away from Carl, reminding me that she played a part in all this too. But for all her attempts to share the blame, I know she wasn't responsible for what happened; she was just the one left to pick up the pieces. Still, it's hardly going to help if I take the vicious sprog and shake him till his brains fall out – attractive as that prospect is – so instead I nod, force my muscles to relax, and slowly lean back.

Carl grins as if he's gained a minor victory.

I shoot him a cold icy glare. So okay, maybe now is neither the time nor the place – there's more important shit to worry about – but one day he'll get what's coming and if I can't express that threat through speech, I can certainly convey it in pictures. I put my right hand on the table and curl my fingers into a hard tight fist.

He sees the gesture all right, pales and looks towards his mama. But no joy there: she's got her face stuck firmly in her glass.

And I'm not finished yet. 'What about the rest?' I ask provocatively. Now I'm staring straight into his eyes. 'You think you left nothing behind? What about the hairs, the skin, the blood? I mean, there was a struggle, wasn't there? There was a fight. You must have heard of science, Carl. Eddie's body must be crawling with your DNA.'

He falters, a quiver invading his wide sulky mouth. I've hit him where it hurts. He stares down at his feet. It's not as though he's ashamed or disgusted by what he's done – far from it – he's only afraid of the consequences. Dee, as usual, rushes to his rescue.

'He's never been arrested. He's never . . . he's not even had a test, so unless they've got a reason to suspect him, why should they come looking?'

I frown, shrugging her objections aside. 'Well . . . ' I don't want to let him off the hook so easily. I want him to sweat, to think about it.

Although she's right – to a point. It doesn't matter how much DNA they retrieve if they haven't got a match for it, a suspect. So long as no one saw them, so long as no one saw the car, so long as no one knew about the connection to Eddie, so long as Carl never makes the same mistake again ...

Dee repeats, 'Why should they?'

There's an answer to that although I'm not about to say it: *Because your son's a fucking psycho. Because his brains are so far up his arse he can't see sense for shit.* Even with Dee covering his tracks, I can't quite believe he hasn't left a trail of evidence. And even if he hasn't, even if by some freak chance he's managed to get away with it, how long before his crazy braggart mouth runs riot?

I don't want to be here when that happens.

Ignoring her question, I ask one of my own: 'So how's Jim? How's he dealing with this?'

Carl snorts. 'How do you think?' The gin's getting to him now, giving him false courage. While Dee's around he knows he's safe. 'He's off his head. He's fucking freaked.'

She throws him a look, a warning glance. 'Jim's okay,' she says, turning her attention back to me. 'He's fine. He'll be fine. He just needs a bit of space.'

Which tells me everything. I can't help smiling. And although my instincts keep insisting I should leave tonight, cut my losses, pack my bags and run, I can't resist the temptation of seeing Jim suffer. At least for a day or two. Why not? I've waited eighteen fucking years for the pleasure.

And yeah, of course it isn't smart; if the cops come calling

I won't stand a chance. They'll hang me out to dry. They'll dig my grave for me. But if all goes tits-up they'll be doing that anyway so I might as well enjoy myself in the meantime.

Maybe I'm heading for trouble – but hell, it's hardly a novelty.

Chapter Eleven

Simone

God alone knows what's wrong with Marc; moody isn't the word for it. He's acting like a bear with a sore head and if it wasn't for the fact that he hasn't touched a drop of alcohol I'd suspect he had a lingering hangover. I've tried to talk to him but the more questions I ask the more defensive he gets. I've tried kind, persuasive and even downright stroppy, but without any noticeable success.

Then late this evening, just as I'm starting to wonder if he's embarked on a terminal mid-life crisis, he finds his voice again. 'I think we should go to Spain, Sims.'

My heart sinks. Now this is a conversation that I don't want to have. 'Mm,' I murmur vaguely, turning on the TV in the hope of distracting him.

'What are you doing?' As if I've just set the timer for a nuclear device, he leaps forward and grabs the remote. In a second the screen has dissolved into darkness again.

I stare at him, bemused. 'The news is on.'

'So what? I'm sick of the news. What's the point? It's always the same.' He leans forward, putting his head in his hands. He rakes his fingers roughly through his hair. He glances at me, 'Sorry. Sorry, but it's all so . . . ' He rubs his forehead and sighs. 'Can't we just talk?'

Which is pretty rich seeing as he's the one who appeared to have taken a vow of silence. But I nod anyway. At least he's trying to communicate and, much as I dread the idea, this is probably as good a time as ever to make my position clear on the whole expatriate venture. I take a deep breath. 'Look, I understand what this Spain thing means to you, a new future, the chance to start again but I'm really not sure if—'

He doesn't give me a chance to finish. 'That's exactly what I mean,' he insists. 'We won't know, will we, until we give it a chance? That's why we should take a trip, check it out, get away for a week or two.' His eyes are shining now, almost crazily bright. He jumps off the sofa, walks over to the window, and back. 'Sims, we should go this weekend. We should go on Friday. No, we should go tomorrow. I'm sure I can get some cheap flights off the Net.'

Tomorrow? Friday? This is madness. What's he talking about? I flail around for an excuse. 'But we can't . . . what about the shop, what about Dee, what—'

Marc leans over and wraps his arms around my shoulders. 'Don't worry, I'll sort that out. She'll understand. Mum won't mind. I mean, when was the last time we had a holiday?' His warm breath whispers against my neck. 'Please.' He pauses, gently kissing the top of my head. And then suddenly there's a tremor in his voice. 'Please, Sims.'

I hear the plea and my hand reaches automatically for his. I turn to him. 'What's wrong?'

He twists my fingers round his, linking them in that old familiar way.

'Marc?'

At first he won't even look at me but gradually he raises his gaze. His expression has changed; it seems almost bereft. He slides his tongue cautiously along his dry lips. There's a short brittle silence and I think for a second that he might talk, that for once in his life he might actually share what he's thinking. But he doesn't. He can't. He only shakes his head and smiles. 'It's nothing.'

And then he's broken free. He's off again, pacing round the room. He's done three brisk circuits before he stops by the window, flinging it wide open to let in a blast of freezing winter air. He breathes it in like a dying man desperate for oxygen. Then he starts to laugh. 'Yeah, come on. Let's do it. Let's go get some sun. Let's get away from here.'

I don't have the heart to say no. I could claim my courage has failed me but it's more than that. Guilt has kicked in too. He's behaving so strangely – even by *his* standards – that I'm starting to wonder if it's down to some kind of depression. Marc has always had his moods but this is different; perhaps it's a form of post-prison blues. There's an edge to him, a kind of mania. It's like he's poised on the edge of a cliff, waiting for someone to push him off.

And I don't want to be the one to do it.

I join him by the window. 'Okay.' I gaze down into the garden. I get the feeling he was looking at something, at someone, but there's only drab emptiness now. I slip my arm around his waist. 'But maybe next week rather than this one, huh? At least give me time to buy a pair of shades.'

Smiling, he leans down and skims his lips against my throat. 'You can get those at the airport.' I mean to protest but he stops me with another kiss. 'Come on. Say yes.' He assails me softly, butterfly kisses leading all the way to my mouth. 'Let's get out of here, let's get away.'

'Marc . . .'

I should stop it but I don't. I should know better but . . .

I wake early in the morning. Marc is still asleep and I lie for a few minutes watching his chest rise and fall, listening to the rhythmic sound of his breathing. In the early days of our marriage it was something I often used to do, filled with a vague feeling of astonishment that this smart sexy guy was actually my husband. Now what do I feel? An enduring affection, I suppose. A kind of love. A desire not to see him hurt.

Carefully, I slip from under the covers, grab my clothes from the chair and tiptoe into the bathroom. It's the first night in a while that he's slept peacefully and I don't want to wake him. Although, if I'm being honest, it isn't a completely selfless act; I'm hoping to escape before he starts planning that holiday again.

I brush my teeth, take a quick shower and towel myself dry. Then, wiping the mist from the mirror, I run a comb through my hair and gaze at my reflection. Not the most encouraging sight in the world. I could swear those frown lines are getting deeper. In less than eight years I'll be forty. Lord, that's not a thought to dwell on. Delving into my make-up bag, I make an attempt if not to repair then at least distract from nature's damage – a little shadow on the eyes, blusher, a smudge of lipstick.

I pull on jeans and a jumper and wander into the living room. By now I'm craving a cup of tea but best not to hang around. He could wake up any moment. There's a cafe on the corner of the High Street where I can pick up a takeaway cuppa and a roll.

I lift my jacket from the peg and throw it over my arm before cautiously opening the front door. I pause, listening intently, but there's still no sound from the bedroom. The click as I close it behind me sounds as loud as gunfire in the silence of the morning. I wince, holding my breath, and then, like an embarrassed lover creeping away from a drunken assignation, slink quietly down the stairs.

I'm almost out of the house when I glance back and see Jim sitting in the kitchen. He's noticed me so I give him a wave. 'Morning.'

I'm hoping that will suffice but he raises a pair of bleary eyes and shouts loud enough to wake the dead: 'What happened to Marc last night? He was supposed to be at work.'

Reluctantly, if only to get him to lower his voice, I walk along the hall. 'Was he?'

'Damn right, he was,' Jim insists. 'We've got a bloody business to run. What does he think, that he can just stroll in and out whenever he feels like it?'

I shrug. I've no idea what Marc thinks at the best of times.

Although I do know he's not a shirker; he hasn't missed an evening's work since he started the job.

'At some bloody poker game, I suppose,' he grumbles.

There's a bottle of whisky on the table and an empty glass. The smell of booze drifts through the air. How drunk is he? It's hard to tell. All I am sure of is that Jim, never abstemious at the best of times, currently seems to be drinking for Britain.

'No. He was with me, actually.'

'Ah, the perfect alibi,' a soft voice declares.

I swing round to see Johnny standing there. He must have been in the living room. Aware that he's surprised me, his mouth slides into a thin knowing smile. 'Good morning, Simone. And how are you today?'

I nod, instinctively taking a step back. 'Fine, thank you.'

He hears the stiffness in my tone and stares at me for a few seconds longer than he should. Then, just as I'm starting to enter the zone of high discomfort, he glances away towards Jim. He sighs, taking in the bottle and his general state of dishevelment. 'You've forgotten,' he says.

Jim looks up and frowns. 'Uh?' I don't know how many Johnny Franks he sees but possibly more than one for he instantly lowers his head and rubs his eyes before raising them again. His earlier belligerence has suddenly slipped into confusion.

Johnny sighs again. 'You were supposed to be giving me a lift.'

That Johnny ever goes out is news to me but then I'm hardly up to date on the latest headlines. Looking more closely at him now, I see that he's washed and shaved and even wearing a tie. I'm curious, but not so curious that I want to prolong the encounter.

I glance at my watch. 'Well, I'd better be going.'

I'm just about to retreat when Jim, drunkenly inspired, drops the bombshell. 'Ah,' he announces triumphantly, 'Simone's going that way. She can drive you.'

Simone can *what*?

'Sorry,' I say hurriedly, 'but I'm on the bus. Marc may need the car later.'

Jim ponders on this, then slowly reaches into his pocket and pulls out a set of keys. For a second he stares at them as if he's not quite sure how they got into his hand but then, hit by a wave of clarity, he smiles and slides them across the table. 'Take mine, love. I won't be needing it.'

There's one of those long awkward pauses where, although I'm well and truly stymied, I still frantically struggle to find another excuse.

'It doesn't matter,' Johnny says brusquely, 'I'll get a cab.'

I'm sorely tempted to let him – his company's the last thing I need this morning – but there's such obvious irritation in his voice that I can't help feeling a bit sorry for Jim. For all the talk of them being old friends I don't really believe it; there's no love lost between these two. And I, for one, wouldn't like to get on the wrong side of the chilly Mr Frank.

'It's okay,' I reply, forcing a smile. I lean forward and pick up the keys. Through the years Jim has been decent to me and now it's payback time. 'See you later,' I say to him, 'and don't forget to tell Dee.' There's only one parking space attached to the shop and she'll be far from impressed if she has to leave her own car on a meter.

He grunts in reply, his hand reaching out for the bottle.

I'm halfway down the hall before I sense that my passenger isn't following. I glance over my shoulder to see him still standing by the kitchen door. 'Johnny?'

'I told you,' he says icily, 'I'll get a cab.'

A shiver runs through me. No, I'm not leaving them alone together. Jim's barely capable of standing up, never mind facing the wrath of Johnny. I glance at my watch again. 'Well, I hope you haven't got a pressing appointment because it's almost eight o'clock and your chances of getting a cab in the next half hour are about a million to one.'

It seems to hit the right nerve. For the first time ever, I see him falter, his gaze flickering down to his own watch. Wherever he has to be, it must be important. He looks from me to Jim and back again. Eventually, he nods. He gives Jim one last glare of disgust before heading for the door.

Silently, we get into the car. We've passed along the drive and through the gates before he speaks to me again. 'I'm going to Grove Street.'

'Okay.' I remember where it is, a thin winding road off the High Street, but I've rarely been down it. Who could he be visiting there? One of his old pals perhaps, an old friend, an old villain who he *would* like to see again. From what I can recall, there's only a scattering of shops and offices, a few houses and flats . . .

I've spent a minute or two considering the possibilities

when his voice cuts abruptly across my thoughts. 'Why don't you just ask?'

'What?'

He snorts. 'It's a simple question.' Taking a small leather pouch from his pocket he picks out some tobacco and starts to roll one of his skinny cigarettes. 'If you want to know why I'm going to Grove Street, why don't you just ask?'

'I don't,' I retort too quickly. 'Why should I?' Even to my own ears it doesn't sound convincing.

He dampens the paper with a fast lick across his tongue and then seals it. 'Do you mind if I smoke?'

I shrug. 'Whatever.'

As he raises the cigarette to his lips, I notice the nasty scrape across his knuckles. How did he do that? The skin's swollen and bruised, blue around the edges. I'm so busy staring that I don't notice the traffic slowing in front and almost bash straight into the rear end of a very flash Mercedes. Braking just in time, I stop with only a few inches to spare. The driver turns his head and glares at me. I smile apologetically.

Johnny laughs. 'Who are you trying to kill – me or him?'

I turn and glower. 'What happened to your hand?'

His laughter quickly fades. 'Nothing.'

'It doesn't look like nothing. It looks like you've been in a fight.'

Now suddenly he's the one on the defensive. 'Does it?' He frowns but doesn't deny the allegation. He glances down and flexes his fingers.

The traffic's moving again. We shift slowly forward,

passing over the crossroads, before coming to another grinding halt. I wind down the window and peer ahead; there's a tailback but I can't see the cause. There could have been an accident or it might just be the usual rush-hour chaos. Whatever the reason, I'm still stuck in a jam with a man who sets my nerves on edge.

He looks at me. 'What's the hold-up?'

I shake my head. 'God knows. When do you need to be there?'

'Eight thirty,' he says.

I glance at the clock on the dashboard. It's only quarter past. 'You've got time. You could walk it from here.'

But he doesn't take the hint. Instead, he sits back, draws on his cigarette and stares out through the window. We sit in silence, the minutes ticking slowly by, until he speaks again. 'If you really want to know, I'm seeing my probation officer.'

'Oh.' Somehow that wasn't what I expected to hear.

He smiles drily. 'Life is full of obligations.'

I should have guessed. He's on life licence, of course he is. He killed a man. For a while at least, he'll have to check in every couple of weeks. Even Marc had to jump through the hoops when he finally got his parole. I glance at him. 'Sorry.' Although God knows why I'm apologizing; it's not my fault that he's in the place he is.

'So what did you think I was doing, robbing a bank?'

I ignore the question, looking at his hand again. 'They won't be too impressed with that.'

'How's Marc?' he retorts.

I narrow my eyes and stare at him. 'He's fine. Why shouldn't he be?'

He shrugs. And I get that weird fluttery sensation in the pit of my stomach, the feeling that something is oh so very wrong. I open my mouth to ask again but quickly bite my tongue – I don't want to give him the satisfaction.

The vehicle in front has started to move off. I keep my distance, unwilling to scare the driver any more than I already have. I hate negotiating busy traffic. And it's made even more stressful by driving a car that doesn't belong to me.

It's almost eight twenty-five by the time we reach the High Street. As we come adjacent to the shop he says, 'You can drop me off here.'

I pull into the parking space. 'Are you sure? I can always—'

'No, this'll do.'

He unfastens his seatbelt. He's halfway out when he turns to look at me again. I'm sure he's going to say 'Thanks' or 'See you later' or any of those usual banal niceties. But he doesn't.

He doesn't say a single word. He just smiles, closes the door and walks away.

'Who was that?' Kerry Anne asks, before I've had time to hang up my coat. I arrived to find her standing on the doorstep.

'Who?'

'Him,' she says, staring out of the window.

I follow her gaze but he's long gone. 'Oh, just an old friend of Jim's. He needed a lift. Why are you here so early?'

'It's not *that* early,' she replies. Which is true, although it's still thirty minutes before she usually starts work. 'What's his name?'

I frown. An uncomfortable car ride with Johnny followed by an interrogation from Kerry Anne isn't the ideal start to a day. 'What's with the twenty questions?'

'I just wondered,' she says but her eyes continue to scrutinize me.

Forcing a laugh I reply, 'Well, how about wandering over to the kettle and making a cup of tea instead. I'm parched. You do that and I'll start sorting the deliveries.'

She makes a quiet huffing sound in the back of her throat before her mouth slips into a prim thin line. 'If that's what you want.' Flouncing into the kitchen, she clatters the mugs down and slams the fridge door.

What on earth is wrong with everyone? Marc's manic, Jim's permanently drunk, and Dee's so irritable you can barely talk to her without getting your head bitten off. Carl's got the sulks; something to do with Melanie, I think. And now even Kerry Anne's behaving oddly.

'Are you okay?' I ask, when she returns.

She almost hurls the mug down in front of me. Some of the tea slops out and spills over the counter. '*I'm* okay,' she stresses. 'Why shouldn't I be?'

'Because you seem upset. Have I offended you in some way?'

'No,' she replies shortly, although her eyes say different. She's glaring at me like something revolting she's seen on a pavement – and almost stepped in. Then, suddenly dropping the attitude, she shakes her head and smiles. 'No, really, it's nothing to do with you.'

Maybe it isn't. Maybe it's just boyfriend trouble but I'm not entirely convinced. I nod and get on with my work but for the rest of the morning she keeps giving me these strange little looks, watching me when she thinks I'm not aware of it.

At lunchtime she goes out for sandwiches and I stand at the counter, flipping through the local paper. The shop's busier than it was but there are still long stretches of quiet. As the month goes on, trade should pick up although by then, of course, Dee may have sold the business. Yesterday, I tried to talk to her about it but she impatiently waved me away. 'I haven't got time for this, Simone.'

I turn the pages until I reach the job ads. I'm not sure what I'm searching for – another position with a florist, a return to accountancy? I don't even know if I want to stay in the area. If the Buckleys go to Spain, maybe I should move too. Which reminds me that I haven't heard from Marc. Surely he'd have rung if he'd bought the tickets?

I'm still scanning the situations vacant when Kerry Anne comes back. I casually turn to the news section and pretend to look absorbed. And then suddenly, shockingly, there he is, staring straight up at me: a black and white version of the man who came into the shop. Eddie Tate. But worse than that – a *dead* Eddie Tate. A *murdered* Eddie Tate. Christ! My stomach hurtles towards the floor. I can feel my heart pumping wildly while every drop of blood drains out of my face. A hundred voices start screaming in my head: Is this why Marc so desperately wants to get away, why Jim's been stupid drunk, why Johnny's hand is covered in bruises . . . ?

Quickly, I snap the paper shut; Kerry Anne's approaching and I don't want her to see it. What if she recognizes him? What if she suggests we call the police?

She dumps the sandwiches beside me. 'They didn't have tuna so I got you chicken.'

I stare wide-eyed at the bag, at the corner where a fat stain of grease has leaked through the wrapping. A wave of nausea hits my throat and for a second the room begins to spin.

I grasp hold of the counter until the world slips gradually back into focus.

'Have you finished with that?' she asks, glancing towards the newspaper.

'No!' I almost yelp at her. Then, moderating my tone, hurriedly mumble, 'Sorry. No. Sorry, look, I've got to go out. There's something I've got to do.' Forcing my legs into a movement they quite clearly have no wish to make, I stagger into the kitchen and grab my bag. Still clutching the paper to my breast, I dash clumsily back through the shop, clipping the heads off several narcissi in my rush to get away. 'I won't be long. Half an hour.'

Kerry Anne stares after me. She's wearing an expression of astonishment.

In the street the cold blustery wind comes as some relief, tearing at my clothes and blowing me partially out of the cocoon of shock. I stand for a moment, taking deep breaths of air, before fumbling for the keys and getting into the car. Throwing the paper on the passenger seat, I start the engine and pull out into the traffic. I don't know where I'm going. The impulse is to speed home, to talk to Marc, but first I need some time alone. If nothing else I have to read that article properly.

I drive to the nearest refuge I can think of, the local recreation ground, and park untidily on the gravel forecourt. There's a scattering of cars but no other evidence of life. The place has a dreary abandoned feel to it. The swings are empty, the slides deserted. Even the clouds are gloomily grey, the wind sweeping them sluggishly across the sky.

Tentatively, I reach out and pick up the paper. As if it might burn, I turn the pages with the tips of my fingers. My heart has restarted that scary anxious thump. Three pages, four. And then, just as I'm hoping that it's all been some mad mistake, there he is again – Eddie Tate. Still staring up at me. Still dead. Still murdered. The words dance in front of my eyes, tripping in and out of focus. I swallow hard. *Concentrate*.

Killed.

Where? In Dalston. That's in London, not Essex. That's miles away from here. For a moment my spirits rise but as quickly fall again . . . it's in the East End and not so far from The Palace.

How? I scan down the paragraphs but they don't make for easy reading. He was beaten, cut and tortured; not too much detail but enough to make my skin crawl. A slow and vicious murder. A gangland type of killing. And then his body moved and dumped like some lousy piece of trash. I can't pretend I liked the guy but God, Holy God, surely no one deserves to die like that.

When? On Tuesday night. Sometime late that evening or early Wednesday morning. Only a day after he came into the shop. Only a day after I talked to him. Only a day after Johnny said: *I'll make sure it doesn't happen again*. A thin film of sweat breaks out on my forehead. No, he wouldn't, he couldn't. It's inconceivable. He's only just got out of jail.

I wind down the window to let in some air.

But then there's the bruising to his hand ... the damage he has no explanation for. And he's killed before. There's no doubt about that. He killed a man called Roy Foster. And maybe, just maybe, he killed Sarah too ...

Shit, I need a cigarette. Rummaging in my bag, I find my secret stash and shakily light up. I try to trace the hours back to Tuesday evening, to what time Marc came home: it wasn't late, I'm sure of it. And he was okay then.

I scan the article again. Eddie was found yesterday, wrapped in a blanket, dead in the back of his car. No, Marc couldn't have had anything to do with it. He may be good at hiding things but he couldn't have hidden that.

But that's not to say he doesn't know about it now. He does. I'm certain he does. And everything makes a horrible kind of sense – his panic, Jim's drinking, Dee's agitation ... the whole God-awful crazy atmosphere. They're all walking on egg-shells. They know what Johnny's done.

They're shielding him. They're covering his tracks.

But why? Why should they? Friendship's one thing – but murder's quite another.

There's only one way to find out. I reach for my phone and press 1, Marc's mobile number. It rings three times before switching to answer mode. I listen to his recorded voice – please leave a message – before shutting it off again. Should I try the house phone? No. If I want an honest answer I'll have to ask him face to face.

I put the engine in gear and quickly reverse out of the car park. It's not the most perfect of manoeuvres but I don't give a damn. Who cares if I'm driving like a maniac, I've got more important things to worry about.

By the time I pull into the drive it's almost two o'clock. There's a light on in the kitchen. Johnny must be back by now. Do I dare go in and ask him straight out? But what if I've got this all wrong – you can't just go round accusing people of murder. But then what if I'm right?

My hands are shaking as I get out of the car. Shivering, I walk slowly round to the front of the house. What has Johnny done – and why? And how am I going to deal with it?

But all of these thoughts are wiped clean from my mind as I open the door and hear the cry. A thin prolonged keening, high-pitched, almost unearthly, it floats along the hall and turns my blood to ice.

Something terrible has happened.

And I know instinctively that it has happened to Marc.

Chapter Twelve

Johnny

Jim hasn't moved for the past twenty minutes. As if transformed into stone he's been staring blankly at the table, one hand still around his glass, the other cupped around the thick fleshy folds of his chin. His eyes have a thick glazed expression.

Dee, however, has taken an opposite role. Like a woman possessed, she's pacing the kitchen, tearing at her hair, her voice slowly rising to a fever pitch of hysteria. Her wailing's starting to get on my nerves. How can anyone think straight with that fucking row going on? What she needs is a good sharp slap to shock her out it.

And then abruptly, she falls quiet. I feel a spurt of gratitude but then, following her gaze, glance over my shoulder.

Simone is standing by the door.

Like a rabbit caught in headlights, she has a stunned bewildered look. Her wide shocked eyes are staring blindly at Dee. A series of tiny gulps emanate from her throat. Shit,

I hope she isn't going to cry. One weeping female's enough for any man to handle.

'What is it?' she eventually manages to croak.

No one speaks.

'Tell me. You've got to tell me. It's Marc, isn't it? Is he ... is he ... ' She can't bring herself to say the word.

So what lucky soul's going to have the pleasure of breaking the news to her? I sit back in my chair. Not me, that's for certain.

Surprisingly, it's Jim who steps into the breach. He rises from his stupor and slowly shakes his head. 'No, love. He's not ... ' But even he can't wrap his lips immediately around it. Instead, he reaches for his glass and knocks back another inch of whisky. Then, courage restored, he gently continues, 'He's not dead, love. It isn't that.'

Simone steps forward, relief flashing briefly across her face, before Dee swiftly eliminates it again.

'As bloody good as,' she cries out, slouching down and dropping her head into her hands.

Simone stumbles towards the table. 'What? An accident? Has he ... '

Fuck, at this rate we'll be here all day. And I can't take any more of these histrionics. 'For God's sake, will someone just tell her!'

She turns, her eyes tearfully pleading. '*You* tell me.' Almost falling into the chair beside mine, she half reaches for my arm before withdrawing. Even now, in this moment of pure unadulterated terror, she can't quite bring herself to touch me. 'Please.'

I glance towards Dee and Jim but there's no hope of salvation there; she's sobbing like a widow and he's resumed his coma status.

'Please,' Simone begs again.

So what choice do I have? There's no easy way to do this and no point either in creeping round the truth. Prolonging the agony isn't going to change it. On the table, there's a folded sheet of paper. I pick it up and pass it over. 'I'm sorry.'

She takes it cautiously between her fingers.

There's a protracted moment of silence, thick and heavy. For a few seconds everyone seems to be holding their breath. It's so quiet I can almost hear her brain ticking over, the frenzied clicks of incomprehension as she tries to make sense of the sentences in front of her:

WE HAVE YOUR SON. DO YOU WANT HIM TO JOIN EDDIE?

YOU HAVE SEVEN DAYS TO GIVE US THE DIAMONDS.

NO COPS.

She looks up, frowning. And then, as if it might be some gruesome practical joke, her mouth quivers into a smile. 'This is . . .'

But by now everyone's refusing to look at her. Even I can't stand to go there – and bearing bad news is a speciality of mine.

She looks desperately towards her mother-in-law. 'I don't understand.'

'They're going to kill him,' Dee moans into her fingers. 'They will. They're going to kill my son.'

Simone turns towards me, her eyes bright and frightened. 'Johnny?'

Shit, what am I supposed to say? I've already done my share. I've done the hard bit; I can't be expected to explain the whole fucking story. I can't be responsible for picking up the pieces.

She's still talking but I'm barely listening. 'What diamonds? What's happening? Where's Marc?' She has a crushed desolate expression on her face. It reminds me of Sarah's. It reminds me of when Roy Foster died, when she came to see me in jail, when . . .

Dee shifts in her chair. She glances up at Simone and wipes her tears away. 'Ask him,' she mutters, 'if you want to know – ask him!'

Which is fucking rich after everything *she's* done. I glare at her, although God knows why I should be amazed – she always was the greatest bitch on earth. And the most selfish. And yes, okay, I know that she's going through hell, but that doesn't alter the fact that she's still searching for a way to shift the blame.

Simone stares at me.

'Tell her,' Dee urges, 'she's got a right to know.'

You tell her, I want to yell back. But I don't. What's the point? We're already up to our necks and no amount of shouting will change that. The past has caught up faster than I anticipated.

'Okay,' Dee says, as if I've stood my ground and blatantly refused. 'I'll do it then.'

And she does – slowly, falteringly, like blood being drawn from a stone. She leans across the table and takes Simone's hand. She tells her about Hatton Garden. She tells her about the robbery, the ice, about how Eddie was the driver. She explains how they agreed to help me get the diamonds back. There's only one subject she unsurprisingly fails to cover.

And after she's finished there's one of those long uncomfortable silences.

'What have you done?' Simone eventually asks. Her voice has acquired a disquieting calm. She's glaring at me now like I'm the devil incarnate. And she's staring down at my hand, at the knuckles, at the bruises I got from hitting Carl. I know what she's thinking.

She deliberately pushes the paper in front of me. It's open at the appropriate page; the grainy image of Eddie Tate gazes out accusingly.

'Hey, I didn't kill him, right?' I glance at Dee but she quickly looks away. She isn't going to come clean about her part in it or Carl's. That information's clearly going to remain on a need-to-know basis.

Simone says, 'You didn't like him.'

'There's a lot of people I don't like, sweetheart, but I'm not a fucking butcher.'

Dee flinches at the comment but still provides an alibi. 'He didn't, Simone. He couldn't. He was here on Tuesday night.'

But I can see it doesn't wash. Maybe she wants me to be

guilty. In her mind I've already been tried and convicted – once a killer always a killer.

'So what happened to your hand?'

There's no point lying about it; one look at Carl's face and she'll make the connection. I shrug. 'You were right, what you said in the car. I had a fight – but not with Eddie Tate. I've not been near him. It was—'

'It was with Carl,' Dee interrupts. 'It was something and nothing, love. A scrap. I promise. It's not to do with ... with this.' She bends her head and starts to cry again, a slow horrible weeping.

Confusion sweeps into Simone's eyes. Suddenly, as if the implications of the ransom note have just sunk in, she scrapes back her chair and stands up. Her face has gone ashen. 'So who ... why have they ... ?' She turns and stumbles towards the sink, her fingers clutching for its rim. She leans over the basin, a thin pathetic retching sound emerging from her throat, and stays there for a minute, visibly shaking, even the chatter of her teeth clearly audible above Dee's crying.

No one moves. We sit and watch her.

Finally, she takes two, three deep breaths and flips on the tap. She lets the cold water pour into her hands and splashes it over her face. Some of it spills down her jumper and on to the floor. Then, with her hair dripping, she turns and asks with renewed hope: 'The police. What do the police say?'

Dee shakes her head and moans.

'They've been here, haven't they?' She looks from Dee to Jim. 'They must have.' I can hear the rising panic in her voice, the bewilderment. 'You've told them?' But she already knows the answer. She can read it in their eyes. 'But you must. It's Marc. You've got to—'

'No!' Dee wails.

And her cry brings Jim temporarily back to the world of the living. 'We can't, love. We can't get them involved. If we do then—'

'You've *got* to,' Simone insists. 'For God's sake, what are you thinking?' She starts rooting in her bag, spilling its contents across the table: perfume and lipstick, an address book, a handful of tissues, before finally retrieving her phone.

Dee reaches out and grabs it from her. 'No,' she says again, 'no cops. You can't.' She's sobbing like a child now, gulping out the words. 'Please. You don't understand these ... these people. They'll k-kill him. They'll kill my baby.'

'We'll get him back,' Jim mutters unconvincingly into his glass.

'How?' Simone shouts back at him. '*How* are you going to get him back?'

Jim glances nervously at me.

And suddenly all eyes are turned on me.

White knight Johnny rides to the rescue. It's great to be so popular. And seeing as I've now got an image to sustain, I try to sound suitably confident. 'I'll do it. Don't worry. I'll sort it out.'

But the words don't provoke quite the level of swooning gratitude I expected.

'You?' she asks.

And I could say her tone was sneering but that hardly

begins to describe it. Even under pressure, Simone's got the finest line in contempt this side of Watford.

'He will,' Dee insists. 'He's got what they want. He'll give them the diamonds. He'll help us get Marc back.'

'Why should he?' she asks, stating the obvious. 'Why should he give up anything to save Marc?'

Which more or less hits the nail on the head. Simone may be petrified but she isn't stupid. She knows I don't give two shits about any of them. But what she doesn't know is that Carl killed Edie Tate and I can't afford to have the cops sniffing around. Dee, however, understands exactly how precarious my position is. I'm in as tight a corner as she is. If I won't cooperate, they'll have no choice but to call in the Law, and then questions will be asked. First the ice will have to be explained and that, perhaps, will lead to Hatton Garden and that, in turn, may lead to the nasty little business of Eddie Tate. Dee's desperate enough to believe that I won't take the risk of going back to jail. I know what she's thinking, even if she's not saying it out loud – that my future's as much in the balance as hers.

'I'm on life licence,' I mutter. 'You think I want to go back inside for robbery?'

Dee turns her black-stained eyes to gaze pleadingly at me and at the same time reaches out to grasp my arm. Her fingers dig desperately into my flesh, an unpleasant reminder of when she told me about Carl. 'You will, won't you, Johnny? Tell her. Tell her you're going to help us.'

Her fingernails are red as blood. I gaze down at them, disgusted. I want to pull away, to disengage, but force myself to keep the contact. 'Of course I will.' And then, in case that doesn't sound convincing enough, I lay my own hand reassuringly over hers. I even manage a squeeze. Her skin is freezing, cold as death. 'You know I will.'

Of course, I've already made up my mind. I'm going to take my chances and get as far away as possible. But it's a gamble. If the truth comes out, I could end up running for the rest of my life. Simone stares at me as if she doesn't believe a word. But at the same time she's busy weighing up the options, making frantic mental calculations while she tries to figure out the best way of keeping Marc alive. The seconds tick by. 'I still think we should call the police,' she says.

Dee hurls the mobile down on the table. 'Okay. You do it then. You call them. You do what you like.' Her tone is slipping back into hysterical mode. 'But don't come crying to me when ... when ... ' She raises her twisted face. 'It'll be *your* fault.'

And although Simone stares at the phone, she doesn't make a move to pick it up. She's afraid. There's some sense to Dee's reasoning and she knows it. She can't take the risk of being wrong. But it all comes down to whether I can be trusted ... and that's a different matter altogether.

Reluctantly, she transfers her attention to me. 'So what's the idea?' she asks cynically. 'What's the great plan?'

I shrug. 'There's no great plan, just a straightforward exchange. I give them the diamonds and they give us back Marc.'

'That easy, huh?' she almost snarls.

Now that's no way to treat your potential saviour. A little respect is called for at the very least. 'Well, if you're not interested ... '

Dee begs, '*Please*, Simone.'

She falters, biting on her lower lip. 'I'm sorry. I didn't mean ...' She hates my guts but she knows she shouldn't show it; I might be her only chance and she can't afford to piss me off. 'I'm sorry,' she repeats, slumping back into a chair. 'I'm just scared.'

It's not the most heartfelt apology I've ever heard but it'll do for starters; there's time enough to make her grovel. And I've got to say, there's a certain amount of heart-warming satisfaction in this whole scenario. It couldn't have gone better if I'd planned it myself.

Especially when it comes to Jim.

There he is, huddled over his whisky, a big man looking small. I can't resist a smile. I've come a long way to have this simple but extraordinary pleasure. Perhaps he's finally beginning to understand what grief brings, what it might actually mean to lose someone you love. I lost my wife – he might lose his son. A fair exchange? Too fucking right. I've got no idea who's abducted Marc and I don't give a damn – but if they walked into this room, right here, right now, I'd stand up and shake their hand.

Simone's strident voice cuts across my thoughts. 'So where are they?'

'What?'

'What do you think?' She's trying not to lose her rag. 'The diamonds, of course.'

I laugh. She's got a fucking nerve. 'You think I'm going to tell you that?'

'You think I'm going to trust you with my husband's life?'

She reaches again for her phone and dials the first couple of digits.

'Go ahead,' I taunt. 'Call the cops. Call them.'

'Why shouldn't I?'

Jim sighs, lurching for his glass. Dee moans softly into her hands.

'Because I'm your last chance,' I answer calmly. 'But if you want to throw it away – just go ahead.'

Her face crumples into indecision. She wants to call my bluff but doesn't dare; her husband's life is in the balance. The seconds tick by. Slowly, frowning, she lays the phone back down on the table.

I try to hide my relief. The last thing I need is a knock at the door, a posse of cops. One glance at that ransom note and even the most cretinous of pigs would eventually find the Eddie Tate connection. There'd be some explaining to do then. And don't get me wrong, I'm more than glad that the Buckley sins might finally be coming home to roost – but I've no intention of being here to welcome them. I'm packing my bags and getting out.

'Johnny's going to London,' Dee says. 'Tomorrow. He's going to get the diamonds.'

Simone turns her gaze on me. 'Oh yes?'

I don't need to be Einstein to recognize the incredulity in her voice. 'Yes,' I repeat. Our eyes meet in a pool of mutual suspicion.

'And are you coming back?' she asks.

'You think I want to see Marc dead?'

And there's not much she can say to that without insulting

me, without deliberately destroying whatever fragile hopes may remain. Her eyes blink closed while her body folds into a shudder. If I had any feelings left I might almost feel sorry for her – but I don't. My compassion ran out years ago. Any remaining fragments I need for myself.

'No,' she says, defeated.

Smugly, I rise to my feet. 'Well, that's settled then.' I depart for a much-needed slash and as I return the room falls into an uneasy silence. It's clear they've been talking among themselves. So what now? A few furtive glances are exchanged before Simone finally speaks.

Her voice is low but determined. 'I'm coming with you – tomorrow.'

So that's what they've been cooking up between them. Perhaps Dee doesn't trust me quite so much as she makes out – or perhaps Simone's just managed to exert her influence. I snort. 'I don't need a bodyguard, love.'

'No,' she replies quickly, 'but you do need a driver. You haven't got a licence. What are you going to do – bring the diamonds back on the train?' She gives me a small unfriendly smile. 'That doesn't seem very safe.'

'She's right,' Dee adds supportively. 'Anything could happen.'

'What, to me or the ice?' Although the answer to that is pretty self-evident: if it came to a choice they wouldn't hesitate for a second. If I was dying in the gutter they'd happily step over me.

Simone gazes straight into my eyes and asks provocatively, 'So what's the problem, Johnny?'

I can't afford to raise their suspicions. And what the hell, a lift into London isn't going to do me any harm. In fact it could be positively useful. I shake my head. 'Nothing. Nothing at all. If that's what you want, it's fine by me.'

It won't take me long to lose her once we're there.

Chapter Thirteen

Simone

I wanted to leave last night but Johnny wouldn't agree. He had calls to make, he said, meetings to organize. And when I persisted he argued, 'Come on, Simone. We're all exhausted. No one's thinking straight. We need a good night's sleep.'

Sleep? As if sleep was an option with Marc out there somewhere, terrified, probably wondering if he'd ever see daylight again. And all this stuff going round in my head, about how he'd wanted to get away, almost begged – as if he realized he was in danger – and I'd just brushed it all aside. If only I'd forced him, made him speak to me, none of this might have happened. He must have known about Eddie Tate's killing and its implications. He must have realized someone else was after the diamonds, someone so ruthless that... Why else was Eddie tortured, unless it was to find out what he knew? Why else would Marc have been so eager to go to Spain? He was scared he'd be the next in line. And what had I done to help? Nothing, bloody nothing. I'd just put it down to one of his moods.

I was pacing the floor when Dee knocked on the door around midnight. 'Can we talk?' She looked worse than I did, pale, ghost-like, hovering on the edge of that precipice of fear. I wanted to be alone. I didn't want to talk, not to her or to anyone, but I still waved her inside.

She sat down on the sofa and stared uncertainly at her feet.

Far from feeling sorry for her, I had this sudden urge to shout, to scream: *What did you think you were doing?* This was all her fault. Hers and Jim's. Johnny may have stolen the diamonds but they'd agreed to help him get them back. Marc was barely out of prison before they'd hatched their stupid little plan. And now look where it had led.

Sensing my mood, she raised her tear-stained eyes. 'I know what you think.' Her mouth quivered and she swallowed hard. 'And you're right, love, you're right to blame me. It was ... I should never have ... ' She shook her head and dropped her face back into her hands.

But my anger was gradually dissolving. I only had to hark back a few weeks to recall how hard she'd battled to keep Johnny away. No one could have put up a more spirited fight. At some point since, yes, she'd made a foolish decision but she could never have anticipated the outcome. All I was doing was transferring my own guilt. This felt like some cruel and terrible punishment for not loving Marc enough.

'It's not your fault,' I said, resignedly. How she'd been persuaded to embark on this madness was anyone's guess but, if I was being painfully honest, I doubted if Marc had been last in the queue of those trying to influence her. A hidden stash of diamonds was just his sort of crazy dream.

'We shouldn't have kept it from you,' she murmured into her fingers. 'I'm sorry. I'm so sorry.'

I sat down heavily beside her. 'So why, Dee? What made you even agree to it?'

She sighed. 'It just seemed like such an easy way out. The Palace has been ... well, you know, and we've tried, we've really tried but ... and we thought ... Well, it all happened such a long time ago and ...' She faltered again, her mouth, then her eyes and then her whole face collapsing. 'What have I done, Simone? They'll kill him. They'll kill him, won't they?'

She leaned in against me, a sobbing weight of despair.

'No,' I insisted, 'they won't. I promise. I'm sure.' Perhaps it was just the fact of having to be strong for someone else, for having to put on a brave face, but for a moment I really believed it. 'It's not your fault,' I said again.

'You don't understand,' she muttered.

Which brought my high hopes clattering back to earth. 'What do you mean?' I touched her cheek and forced her to look at me again. 'Dee? I can't do this unless you tell me everything. Please, you've got to help me if we're going to help Marc.'

She hesitated, her eyes roaming restlessly around the room until they finally came back to settle on mine. 'These people – whoever's got him – well, what if Johnny ... I know what he said but what if he doesn't—'

'You don't trust him,' I interrupted, blurting out my suspicions if not hers.

It was probably the worst thing I could say, but then the

truth often is. Her brow furrowed into a terrified frown. 'No. He wouldn't. He wouldn't desert Marc ... he couldn't. No, he's got his faults but he'd never do that.'

So why didn't I believe her? It sounded to me like she was trying far too hard to convince herself. 'Are you sure?'

She shook her head again. 'Unless ...'

'Unless?'

I watched her bite down hard on her lower lip. 'He might get worried, about the police, about Eddie. He might ...'

'Do a bunk?' I suggested brutally.

'No!' Dee cried again. But despite the remonstration her eyes said something different.

It was hardly news. I didn't trust Johnny one single inch. Even as we spoke, he was probably planning a surreptitious escape. But if he thought he could shake me off, take the diamonds and run, he had another think coming. 'Don't worry,' I told her, 'I won't let him disappear. I won't let him out of my sight.'

She grabbed hold of my hand and held it firmly between hers. She forced a thin tight smile. And then she said something I didn't expect. 'Of course you won't. And as long as you're there, love, he won't let us down. You know how he feels about you.'

I stared at her. 'What?'

'If we want to get Marc back ...' She squeezed my hand tighter. 'You'll be nice to him, won't you? It's our only chance. He'll do it for you. I know he will.'

And now the nightmare was slipping into something more surreal. What was she suggesting – that Johnny ... no,

I couldn't even think about going there. And it wasn't true. It couldn't be. 'Look, Dee, you're wrong. He doesn't . . .'

But she wasn't listening any more. Turning my hand around in hers, she was lost to another world. 'It's okay. It'll all be okay.'

It's morning. I watch as the sky pales into dawn. Rain is falling, a heavy steady beating against the window. For a moment I can't recall what the urgency is, why I have to get up, but slowly the panic wakens in my gut, a hot sick feeling that rises to my chest and then my throat and then . . . Oh God.

I stagger to the bathroom and lean my head against the cool tiles. I take some long deep breaths and the nausea passes. I brush my teeth and step into the shower where I'm greeted by a stream of barely lukewarm water – the perfect start to a perfect day.

I can't believe it's morning already. It's a miracle I managed to sleep at all. In the end, worried I'd be in no fit state to drive, I resorted to the pills in the bathroom cabinet, a legacy from Marc's post-prison insomnia. Just half a pill had been enough to deliver me into a weird dreamless state of unconsciousness.

Lord, how I'd like to be back there now.

As I wash, my mind's starting to spin again, providing a dizzying recital of yesterday's events. What I need to do is concentrate, to try and think straight, but it's easier said than done. And on top of everything else, there's that crazy thing Dee spoke about last night.

Shivering, as much from the memory as the cold, I step out from under the water and grab a towel. Had she been serious? No, she couldn't have been. She was just upset, confused. She was clutching at straws. Johnny doesn't have any interest in me, the very opposite ... except, well, there was that weird thing Marc had said at Christmas, about his wife, about Sarah, about how I ...

No, this isn't the time to struggle with that. I'm messed up, scared enough already. I have to stay focused. I need some caffeine. I take a detour via the kitchen to switch on the kettle and then head back to the bedroom.

What to wear is the least of my worries but I'm still incapable of making a decision. I open the drawers and stare at their contents. As if they belong to someone else, the garments lie in clean neat layers. I feel odd, disoriented, like a stranger in my own home. A minute passes. Then another. What am I doing? Unless I want to walk the streets naked, I'd better make a choice and quick.

In the end I drag on my usual jeans and boots, pair them with a T-shirt and a thin black sweater – it'll be warm enough in the car – and make a vague mental note to pick up my winter coat on the way out.

I look at my watch. It's close to eight o'clock. Damn! A sense of urgency suddenly kicks in. I've only got ten minutes. Grabbing a bag from the bottom of the wardrobe I quickly throw in some underwear, a change of clothes, toiletries and make-up. What else will I need? God knows. I'm not even sure how many days we'll be gone.

Rushing back to the kitchen, I make a fast strong cup of

instant coffee. I should eat, a slice of toast if nothing else, but I can't. Fear is churning at my stomach. I reach for the cigarettes, resorting to that old familiar comfort, and light one with a shaky hand.

Everywhere I go, everywhere I look, there are reminders of Marc: his clothes, CDs, books, even a mug that he drank from yesterday. I don't have the heart to wash it up. Instead, like a clairvoyant trying to read invisible tea leaves, I stare intently into its dregs. It doesn't help. As if he's already dead, a wave of desolation floods over me.

I try to shake it off, to think along more positive lines. Why would they kill him? They wouldn't. He's their key to the diamonds, their bargaining tool. He has to be safe. He's got seven days' grace if they stick to their side of the deal.

But what if Johnny doesn't stick to his?

I lean my face against the window and stare down at the garden. It's filthy dark, filled with shadows. Even the cyclamen, pale as they are, are no more than a blur.

What if he reneges on his promise?

I shudder and look at my watch again. There's no time left to think about it. I have to make a move. After a few last gulps of coffee, I stub out the cigarette, pick up my bag, my purse and coat, and head out of the door.

It all seems quiet until I reach the first floor. Then, as I head down the last flight, Dee appears from the kitchen and stumbles along the hall. It's clear she's spent the night with a bottle of gin.

'Take care of yourself, love,' she says, holding me tight in an alcoholic embrace.

'I'll call,' I promise, gently extricating myself. 'Try not to worry.' I can't remember the last time Dee showed me so much affection but then it's not every day that your son gets held to ransom.

She's about to say something else when Johnny appears and she instantly closes her mouth.

'All set?' he asks cheerily, as if we're about to embark on a weekend jaunt to the country.

He's carrying a bag that's only slighter larger than mine and I try to figure out how much he's bringing with him: everything he owns or just some of it? But then how many possessions does a man have after eighteen years in prison? And if you're about to pick up thousands of pounds' worth of diamonds then I doubt you're too concerned about the odd abandoned shirt.

'Here,' Dee mumbles, 'have these.' She pushes a set of keys into my hand. 'You can take Jim's car.'

I shake my head and pass them back. 'It's okay, really, I'd rather drive my own.' Jim's BMW may be faster, more comfortable, and probably a darn sight more reliable than our old Fiat, but I prefer what I know. And anyway a small car's got its advantages, especially in London.

As we're about to leave, Jim and Carl join the farewell committee, the former looking hung over, the latter like he's been a few bad-tempered rounds with Tyson. It's not the most Christian response but I can't help feeling a rush of satisfaction; if anyone deserved a taste of his own medicine it's Carl Buckley.

Neither of them speaks. Jim makes the effort to nod but

Carl just stares sullenly at his assailant. There's a mountain of hate in that gaze but Johnny doesn't seem too bothered.

Fortunately the rain prevents any lingering goodbyes. As soon as the bags are deposited in the boot, I give a wave, climb into the driving seat, and start the engine. Johnny curls in awkwardly beside me, his long legs bent into the limited space.

We're halfway down the drive before I mention, 'If you need more room you can push the seat back. There's a lever to your left.'

I stop and wait for the electric gates to open. He's still fumbling unsuccessfully, a series of slight frustrated sighs escaping from his throat. If it was anyone else I'd lean across and do it myself but I don't fancy being so close. The only other option is to get out of the car and walk round his side but thankfully I'm saved from this foray into the rain as, with a jolt, he suddenly shoots backwards. I try not to smirk.

Before moving off again, I ask, 'So where are we heading?'

'The City,' he replies shortly.

'Okay.' I wait but no further information is forthcoming. 'Any chance of something more specific?'

'I'll direct you when we get there.'

'Oh great,' I reply, pulling out into the traffic, 'so you've kept up with all the one-way systems then? That'll be useful.'

He gives me a look, a sarcasm-is-the-lowest-form-of-wit kind of look, before eventually capitulating. 'Old Street,' he says reluctantly.

It's another ten minutes before he talks to me again. Of course he chooses the moment that I'm negotiating a tricky exit off a roundabout to resume the conversation. And not just any old small talk, oh no; while cars are hurtling from every direction, he has to come straight out and ask, 'So why exactly did you marry Marc?'

I glance at him, startled. *What kind of a question is that?*

The answer is clear almost immediately – the sort guaranteed to cause a major accident if you don't keep your eyes on the road. Swerving to avoid a lorry, it's only by some miracle that we finally make it safely on to Eastern Avenue.

While my heart's pumping, he continues to look impassively out of the window. Glaring straight ahead, I silently curse him.

'Sorry,' he says smugly, 'I didn't mean to upset you.'

Upset me? He almost just bloody killed me. But recalling what Dee advised – *Be nice to him* – I make an effort to rein in my temper. Not that I believe her ludicrous notion but there's no point either in being deliberately antagonistic. He's the one who's holding all the aces. If he decides to bail out then ...

'Look,' I reply bluntly but softly, 'my life's been turned upside down, my husband's been taken hostage, a man's been murdered, my family's been plotting behind my back to retrieve a stolen stash of diamonds – and now I've almost been squashed beneath the wheels of a truck. Just how much more upset do you think I'm capable of being?'

He gives me one of his weird unintelligible smiles. Whether he's amused or sympathetic is impossible to judge although, going on past experience, it's unlikely to be the latter.

The traffic grinds to a halt and stays that way for the next few minutes. This is one of those infamous snarl-up locations, a rush-hour disaster area I should have found a way of avoiding. Sadly, it's too late for that now. And although it's not the first occasion I've been stuck with Johnny in the tight confined space of a car, I can't quite figure out why it feels so much worse this time.

I drum my fingers on the steering wheel, willing the road ahead to clear. Perhaps I *do* know what's bugging me: I'm too aware of him, too disturbed by his sitting so close. Perhaps I should have taken up the offer on the BMW. At least I could have kept a reasonable distance. Even the small things, like his smell, set me on edge. There's nothing bad about it, nothing malodorous – there's even a fragrant whiff of shampoo and soap – but somehow, overlain by the tobacco, it's just too unpleasantly distinct.

Mind, for all my discomfort he doesn't seem too easy either. Despite the rain, he winds down the window and leans out. Maybe he's just checking on the traffic but from the paleness of his face, and the quickness of his breath, I'm more inclined to suspect an attack of claustrophobia.

'Are you all right?' I ask. I'd like to claim that it's a purely humanitarian response, an act of kindness, but it isn't. If Johnny's got a weakness then I want to know about it. Any weapon, however big or small, could be useful in the days ahead.

But he doesn't reply. He doesn't even look at me.

And before I get the chance to pursue any lurking devils, the car ahead has shifted and we're slowly crawling forward again. Gradually we pick up pace until we're rolling along at a respectable 20 mph. Still he doesn't say anything and, as much to break the silence as in any hope that I might get an honest reply, I ask, 'So why are you really doing this, Johnny? No offence, but what's in it for you?'

'We've already had this conversation. I get to stay out of jail.'

I suppose there's some truth in that – but I'm still not convinced. 'Oh come on, those diamonds are worth a fortune.' I try to keep my tone light rather than accusatory. 'They're your future. They're your way out, your chance to escape from ...' I pause, looking around. The bleak grey street seems to say it all. 'What's to stop you from just taking off? It's not as if you even like the Buckleys.'

He smiles. 'You're a Buckley.'

I ignore the implication. 'You see, unless I'm missing something, it doesn't make any sense.'

Johnny lifts his eyebrows and sighs. 'Then perhaps what you're missing is an old-fashioned sense of loyalty.'

Forgetting my intention to stay calm, I glare at him and snap, 'And what's that supposed to mean?' He's hit a sore point, reminding me of my plans to leave Marc. That guilty secret hasn't just been playing on my conscience, it's been eating away at my guts too. There's this sharp remorseful pain that grows more intense by the hour. His kidnap feels like a punishment, divine retribution for my intention to renege on my marriage vows. *For better or for worse*. And it's not as though I ever stopped caring. I didn't. The thought of Marc being hurt, *killed*, fills me with unadulterated terror.

Which maybe goes to prove, now I'm in danger of losing him, how much I still love him.

Johnny takes a moment to absorb my retort – or perhaps just the evidence of my guilt – before continuing. He doesn't answer directly, harking back instead to my earlier comment. 'You're right. Well, about Jim for sure; we never were the best of mates. I was always much closer to Dee.'

He stops. Is that it? I'm tempted to prompt him – but wisely keep my mouth shut. There's a time and a place for interrogative interruptions. Occasionally, if you keep quiet for long enough then ...

'Yeah,' he eventually begins again, 'we go back a long way. And if you think that doesn't count for anything, that it's all just ancient history, then you're wrong. It's the old ties that are the strongest. When you've been inside for as long as ... well, you don't ever forget your real friends, the ones who've stood by you. No, Dee's been good to me. I'd do anything for her.'

And now I know for sure that he's lying! Dee didn't stand by him. She was as shocked as I was to hear that Jim had invited him to stay. She didn't even want to *see* him again. I swing the car left on to Mare Street, trying to think of what to say next.

Perhaps he reads my expression because he gives a soft disconcerting laugh and averts his face to stare out of the window. 'Sorry. I thought you realized.'

It takes a while for the words to settle in my brain. Realized? Realized *what*? The driver in front is doing the indecisive jig of the lost. Now, while I'm not completely incapable of simultaneously driving and thinking, I've already had one near-death experience today and am loath to encourage another. For the next thirty seconds, I keep my mind and my eyes fixed firmly on the road ahead.

'What?' I eventually ask, as I take a right into Hackney Road and our future feels a little more secure.

He shrugs. 'At Christmas. When we talked. I thought you'd guessed; women's intuition and all that.'

Frowning, I glance back at him. Christmas is one of those days that I've already put firmly behind me. Best forgotten as the bad ones always are. Reluctantly, I resurrect the memory, trying to remember what he told me. The only time we really talked was outside, after the row, after it all kicked off, after Jim said that stuff about people in glass houses, after Dee stormed out ... and when I was curious, too curious perhaps, as to what lay at the heart of it all. And what I'd presumed was that she'd once had an affair, that ...

The light finally flicks on in my brain. 'God,' I whisper, 'it was you.' And I don't know why I'm shocked but I am. He doesn't deny it. 'It was a long time ago and no, in case you're wondering, there's nothing going on now.'

'But you still have feelings for her?'

'Not like that,' he replies. He's got a faintly embarrassed expression on his face, the kind of look that men often assume when the ugly subject of emotion raises its head. 'I'm not proud of what we did. It should never have happened but ...' He shrugs. 'So you see, there *is* a reason why I'm doing this.'

Do I believe him? Not entirely. He may be telling the

truth about the affair but as to the rest ... well, the jury's still out on that. 'For old time's sake then?'

'Partly,' he agrees, 'but don't forget they took me in when I needed a place to stay. They gave me the chance to sort myself out. If it wasn't for them, Lord knows where I'd be now.'

'You gave them money to do that,' I retort, taking a shot in the dark.

It hits the mark. He glances at me, startled. 'What makes you say that?' It's good to see him wrong-footed for once, on the defensive.

'Why? Are you denying it?'

Johnny laughs. 'You ask a lot of questions.'

'I've got a lot to learn.'

We're approaching Shoreditch High Street and it occurs to me that we're not so very far from Dalston, from where Eddie Tate met his gruesome end. Glancing down at Johnny's hand, I wonder if Dee was lying about Tuesday night, if he really was at home or if ... No, I can't start thinking like that, not when I'm trapped in a small metal box with nowhere to go. Whatever their history she wouldn't cover up a cold-blooded murder. I can't believe that. Well, not unless she was doing it for Marc ...

Is that the deal – they keep quiet about the killing in return for Johnny handing over the diamonds?

'Why did you hit Carl?'

He's in the process of rolling a cigarette. As if the task takes all his concentration, he waits until he's formed the skinny cylinder, until it's been dampened, sealed, examined and lit, before finally replying. His lips slide into a thin cruel smile. 'Does anyone need a reason?'

In Carl's case, probably not, but it's hardly an adequate answer. 'I thought you two got on like a house on fire. You spent enough time together.'

'Let's just say we had a difference of opinion.'

'You always solve your differences with your fists?'

He exhales a thin stream of smoke out of the window before turning to look at me again. 'No, not always.' There's a short pause before he adds softly, 'And no, I didn't kill Eddie Tate either.'

God, I hate the way he does that, reading my thoughts as if they're sitting in a cartoon bubble right above my head. Too quickly I retort, 'I didn't say you did.'

'But you can't help wondering.'

He doesn't seem so much offended as amused. Perhaps he's one of those men who get a kick out of women being scared of them. And I am afraid although I'm desperate not to show it. I'm trying to keep it buried not just from him but from myself too. I'm secretly praying Dee wouldn't be so mad as to pack me off with a psychopathic killer, but if it came to a choice between my life and her son's . . .

'You don't need to worry,' he continues, interrupting my thoughts. 'Trust me.'

Easy for him to say. But I force a smile and make a determined effort to wipe the frown from between my eyes. 'Sure,' I reply, in what's intended to be a comfortable easy tone but which emerges as more of a squeak.

He grins as I sneak a glance at him. I quickly look away.

It's only as we're approaching Old Street that I finally register the congestion charge signs. 'Damn!' I mutter under my breath. I should have remembered we'd be entering the pay-for-the-privilege zone but it's been so long since I was in central London it's gone clean out of my head. I pull in at a garage, fill up with petrol and pay my dues.

As we move back out on to the street he says, 'They should charge to get out rather than in.'

It takes me a moment to pick up on the joke. Surprised, I reply, 'I thought you liked London.'

'Whatever gave you that idea?'

'I don't know.' Now it's my turn to shrug. 'I guess I just presumed. I mean, you used to work here, didn't you? You used to live here.'

He expels one of his long world-weary sighs. 'Well, perhaps that's the trouble with presumptions, love – they're often a fair distance from the truth.'

Now there are plenty of people who can call me *love, dear, sweetheart* or any of those meaningless endearments and I won't get the slightest bit bothered by it. But there are others – like Johnny for example – who can imbue those words with such stunning condescension that it makes my blood boil. Hackles raised, I'm about to snap back, to say something I may later regret, when—

'The next right,' he urgently instructs. He points a finger in front of my face. 'Here, quick, this one.'

For God's sake, he could have given me more warning! Veering dangerously across the street, indicating too late, I provoke the predictable road-rage of at least three other motorists. And with the window still wound down I get the full force of their horns *and* their unrestrained Anglo-Saxon vocabulary. Hunching lower in my seat, I try to pretend I'm invisible.

Once I've gained access, narrowly avoiding those pearly gates of heaven, I turn to glare at him. It's the second time today I've almost met my maker.

'It's okay,' he says, 'you don't need to apologize. I'm getting used to your driving.'

Too angry to speak, I grind my teeth and slowly count to ten.

He doesn't seem to notice – or maybe he just doesn't care. 'You can park anywhere round here.'

I pull in at a meter near the swimming baths, still seething. 'You know, I hate to be fussy but a bit of notice would have been useful, a hint that you wanted to turn right.'

'I told you,' he says, shaking his head. 'It's not my fault if you've got slow reactions.'

What? I take a few deep breaths. I know he's deliberately winding me up and I'm determined not to rise to it – at least no more than I already have. I simply ask, 'So where to now?'

He nods towards the end of the road. 'I've got a meet in the caff. I'll see you back here in . . . ' He examines his watch. 'What? Shall we say about thirty minutes?'

I laugh. What does he think – that I was born yesterday? I might not be an expert but I know a simple con when I hear it. Slipping off my seatbelt I say, 'Great, I'm starving. I could do with some breakfast myself.'

And that stops him short.

'To be honest,' he replies, 'I'd rather go on my own.'

I bet he would. A quick hike around the corner and he'll be back on Old Street, straight on the tube or in a passing cab, and gone before the dust has even settled.

I don't think so.

'That's okay,' I agree, sliding quickly out of the car. 'I won't get in your way.' I slam the door closed before he can argue the point, then walk to the meter and feed it with enough small change for an hour.

When I turn around he's standing behind me.

'Look,' he explains, 'I've got a meeting, an important meeting – you *know* how important. It's a one-to-one, it's been arranged, and if I suddenly turn up with a stranger then—'

'You won't,' I interrupt. 'Don't worry. I'll keep my distance. I won't sit anywhere near you.'

Johnny blinks his cold grey eyes. 'It's not a good idea.'

I know exactly what he thinks, that he can lose me in a second, that he can spit me out as easily as a piece of chewed-up gum. But I'm not going to make it that simple. Strolling back, I lock the car doors, and turn to smile at him again. 'I promise. They won't even know I'm there.'

'It's really not—'

I drop the keys in my pocket. Leaning towards him, I lower my voice. 'I'm coming with you, okay? We can argue about it here, along the street, or in the cafe – it's your choice how public we make it – but I'm still going to be there.'

The expression in his eyes doesn't waver – but my courage does. What am I doing? Threatening a man like Johnny

Frank, a convicted killer, isn't the smartest move in the world. If I wasn't in danger before, then . . .

But suddenly he looks away. 'Okay,' he agrees, 'but you don't sit anywhere near me, right?'

I nod, relieved. 'It's a deal.'

We walk together towards the end of the road. It's all a pack of lies, I'm sure it is. There won't be anyone in the cafe, there won't be any meeting and there won't be any reason to keep my distance. What will I do then? What will I do when we've been sitting for fifteen minutes waiting for his invisible friend to arrive?

We enter a small square lined with shops. 'Over there,' he says. 'You want to go in first?'

'No.' I spot the place he means, more a sandwich bar than a cafe. There's a short line of people queuing for takeaway coffee and rolls. Once he's inside, there's nothing to stop him from clearing off, creeping out the back door, or going to the Gents and sliding through a window. I can't always be by his side. But whatever those escape routes, I can't let him take the most obvious one – if I go in first then the minute I turn my back he could scoot off down the street. 'No, you go on. I'll give you a couple of minutes.'

Even as he starts to walk, I'm reluctant to let him get too far ahead. He looks over his shoulder and glares at me. I fall back a few paces.

But as he passes through the door, I'm not so far behind; like a shadow I'm sticking to his heels. Scuttling past the queue, I'm still convinced I'm right, that he's playing some perverse unholy game that's finally about to unravel.

So it's something of a shock, as I follow him through to the back, to see the man rise suddenly from his chair. He's as tall as Johnny but older and with hair as white as snow. The stranger rushes over to embrace him with one arm and pump his hand with the other. 'How are you? How are you? It's good to see you again.'

I slide into the nearest seat and try not to gawp.

I'm more than surprised. I'm shocked. But for the first time in what feels like forever there's a tiny spark of hope.

Chapter Fourteen

Johnny

It's true I meant to take off as soon as we got here but some opportunities are too good to miss. Anyway, what's the rush? We've got six days until the deadline, plenty of time to have a little fun.

And I can't deny that it's been one hell of a day. We've done Old Street, Spitalfields and Soho: a nostalgic tour round all the old haunts and a chance to catch up with a few pals. Mind, the highlight's got to be this morning when she walked into that caff and saw Patrick standing there. Christ, the look on her face was bloody priceless.

So Simone's dropped the attitude, at least temporarily. She's doing her best to be nice to me. It's an effort, I can tell, but you've got to give her points for trying. Although if we're being honest, I am her only hope of saving Marc so she can't afford to piss me off. And her trust levels haven't risen that spectacularly – as I found to my advantage when we booked into the hotel.

'Two single rooms,' I told the guy at the desk.

'No, one room,' she insisted, adding promptly, 'with twin beds.'

The guy raised his head and threw me a surreptitious *Seems-like-you-just-got-lucky* kind of glance which, being the gentleman I am, I naturally ignored. Anyway, it's surveillance she's got on her mind, not seduction.

So here we are, within spitting distance of King's Cross, which I have to say hasn't vastly improved since I was last in the vicinity. We could easily have driven to Essex, been back at the Buckleys' in less than an hour, but I swear I'm never returning there. No, now I've got Simone to myself I may as well make the most of it. So I told her I had to stay over, that I might need to go out later this evening.

'How long is this going to take?' she asks, throwing her bag on the bed nearest to the door. She's not taking any chances. If I'm planning on sneaking out in the dead of the night, I'll have to get past her first.

'Three or four days.'

She doesn't look best pleased.

I try not to feel too heartbroken about it. 'These things take time,' I explain, 'they need to be *arranged*. What did you imagine – that I'd dumped the diamonds in a left luggage locker at Paddington?'

It's great to be able to wind her up and know that she can't say anything back. She'll have to keep that smart mouth of hers in check if she wants me to cooperate. Still, it doesn't stop her narrowing her eyes and giving me a condescending glare. I take it on the chin. After all, a completely docile Simone wouldn't be much of a challenge.

She disappears into the bathroom, hesitating before she finally closes the door. Clearly the choice between risking my doing a runner or having me listen to her pee is a close one but dignity wins out in the end.

While she's gone I take the opportunity to look around the room. It's clean for sure, the surfaces pristine, but they haven't been too generous with the space. Not that I'm complaining. No, the very opposite; I'm used to living in a box and at this present moment, cosy suits me just fine.

There's a TV, radio and a kettle, with teabags, sachets of coffee and several tiny containers of long-life milk. A nice cup of tea is exactly what we need.

When she comes back I'm busy emptying the contents of my bag. She gives me another of her suspicious looks, not sure if this is evidence of my intention to stay or just a clever ruse. Trust, as I'm rapidly discovering, doesn't figure large in Simone's vocabulary. Maybe I should have a little more sympathy – she has more reason than most for being cautious – but I don't. She's old enough and smart enough to take care of herself.

'Tea?' I ask, all wide-eyed innocence.

As if I've offered hemlock, her nose wrinkles at the prospect. 'No thanks.' She sits down on the bed, rummages in her bag, and gets out the A–Z. 'So where are we going tomorrow?'

Ah. Now I haven't exactly worked that one out. Another day in London perhaps or should we go further afield? Come to think of it, I wouldn't mind a trip to the coast. It's been bloody years since I saw the sea. Not the perfect month for it perhaps but a breath of fresh air wouldn't go amiss. And the further we get from the Buckleys the better. I don't want Dee suddenly deciding that she's going to join us.

'Norfolk,' I reply.

She stares at me as if I've just said Tibet. 'What?'

'It's not that far. Only a few hours.'

'Why do we need to—'

I shake my head indulgently. 'That's okay, love, I understand. If you don't think you can manage it, I can always get the train.'

I watch her face turn slowly pink.

God, she hates it when I call her *love*. And she hates it even more when I question her driving ability. Combining the two is like mixing dynamite with a particularly vicious Molotov cocktail. Under any other circumstances it would be a case of stand back and watch the fireworks – but she can't afford to light that fuse. She can't afford to burn her bridges.

'The north coast,' I say casually. 'I've got to meet someone.'

Simone takes out her frustration on the bedcover, twisting it tightly between her fingers. 'The north coast?' She chews it over for a minute, clearly horrified, but eventually forces her mouth into a small tight smile. 'Okay, if that's what it takes.'

You've got to give her credit. She's doing everything she can to help that loser of a husband. Although why she ever married him is a mystery to me.

'I'm sorry,' I sigh, in my most apologetic tone, 'but I never said this was going to be easy.'

Simone raises her eyes and stares at me.

Well, okay, maybe that *is* pushing it a bit. Sarah always claimed that I overplayed the drama. 'Don't go to town, honey,' she used to say, 'have the sense to quit when you're ahead.'

So I do.

I fill the kettle, make myself a cup of tea and then sit down on the bed. It's quiet in the room, just the distant sound of traffic buzzing gently in the background. I roll a cigarette and wait for her to fill the silence.

It doesn't take too long.

'I'll need to get the road atlas, check out the route. It's in the car.'

'Would you like me to get it?'

'No!' she retorts, as if I'm about to embark on the second step of the Great Escape. 'No, really, it's okay.' She glances at her watch. 'It's almost seven. Why don't we go and get something to eat. I can pick it up on the way back.'

I'd like to feel flattered. I mean it's been a while since a woman wouldn't let me out of her sight but hey, let's get real, lovely as she is she's only got one thing on her mind and it has nothing to do with my masculine charm. 'You want to try one of those fancy restaurants in Islington?'

'No,' she snaps again, like an irritable wife. 'I'm tired. I'm not in the mood.' Then, recalling her obligation to keep me happy, she sighs and adds reluctantly, 'Well, not unless you really want to.'

Just for the hell of it, I'm tempted to insist, but there's time enough to see how far I can push her. Maybe tonight

I'll start muddying the waters, introducing a little sympathy and understanding into the mix. Not too much though; I wouldn't want her to die of shock.

'Sorry,' I say apologetically, 'I should have thought. I guess you've got more important things on your mind.'

She's not sure how to respond to that. After a second's thought her mouth stretches into a small pained smile.

There's only a scattering of guests in the hotel restaurant. It's seven o'clock, too early for most people, but I'm still trying to get used to eating so late – and in company. Inside, I mainly ate my meals alone so God knows how badly my table manners have deteriorated.

When the waiter arrives, she's still frowning at the menu. 'Simone?'

'Erm ...' She stares down at the words as if they're in a foreign language. 'Okay, I'll just have an omelette, thanks. Mushroom.'

I order the Beef Wellington and a beer. 'You want anything to drink?'

She opts for a slimline tonic, ice and a slice.

We sit by the window and gaze silently down at the street. It's prettier by night, the glittering lights disguising the dinginess. But I still can't wait to get away. No, I've fallen out of love with London. Once it was the only place I wanted to be but now I feel like a stranger. Has it changed or have I? Hard to tell. A bit of both, maybe.

I glance at Simone. She's got a distant anxious look on her face. She might be staring at the street but that isn't what she's seeing.

'Don't worry,' I say, reassuringly, 'he'll be okay.'

She shakes her head. 'Will he? You can't know that for sure.'

Despite the fact there's no one sitting near, I lean over the table and lower my voice. 'What do you think matters more to them, a thirty-five-year-old accountant with a bad gambling habit and a roving eye, or a glorious fistful of diamonds?'

Her mouth clamps shut. She gets the gist but doesn't like the references. Or maybe she's just shocked that I'm aware of her husband's weaknesses. She's probably already embarked on that idealization nonsense, rewriting his character, and seeing the past through rose-coloured glasses. Women are good at that kind of thing.

I raise my hands. 'Sorry. I wasn't having a go, just trying to put things in perspective.'

'What about Eddie Tate?' she retorts. 'How's his perspective doing these days?'

Fair point.

'Look, all I'm saying is that we shouldn't jump to conclusions. Anyone could have . . .' I pause as the waiter brings the drinks. Before I start speaking again, I take a few welcome sips. After all that crap I drank inside, fermented piss the most of it, it's such a pleasure to taste real alcohol. 'They might not be connected. Eddie was a villain and villains always have enemies. He could have been killed for any number of reasons.'

But she isn't letting go that easily. 'So why is he mentioned in the note?'

'Someone taking advantage, someone spotting a useful opportunity?' I shrug. 'Eddie could have talked to anyone.'

She turns her glass slowly around in her fingers. I can almost hear her brain ticking over. She hesitates, weighing up the options, and then comes straight out and says it. 'Do you know who killed him, Johnny?'

Her eyes are boring into me. But I do that thing that good liars always do – I stare straight back. In my experience, it's usually a sign that someone's got something to hide but common understanding is quite the opposite. 'No,' I reply firmly, with just the right level of aggrieved resentment. 'You think I wouldn't tell you if I did?' There's not even a hint of a quaver. But then lying is second nature to me now; I can do it in my sleep.

Our eyes remain locked tight.

She's the first to look away.

And then the food arrives. Christ, I didn't realize how ravenous I was; deception's a drain on the energy. I dig in with all the gusto of a guilty man's last meal. I've cleared almost a third of my plate before I glance up again. She's toying with her omelette, moving it around like a piece of toxic waste. And while she plays with her own food, she's watching me eat mine, her gaze absorbing every mouthful, my appetite clearly providing irrefutable proof of my moral turpitude.

'Is that no good? You want to order something else?'

She glares at me. 'I'm not hungry.'

'You need to eat,' I insist.

Christ, I sound like some fussy parent.

As soon as that thought enters my head, I find myself

gazing around, wondering how we appear to other people. The place has filled up since we first came in, single males mostly but also a few women. How do they see us? We could pass for a couple – couldn't we? Sure, there's an age difference but that's not unusual. And I don't know why it should even matter except that I've noticed the way some men are looking at her, their eyes roaming over her body, their eyes searching for hers. And for a moment, as if I'm with Sarah again, I feel that old proprietorial rage.

Simone drops her fork. It clatters against her plate. She doesn't bother to pick it up. 'So what do you think we're dealing with here, what kind of people?'

'Sorry?' I'm still staring at the smart-suited guy in the corner. He's been eyeing her up for the last five minutes.

'You must have some idea. Who knows about the diamonds? Who knows you're out? Who do you think is behind all this?'

I try to look as though I care. 'Word gets around about these things. It could be someone from the past – and that wouldn't be a short list – or maybe one of Eddie's cronies, or maybe just someone who's heard the story and . . . but come on, this is pointless; we know what they want. So long as they get it, Marc will be fine.'

'You like him, don't you? You *will* help him?' Her voice has slipped to a pleading whisper. There's a tremor in it too. Shit, I hope she isn't going to blub.

'Of course I will. You don't even need to ask.'

Sacrificing the rest of my meal on the altar of the greater good, I push my plate away as if I can't bear to eat either. I stare down at the table, rearranging my features into a semblance of sympathetic grief. 'Simone, I know what it means to be afraid of losing someone.'

She gives me a long hard look. She wants to believe but can't quite overcome those inner doubts. We sit in silence for a while. Then, just as I'm beginning to suspect that I may have overdone the schmaltz, she reaches out and lays her hand lightly over mine.

'I'm sorry ... about Sarah.'

It's a calculated gesture rather than an emotional one but at least it's a start. And it's also one in the eye for Mr fucking Armani; he drops his gaze immediately. I stop myself from blatantly gloating but can't resist a moment of indulgence, of self-congratulation; this must be the first time she's voluntarily touched me. All in all, this is working out better than I could ever have imagined.

Simone's still watching closely, waiting perhaps for me to talk about the wife I lost. I wonder how much Marc has told her. Best tread cautiously here. And not just because I might blow it by saying something stupid but if I think too much about Sarah I may be tempted, sorely fucking tempted, to take those car keys and drive straight back to Essex tonight ...

Keep it short. Keep it simple. 'It was all – a long time ago.'

She nods, slowly withdrawing her hand. I can feel her fingers slipping away. Shame, I was just getting used to having them there. At least she has the good sense not to say *It must have been terrible*. Instead, she leaves a short respectful pause.

Her next question takes me by surprise. 'You used to own The Palace, didn't you?'

'Yeah, for a few years.' I give a sardonic smile. 'Before my dramatic fall from grace.'

'Have you been back?'

'Why should I want to do that?'

She shrugs. 'I don't know. Curiosity?'

Christ, I'm sitting here trying to appear simultaneously strong and sympathetic, a pretty shit juggling act for any man to deal with, and she's managed to hit on yet another subject I don't want to dwell on. Does she suspect? Has Dee told her anything? No, she made it pretty clear that Simone was well and truly out of the loop.

'It's in the past,' I reply abruptly. 'Some things are better left there.' Then, worried that might sound too defensive, I add, 'It's changed a lot since my day. I doubt if it's my kind of place any more.'

She raises her eyebrows. 'Really? I'd have thought any place full of half-naked females was every heterosexual man's dream.'

As if to provoke me she lays a slight emphasis on the word *heterosexual*. It has the desired effect. I flash her a look. What's she suggesting? That maybe I've gone over to the other side, turned into a fucking gay boy while I've been inside? I'm about to make a crude retort but quickly bite my tongue. That's what she wants, to rile me, to make me lose my cool – to try and get inside my head. She's digging for information. Probably wiser not to try and change the subject too quickly. Instead I laugh, turn the spotlight back on her, and ask, 'So did it bother you, Marc being there so much?'

She knows what I'm doing, tit-for-tat, and accepts it with a smile. 'Why should it?'

Her nonchalance isn't entirely convincing. I suspect there aren't many women in the world who could happily wave their husbands off to that kind of work without small seeds of doubt lurking in their minds. I mean, shit, Sarah would have broken both my legs if I'd gone within ten paces of a stripper.

I can't resist sticking the knife in. 'No, I guess he had everything he needed at home.'

That wipes away her self-satisfied smile. She already knows that I'm aware of his affairs, of how many times he's cheated on her. And sure, it's a cheap shot, but worth it just to see the change in her expression.

And I wait, grinning, thinking she's going to come back with one of her smart-arse Simone retorts but she doesn't. In fact the very opposite happens. Slowly, horribly, she does one of those curious crumpling things, everything falling, her eyes closing, her mouth curling down, even her hands trembling as she raises them to cover her face.

My heart sinks. Fuck! So much for the sensitive Johnny Frank.

'Sorry,' I plead. This time I'm the one who's reaching out, trying to make amends. But even as my hand folds over hers, she's pulling back. Am I that awful, so vile that she can't even bear to be near me? Perhaps I am. Because even as I'm doing it, even as I'm trying to comfort her, it's not out of care or regret – all I'm wondering is if I've well and truly blown it.

Is this the end of the road? Have I just destroyed any vestige of trust she might have had in me? Perhaps she's already in the process of giving up, of doing what she really wants to do – calling in the filth. And then what? A pile of bloody grief, that's what.

While she rummages in her bag for a tissue, I make a desperate attempt to try and heal the rift. 'I'm sorry,' I say again, 'it's all this stuff, The Palace, the past – it gets to me. It gets under my skin. It shouldn't, I know it shouldn't. I need to let it go but I can't.'

They're probably the most honest words I've spoken all night.

And perhaps she realizes it. She raises her head and looks at me. It's like being stared at by Bambi. Two matching smudges of mascara lie under her liquid hazel eyes and she looks so sad, so fucking vulnerable, that if I wasn't such a bastard I might almost feel a pang of guilt.

'I could do with a drink,' she says.

Summoning the waiter, I order a couple of large brandies. While we wait, although I'm tempted to keep on apologizing, I take the sensible option and keep my mouth shut. The greater advantage usually lies in silence. She dabs gently at her eyes in the way that women always do, quietly if accusingly repairing the damage.

We don't speak again until the drinks arrive.

She takes a sip, sits back, and asks, 'Have you got a cigarette?' Then she glances round. 'Are we allowed to smoke in here?'

The idea that we couldn't hasn't even occurred to me. In

my day you had a meal and then a fag but there's been a fair few changes since I was last let loose on the world – and not all of them good. There's not an ashtray in sight so I guess the answer is no.

'There's probably a lounge somewhere,' I suggest.

'Or we could just go back to the room.'

Twenty years ago I'd have viewed that as a promise, as a definite green light, but sex is clearly the last thing on her mind. She'd rather crawl naked over red-hot coals than share a bed with me. 'Sure, why not?'

We both stand up. I throw the creep in the suit a dirty look as we leave.

Out in the corridor she passes me the car keys. 'Do you mind? The atlas is on the back seat.' She takes the drink from my hand. 'I'll see you upstairs.'

I'm not sure if this is supposed to be a test, a gesture of trust, or whether she's certain that I won't let a perfectly good glass of brandy go to waste. Maybe she's just decided that if I am going to run out, she'd prefer I do it now rather than prolonging the agony. And as I walk across the forecourt, I can't claim I'm not tempted. I've got everything I need with me: money, phone, a convenient set of car keys.

I open the door and reach in for the map. It's got to be one of those split second decisions – yes or no? The longer you hesitate, the more difficult it becomes.

She turns as I come into the room. Does she look relieved to see me again? It's hard to tell with Simone. I've clearly taken a little longer than I should have. Maybe it's disappointment that forces her mouth into a smile. Perhaps she was hoping I *would* go. She'd be absolved of all responsibility then; she could ring the cops with a clear conscience.

But she can't get rid of me that easily.

I put the map down beside the cabinet, dig out a packet of cigarettes that I bought in the bar and offer her one.

'Thanks.'

'I didn't know you smoked.'

'I don't,' she claims, accepting a light. 'I've given up.'

As she leans towards me I can smell her hair, a light trailing fragrance like vanilla. I'm still getting used to this again – the scent of women. She seems to linger for a second longer than she needs to before taking a step back and retreating to her bed.

I take off my shoes and stretch out on the other one. I'm not sure what to say next, where to go. I've already made one major mistake and don't intend to make another.

But I don't have to worry. Almost immediately she begins to talk, asking about my past, telling me about hers, doing that subtle bonding/interrogation routine. This is my story, what's yours? Knowledge is power – but only if you're getting the right information. I make up most of the answers, a good creative exercise for my brain.

'You must feel bitter. I mean, about all the years that you've lost.'

Fuck, it's like being back with the prison shrink. And of course the years aren't the only thing I've managed to lose. I shrug. 'You've got to try and move on. Make the most of what you've got. It's the future that matters.'

You have to take responsibility for what you've done. Isn't that how the dictum goes? Although it strikes me that the Buckleys haven't done too much of that – and aren't intending to either. I should have finished Jim off when I had the chance.

After a while she starts telling me about Marc, how they met, what he's like, what a decent guy he is at heart. And sure, he isn't perfect, far from it, but he doesn't deserve this. He's kind, he's smart, he's . . .

As if I give a damn.

'I couldn't bear it if . . . if anything happened to him.'

Looking at me with those big sad eyes, trying to lay on the guilt trip. I know what she's really saying: If you won't do it for him, then do it for me. What's a few diamonds between friends? I nod and make all the right sympathetic noises.

The subject is starting to bore me – there's only so much you want to hear about a woman's husband – but her presence is having the opposite effect. There's no denying she's a looker and no pushover either. I like a female with a bit of spirit. Still, I'd better be careful; sneaking glances at her tits probably isn't the best way to ingratiate myself.

'Well,' she says, reaching down for the atlas, 'I guess we ought to sort the route for tomorrow. You want to show me where we're going?'

I slide off my bed and walk the few steps across to hers. Not sure if I should sit down, I hover instead around her right shoulder. She flips to the relevant page.

'There,' I tell her, leaning over. I put my finger on the spot.

'Cromer?'

'No, just along the coast – there.'

My hand brushes briefly against hers. I can smell her hair again or perhaps it's the scent of her soap. I breathe it in. And maybe this time I'm the one who lingers for a little longer than I should because she suddenly turns and glares up at me.

'Okay,' she says. Her tone is dismissive.

And like a chastened dog I skulk quietly away.

Rolling a cigarette, I pretend I'm not watching her. But there's a mirror directly opposite and I can't resist the occasional glance. Now is it just my imagination – or a severe case of wishful thinking – that she's deliberately drawing attention to those long legs? While she's studying the map, she's slowly stroking one thigh with the palm of her hand.

And a part of me longs for the old days, when I wouldn't have thought twice, when I'd have known instinctively what to do and what to say. But I was a young man then, a different man – and he's dead and buried.

The minutes tick by. At ten o'clock, I take a shower. A cold one. Standing under the water, I feel like one of those ancient monks attempting to drive away his devils. *Don't think about her breasts.* Raise your mind to greater things. *Don't think about her mouth.* Concentrate. *Don't think about your fucking cock.* It's revenge I'm after, not some roll in the hay. *Keep your mind on the job.*

And so I close my eyes and try.

It's a been long day but a useful one. Patrick bunged me a monkey this morning, enough cash to keep me going for a while. And I picked up a few extra quid from the others.

They'll get it back – as they know – with interest. In a couple of days I'll have the diamonds. And then ... well, it'll be time to start running.

It's only as I turn off the water that I hear the murmur of her voice. Is there someone else in the room? No, she's on the phone. Talking to Dee, no doubt, updating her on all the latest news. Shit, if she only knew what she'd done, what Carl had done, she wouldn't be so quick to confide. I lean my ear against the door but she's only uttering those neutral phrases:

Yes, I know. No, I'm sure. Don't worry. Do you think so?

Fuck knows what kind of crap Dee is feeding her. Anything to keep her on side, anything to keep her precious son alive, while she clings vainly to the hope that I value my freedom too much to betray them.

I'm still listening, slowly drying myself, when I hear her say, 'Honestly, I don't think he will.'

What does she mean – that I won't cooperate, that I won't give up the diamonds, or that I won't run out on her? It's impossible to tell from the tone of her voice. And then, as if she's suddenly become aware of the silence from the bathroom, she murmurs, 'Look, I've got to go. I'll ring you tomorrow.'

I head towards the basin and vigorously brush my teeth. It suddenly occurs to me – hell – that I've left my phone in my jacket pocket. What if she's found it, if she's already going through the address book and checking out the numbers – what if she's discovered Mel's? That's going to be a hard one to explain. But no, she wouldn't dare get caught in the act. I could walk back in at any minute.

And I do walk back, faster than I intended, with only a towel around my waist. I'm hyped up, ready for a showdown, but she's still lying on her bed staring innocently at the map. She glances up at me, her eyes skimming over my chest, before lowering her gaze again.

'Are you done?'

I get that feeling, that grievous self-conscious feeling, that I'm a touch more naked than I ought to be – and a damn sight older. I've kept myself in shape but I'll never be young again. You can work out in the gym, you can shift the weights, but you can't reclaim time. 'It's all yours.'

What does she see when she looks at me?

Nothing to light her fire, that's for sure. She disappears into the bathroom as quickly as a rabbit down a hole.

By the time she comes back I'm already in bed, my back turned to her. She turns off the light but half an hour later she's still awake. She rolls over, the crisp sheets rustling. Even in the dark I can feel her eyes on me. She's clearly thinking hard – but trying to decide what? If I'm safe to be trusted? No, she'll never believe that. But maybe if I've got another reason for wanting to stick around – that if she's nice enough to me, *friendly* enough, I might finally do what she wants.

It's an interesting thought.

How far will she go to save her husband?

Chapter Fifteen

Simone

I'm starting to wonder if Dee was right about Johnny. All the looks he keeps giving me, the sneaky glances when he thinks I'm not watching. What's that about? Perhaps there is some truth in what she says – *You know how he feels* – but if there is, he's got a funny way of showing it. And how do I even begin to get inside his head? At least half of what he said last night was lies. Although I'm not sure who he's trying harder to hide from – himself or me.

But if it is true, if Johnny does hold a torch – however faint – it could be useful, a road out of this nightmare. Unpleasant as the prospect is, getting close to him might be the only way to save Marc. But not *too* close. Just close enough for him to believe that I've got an interest too, that maybe, just maybe . . .

Ugh. Even the thought of it sends a shiver down my spine. Did he notice? Hopefully, he'll just put it down to the fact the heater isn't working properly. I've been driving for over three hours now and the rain still hasn't stopped. I don't like being this far from London. What will I do if he disappears with the car? I can't watch him every minute of the day. Yesterday, he could have gone – I gave him the perfect opportunity – and a part of me hoped that he would. It was the selfish part, the part that wanted rid of him for ever. But for Marc's sake, for Dee's – God, she sounded terrible last night – I've got to stick it out.

So I'm feeling pretty down but Johnny seems the opposite. Ever since we left the city, he's had a smile on his face. Maybe he's a country boy at heart or, more likely, he's just pleased to be a step closer to retrieving his diamonds.

'Don't you like the sea?' he asks, as the slate-coloured waves tumble into view. He's staring out of the window, his nose almost pressed against the pane.

Personally, I don't think there's anything as bleak as a seaside town in the middle of winter but I keep that opinion to myself. 'Sure, it's very . . .' Cold? Wet? Dismal? Eventually, I settle on ' . . . invigorating.'

He laughs. 'You'll get used to it. Hell, you may even get to like it.'

Not too used to it, I hope. Just how long is he planning on staying here?

'So has it changed much?' I ask, as he guides me towards a hotel on the front. He's either got a good memory or someone else has provided him with directions. 'I presume you've been here before.'

He hesitates. 'With Sarah,' he eventually replies, but doesn't elaborate.

There's an opening there, a way in, but I don't grab it fast enough. Even before I've turned off the engine he's unlocked the door and leapt out. Leaning down, he says, 'There's no point the two of us getting wet. I'll check, see if they've got any rooms.'

I watch as he strides quickly up the steps. In fact the rain has slowed now; there's only a fine drizzle spattering the windscreen. But I'm not worried about him slipping away. Whatever Johnny's game plan is I'm certain, at least for the time being, that it still includes me.

And right enough he reappears a few minutes later. He has that way of walking, a kind of confident strut as if he owns the pavement. Perhaps it's something he learned in prison or, more likely, it's always been his style.

I wind down the window.

'Okay,' he says, extending his left hand, palm up. 'No problem. If you give me the keys, I'll get the bags out.'

And I wonder why I've never noticed before – the pale scars running up the inside of his wrist, the brutal white lines that look so much like . . . I know what they are but somehow they don't fit in with my image of him. I feel uncomfortable, faintly shocked, as if I've inadvertently witnessed something I wasn't supposed to.

He sees me staring and quickly pulls his hand away.

There's one of those awkward elongated pauses. Then, to cover my embarrassment, I get out of the car and open the boot myself.

As we go inside, the receptionist looks up and smiles. 'Good morning.'

I say good morning back, everything pleasant, everything

normal, as if we're some perfectly ordinary couple on a weekend break. What would she think, this girl, if she knew what was really going on? Not that she'd believe it. I can hardly come to terms with it myself.

I've got that bad sick feeling in my stomach again.

'You all right?' he asks as we go up in the lift.

No, I'm not all right. Eddie Tate is dead and my husband might be next. And I'm relying on a man who can't be trusted, a man who's already served a hefty sentence for murder, to come riding to the rescue.

What kind of a fool does that make me?

'Fine.' I nod.

And suddenly it all seems so impossible, so beyond my control, that I can barely stand up. My legs feel like jelly. I try to steady myself by leaning against the side of the lift. Shit, I'm so tired of pretending I can deal with all this. It won't change anything. It won't make anything better. He already knows I'm scared witless.

The words have escaped before I can stop them. 'Okay, so I'm not. I'm worried sick. I'm terrified. Is that what you want to hear? It's been a couple of days and Dee still hasn't had a call … and so something's got to be wrong, hasn't it? What if—'

'They will,' he interrupts, 'they're just making us sweat.'

'You can't be sure.'

I want him to tell me that he is, that he knows it beyond a shadow of doubt, but of course he can't. Instead he lifts his shoulders in that familiar shrug and tries to do the next best thing. 'That's the way these people work.'

The lift doors open and the corridor beckons.

I have to force my feet to move. I've got this sudden urge to hang on his arm, to plead with him. *Please help me. Please don't turn your back and walk away.* I'd be willing to get down on my knees and beg if I thought, for even a moment, that it might save Marc's life. But that isn't the way to keep Johnny on side. I've got to play a smarter game than that.

He's still looking at me as we enter the room, wondering perhaps if I'm about to lose my nerve, to cross that discomfiting line into hysteria. I can't have him thinking that. If he starts imagining I'm more of a liability than an asset, he'll drop me as fast as a bag of rats.

'Sorry,' I say, with what I hope sounds like renewed confidence. 'I'm sure you're right.' I even manage to dredge up a smile. Making an effort to pull myself together, I cross over to the window and stare out. There's a glorious sea view. 'Hey, look at that.'

He comes and stands beside me.

As we both stare out towards the horizon, I have this mounting dread that he's about to touch me, to lay his hand sympathetically on my shoulder, but he doesn't. Instead he glances at his watch. 'We've got an hour – do you fancy a walk or would you rather stay put?'

I'm hardly an outdoors sort of girl – and outside looks about as inviting as a stroll through Siberia – but anything's better than staying here. The room might be more spacious than the car but it still feels as suffocating. 'Yeah, let's go for a walk.'

I glance back as I close the door behind me. It's a nice

double room, a *large* double room, with a view to die for. That can't come cheap. But then is he paying for the privilege or am I? The question of the bill remains unresolved. He paid for last night so maybe it's my turn today. And it's not the money that bothers me – I don't give a damn how much it costs, or what it takes, to get Marc free – but there's still that nagging doubt that Johnny might be taking me for one almighty ride.

It's icy outside, a freezing wind blowing briskly off the North Sea. Lord, does anyone come here for pleasure? I'm glad I brought my heavy coat. As we make our way towards the shore, the tips of my fingers already white, I lower my chin into my collar and dig my hands deeper into my pockets.

'You see,' he says, as if I might actually be enjoying it, 'it's not so bad, is it?'

Well, he's clearly happy. The wind has coloured his cheeks, a blush of pink relieving their usual pallor. He's even wearing a different smile. We don't descend to the sand – the tide's in, covering the beach – but stroll instead along the raised concrete walkway.

Now might be a good time to embark on the charm offensive, to test Dee's theory, but I don't know where to start. *Did you come here often?* Flirting hardly seems appropriate when someone's holding a gun to your husband's head.

He wanders over to the rail, and stares down.

It's not even midday but already the light is fading. Gloomy as dusk, the sky lies heavily above us. And okay, I'm not denying it, there *is* something compulsive, almost mesmerizing, about watching the waves crash around the boulders. Despite the cold, I don't have any inclination to move. And it's not just the image, it's the sound too – that rhythmic flow and ebb, the rise and fall, the impression that there's a power so much stronger than the human will.

And Lord, I hope that's true – because whatever's driving Johnny, I sure as hell can't compete. I only have to look at his face to realize that. His grey eyes are suddenly furious, his lips slightly open, his teeth clenched tightly together. His hands are lying on the rail in two closed fists.

Perhaps divine intervention is the best I can hope for.

He pulls away abruptly and starts walking. He doesn't even look back. Should I just let him go? No, I can't afford to let him leave like this. Running and stumbling on my heels, I eventually catch up and fall in with his stride, step for step.

He doesn't speak.

I keep my mouth firmly shut too. Silence. If that's what he wants – fine. I can do that.

We've walked the length of the front, and doubled back, before he looks halfway human again. What's going through his mind? Sarah, perhaps, the times he spent with her here. That can't be easy. Or maybe just all the years that have washed through his life. And I can't begin to imagine what eighteen years in prison does to someone, what it means, how it alters and destroys, how it . . .

But forget it. No. The last thing I'm going to do is to start feeling sorry for him. That's the road to nowhere. For all I know he could have killed her too. He could have had Sarah murdered as easily as he killed Roy Foster.

He stops suddenly. 'Do you want to come with me?'

And for a second, lost in too dark a place, I don't have a clue what he's talking about. I raise my eyes and look at him.

'I've got a meeting at one. Do you want a quick drink or would you rather go back to the hotel?'

I'd rather go back. I'm tired, exhausted. I barely slept last night, tossing and turning, falling in and out of restless dreams, too worried that he'd pack his bag and run. And on top of that there was the three-hour drive to Norfolk. So yes, I'd dearly love to slip between those clean white sheets and slide into oblivion. But I can't. I won't. I'm too afraid.

'I'll stay – if you don't mind.'

'Why should I?' he asks. Now he's smiling again, returned to normal – or at least as normal as Johnny ever is. He's back in control, his emotions safely barricaded. After one last lingering look at the sea, he turns and heads up the steps. I follow behind, trailing at his heels.

The pub's only a short distance away. As soon as we walk in, I feel heartened. And it's not just to do with the blazing log fire throwing out its rays of warmth – grateful as my extremities are – but that it's such a relief to be with other people again. Being alone with Johnny frays my nerves. I never know what he's thinking, what he's planning. Here, in the company of strangers, surrounded by the gentle buzz of midday chatter, there's reassurance: surely nothing too terrible can happen while this tiny part of the world spins so comfortably.

We find an empty table and he asks, 'What would you like?'

What I'd like is something strong, something to keep me feeling optimistic. 'Will I need to drive again today?'

He shakes his head. 'You want a whisky?'

'That sounds good.'

I watch as he goes to the bar. The woman comes to serve him straight away. She's a pretty, slim brunette in her mid-thirties, her blouse opened just far enough to show a hint of cleavage. After he's given his order he makes a comment and she leans forward and laughs. Even as she's pouring the drinks, they keep on chatting and smiling, trading words I'm too far away to hear. I watch her dark eyes lift and search out his. She's engaged in that subtle routine of female appraisal. I'm not sure why it offends me so much or why I can't stop staring. Perhaps it's because I don't think of Johnny as an object of desire, as a man that women might find attractive – or perhaps I'm just amazed that he can even imagine flirting at a time like this.

Which brings me unwillingly back to my own hypocrisy. Wasn't I intending to do exactly the same thing? So maybe I'm just annoyed that she got in there first. Frowning, I strip off my jumper and glance down at my T-shirt. Perhaps it would help if I slipped the front zip down an inch or two . . .

But by the time he returns, my modesty – along with my zip – has returned to a more conventional position. Johnny might be happy to take advantage of anything offered on a plate but it won't alter his intentions. I've got to be cooler than that and more cunning. I gaze sweetly up at him, accepting the drink with a smile. 'Thanks.'

He takes the chair opposite and sits down.

He's bought doubles. And not the cheap stuff. I'm hardly an expert but it only takes a sip to tell the difference. This is the kind of whisky that slides gently down the throat, calming and soothing, making everything seem temporarily better.

I lean back and let it do its work.

He crosses his long legs and sits back too. I follow his gaze, towards the flames of the fire, the other tables, the people around us. What does he see? I can't read those cold grey eyes of his. Then, as if an unexpected memory has caught him off guard, his face twists a little and he sighs. Quickly he drops his head, gets out his tobacco and starts to roll a cigarette.

'Is it difficult for you – being back here?'

He looks up but evades the question. 'I didn't exactly have a choice.'

Didn't he? I rather got the impression that he *wanted* to come. He certainly seemed keen enough when we arrived. Or is he trying to claim that he's doing this for me, for Marc? Perhaps he's fishing for some gratitude.

The whisky helps the lie slip easily off my tongue. 'I understand.' I even make myself lean forward and lay my hand briefly over his. His fingers are warm but, like last night at the restaurant, it still takes an effort to touch them without recoiling. 'And I appreciate it. Honestly.'

'It's a pleasure,' he replies. 'That's what friends are for, Simone. Perhaps one day you can return the favour.'

Which has a fairly ominous ring to it. But I nod and smile. Because isn't that what friends do too?

There's a short expectant silence as if he's waiting for me to continue.

I rack my brains trying to scramble something suitable to add. In the end all I come up with is a rather weak, 'I hope so.'

His gaze flickers over my face, perhaps searching for signs of insincerity. They can't be too hard to find. He lights his cigarette, exhaling with a sigh. 'So, it's looks like we're stuck together, you and I. Well, at least for a while. That's a turn-up for the books.'

It's that all right. 'Who'd have thought?'

'Who'd have thought,' he echoes softly. 'And imagine – a few days ago, you couldn't even stand to be in the same room as me.'

The heat from the fire has nothing on the inferno that rages on to my cheeks. You can't beat the truth for major embarrassment. Mumbling, I reply, 'I wouldn't say that exactly.'

But even to my own ears it doesn't sound convincing.

Surprisingly, he leans forward and laughs. 'Oh, don't worry. I don't blame you. In your position, I'd have been pretty dubious myself. I'm hardly the houseguest from heaven.'

Grasping at this straw, I reply, 'I didn't know you then.'

'And you do now?'

'Perhaps. No. I don't know.' I take a swig of whisky and force myself to look into his eyes. 'Better than I did.'

He stares back at me. I try to decipher his expression but I can't; it's as empty as a blank sheet of paper. He opens his mouth but whatever he intends to say next is lost. A hand clamps firmly down on his shoulder.

'Johnny, mate!'

He turns. 'Alan!'

Instantly he slips into a different mode; rising briskly to his feet, even his movements are altered. There's a frenzy of handshakes and exclamations. They heartily slap each other's backs, separate, and then move together again. He's suddenly acquired a rougher edge to his voice, that man-to-man exclusive tone.

'Fuck, it's great to see you! You're looking well. You're looking good.'

'You too! Shit – how long has it been?'

'Too long.'

'How are you doing?'

'Not bad, not bad.'

And so it continues for the next few minutes while I wait – the perfect image of womanly patience – until they calm down. 'This is Simone,' Johnny says, remembering me. 'Simone, this is Alan.'

We reach across the table and shake hands.

'Good to meet you.'

'You too,' he replies. He's a red-haired ruddy-faced guy about the same age as Johnny but half a foot shorter. He winks at his old friend. 'You should have told me, mate. I'd have brought the missus. We could have made a day of it.'

It's clear what he thinks – that we're together, that we're a couple. I glance towards Johnny, expecting him to make the correction, but he doesn't. He just engages his Mona Lisa smile. This is probably my cue to leave.

I pick up my coat. 'Well, I'm sure you two have a lot of catching up to do.'

'Don't go,' Alan insists, 'stay and have another drink. You're not going to let this lovely lady rush off, are you, Johnny? We've only just met.'

Johnny looks like he'd willingly stride across the pub and open the door for me but says instead, 'Of course not. Same again, love?'

Is that *love* thing for Alan's benefit or for mine? He obviously doesn't want me here but what the hell, this might be the perfect opportunity to dig up some information. And he can't get that annoyed over it; it's hardly as if *I* suggested staying. I'm only being polite. 'Oh, okay. Better make it a single, though.'

While he goes to the bar – where it seems, fortuitously, that he might have quite a wait – I lean towards Alan and ask, 'So, I take it you two go way back?'

'And a few years further than that.' He folds his burly arms on the table. He's short and stocky with a well-developed paunch but I get the impression there's still enough muscle left to inflict some major damage. Not a man you'd want to cross. 'One of a kind, Johnny,' he continues, shaking his head. 'It's a terrible business. Eighteen years, he never deserved that.'

'God, no,' I reply sympathetically. I wonder what he thinks killers do deserve – a pat on the back and a bunch of flowers?

He glances over his shoulder and lowers his voice. 'So look, how's he really doing? Johnny's not one to complain but I know how tough it can be when you first get out.'

I dare say he's speaking from personal experience, but the idea that I may be sitting drinking with *two* murderers isn't one to dwell on. Still, he's given me the perfect opportunity to find out about Johnny's background. Although I'll have to be careful how I phrase it; I don't want him to suspect just how little I know. Carefully, I say, 'Well, I guess it's easier if you have some family support.'

He nods. 'That's true enough.'

For a second I think that's going to be it, my cautiously sown seed has fallen on stony ground, but then he sighs, shakes his head again, and carries on.

'Yeah, it hit him hard when Dixie died. They were like brothers, those two. He's never got over it. I mean, you don't, do you?'

'No,' I agree solemnly, even though I don't have a clue what he's talking about. Who was Dixie? I'm about to start probing but Alan hasn't finished yet.

'Thank God he's still got Melanie. That girl's like a daughter to him.'

The name descends like an axe. *Melanie*? I can feel the air rush painfully into my lungs producing a gasp of dismay. Quickly, I try and cover it with a cough. Melanie? No, he can't be talking about the same one. Come on, get real, there must be thousands of Melanies in the world. There's no connection to Carl's girlfriend. How could there be? No, it has to be a coincidence. Unless . . .

But there isn't time to pursue it. Already Johnny's on his way back, weaving a way through the crowd. His earlier conquest at the bar must have pushed him up the waiting list. My heart begins to thump. I don't want him to know what I've heard, not until I've been able to think it through, to be sure that they *are* two different women. Because if they're not, if they are one and the same, then . . .

'So what about you, Alan? Do you have any kids?' My voice comes out at a higher pitch than usual.

Thankfully, by the time three large whiskies appear on the table, he's already embarked on the saga of his offspring. I'm glad Johnny's bought me another double; like a thirsty alcoholic I've got the urge to knock it back in one. But I don't dare lift the glass. What if my hand shakes? *Act normal*, my brain is telling me, but I'm not even sure what that means any more.

'Alan's been telling me about his family.'

Johnny throws me a glance. His eyes seem to narrow but that might just be a figment of my imagination.

'How is Ruth?' he asks, sitting down.

And as Alan proceeds to tell him, in detail, I feel I've gained a temporary if uneasy reprieve. All I have to do now is look fascinated and make the usual polite and encouraging comments. 'Three grandchildren? Really? That's great. How wonderful.'

And eventually, after several long minutes, I'm confident enough to pick up the whisky. I take a few hasty gulps. I need to get out, to get away from here before *her* name is raised again. Melanie, Melanie, Melanie. I'm nodding and smiling while all the time it's going round my head like some bloody awful mantra. No, they can't be ... they can't know each other. I've seen them together and there wasn't any indication that ... except, well, there wouldn't be, would there? Not if they wanted to keep it quiet.

'Simone?'

I've let my attention slip. Johnny's leaning forward, offering me a cigarette. 'Thanks,' I respond, automatically taking one and then instantly regretting it. He's poised with his lighter and I worry again about a shaking hand.

Fortunately, Alan creates a distraction. 'Christ, Johnny, did you hear about Eddie?'

And this time it's his turn to falter. I see him jump. The flame shifts an inch and I have to grab his hand to bring it back. Has Alan noticed? Perhaps, even if he has, he thinks it's just a loving gesture.

'Yeah,' Johnny says, 'what the fuck was all that about?' And he gives me a long hard look — a warning or a plea for silence?

I glance from him to Alan, my ears about as pricked as they've ever been.

But Alan just shrugs. 'I don't get it. I know he could be ... but why? Why would anyone do that to him?'

Johnny shrugs too. 'God knows.'

I glance into his eyes, searching for some small nugget of truth. A moment ago there was a flash of alarm, a definite reaction, but there's nothing there now. He's closed down as securely as he did on the promenade. And the grossly unwelcome memory of Eddie Tate rises up to haunt me — not the day he came to the shop, not the things he said or did, but just that stark black-and-white image in the newspaper: a dead man, a man murdered.

God, I need to get out of here.

I pull my hand away and try to keep on smiling. I'm getting good at this smiley stuff. It's the perfect mask for anything too hard to face. Grabbing my glass, I swallow the rest of the whisky and look at my watch. 'Hey, I've got to go,' I announce, as if I've got an urgent appointment and time has run away with me. I turn to Alan. 'It's been great to meet you.'

'Oh, you don't have to—'

'I do, I'm sorry,' I lie, standing up, 'but I'm sure we'll catch up soon.'

Johnny also rises to his feet.

'It's okay,' I insist, waving him back down. I'm still smiling so hard my lips are starting to ache. 'I'll see you later.' And then I shake Alan's hand again, exchanging the usual banalities.

They seem to go on for ever.

With a final friendly wave, I walk demurely across the pub and out of the doors. For all my city ways, I can barely wait to get outside. As if I'm the one who's been imprisoned, I stumble gratefully into the cold, gulping in the fresh freezing air and trying to get my thoughts together.

Now I've got two names careering through my head: Melanie and Eddie, Eddie and Melanie. And I can't make sense of either. I stare up at the darkening sky, hopelessly searching for any kind of insight. Then, absurdly worried that Johnny might decide to follow me, I take to my heels and head off up the street. What I need is nicotine. What I need even more is to get away from *him*.

In the summer this is probably a bustling place but now the town has a forlorn abandoned air. Even the arcades near the front are empty, their flashing lights playing to an empty auditorium. I hover for a moment, tempted to step inside, to waste my loose change on some defiant wasteful gamble. But I don't. My hopes are already riding on too many crazy odds.

I walk on into the centre. There's only a few hardy souls here, huddled in their coats and scarves, their bodies braced against the wind. I find a newsagent and buy a pack of twenty and a disposable lighter. As I pace the streets, I start thinking about Christmas Day. Didn't Johnny deliberately sit next to Melanie? No, I can't be sure. At the time, I would have claimed he deliberately sat opposite to me. But then there was the row and it wasn't just him being provocative – wasn't *she* going on about fidelity? I'd put it down to crass stupidity but maybe I'd underestimated her.

Why would they do it though? Why would they pretend to be strangers? But then nothing's beyond Johnny. I may as well ask why he paid Jim and Dee to stay with them. Why didn't he choose Alan or any of the other guys who slapped him on the back and seemed so pleased to see him yesterday?

But I suppose the most pertinent question is: if this Melanie *is* a different girl, and if she is so very close to him, then why hasn't she been to visit? He hasn't even mentioned her. And Johnny may not be the chattiest bloke in the world, but that doesn't make sense. No, it goes well beyond that; in this vicious new world of ransoms and death threats, it quite definitely enters the sphere of the highly suspicious.

Or am I finally losing my marbles, seeing conspiracy anywhere and everywhere? Perhaps, like one of those Roman emperors forever waiting for the poisoned chalice or the stab in the back, I'm slipping into paranoia. Except, now I come to think of it, they were usually right to be concerned.

But where *is* Carl's seductive little Barbie doll? I haven't seen her since – well, since I read the news about Eddie Tate. And the memory of that day reminds me again of Marc, of the danger he's in, of how ... I suddenly get a suffocating sensation, a tightening of my throat. Panic sweeps over me, and for a moment the street shifts out of focus. I'm beginning to feel as faint as I did in the lift. Desperately, I look for somewhere to sit, for somewhere I can take the weight off these treacherous legs, but there's nowhere. The best I can do is to find a wall and lean against it. Struggling for air, I raise my face to the sky.

Breathe, breathe.

And for the first time, as the world swims around me, I'm aware of how utterly alone I am. There's no one coming to the rescue – no husband, no friend, no passing stranger. If I were to collapse now ... but I can't afford to let that happen. I can't give in.

Breathe.

Eventually the cold air drags me back to reality. The mist starts to clear and the pavement to regain its solidity. Dazed, I glance around. Across the street, there are people passing by but no one's looking at me, nobody's staring – or caring.

Already the daylight is fading, the heavy shadow of dusk creeping over the town. If I were sensible, I'd head straight back to the hotel. But I need to calm down first, to achieve at least a minimal level of composure before facing Johnny again.

That's if he ever comes back.

As I stumble down the steps to the sea front it's clear the temperature has dropped a few degrees. There's an extra harsh bite to the wind. I'm almost grateful for the cold, for its icy bitterness, for its ability to chase away all but the most basic survival instincts. Keep your head down, keep your hands in your pockets. Don't think. Can't think.

It's even more deserted here than in the town. There's only a few disgruntled dogs walking their owners. The wind throws back my hair. I raise a hand, pointlessly, to wind a few strands back behind my ears. What am I doing? Fear twists my stomach into a knot. Marc – where are you? Are you safe? I lean over the rail that Johnny leaned over and stare out towards the sea.

I can smell the salt, the brine. I stand and watch until the last flash of silver dissolves across the waves. I'm beginning to understand why he wanted to come here. There's something weird and wild, almost primitive about this place. You can put your soul on the line. You can lose yourself in the sound of the sea.

But not for ever.

It doesn't change anything. It doesn't change the fact that Marc could be murdered, that his life is entirely dependent on Johnny, on some diamonds, on some bloody stupid hope and a prayer. I reach for my phone – surely the best thing I can do is to ring 999. But then Dee's voice comes back to haunt me: *Don't come crying to me when ...*

I don't know what's right or wrong any more. I'm incapable of making a decision. I roll back from the rail and slump down on a bench. Leaning forward, I bury my face in my hands. The tears roll down my cheeks. If I were halfway smart, if I had even half a brain, I'd be back in the room by now searching through his bag for evidence. But it's too late for that; I've already blown my chance. And what could I hope to find anyway – an incriminating note from Melanie or an entry in a journal reading, *Yesterday I killed Eddie Tate*?

I find a tissue and wipe my face clean. This isn't doing any good. Instead of wallowing in self-pity I should be taking the opportunity to make plans, to plot, to work out how to get closer to Johnny. If I want him to help I'll have to provide an incentive. I'll have to give him a damn good reason to stick around.

Reluctantly, I get to my feet and start back. There's no point putting it off. Time's ticking away, maybe even running out. Tonight may be the last chance I get to make a difference. I've got to make the most of it. I've got to do whatever it takes.

And then, surprisingly, as if just by thinking about Johnny I've magically managed to conjure him up, there he is, standing two hundred yards along the esplanade; he must have cut down the steps near the hotel. He's standing very still, gazing out towards the sea. I can make out the profile of his face but not his expression. Pensive? Angry? It's too dark to tell. If I keep on walking I'll have to pass right by him and, whatever his mood, I don't imagine he'll welcome the intrusion.

Accordingly, I hold back, slinking into the shadows. The wind whips around my face and my teeth start to chatter. I hope I won't have to wait too long. The art of seduction is rarely enhanced by impending pneumonia. The shock of this thought temporarily distracts me from the cold. Am I really planning on seduction? No, that's too strong a word. *Temptation* is nearer the mark. Or *leading him on*. Although that can backfire, and pretty dramatically, if you don't have your wits about you. And I'm hardly an expert – when was the last occasion I hooked a man with my deeply sensual and captivating charms?

Shivering, I wrap my coat tighter around me. How much longer should I give him? Five minutes, ten? I'm starting to feel like a stalker. No one in their right mind would loiter in a place like this on such a freezing day. Perhaps he wouldn't notice if I slipped quietly behind him.

I'm still considering this option as the two men loom into view. They've got their collars turned up high and their heads bent down. I don't think anything of it until, as they draw nearer to Johnny, they gradually slow down and stop. He turns as one of them speaks. I can only hear a faint mumble. Maybe they're just asking for directions or a light. No, they're still talking. They're drawing closer together. Ah, the truth dawns! So Johnny has another meet, a secret assignation. I should have guessed. Still, I shouldn't hang around; if he spots me, he might think I'm spying. I'd better retrace my route and use the other flight of steps.

And then in a second everything changes. I'm just about to leave when a pale hand rises out of the twilight, driving quickly and viciously through the air. I hear the crack and then the exhalation of Johnny's breath, sharp and pained, as he falls to the ground. What? And suddenly they're both leaning over him, one of them almost on top, fists still flying, the punches delivered with a gross and forbidding regularity.

Shit, they're going to kill him.

And I'm still staring, wide-eyed with disbelief. It's unreal, removed, like a scene from a movie. First I'm paralysed, too shocked to move, and then I do that mad, frantic, looking-around routine but there's no one else in sight. Of course there isn't. These two have chosen their moment with care. They've overlooked me because I've been skulking in the shadows.

How long have I been watching this? It feels like an eternity.

And now one of them is standing up, standing over him, kicking him. Like a madman he's driving his boot into Johnny's body, over and over again. The dull relentless thump is almost drowned out by the sound of the waves. If I don't do something soon, if I don't act, if I don't ...

All I hear next is my own hysterical scream. I'm scared, terrified, but the fear of losing him, and effectively losing my last chance of saving Marc, obliterates everything else. Doing a fair impression of a banshee I launch myself forward, waving my arms. Even as I'm running towards them I have this dread, this agonizing fear, that I'm about to meet the same fate. Won't they turn on me too?

But luckily my assault has the opposite effect. As if the Furies are descending, they glance up, pause for one long moment, and then take to their heels. Escaping up the steps, they disappear into the dark.

Thank God.

I drop quickly down beside him.

I'm not sure if he's alive. He's lying, curled up tight in a ball. There's blood pouring out of his nose. I lean towards his mouth. Is he still breathing? Yes, there's a thin rasping sound emerging from his lips.

'Johnny. It's me.' I shake his shoulder. 'It's Simone.'

Even as I'm doing it, I know I shouldn't. I shouldn't try and rouse him. There might be internal injuries; I could be doing more harm than good. I should leave him be, call an ambulance and let the professionals deal with it. I reach for my phone. But as I'm punching in the number, he suddenly shifts and groans.

'Simone?'

I lean over him, smiling with relief. 'I'm here. Don't worry. I'm getting help.'

'No,' he whispers. The word's barely audible. His mouth's already swelling, his lips so bruised he can barely speak. He groans again. His eyes are opening and closing, flickering, searching for some point of focus.

'Don't move,' I insist. I put a hand on his arm, attempting to restrain him, but he slowly begins to drag himself up. I try to stop him, to hold him down.

'No,' he murmurs, reaching out. He folds his fingers around mine. It's not help he's searching for, not kindly reassurance, but only the hard cold metal of my phone. 'Leave it. Please.'

How can I? He's clearly in agony, maybe bleeding to death. 'Johnny, I need to—'

'Just get me back,' he insists. 'Please. Just get me back.'

I hesitate, staring down at him. What the hell can I do? He needs proper help. This isn't something that can be covered by a few comforting lies and a strip of Elastoplast.

'I can't.'

He lets go of my hand and grabs the rail to drag himself to his feet. I watch his face scrunch into pain. His breath emerges in a series of short sharp pants. 'You see,' he claims ridiculously, swaying in front of me. 'I'm okay. I'm fine.'

Except he looks like he's been hit by a freight train. There's blood everywhere, on his face, down his shirt, even on his shoes. He's drowning in red.

'Johnny, don't be crazy. I have to—'

'Please,' he says again, and when I don't respond, when I just continue to stare at him, he turns his back and starts to stagger towards the hotel.

I run the few steps necessary to catch up and grab his arm. 'What the hell are you doing?'

But he doesn't stop. He doesn't even reply. He just keeps on walking.

Chapter Sixteen

Johnny

The world's doing a dance, a vicious tango of revenge and retribution. Just to move requires an effort, a triumph of will over body, but if I stop walking I may never start again.

Fuck. I should have seen it coming.

Simone's right beside me, fussing, panicking, trying to hold me up, trying to persuade me to sit down, desperate to call an ambulance. But if she does that then the cops won't be far behind. And the last thing I need – with the ghost of Eddie Tate still lurking – is to draw attention to myself.

'Just get me back,' I keep on mumbling.

There are lights strung along the esplanade. I can't remember when they came on. Like a series of tiny magnesium flares, they're exploding in my eyes, hurting, burning. I raise a hand to shield my face.

Someone's approaching. Quick footsteps on concrete. Perhaps they heard her screams. I turn away, lurch towards the steps and start to climb.

'It's okay,' I hear her murmur. 'Thanks. He had a fall but he's all right.'

A pause before the footsteps eventually retreat.

She clambers after me. Now she's quiet, accepting, trying to assist rather than impede. She lets me lean against her, producing small sounds of encouragement as we slowly struggle up. Her shock's beginning to wear off, to be replaced by a more brutal pragmatism: better this than the alternative – I won't be much use to her in Accident and Emergency.

No, that's not fair. *I'm* the one who's refusing to go.

But I'm still going to get the interrogation. A hundred questions are poised on her lips – questions about who did it and why – but she has the good grace, at least for the moment, to keep them to herself.

What the fuck will I tell her?

We halt at the top where she roots in her bag and gets out a roll of tissues. The faint glow of a street lamp fizzes in my brain. I don't want to stop. I'm afraid to stop. The hotel's within sight but without her help I'm not sure if I can reach it. One last burst, that's all we need. 'Come on,' I urge.

'For God's sake,' she mutters, holding me back, 'you can't go in like that.'

And she's right. She's thinking more clearly than I am. If there's one thing hoteliers hate – apart from arson, vomit and reneging on the bill – it's guests bleeding all over the carpet. Someone'll be on the blower, calling the filth, before the first drops have even hit the shag pile.

'Here,' she says, peering into my face, and making soft dabbing motions round my nose. 'Christ, you look awful.'

'Hey, skip the sweet talk. Just say it like it is.' It comes out in a slur, barely decipherable. My mouth seems to be speaking a foreign language. I try a wry smile instead. Johnny Frank: always the hero. A big mistake. My jaw hurts like hell. Is it broken? Tentatively, I reach up to touch it. I don't think so.

She scowls, pushing my fingers away. 'Leave it.'

I'm hanging on to the rail, still trying to look tough, while she mops up the damage. Shit, if I stand here much longer my legs are going to collapse. The pain's starting to kick in on a deeper level. I need to sit down before I fall down.

'Okay,' she finally declares, 'that's not so bad.' Well, that's what her mouth says but her eyes say something different. She's clearly seeing road kill. Leaning closer she turns up the collar of my coat. 'Let me go in first. If there's anyone on reception, I'll keep them talking. You take the side stairs. And keep your head down.' She pauses. It's a long distant pause. 'Johnny, are you listening?'

Listening? Of course I'm fucking listening. I just got distracted for a second, wondering why I ever came here, what I'm doing, why it hurts to breathe, why the fuck I've got stars dancing in front of my eyes.

'Sure.'

She doesn't seem convinced. Gazing up at me, there's God knows what intentions running through her head. Before she can find her way back to 999, I grab her arm and force her forward. Only twenty feet until we reach our destination. I'm starting to slump, to lean too heavily against her. I can make it. Or can I? Even when I get inside there's another flight of stairs to negotiate. I'd forgotten. How could I have forgotten? She's only just told me.

'Can you manage?' she asks.

I'm suddenly standing, swaying, squinting in through the doors. It's light inside, too bright. I've no idea where the last few moments went. I can't remember walking here. I open my mouth but nothing comes out. I can see the stairs – they look like the winding ascent to Everest. *How the fuck am I going to get up those?*

She hesitates, uneasy. 'Look, you don't have to do this.'

I glare at her. Jesus. What does she want – a fucking debate?

'Okay,' she says, frowning, getting the message loud and clear. 'Just give me some time. Give me a minute before you come in.'

With one last backward glance, she swings through the doors. And as soon as she's left I wish that she hadn't. Courage is easier to sustain in company; without an audience, it hardly seems worth the bother. Sixty seconds. I begin to count them off. One, two, three ... My nose has started to bleed again. I can feel it, taste it. The blood's running into my mouth. Raising a wad of damp tissue to stem the flow, I hunch back into the shelter of the doorway. It would be faster, easier, once I got inside to take the lift but to do that I'd have to walk straight across the foyer.

It must be a minute by now. I look in through the glass again. Simone's deep in conversation with the receptionist, a series of maps laid out on the desk. Excellent. Time to go. Huddling as deep into my collar as I can, and keeping my face averted, I quietly open the door and, using every last inch of energy, launch myself up the red-carpeted stairs. It's only five shallow excruciating steps before I'm out of sight.

Did anyone notice? Well, no shouts or screams; that has to be a good sign. I can hear Simone's voice, winding things up now, expressing her thanks. She'll be here soon. Breathing heavily, I hang on to the banister and wait for the dizziness to pass. After the cold outside, the warmth feels almost tropical. Stifling. I can feel myself slipping, consciousness blurring into a semi-dream, solidity becoming liquid . . .

The next thing I'm aware of is being in the room. How the fuck did she get me here? Perhaps she bounced me up two flights, dragging me by my hair. I couldn't feel any worse if she had.

Every muscle, every joint, cries out in protest. To move is to hurt. So I try to stop moving, to sit very still, to give my central nervous system a break.

The curtains are drawn and there's a thin lemon light drifting from a bedside lamp. How long have I been here? Five minutes, twenty? My jacket's off, hung over the back of a chair. Ruined. I'll never get those bloodstains out.

There's a knock on the door. I jump, kick-starting the pain again.

But Simone answers it, unconcerned. I hear a murmur of voices before the door clicks shut. She comes back with a bottle of brandy and two glasses in her hand. Who says women aren't good in a crisis? As if she's about to perform a major operation without the aid of anaesthetic, she solemnly pours me a large one.

'Here, you'd better drink this.'

I'm not about to argue. I take half of it in one large gulp. Like liquid fire it sweeps through my body, burning and then slowly numbing. I can feel the sweat prickling on my forehead. Another mouthful and the glass is empty.

She instantly refills it.

Now I'm beginning to feel almost human again. Not in peak condition but a little less like a piece of garbage. There seems every possibility, major organ failure notwithstanding, that I might even live.

'We need to get you cleaned up.' Poised with a bowl of water, cotton wool and a bottle of antiseptic, she adds ominously, 'And while I do that, you can tell me what happened.'

I squint at her, shaking my head as if the memory's too vague. My tongue still feels too large for my mouth. 'I don't know. I can't ... They jumped me. They were after money, I guess.'

'What? Are you saying they were a pair of muggers?' Her tone has suddenly slipped out of the sympathy zone and into the incredulous.

I flinch as the antiseptic makes contact with an open wound. A hissing sound escapes from my lips. 'Jesus, Simone. What is that stuff, acid?' I gaze at her with all the tearful despair of a man about to lose his dignity. But indifferent to my agony, she just keeps dabbing away.

Florence Nightingale she fucking isn't.

'So how come your wallet's still in your pocket?'

I shrug, a movement that's more trouble – and more

pain – than it's worth. 'Is it? I don't know. You must have scared them off.'

'Don't mess me about, Johnny.'

She finds another sensitive spot and proceeds to attack. Perhaps this isn't the best time for prevarication.

'Look, it's not what—'

'It's to do with Eddie Tate, isn't it?' she interrupts. 'It's to do with Marc. Why don't you just tell me? You owe me that much. I saved your skin out there.'

Well, she's making up for it now. Another few minutes and I doubt there'll be any flesh left on my bones. 'It's nothing to do with that, with them. It's not connected. I promise.'

'So how come I don't believe you?'

'Why would I lie?' I reach out for my drink.

She sighs, despairingly. 'I've no idea. Why do you usually lie?'

And from the way that she says it I get this instinctive feeling that she knows something more than she should, that one of my sordid little secrets has wormed its way out into the open. And that should make me uneasy but it doesn't. In fact it has the opposite effect. I find the concept intriguing, challenging, even vaguely erotic.

A disturbing thought to have at a time like this.

I raise my eyes to gaze straight into hers. I didn't intend to tell her – but nothing else will shut her up. And perhaps a part of me wants to share it, to speak it out loud. 'Okay, you really want to know?' I pause for that extra effect, a distinctly dramatic pause. 'It was payback.'

She frowns, then wrinkles her nose as if she can still smell deceit. God, this girl's got a definite trust problem.

'What do you mean?'

At least I've gained a reprieve from the sadistic ministrations. She's standing motionless, waiting for an answer. I take the opportunity to grab another gulp of brandy. 'My past sins coming back to haunt me.' And when she still continues to look both suspicious and confused, I touch my jaw with the tips of my fingers. 'A gift from Roy Foster's family, my dear – a reminder that I might have been gone but I've never been forgotten.'

There's a short silence.

'Shit,' she says eventually.

'Shit,' I agree wryly. Then, as I seem to have caught her off guard, I decide to exploit it. I mean, this hardly qualifies as one of the greatest days of my life; provoking Simone may be its last remaining pleasure. 'But I'm sure you think I deserve it.'

She has the decency to blush before turning away. 'You served your time,' she mutters, like some pinko-liberal reading from a manifesto.

Strange, though, how she can't meet my eyes.

But I pour her a brandy anyway. It's the least I can do. A tiny pang of guilt has broken through. Loath as I am to admit it, if it hadn't been for her I'd be drinking intravenously by now, probably with a catheter stuck up my cock, caught within four bland magnolia walls, eating jelly and dreaming morphine.

'That's one fucking scream you've got.'

'Yeah, well I've had a lot of practice.' She lights two cigarettes and passes one to me.

You don't get this kind of service on the NHS. I take off my shoes and lie carefully back against the pillows. If I don't breathe it doesn't hurt too much. Maybe I'm getting better or maybe it's just the booze. 'You want to tell me about it?'

She glares at me. 'No.' Considering her usual repertoire of scowls and frowns, this effort's barely second-rate. She isn't sure what stance to take – sympathetic, cold or merely cynical. Whatever I've done in the past, I'm still her only hope. She has to make the best of any existing chances. 'But what makes you so sure they're not a part of this, that they're not—'

Before she can complete the question, I've already jumped in. 'Come on. Would you beat the living crap out of someone about to lead you to a stash of diamonds?' I grin and shake my head. 'This was purely personal, sweetheart, nothing more, nothing less.'

She winces at the *sweetheart*. It gets her every time. She takes a sip of brandy, glancing over the rim of her glass. 'Trouble seems to follow you around.'

'It's a curse,' I agree.

Perhaps it's the tone of the comment, its flippancy, or just my unwanted and thoroughly undesirable presence that nudges her closer to the edge. Whatever the cause, she reaches for the dreaded antiseptic again. 'We haven't finished. You need to sit up.'

Is she kidding? I'm finally getting comfortable. 'I'm fine. I just need some rest.'

Simone puts her head to one side and stares at me. Her eyes are bright. She looks like one of those wild predatory birds, an eagle or a hawk, observing its prey and preparing to swoop. There might be grace, there might be beauty, but above all there's an overwhelming sense of hunger. If she had the choice she'd tear me apart, limb from limb. Instead, she assaults me with words. 'Do you want an infection? Do you want to die of blood poisoning?'

She's got the sweetest way of putting things.

Reluctantly, I drag myself forward.

After a few minutes more of her less than gentle repairs, she covers the cut above my eye with lint and a plaster. 'You'd better take your shirt off.'

Now that's an offer that doesn't come along every day. But even as the thought arrives, it's extinguished. Just moving my arms reminds me of every bruise and cut. I struggle, wincing, out of the sleeves. There's nothing like pain for focusing the mind.

Well, except for one thing – watching someone else's eyes roam over the damage.

She throws my bloodied shirt aside and gazes long and hard at my abdomen. Her expression borders on disgust.

I force a laugh. 'That impressive, huh?'

She doesn't answer. Instead, she asks, 'Do you think they'll come back? Do you think they'll try again?'

As if I have a fucking clue. It's the last thing I want to think about.

'They could have killed you,' she says.

'Thanks for reminding me.'

She lowers her eyes. 'Sorry.'

But she's not wrong; they could have. The fact they didn't suggests they're not likely to. All it would have taken was a blade, a gun – two seconds instead of two minutes. Fuck you. Finished. No, they were just wreaking their own private form of revenge. It's over and done with.

Isn't it?

Where's the brandy? I fumble for my glass.

When I glance up again, she's poised with yet another of her vicious antiseptic swabs. 'It might be easier if you do this yourself.'

Is this her idea of being kind – or just another way of saying she can no longer bear to touch me? I take it off her and make some vague swipes across my chest and stomach. It hurts like fuck but I try not to whimper.

She stands a safe distance away, watching. 'Look, Johnny, are you sure these ... these people ... aren't connected to Marc? They must have followed us. There's no other way they could have known where we were. They might have thought you'd already picked up the diamonds.'

It's an interesting theory and she's right on one score – they must have followed us up from London. And probably all over the city too. Once I would have spotted them in a second, felt their presence instinctively, but I was so wrapped up in my own fun and games that I never thought to look over my shoulder. I shake my head. 'No, they didn't even search me. And anyway, they wouldn't take that kind of risk. What if they were wrong? They wouldn't get a second chance.'

'I suppose,' she agrees, disappointed that she hasn't stumbled on the perfect clue. And then, as if the sight of my bruised semi-nakedness offends her, she turns and disappears into the bathroom. She's back a few seconds later with a white hotel dressing gown draped over her arm. 'Put this on before you freeze to death.'

I do as I'm told.

She curls up on the other bed, her hands wrapped tight around the brandy glass. 'So where do we go from here?'

I'm not sure if it's a purely geographic or more general query. 'Nothing's changed.' I bark out a small laugh. 'Well, except I'll be watching my back with a little extra care and attention. No, we'll carry on. We'll head back to London on Monday.'

Patrick will have the diamonds by then, everything done and dusted, and I'll be able to fuck off for good. No more mistakes. No messing around. And no more fucking Buckleys or Fosters to cause me grief.

'How are you feeling?' she asks.

I don't answer.

'Johnny?'

Slowly, lazily, I open my eyes and look at her. 'Like someone's nailed my wrists to a cross and beaten the crap out of me but apart from that . . . yeah, pretty good.'

As if I've just told a particularly distasteful joke, the corners of her mouth curl down. She pulls her knees up to her chest and wraps her arms around them. She looks quietly reproachful. She's got that ability, that disturbing female skill, to make you feel – no matter how innocent you are – as guilty as hell.

It's a talent.

Am I acting like a tosser? I know I should be more appreciative. But gratitude doesn't come easily. I'm not used to expressing it. I'm not good at being beholden. I'm not good at *owing*.

I search for something encouraging to say. 'Try not to worry,' is the best I can come up with. It's hardly original but I'm barely sober. The brandy's soaking through my blood, reducing my vocabulary to the basics.

She sighs. 'Marc knew he was in danger. The night before it . . . the night before they took him, he was desperate. He wanted us to go to Spain, to get away.'

You bet he fucking did. And he must have been crapping himself, wondering – just like I did – if he was about to end up inside again. 'So why didn't he tell you?'

'Because he didn't want to scare me.' She pauses and smiles wryly. 'And I guess he didn't want me to find out about the diamonds either.'

My eyebrows do an upward lift. 'Have you two always been so straight with each other?'

'Did you tell Sarah everything?'

'Touché.'

'No,' I agree, 'but that was different. She wasn't under any illusions; she *knew* she was marrying a bastard.'

Simone twists on the bed and briefly looks away. Her cheeks flush that giveaway shade of crimson. Why can't I resist putting in the boot? It's becoming a compulsion.

For a few minutes we fall back into that familiar silence. I can hear a faint crashing noise. It could be down to the waves or maybe just to permanent brain damage. I lean carefully back against the pillows.

'Still,' I murmur provocatively, 'I suppose we all learn from our mistakes.'

'And what have you ever leant?' she snaps back. 'What do you know about anything?'

Then, as if she can no longer bear to be even within three feet of me, she jumps up and walks across the room. Sliding back the curtain, she opens the window and stands there with her back turned.

I think this is what they call the cold shoulder.

And I'm sorely tempted, for one mad impetuous moment, to spill the truth. At least the part about Eddie Tate – about what Carl did, about what Dee's covering up. That would curl those pink-socked toes of hers. But I know I have to fight it; it's just a knee-jerk reaction, an impulsive desire to retaliate. Other than a brief satisfaction, there's nothing to be gained.

Best to keep my mouth shut.

And she seems to have the same idea. For a while the noises are purely external: the echo of footsteps, the occasional voice, the distant ebb and flow of the waves. Floating up from an open downstairs window, the clatter of plates and cutlery heralds the start of evening dining. Ordinary people doing ordinary things. It's only gradually that I begin to tune in to another sound, a series of soft desperate breaths as she gulps in the sea air.

Fuck, she's not crying is she?

Sighing, I stub out my cigarette and peer at her. Hunched

against the window she has the closed restrained stance of someone fighting the inevitable, one hand clenched against her thigh, the other wrapped too tightly round the sill. My gaze skims quickly over her body. Not the right time or the right place but ... well, she's worth the scrutiny. She's wearing a black sweater and faded blue jeans. My eyes linger for longer than they should, tracing the contour of her spine, her waist, her long slender legs. Bearing in mind the sensitivity of the situation, I try not to stare too hard at her arse.

'You're such a shit,' she mutters. Her voice is hushed but emphatic enough to carry.

Bearing in mind my current disabilities, this seems a touch callous and I'm about to assume my state-of-the-art bewildered expression when it suddenly occurs to me – oh Christ – that she can see my reflection in the glass. She's observed it all, every look, every slow lascivious glance. She's followed my gaze all over her body. I've been well and truly caught in the act. Before I can think of an adequate excuse she turns to face me again.

'This is just some kind of game to you, isn't it? You don't really care if Marc lives or dies.'

I make the effort to meet her eyes and to do the only decent thing I can – lie with conviction. I shake my head. 'That's not true. I've told you why—'

She barely waits for me to finish. 'Oh, don't give me that bullshit. I'm sick of it.' She flashes me an angry look. 'This isn't anything to do with friendship ... or past love affairs. And you won't go back to prison if they can't find you. All you want are your bloody stupid diamonds. So save your breath. I'm not a complete idiot.'

She glares at me.

I stare directly back. This kind of confrontation is small fry, amateur, compared to the stand-offs I've been used to. You can't afford to be weak when you're defending yourself on a prison landing, face to face, knowing one false move could send you to purgatory. It's simple, basic. Stay cold and angry. Hold your ground, hold your gaze, and never look away. Give an inch and they'll take a mile.

Except those guys' eyes didn't fill with fucking tears.

And the minute I see them I'm screwed. She's trying to hold it together but as she walks towards me, it just gets worse and worse.

She sits on the edge of my bed, tears running down her cheeks. 'Will you promise me something?'

I'd promise her the whole fucking world if she'd just stop crying.

'Promise you won't run out on me?' She takes a deep breath. 'Even if ... if you decide you don't want to go through with it, will you tell me?'

I can hardly move, never mind run. It would take three paramedics with a heady dose of Valium to drag me out of here. 'I'm not going anywhere.'

She does that trembling lower lip thing again. 'It's just – if that's what you intend to do, I'd rather know it now.'

This is crazy. It's Jim I hate, want to punish. I'd like to string him up by his neck and watch him swing. He's the one who should be sitting here now, in pain, suffering, *afraid*.

Not her. How the fuck did it come to this? One big bloody awful mess. I should have bailed out when I had the chance.

Simone wipes her face with the back of her hand.

There's only one thing for it. I do what I always do best in times of emotional emergency, pour another drink – and lie. 'Sure,' I say, with all the sincerity I can muster. 'I give you my word.'

After all, there's nothing legally binding about a promise made under the influence of alcohol.

Chapter 17

Simone

It's morning – and I feel like a brick has been dropped on my head. Too much brandy on an empty stomach and far too many cigarettes. Just to add insult to injury, the local church bells are ringing in my ears, a loud and unnecessary reminder of all my earthly sins. Perhaps I should crawl out of bed and find someone to confess to.

A few feet away, Johnny's still asleep, his mouth slightly open.

From what I remember, it didn't go too badly last night. At least I was spared the trial of seduction; a man's hardly ever in the mood when he's just had his head kicked in. And I did discover one useful weakness – he isn't too keen on displays of emotion. Shed a tear and he's mortified. He'd have promised me the moon and stars to put a brake on the waterworks.

But whether he'll be true to his word is another matter altogether.

I swing my legs carefully over the side. Sudden movements

and hangovers aren't the best of soulmates. I dig some fresh clothes out of my bag, creep softly past him and lock myself in the bathroom. After a long hot soak I may be able to force down some breakfast. Coffee would be good too, strong and black. I start the water running and pour in some gratis hotel smellies. Then I scrub my teeth, trying to avoid looking in the mirror. Once the steam has done its work, my reflection will be safe.

Now would be a good time to call Dee. But I need five minutes to get my throbbing head together. Aspirins first, with a glass of water. Is it safe to drink from a bathroom tap? I stare down into the basin. What the hell, it's a bit late to start worrying about poisoning.

Sitting on the edge of the bath, I review the events of last night. Some of it's bordering on the hazy. What did we talk about? The Fosters, of course. It's only taken a few weeks for Johnny's past to dramatically catch up with him. But then he'll never really be able to escape it; like a dark shadow attached to his heels, it will always be there. How can he ever move forward when ...

I pull myself up sharp. Don't start feeling sorry for him. Johnny's a manipulator, a criminal, a man who lives outside the boundaries of common morality. He's a law unto himself. And he's only interested in taking care of Number One. All I can hope for – and let's face it, it's a slim hope – is that he'll feel he owes me *something* for yesterday.

The bath's three-quarters full. With a sigh of relief, I lower myself into the bubbles. Heaven. Closing my eyes, I lean back against the cool white porcelain and dream of sobriety.

Then, just as I'm slipping into a doze, I remember Dee and a shock of guilt jolts through my body. I sit up too quickly, reviving the jackhammer in my head.

Moaning gently, I scrabble for my mobile and turn it on. *Five missed calls.* All of them from Dee. And a text message: *Ring me.* My guilt moves swiftly into alarm. It must be bad news. Is it Marc? Please God, no. With trembling fingers I push the button to return the call.

It's answered straight away. 'Where have you been?' she shrieks. Her voice is so loud, and the pitch so piercing, I have to hold the phone away from my ear. 'I was ringing all night. I thought ... we thought—'

'Dee, what is it? What's going on?'

I can hear her taking deep breaths, trying to calm herself. My heart pounds in rhythm to the pain in my head.

'We heard,' she manages to splutter.

And for a second relief flows through me. Stupidly, I think she's talking about Johnny, about the attack. 'It's all right,' I start to say but she's already talking over me.

'We got another note. It was left at the gate last night. Simone, they need the diamonds by Thursday or they'll ...' She makes a thick choking kind of sound. 'And I've been trying to ring you and when I couldn't get through, I thought ... Where are you? When are you coming back? Are you still with him?'

So it's finally happening. Perhaps a part of me thought it never would – that somehow this bloody awful nightmare would just melt away. But all the time it's been creeping closer and closer. A wave of nausea renders me speechless.

'Simone? Simone, are you there?'

'Yes,' I manage to murmur.

'And Johnny – is he still with you?'

I try to keep my voice steady. 'Yes. It's okay. It's fine. We'll be back ... I'm not sure when exactly. But soon. A couple of days. We'll be in London again tomorrow.'

There's a brief silence. 'So where are you now?'

'Norfolk.'

'Where?'

'Norfolk,' I repeat, although I know she's heard and that she means *why* not where. Except I haven't got the energy to explain. I want to get off this phone as quickly as I can. I want some time to myself, some time to think before I pass the news on to Johnny.

'I don't understand, what are you doing in ... '

Her voice is starting to falter again, to lose the battle against her emotions. I can't bear to listen. My own fear and dread are hard enough to deal with. 'Look, I've got to go, Dee. He's waiting for me. Try not to worry. I'll call again. I'll call tomorrow. And I won't let you down. I swear.'

As I hang up the only thing I'm hoping is that it isn't an empty promise.

I haul myself out of the bath, get dried and dressed. I've switched to automatic pilot, going through the motions, barely aware of what I'm doing. I pull on my jeans and a T-shirt. I feel like I've been dragged to Hades and back. With the edge of a towel I clear a wide stripe through the condensation on the mirror and stare at my face. My hair needs washing. Jesus, how can I even think about my hair at a time like this? Except it's a way of not concentrating on the real horror, that mighty boulder rolling slowly towards me.

When I walk back into the room Johnny's awake and sitting up.

'How are you?' I ask.

He nods. 'Alive, I think. You want to check my pulse?'

His face doesn't look so bad, all things considered. There's still heavy bruising around one of his eyes, an artistic swirl of ochre-reds and mauves, but the swelling has reduced. Even the cut on his lip has begun to heal. Now, at least from the neck up, he only looks like he's been in a minor car crash. And from the neck down – well, that's his business.

'Shall I order breakfast?' I scan the menu. 'What would you like – eggs, toast, coffee? Full English?'

He gives me a penetrating stare. 'What's wrong?'

'What?'

Shifting on the bed, he half-suppresses a groan. 'I might be crippled,' he says, 'but I'm not blind.'

Am I that transparent? I was hoping for some space, a chance to think, and an opportunity to shovel some food down his gullet before spilling the information. It's been my experience that men usually respond better to any kind of news on a full stomach. 'Nothing. Nothing, really. Only, I just heard from Dee and ... ' I stop abruptly, gazing down at the menu again. *Nothing?* What am I talking about? This is as serious as it gets. But my eyes are still relentlessly scanning the words – bacon, eggs, sausages, beans – chewing them over, absorbing them, feeling increasingly sickened by them ...

'So she's heard.'

My gaze flies swiftly up to meet his. 'What?'

'I take it she's heard from the bastards holding Marc.'

How does he know that? 'What?'

He frowns. 'Please stop saying that.'

'What?' It takes a moment for the request to sink in. My legs have acquired that weird jelly sensation. Slowly, I lower myself down on the corner of his bed. 'Sorry.'

'So have they? Is that what this is all about?'

I open my mouth but quickly close it again. I nod. Eventually I manage to murmur, 'Thursday.'

'Good. Okay. Well, that was what we were expecting, wasn't it?' He moves forward a little and smiles. 'Don't you see? This is good news, not bad. The very fact they've made contact means that Marc's still alive. The deal's still on. You should be pleased.'

Lifting my head, I stare into his cold ambiguous eyes. 'Oh, excuse me if I'm not doing handstands, but for some reason I find it hard to view this as a cause for celebration.'

He expels a low patient sigh. 'Believe me,' he insists, 'the time to start worrying is when they *don't* get in touch.'

And I know he's right. Better this than silence. But I'm aware as well that if we can't deliver, if he reneges on his promise, then ...

'You have to trust me, Simone.'

I only wish I could.

While Johnny tucks into a hearty breakfast of bacon and eggs – he must have the constitution of an ox – I force down a slice of toast. Already I'm starting to wonder how

I'll get through the day, trapped within these four walls with him. What are we going do – play charades? I want to get on the road and head back to London but he's clearly in no state to travel. His appetite may be unaffected but he can barely walk; I even had to help him to the bathroom, although thankfully only as far as the door. Anyway, I'm in no fit state to drive. God alone knows what my blood alcohol levels are.

'So how are Jim and Dee?' he asks, pouring out his third coffee. 'How are they bearing up?'

I shrug. 'As you'd expect.'

He glances over the rim of his cup. 'Did you tell her what happened yesterday?'

'No.'

'Why not?'

'Because she's terrified enough already. I don't want to push her over the edge. She's just got that letter and if she starts to panic then ... '

'Yeah, you did the right thing.'

And the minute he says it, I start to think the very opposite.

'It'll be over soon,' he continues with irritating cheeriness. 'Come Thursday you can put it all behind you, get on with your life.'

'And you?'

He raises an eyebrow.

'What are *you* going to do? I mean, you're the one about to sacrifice your pension plan. That must have some bearing on your future.' It's supposed to sound casual but doesn't quite hit the right note.

'How sweet of you to worry,' he replies, grinning.

At which point I could happily slap him but it seems inhumane to add to his injuries. Instead, I do something even more destructive. Before I can stop myself, in an act of petty revenge, the retort flies like a cruise missile from my mouth. 'And how's Melanie?'

That wipes the smirk off his face.

Now it's his turn to take refuge in the monosyllabic. 'What?'

And from the way he barks it out, I'm sure I've hit the jackpot. But the satisfaction is short-lived. I wish I could take the question back. His eyes are fixed in a hard cold glare and I can feel the temperature sliding down to zero. Damn! What have I done? My gaze darts around the room, desperately searching for some inspiration, for some way out of the hole I've just managed to dig for myself.

Then suddenly he relaxes, shakes his head, and asks, 'Melanie?'

A tiny puzzled frown has appeared on his forehead. Christ, he's almost as good as Marc. They must both have attended the how-to-get-yourself-out-of-a-tight-corner Academy of Learning. But if nothing else it gives me the opportunity to go along with him, to try and pretend that I've simply got it wrong. That has to be better than a confrontation.

I force myself to meet his eyes. 'I thought, er . . . that you were quite close to her and Carl, before you . . . you know, before you fell out with him. And she always seemed so nice. You know, friendly. And I haven't seen her for a while, not since . . . and I wondered . . . I thought you might have heard from her and . . . ' Gradually my voice trails off. Why the hell am I bothering?

He slowly shakes his head again.

There's one of those extended uncomfortable pauses. He sits perfectly still while I squirm. Despite having lungs like an ashtray, I reach automatically for a cigarette; I don't really want to smoke it, I just want something to do with my hands.

'No, well, I guess not,' I say weakly.

He's smart enough not to labour the point. He gives a brief dismissive sigh and, instead of issuing any outright denials, calmly picks up his fork and carries on eating.

The subject is closed.

And I'm pretty keen to move on too. Except I'm too nervous to keep my big mouth shut. 'So how are you feeling?' I ask for the second time this morning. I wince even as I say it. It's a pathetic attempt to bury my mistake. 'You're looking much better.'

He glances up again but doesn't speak.

Finding it increasingly hard to meet his gaze, I concentrate instead on his facial cuts and bruises. If I can't be charming, I can certainly strive for caring. 'When you've finished your breakfast, we should change that dressing.'

'It's fine,' he replies shortly.

'No, it should be—'

I watch the expression on his face flicker, change, and then freeze slowly into ice. 'You know, Simone, some things are better left alone.'

And the silence that follows is arctic.

*

It's equally cold outside but much easier to bear. I'd rather shiver out here than spend another second under his frigid scrutiny. I made my escape over an hour ago and am still pacing along the esplanade, up and down, like some frenetic prisoner making the most of their daily allowance of freedom. It's barely afternoon but already the light's failing, growing greyer and dimmer, the sky dissolving into the sea while the rain continues to beat down.

I'm not even properly dressed for it. I haven't got my scarf, my coat isn't waterproof and my boots are leaking. I'm soaked to the skin but can't face going back. Sloshing through the puddles, I'm trying not to think. Except all I can do is think. The morning keeps echoing through my mind – Dee's voice, my voice, *his* voice. And where has it got me?

Absolutely nowhere.

Suddenly Katie slips into my mind. She'll be back any day. Although it's only been a few weeks, it feels more like a lifetime. God, I need a friend right now, someone close to talk to, someone to confide in. I wish she'd ring. And then as soon as I've wished it, I hope the very opposite. How am I supposed to explain all this away? *Hi, how was Oz? Yeah, everything's great here too. It's never been better. A guy called Eddie Tate was brutally killed, Marc's been taken hostage and I'm relying on Johnny – oh, he's a lovely geezer, just done eighteen years for murder – to pay for the ransom in diamonds.*

No, I can't get her involved. I can't tell her anything. What kind of friend would that make me? There are some things that are just too dangerous to share. Leaning against the rail, I gaze down on the shore. The tide's in, the sea crashing so violently against the stones that it throws up a spray. I don't bother standing back. Perhaps, if I'm lucky, a freak wave will carry me off.

But gradually I begin to recall what Johnny said earlier, about moving on, about getting on with life. And he's right. It's not over yet. If it all comes good I might still be able to start again with Marc. Why not? I close my eyes. It's tempting providence to even consider it but if he survives, if he comes through, then surely we've got a chance ... all those years must count for something. He's my husband and I still love him. I do. And suddenly all I can see is his face on Christmas Eve, his smile, his eyes, the way he looked at me – and God, that has to be worth holding on to. It has to be worth fighting for.

Slowly, I make my way back. It was a bad mistake asking Johnny about Melanie, a faux pas as they'd say in polite society. That was clearly a secret he wanted to keep the lid on. He wasn't happy, not happy at all. And although it goes against the grain – he's in the wrong, not me – I'll have to do my best to make amends. *Be nice*, as Dee would put it.

My feet start to drag as the hotel comes into view. The rest of the afternoon stretches ahead, long and grey and gloomy. If Johnny's still got the hump, if I'm still in Coventry, it's going to feel like an eternity. And just to make matters worse, he's going to be extra suspicious of me now, reading between the lines, wondering what I'm really asking. When will I ever learn to keep my big mouth shut?

I pause by the doors, one last minute to breathe in the

fresh air and paint a smile back on my face. Idly, I glance along the street. And then I do a double take. My stomach lurches into fright.

Where's the car? Jesus, where is it?

It was there, right there, just a few yards to the left of the steps. And now there's only a space. Stupidly, I start looking around as if my memory might be playing tricks or it might have miraculously shifted itself. Perhaps it's been stolen? But I already know the truth. I can feel it in my bones, in every tiny trembling nerve. I left him alone for over an hour, plenty of time for him to think, to make a choice, to ...

I'm cursing and praying – *Damn him! Please God, let him still be there!* – as I smash through the entrance and rocket up the stairs, two at a time. In my head I've got a single mental image of the car keys sitting on the bedside table. Bloody fool. Why didn't I take them with me? My heart's thumping, my lungs painfully trying to draw in air, but even as I stumble along the corridor I know what I'm about to find.

I throw open the door – and the room is empty.

His bag is gone, his clothes, every piece of evidence that he was ever here. And of course the keys are missing. Still I persist in the pointless exercise of checking the bathroom. Nothing. I stand for a second, disbelief struggling with anger and fear, before dropping down on to the bed. A hard cold scream rises in my throat. It stifles into a sob.

'You bastard!'

Chapter Eighteen

Johnny

The door's wide open. Simone's perched on the edge of the bed, her body hunched over in a pose of quiet desperation. I watch as her shoulders rise and fall. She's not crying so much as gasping for breath.

At what stage did I change my mind? When I was checking out, when I was strolling down the steps, when I was in the car – or did I always intend to come back?

There are some obligations you just can't walk away from.

I clear my throat and say too loudly, 'Are you going to sit here all day?'

She whirls round, a kaleidoscope of emotions passing over her face: relief, amazement, rage, joy. Jumping to her feet, she breaks into a smile. Fuck, if I'm not careful she may even try and hug me.

'I thought . . .'

She doesn't need to finish the sentence; we both know what she thought.

For a moment, like a couple of awkward teenagers, we stand and stare at each other. Then I step inside, acting casual. 'We should make a move. It's not smart to stay here, not with the Fosters hanging around. We're better off in London.'

'Sure,' she replies softly. She doesn't ask any awkward questions – like where the hell I've been for the past fifteen minutes or how I've suddenly regained the use of my legs – but quickly turns and starts to gather her things. Anxiety makes her clumsy. Objects slip and slide from her hands. As if terrified I might suddenly change my mind, that I might disappear as unexpectedly as I arrived, she keeps glancing nervously up.

This isn't the Simone I've come to know and ... well, whatever. Falling back on a failsafe method of provocation, I dredge up one of my cutest grins. 'Hey, what's wrong, sweetheart? You worried I'd ship out without paying the bill?'

A light flashes briefly into her eyes. 'As if,' she snaps back.

I prefer her angry to grateful. And the exchange, slight as it was, seems to restore the more normal balance between us. Now her fingers are moving briskly, confidently, packing like an expert. She's recovered her poise – and her antagonism.

A few minutes later, we're ready to go.

I reach for her bag but she pulls it away and frowns. 'It's okay, thanks. I can manage.'

I guess there are only so many favours you can do in a day.

'So where's the car?' she asks, as we descend on to the street. She looks left and right. It's raining hard, sheeting down, the water forming tiny lakes around our feet. I see her shiver. Cold, fear, relief? It's impossible to judge.

'Round the corner,' I reply, 'out of sight.'

She forces a smile and follows me.

Out of sight? It's about as hidden as a fucking headline. The battered white Fiat has three wheels on the pavement and one on the road. Even to my own eyes, it bears all the hallmarks of a driver who's either had a stroke – or a violent change of heart.

But she doesn't comment. I open the boot and she finally passes over her bag. I get the distinct impression that she's holding her breath, that she still isn't sure, that she can't relax until we're safely on the road again. And all the while the rain's beating down, thrumming a soft relentless rhythm against the pavement.

She holds out a hand for the keys.

'It's okay,' I insist, 'I'll drive.'

I watch her mouth open, the objections forming on her lips before she even speaks. 'You can't, you haven't got a licence, what if we get stopped, what if . . .'

I flip the keys blithely into the air and luckily manage to catch them again. It's good to know the gods are occasionally on my side. 'What are the odds? Anyway, better me than you. I've got nothing to lose.'

She looks like she's about to argue but then just shakes her head and climbs passively into the passenger seat.

I crawl in beside her and slam the door. I'm determined not to stall the bastard machine. Apart from my recent and precarious five-minute run, it's been eighteen years since I last drove. But once you've learned you never forget.

Or so they say.

Cautiously, I start the engine, turn on the lights and check the mirrors. I slowly edge away from the kerb. All things considered, there's probably no better place to freshen up your driving skills than in a desolate seaside town in the middle of winter. Although I doubt if Simone shares the same opinion; she's got her seatbelt firmly secured and her eyes half-closed.

We're on the main road before she fully opens them again.

By now we've covered a few miles and I'm getting in to my stride. It's good to be behind the wheel again. I'm even in the mood for a little overtaking. Once, twice, no problem... and then I almost clip an oncoming car. She audibly draws in her breath. And yeah, maybe that was a bit close. I haven't quite come to terms with the acceleration.

'Are you sure you don't want me to drive?' she asks hoarsely. Her fingers are gripping the edge of the seat.

But there's no need to panic. We're not dead yet. 'No, I think I'm getting the hang of it.'

'You're going too fast.'

I put my foot on the brake, slow down, and try to look contrite. 'Sorry.' Perhaps I was speeding but the road's so fucking dismal, so dark and gloomy, that I can't wait to escape. The country's all well and good but I've a sudden yearning for the bright lights. I might have fallen out of love with London but I crave noise, action, something to remind me that I'm still alive.

I should never have come here in the first place. What on earth possessed me? I still can't figure out if it was down to a whim or some deeper subconscious desire to revisit a place where I'd once been happy. Maybe I wanted to say a proper goodbye to Sarah. If that was the case, it didn't pan out too well. Although, come to think of it, there were probably plenty of occasions when she wanted to give me a good slap too.

Interrupting my thoughts Simone says quietly, 'I owe you.'

And that's true enough. I didn't have to go back. I could have taken the car, skipped out of town, and left her high and dry. But I'm nothing if not magnanimous. 'That's okay, I guess I owe you too. We can call it quits.'

She pauses, frowns and then says, 'I didn't . . . I meant for the hotel – the bill.'

Shit. Does she do this crap just to make me feel stupid?

Well, two can play at that game. 'Not to worry. They won't notice we're gone until tomorrow. We'll be miles away by then.'

Startled, she whirls round to face me. 'What? What are you saying? God, Johnny, they'll have us arrested, they'll—' She stops dead as she sees my expression.

I'm grinning again. 'Just call us Bonnie and Clyde.'

It's a while before she deigns to speak to me again. 'Do you really think the Fosters will have another go?'

I shrug. I was only using it as an excuse, as a plausible reason for a hasty departure, but it's not beyond the bounds of possibility. 'Maybe. No point waiting around to find out.'

'No,' she agrees. Then glancing quickly over her shoulder, as if they might already be on our tail, she shudders. 'Don't you find that kind of . . . worrying?'

Of course it's bloody worrying but keeping my voice cool, almost indifferent, I reply, 'I guess I'll learn to live with it.'

I like an opportunity to practise my tough no-man-scares-Johnny-Frank act. Although how convincing it is, with my face covered in bruises, my innards mashed and my ribcage screaming in protest every time I change gear, is another matter altogether.

She gives me a look but doesn't pursue the subject.

Something occurred to me while I was in the process of making my earlier exit: if they have been following us around, then they're probably presuming that Simone's more than my personal chauffeur. Which means that *she* could be in danger too. Not that she's my fucking responsibility or anything – I didn't ask her to come with me – but if I deserted her, without a car, she'd be the perfect target for some back-door form of revenge.

And I don't need any more complications.

I should have dumped her in London when I had the chance. Tomorrow. I'll do it tomorrow after I've seen Patrick. I'll get a train and—

'What are you thinking?' she asks suddenly, as if her female radar has sensed an imminent betrayal.

How do women do that?

I shake my head, the picture of innocence. 'I was just wondering where we should stay tonight. It's probably not a good idea to go back to the same hotel.'

'We could go home,' she suggests, almost pleadingly, 'get some rest, a decent night's sleep, and then drive into the City tomorrow.'

I'm about to say no, no way – I don't want to be within a mile of the Buckleys – when I'm struck by a few advantages to this plan. For one it would mean Simone safely deposited, no longer under my duty of care, and for two – well, I've still got unfinished business. Perhaps the recent run-in with the Fosters has reminded me of my own compelling need for vengeance. This could be my last opportunity to add to Jim's misery, to watch him squirm, to push him ever closer to the edge.

'Yeah, maybe you're right.'

'Really?' She smiles, almost laughs, as if I've just offered her a trouble-free divorce.

And now it's too late to change my mind. Do I want to? No. It may be an unnecessary risk – I can only hope the cops don't come calling – but it's worth the gamble. One last evening to scare the fuck out of Jim before I scarper for good.

I give her a sideways glance. 'I hope this doesn't mean that you're tiring of my company.'

She smiles again. 'Not for a second,' she replies, with her familiar edge – a delicate balance that's neither blatantly insulting nor the slightest bit flattering. 'How could you ever imagine it?'

I lift my eyebrows. 'You've got a point.'

She lifts hers too in a mocking, almost perfect, reproduction.

So this is our last journey together. In an odd kind of way, I'm going to miss her. Even the most aggravating of people can leave a gap in your life. By this time tomorrow, I'll be on my own. But that's better. It has to be better. I'll take off tonight, in the early hours, when everyone's asleep. I never was one for lingering farewells.

'Look, could you do me a favour?' I touch my forehead, on the spot where the dressing lies above my left eye. 'Can we keep quiet about this, say I got in a scuffle or something? I've had enough of the past – and, honestly, I can't face an inquisition from Dee. It isn't anything to do with anything else and … and it's not going to help, is it? It's only going to scare her.'

She hesitates just long enough to betray her suspicions. She still doesn't trust me. But the deal's a fair one: in exchange for her silence, she gets to sleep in her own bed tonight. Eventually she nods. 'Sure. If that's what you want.'

We're within spitting distance of Essex when I pull in. I need to take a leak and grab some caffeine before stepping back inside the house from hell. She's been asleep for the last hour, curled up with her face against the window. Slowly she blinks awake and peers at me.

'Where are we?'

'Almost home,' I say, encouragingly. 'Do you mind stopping off for a minute?'

I'm amazed this place is still here, a bleak backstreet sanctuary that in my day was most frequently occupied by small-time villains, thieves and whores. It hasn't changed much. The walls are still a smoke-tinted shade of cream, the atmosphere still furtive. Twenty pairs of eyes rise abruptly as we walk through the doors. Only the women are absent – too early for them perhaps – but if Simone's aware of her solitary status, she doesn't show it. She strolls over to the counter and orders two coffees. 'One black,' she demands, 'no sugar.'

I touch her arm. 'I'm just going for a . . .'

As if bodily functions are beneath her contempt, she wrinkles her nose and waves me away. I walk towards the rear of the room, my gaze drifting sideways, moving slyly over everyone present. But there's no one I recognize. No one to acknowledge and no one to worry about. I visit the Gents and head quickly back.

She's taken a seat by the window. I slide in across the table. 'Are you hungry? Do you want something to eat?'

Her eyes flicker over the grimy surroundings. I can almost see her flinch. 'No thanks.'

And there's something to be said for middle class girls – even when they're disgusted, they're polite. I take a sip of coffee. 'No, well, it's not exactly the Ritz.'

God knows why I even stopped here. There are plenty of other caffs, other restaurants along the road. I could have pulled in anywhere. Never go back. Isn't that the rule? Twenty years ago, I would have walked into this place and seen at least a few familiar faces but now I'm just a stranger, someone passing through. It makes me feel old, removed, like a piece of history that's been summarily deleted.

Sensing my mood she says softly, 'Everything changes.'

I snort into my coffee. 'Not this dive.'

She wraps her hands around her mug and, as if it might be laced with a cocktail of germs, sips cautiously at the dense black liquid. 'Then maybe *you* have.'

There's another of those murky pauses.

She waits but when I don't reply, transfers her gaze and conducts a cursory survey of our surroundings. She's careful to smile, to keep her tone light and amused. 'Well, it's certainly got . . . atmosphere. Is that why you brought me here, to provide a taste of authentic city life?'

I pretend not to understand what she means. That I wanted to make her feel awkward, uncomfortable, to punish her for the unforgivable sin of rousing my conscience, is something I'll never admit. Surely I'm entitled to one last petty act before we go our separate ways? Quickly, I smile back. 'Actually, I just fancied a breather.'

'Right.'

It's amazing how she can imbue a single word with so much scepticism. I wonder if it comes naturally or if she has to work at it. Anyway, if I was hoping to play on her recent discomposure it's certainly backfired. She may be less than happy but she isn't intimidated. I'm the one who feels alienated; if this was ever a part of my world, it isn't any more.

I fumble for a cigarette and light it. Then, remembering, I shove the pack ungraciously across the table. 'You want one?'

She shakes her head.

There's a silence. She sips. I smoke. Our eyes embark on a mutual journey of avoidance, around the room, at the ceiling – everywhere but towards each other. She's the first to speak again. 'You know, we don't have to go back tonight. I don't mind staying in London.'

And I'm not sure whether she's offering it as a consolation prize – like a sweet to a disappointed child – or if she's got some inkling of my intentions. 'Makes no odds to me,' I reply casually. 'Why should it?'

'No, no reason.' She hesitates. 'Except . . . I was just

thinking, maybe it *would* be better to stay away for now, to avoid all the questions – what with Dee and . . . ' She touches her forehead, reminding me of my injuries. 'And it would save us the journey in the morning.'

It would also be a damn sight less dangerous. The filth could be hovering on the Buckleys' doorstep at this very minute, prepared to pounce, ready to triumphantly arrest the killer of Eddie Tate – and all his associates. Why did I ever agree to go there?

'I don't mind,' she says again, 'it's up to you.'

And if I weren't feeling so perverse, so bloody pissed off at everyone and everything, I'd jump at this chance to change our plans. The old Johnny Frank, the one with more thought than instinct, would have snapped her hand off – but this version's got a different agenda. So what if the bastards turn up? I'll deal with that if and when I need to. The game isn't over yet. Jim hasn't suffered enough, not nearly enough, and I haven't waited eighteen years to just walk away.

I shrug, feigning indifference. 'No, we're almost there. And you're right, we need some rest. It's getting late.' In fact it's barely five o'clock, not exactly the witching hour, but any excuse will do in a crisis.

'Are you sure?'

Bloody hell. Now I'm the one having to persuade *her*. Another night alone with the devil incarnate is the last thing she wants but having already lost me once today she's clearly prepared to go to any lengths to ensure my happiness. I ponder on that notion for a second. *Any lengths?* And as she lifts her eyes, as she gazes intensely into mine, it suddenly occurs to me that she might be suggesting more than a night of alternative accommodation.

Fuck, am I currently in the process of passing up an opportunistic shag?

No, it's only wishful thinking. She wouldn't go that far – not even for that cheating rubbish husband of hers. Although it would be interesting to know, if pushed, just how far she *would* go. An embrace? A kiss? Maybe, if I asked really nicely, she'd let me hold her hand.

I must be grinning like an idiot because she asks, 'What's so funny?'

'Nothing.'

I'd love to share the joke but I value what's left of my balls. Which is another crucial issue. Even if she was offering to take me to heaven and back – and hey, a guy can dream, there's no law against it – I'm not sure if this recently shattered body of mine could exactly rise to the occasion.

'Nothing?' she echoes. Those seductive hazel eyes are still fixed firmly on mine.

I'm going have to respond. And as the truth is out of the question, I fall back on ambiguity. 'Only it's kind of strange isn't it – the two us being here together?'

She isn't quite sure how to respond. I could be referring to the general situation or to something more specific. Taking a sip of the strong bitter coffee, she tries to keep smiling. 'I suppose.'

And there's a quality to her voice, about the way she bites gently down on her lower lip, that makes me wish I'd never started thinking about sex. It takes an effort to keep my gaze steady, to prevent it from scrutinizing the places it shouldn't. I'm concentrating on her mouth but that really doesn't help much . . .

Shit. I've got to call a halt to this right now, before I embark on that long and lonely voyage to frustration. Angry is better than aroused. Stay concentrated. Stay focused. Forget it. Think of Jim, of what he did, of why I *have* to return tonight. I'm too old – and far too battered – to be seduced by a fantasy.

Placing my elbows on the table, I draw a deep determined breath. Sex is one thing but revenge is quite another. I know where my priorities lie. I know where they've been lying for the past eighteen years. There are debts to be paid – and Jim has barely started on his first instalment.

By nine o'clock I'm beginning to wish we'd never come back. Dee has been fussing round for the past few hours, flapping like a mother hen, and driving me to distraction. Naturally, I got the third degree as soon as I walked through the door. 'God, what happened? What happened to your face?' She grabbed my arm, horror growing in her eyes. It's great to know you're loved. Except, of course, it wasn't my welfare she was fretting about. She didn't give a fuck about that. Her only worry was that I might have been robbed of the one thing that *was* important.

I didn't see why I should put her out of her misery any faster than I had to. Let her sweat. Shaking her off, I strolled through to the living room, looking for Jim.

'Johnny!'

She tried to chase after me but Simone held her back. 'It's okay, don't worry.' From the hall, I could hear the murmured fragments of an explanation, some fabricated story about a pub, a brawl, a nothing-to-be-worried-about tale of reassurance.

And by the time Dee caught up with me again she was all smiles and consideration. 'Sit down, sit down. Let me get you a drink. Scotch? A large one, right? I'll get some dinner on. You must be starving. Put your feet up – you look shattered. What you need is a good meal inside you. That eye looks sore, Johnny – do you need anything for it?'

And so it went on . . .

I'm on my third whisky before Jim finally gets back. I can smell him before he even appears at the door, the heavy stench of sweat and alcohol preceding his entrance. I wonder if he's been sober at all since we left.

'Good to see you,' he slurs, attempting a smile as he lumbers across the room.

For one piss-awful moment I think he's coming over to shake my hand but thankfully he's heading for the drinks cabinet. I watch as his fat fingers reach eagerly for the bottle. Yeah, he's in a state all right, completely off his head.

He half-fills his glass and looks around for a seat. I notice Simone's nervous glance, her eyes partly closed as if she's praying to God that he won't join her on the sofa. And fortune's smiling on her this evening. Instead he chooses the nearest chair, the one next to mine, and slumps down into it.

Since his appearance, no one else has spoken. Even Dee's endless chatter has temporarily been silenced. But if Jim's aware of the sudden lull in conversation, he doesn't show it. No, he's way beyond the realm of social niceties. Staring intently into his glass, he contemplates its contents and then takes a large greedy mouthful. He licks his lips.

'Good to see you,' he says again, as if it's the only sentence he recalls.

He doesn't comment on the state of my face but maybe he can't see it properly. There's only one lamp on and the room is full of shadows. Or perhaps he's so wrecked he wouldn't notice if I'd had a fucking sex change.

I nod. 'You too, mate. How are you doing?'

The question seems to confuse him. He frowns. His mouth opens, but nothing comes out.

'Stupid question,' I say, apologetically. 'Sorry. It's all such a bloody mess, isn't it? A real nightmare.' Leaving a few seconds for this despairing news to sink in, I embellish it with a sympathetic sigh. 'I can't ... I can't even begin to imagine ... but I'm sure he'll be fine ... I mean, of course he will ... so long as no one panics, and *they* don't lose their nerve and ...'

Jim's features, as they drunkenly catch up with my meaning, gradually twist and fall.

Simone coughs loudly and glares at me.

I look innocently back.

'But it's going to be okay,' she insists, holding my gaze. 'Nothing's going to go wrong. Everything's sorted. In a few days it'll all be over. Won't it, Johnny?'

As if the desire to console is fighting a conscientious battle with the truth, I hesitate. A false quivering smile finds its way into my repertoire. I shift in my chair. 'Sure,' I agree, with an unimpressive excess of enthusiasm.

'You see?' she says, glancing hopefully between Jim and Dee.

You've got to give her credit. She's a trier. But much as I admire her capacity for optimism, she's not doing me any favours. In fact the very opposite. It's an atmosphere of despair I'm trying to induce, not of hope. Suffering is what I'm aiming for – something deep and dark, something that *hurts*. I'm still in the process of constructing that master blow, of finding the right words to completely freak Jim's brains out, when his runt suddenly struts into the room and interrupts my train of thought.

He takes one look at my bruises and his eyes light up. 'What the fuck ...'

And I only have to hear his voice, to see his psychopathic self-satisfied smirk, to lose my cool. I'm already rising from the chair when Dee suddenly finds her voice again.

'Carl! Sit down!'

He pauses. Then, like a vicious but obedient dog, slowly does as he's told. But he's still grinning, still gloating, as he falls back on the sofa. I see Simone flinch as he lands too closely beside her. He turns to study me again. I know what's coming. He just can't resist. Slyly, he asks, 'So, what's the deal, Johnny? You run into a spot of trouble?'

And I wonder if he gives a damn about what happens to his brother. Here I am, holding all the fucking aces, and he's still acting like there's everything to play for. Demented isn't the word for it. Maybe Dee dropped him on his head when he was a baby ... and if she didn't then, shit, I'm more than happy to make up for the oversight.

He growls at me.

I snarl back, waiting for it all to kick off. But as my hand clenches slowly into a fist, Simone jumps up and grabs my glass. 'Let me get you a drink.' She stands between the two of us, creating a slight but effective barrier. While she's turned away from Carl, she stares at me, silently willing me to retreat. *Please*, her eyes say, *don't go there, don't do this*.

While I sink back down, Dee quickly shifts to sit beside her son. She lays a restraining hand on his arm. 'Come on, calm down. We're all in this together.'

Only Jim remains oblivious to what's going on. Addled by the booze, he grunts, belches and gazes into nowhere.

'Another Scotch?' Simone asks.

Carl grins. 'I see your new girlfriend's taking care of you.'

'What did you say?' She swings angrily round. And if he ever thought I was a threat, it's nothing compared to the expression in *her* eyes.

And I leap to my feet again. In truth, it has less to do with defending her honour – gentleman as I am – than having the perfect excuse to rearrange that pretty face of his.

But Dee rapidly intervenes. Now there's more than frustration in her voice, there's fear and panic too. This isn't the kind of welcome you extend to the hero who can save your firstborn. 'I'm sorry, Johnny, I'm sorry. He's drunk. He doesn't know what he's saying.' I notice she doesn't apologize to Simone. Still, I guess she's used to their charming little ways.

Dragging Carl off the sofa, Dee skilfully manhandles him out of the room. He doesn't make any attempt to resist; so far as he's concerned he's done exactly what he wanted – successfully wound me up without having to suffer the consequences.

I listen to his smug diminishing laughter, and her quiet remonstrations, as she leads him down the hall to the kitchen.

But if thinks he's got away with it, he's wrong. *Don't worry, mate, you'll get yours.*

And then there were three; well, if you can count a near-comatose tub of lard as being actually present. The only evidence of life from Jim is the monotonous lifting of his glass to his mouth.

I touch Simone lightly on the shoulder. She's still standing, rigid with anger, glaring at the space Carl recently occupied. It's hard to tell what she's more outraged about, the actual suggestion of infidelity or of that relationship being with *me*. Perhaps it's a potent combination of both.

I offer her a smile. 'It's great to be back, huh?'

In return she gives me a dismissive glance before moving neatly aside and shrugging off my hand. So much for a united front; even in the face of mutual adversity, she isn't prepared to form an alliance. Talking to the devil might be one thing, but waltzing with him is quite another. I sink back into my chair.

Perhaps Jim's got the right idea. There's a lot to be said for being soused.

The seconds tick by. We drift into an awkward silence.

Then without warning Simone shoves a freshly poured drink under my nose and sighs. She even aims for a smile, although she doesn't quite make it. 'Sorry.'

Quite what *she's* apologizing for is anyone's guess. Not that it really matters. That word has been doing the rounds tonight. *Sorry*. I've said it, Dee's said it, and now she has too. But I'm not one to look a gift horse in the mouth. If she's willing to extend a whisky-filled hand of friendship, then I'm more than happy to take it.

We may as well part on good terms.

'Cheers,' I say, lifting my glass, 'here's to the joys of family life.'

She sits down on the edge of the sofa and studies her boots before slowly raising her eyes. 'Perhaps it wasn't the smartest idea, coming back tonight. Everyone's stressed out, upset about Marc and ... Dee's right, Carl isn't thinking straight, he doesn't know what he's doing.'

'Does he ever?'

It's clearly an effort for her to make excuses for him – she loathes him as much as I do – but she feels obliged to try and paper over the cracks. The last thing she wants is for me to start thinking about disappearing again. Her lips slide into a wry upward curl. 'You know, we ought to make allowances; he has got a *very* small brain.'

I snigger into my whisky. 'Can't argue with that.'

Her mouth breaks into a proper smile. We grin at each other. Then she goes and spoils it all by leaning closer and saying, 'Johnny, you do realize how grateful we are, don't you?'

And she's got that plaintive pleading look on her face

again. Christ, I hate this guilt-trip crap. What does she imagine – that if she fastens me with those sad liquid eyes, I'll dissolve into mush and swear an undying allegiance to the cause?

'Don't mention it,' I reply, sincerely wishing that she hadn't.

'I just—'

'Please,' I interrupt. There's only one Simone whose company I appreciate and it isn't the needy version. Where's the smart-arse Ms Independence when you want her? *She's* the Simone I want to leave behind, the one who can cope, the one who won't fall to pieces, the one who understands that I don't give a fuck about anyone.

God, this has all been such a bad mistake. Another one. I seem to have got in the habit recently. I glance at Jim; his eyes are closed, his head lolling drunkenly against the back of the chair. His fleshy lips tremble as a snore rumbles out. What a pathetic bastard! Even if I could get him alone for a while, it wouldn't make a difference. He's way too pissed to appreciate the finer art of innuendo. Still, there's one consolation – if *I* can't kill him, perhaps the booze will do the job for me.

I feign a yawn, placing a hand politely over my mouth. Time to put this farce to bed. 'You know, I'm shattered. I think I'll call it a night.'

She glances at her watch. It's only ten o'clock. 'Sure.' But she hesitates as I stand up and suddenly asks, too urgently, 'When do you want to leave in the morning? I don't mind an early start. Seven, eight?'

The lie slips from my lips with effortless ease. 'Yeah, eight sounds good.' I smile and nod. 'That'll be fine.'

'Okay. Goodnight.'

'Goodnight.'

It's only as I reach the door that I make the fatal mistake of glancing back. There she is, still sitting there, but now her face has assumed an expression of abject desolation. Does she know I'm leaving? Has she guessed? No, she can't. I'm just succumbing to guilt, to self-censure, to the rebuke that might be lying in those soft reproachful eyes.

I stamp bad-temperedly up the stairs. Forget it. There's no such thing as a painless escape – or a pain-free war. It's not my fault if her stupid bloody husband has managed to get himself knee-deep in shit . . . or her brother-in-law gets his kicks out of torture . . . or that Dee's a bitch . . . or that Jim's a fucking waste-of-space grass. She chose to marry into this excuse for a family. I owe her *nothing*.

Well, nothing apart from saving my arse in Norfolk. And how am I supposed to pay that back? I slam into my room and pour another whisky. Shit, if there's one thing I hate it's being beholden. Surely I've paid my dues by bringing her home. At least I didn't desert her. But it's not enough. Even my own twisted logic tells me that.

I walk to the window and gaze down on the black expanse of garden. My hand tightens around the glass. No, what the hell am I talking about? She's a Buckley and when you add up the columns, the accumulated family credit and debit, they're still securely in the red. They owe *me*. They owe me eighteen fucking years of interest. As an accountant Simone should understand those figures. Whatever she might have done, she hasn't negated the debt – she's only knocked a few quid off the balance.

I drink the whisky and nod.

But although I feel better, I still don't feel good. There's only one way to dump these nagging doubts. Grabbing my phone, I light a cigarette and dial Melanie's number.

'Hey, where are you?' she says, as soon as she picks up. 'What's happening? Are you okay?'

'Of course.'

She laughs with relief. 'Where are you?' she asks again.

As if she can see me I shrug and smile. 'I'm fine. I'm sorry, I should have rung but it's been difficult. Everything's fine. I just—'

'Hang on a sec,' she says. I hear a door slamming, the sudden muffling of music. 'Johnny?'

'Yeah.'

'Sorry about that. I'm at work. So come on, tell me what's—'

I cut her short. 'Look, I can't really talk right now. I'll explain it all when I see you. I just wanted to make sure that *you* were okay.'

In fact all I really wanted was to hear her voice again, to be reminded of Dixie, to get my focus back. Sometimes revenge needs a little honing, something to sharpen its edges.

It's getting on for four when I creep down the stairs. As if sleep is equivalent to absence, the house has got that eerie empty feel. Every step I take sounds thunderous. The clock in the kitchen ticks too loudly. The radiators hiss. Like an inverted burglar, one trying to get out rather than in, I hold my breath and tiptoe towards the door. Do I have any regrets? Yeah, a few, but none that are going stop me from getting away as fast as I possibly can.

I put my bag down and take a final glance along the hall. It's been . . . well, I can hardly say fun but certainly an experience. And although there's still unfinished business, it can wait. There's more than one way to skin a cat.

Goodbye, Buckleys. If I had a glass I'd raise it: *Here's hoping you get everything you deserve.*

And then, just as I reach eagerly for the latch, I notice the tiny red light flashing in the box on the wall. My heart sinks. Damn, the door isn't only locked, it's alarmed too. Why didn't I think of that? The minute I try and open it, all hell's going to break loose. Welcome to the apocalypse! I cover my face with my hands. For a second I laugh – I mean, God, you've got to laugh – before a long frustrated groan escapes from my lips.

Fuck, what next?

But even as I turn, I'm already acknowledging the answer to that untimely question. There's a whisper in the air, a movement, a presence. Suddenly the hairs on the back of my neck are rising to attention. Oh God. I don't even have to look to know it.

I'm not alone.

And as soon as I see her, my heart instantly leaps – right into my mouth. If I weren't so fucking brave I'd sink to my knees. Shrouded in a white shirt, like a ghostly apparition, she's standing on the bottom step.

Simone.

Fuck.

Her voice, when she eventually speaks, is a dull monotone. 'Would you like me to tell you the code?'

Chapter Nineteen

Simone

'It's not what you think,' he says.

I try not to laugh in his face. Like there could be *any* plausible reason for him sneaking out in the dead of night.

'It isn't,' he insists. He takes a deep breath and stares at the ceiling. 'Honest.'

Ignoring him, I go to the box and punch in the number. 'There. The alarm's off. You're free to go.' I open the door and stand back. 'You're not a prisoner here, you never have been.'

But still he doesn't move.

'Oh, I'm sorry. You need some transport, don't you? What would you prefer, Jim's car or mine?' I wave towards the keys on the table. 'Help yourself.'

A cold wind sweeps inside. And I'm suddenly aware that this whole dramatic scene would be rather more impressive if Marc's shirt wasn't flapping wildly round my thighs. It's hard to look dignified when your knickers are on view.

'Actually,' he says, 'I was going to take a cab.' He reaches across and closes the door. 'Can we talk?'

'What for?'

He glances uneasily up the stairs, worried perhaps that Buckley reinforcements might be about to make an appearance. Fat chance. It would take an earthquake to rouse them from their slumbers.

'Two minutes,' he murmurs. 'Please.'

He walks towards the kitchen and I follow him. Why not? I may as well hear his feeble excuses. There's little other entertainment on offer at four o'clock on a chilly January morning. But I'm not prepared to beg. If he wants to leave, fine, I won't stand in his way. This travesty has gone on long enough.

And when it's over I'll do what I should have done last week – I'll get on the phone and dial 999.

Moonlight shimmers through the window, turning the room to monochrome. I pull out a chair and slide in behind the table. In the darkness he paces up and down, one hand in his pocket, the other raking through his hair. That sly brain of his must be ticking as forcefully as the clock: what to say, what to do.

'Two minutes,' I remind him. I don't intend to freeze to death. The heating's on low, barely warm enough to cut through the frost. Goosebumps are forming on my skin.

'Okay.' He stops and sits down in the chair opposite to mine. Then, leaning forward, he puts his forearms on the table. Edgily, he clears his throat. 'First,' he begins, 'we need to get one thing straight – I wasn't doing a runner.'

I snort in my finest ladylike manner. 'Oh, sorry. Don't tell me, you couldn't sleep so you and your bag were just off for an early morning stroll?'

As if the sarcasm is undeserved, a wound to his strong and noble heart, he gives a small pained sigh. 'I didn't say I wasn't leaving, Simone, only that I wasn't running out on you. There's a difference.'

'Yeah, between getting caught and not—'

'At least give me my two minutes,' he interrupts. 'Can't you hear me out?'

I'd like to hear him straight out of the door with a boot up his arse but it's not every day you get the chance to observe an expert liar at work. Perhaps I'll pick up some tips. Flapping a hand, I say caustically, 'Carry on. Please. The suspense is killing me.'

'So, right,' he starts again. 'I *was* going, I'm not denying it – but I was also intending to come back.' He's talking to the table but, as if suspecting an imminent interjection, quickly raises his eyes. 'Really,' he insists, 'I give you my word.' He leaves a brief pause to emphasize this honourable declaration. Then he sighs again. 'I know you wanted to come to London with me but I don't think it's smart, not with the Fosters on the loose. You're better off here. You're safe here. What if they have another go? I mean, look at me, I'm hardly in a fit state to defend myself never mind someone else.'

I smile at him. 'How considerate.'

There's a short silence.

I stare at him. He stares at me. It's like one of those childhood games: the first one to look away is a cissy.

'Okay,' he eventually snaps, 'you want the *whole* truth, the unabridged version?' Now his voice is coarser, less apologetic. He introduces another of his shameless pauses. 'I don't want you with me, love. I don't need the stress. I'd rather do this on my own. It's not just the Fosters I'm concerned about, there's Eddie's killers too, not to mention whoever's holding Marc – there are too many complications out there. You think I want to be worrying about you twenty-four seven? Believe me, I don't. I don't need that responsibility. I don't want to be looking over my shoulder a hundred times a day stressing over what might or might not happen.' He shakes his head. 'I like you, Simone, and I really don't want to see you get hurt.'

God, respect where it's due. From bastard to tainted superhero in two minutes flat. Very impressive. If I weren't so angry, I'd be tempted to applaud. Instead, I put my chin in my hands and glare at him. 'And so you decided the kindest, most worthy action was to sneak away?'

'I didn't want a row.' He tries a smile. 'Not one of my greatest moves, admittedly, but I thought if I could just do this on my own, sort it out, pick up the diamonds and get back, then . . .' He shrugs. He reaches out his hand towards mine. 'I'm sorry. It was a mistake. I should have talked to you. I should have explained.'

I pull away before he can touch me. If he imagines I'm going to swallow this wretched fairy-tale, he's got another think coming. Rage and indignation blaze on to my cheeks, the only part of me that's warm. Just how stupid does he think I am? Well, that's a question that hardly needs answering. I'm tempted to cut my losses, to kick him out right here and now, but something he said has begun to niggle.

'You told me Eddie's killers had nothing to do with this.'

Johnny frowns. 'I'm not convinced they do. But that doesn't mean they're not out there, sniffing around, waiting to find whatever scraps they can.' He picks up an empty glass and rolls it around in his fingers. 'That's the thing about villains – they're always on the lookout for the main chance.'

And don't I know it.

'It's not worth the risk,' he says.

I wish I could see him more clearly but he keeps lowering his head, hiding in the shadows. I'd like to see what blatant lying looks like but his cold grey eyes, ambiguous at best, refuse to give anything away. I've had enough. I'm too tired and cold to continue with this. 'Why don't you just go?'

As if we're lovers parting on bad terms, he says, 'Please, not like this.'

'Well, it's been fascinating but I think your two minutes are up.' I can feel the rage growing inside me. I want him out of here before I do something I'll regret.

He puts the glass carefully down on the table, sits back and pulls a face. 'So, what now? Are you going to ring the cops?'

'What do you think?'

'And how, exactly, are you going to explain about the diamonds?'

I shrug. 'That's your problem, not mine.'

'And Dee's, and Jim's.'

I stare at him, astounded. 'You really imagine they're bothered about some lousy diamonds when their son's life is on the line?'

'It's those lousy diamonds that are going to *save* his life.'

'They'll understand,' I insist.

'You think so? You think they'll be happy that you let me walk out, that you called the cops, that you made these decisions without even bothering to wake them?'

'But you're coming back,' I say snidely, 'so there's nothing to worry about, right?'

'You make that call and I *can't* come back.'

I curl my toes against the cold tiles of the floor. 'Well okay, let's wake them then. Let's have a free and frank discussion.' But I say it with more confidence than I feel. Jim isn't in a fit state to make an informed decision about what day of the week it is and Dee may well believe his story. Johnny can be very persuasive when he puts his mind to it. Ringing the police as a knee-jerk response to his doing a runner is one thing, ringing them against Dee's express wishes is quite another. But God, no, surely even *she* couldn't fall for this pile of tosh.

'As I see it,' he continues smoothly, 'you've got two choices. You either trust me or you make that call. But if you choose the cops then once it's done, it's done. There's no going back.'

He's got a bloody nerve. *Trust him?* I'd more likely jump from a plane without a parachute.

He must see the incredulity in my face because he quickly adds, 'Or there could be a compromise. Give me twenty-four hours and if I've not returned by then—'

'You can get a long way in twenty-four hours, Johnny, halfway round the world in fact.'

'Yeah, okay, but look at this from *my* point of view for a moment. What's going to happen if I do a bunk? You're going to get the cops involved, it's all going to come out about the diamonds, about the robbery, about the connection to Eddie ... and I'm going to be up to my neck in shit. You think I want to be on the run for the rest of my life, worrying when they're going to catch up with me – you think I *want* to go back inside?'

I raise my shoulders in a brief dismissive shrug. 'Oh, come on, the robbery was years ago. Unless they catch you with the diamonds, how are they ever going to prove you were involved? And you had nothing to do with killing Eddie Tate.' I hesitate for a second, that nasty suspicion still lurking in my mind. 'Did you?'

'Jesus,' he says, sounding genuinely frustrated, 'of course not. How many times ... You don't know much about the law, do you? With my kind of record they'd bang me up as soon as look at me. Just being associated with Eddie will be enough to put me in the frame; it won't take them long to put two and two together and make a very convincing five.'

There may be *some* truth in that but not enough. Johnny Frank the victim – original but not entirely convincing. 'Except that won't be so easy if you're sunning yourself on foreign shores.'

He half sighs, half laughs. 'For fuck's sake, I'm not Ronnie Biggs.'

I gaze towards the window, avoiding his eyes. I'm so cold

my teeth are starting to chatter. Clenching my jaw, I try to figure out where to go next. We seem to have reached an impasse, to be joined in a tug-of-war that neither can win. He's got the pull of the diamonds, the potential to set Marc free, and I've got the threat of calling the cops, of causing him major grief. Who's got more to lose? On first reckoning I'd say it was me – this is my husband's *life* at stake – but then, isn't it true that Johnny's future is hanging in the balance too? He's so mixed up in this mess that whatever happens he's hardly likely to walk away scot-free.

'Come on, Simone,' he urges. 'Twenty-four hours. What have you got to lose?'

That's easy to answer. 'Twenty-four hours when the police could be searching for Marc.'

It's his turn to snort. 'Yeah, right. And you really want to take that road, take that chance? You think the house isn't being watched? The minute those cop cars come rolling into the drive, no matter how disguised they are, that'll be the end of it. But go on, you do it, so long as you don't mind signing his death warrant . . .'

His words shouldn't hurt me but they do. I recoil, wrapping my arms around my chest. And so we've come full circle again, to last Thursday, to the day it all began. The situation may be different but the song remains the same: trust Johnny and take the consequences or call the police and take the consequences. Which makes me – what? Either Simone the fool or Simone the executioner.

'That's crap,' I retort, 'you don't even know if they're watching.'

He shrugs again, stands up, takes the glass to the sink and rinses it under the tap. I watch him, silhouetted against the window, the outline of a stranger. I've been alone with him for three days but as to who he is, I'm still as much in the dark as when we first met.

The splash of water drowns out an angry silence. He fills the glass, takes a mouthful, and walks back to the table. He sits down, bringing his sly smile with him. 'No, you're right, you can never know anything for sure. But it pays to look at all the angles. Never go in blind. Never make rash decisions.'

But he's wrong there. There's one thing I *can* be sure of – that he's trying his best to scare the hell out of me. The trouble is, he's succeeding. Now fear is wrapping round the cold, biting at my resolve, and every bone in my body from my toes to my skull is starting to shake. Let's be honest, he could have a point – what if I call the cops and it all goes wrong and … I want to hide, to cover my face with my hands, to think, to reason, but I can't. If I drop my guard for even a second he'll walk all over me.

'Simone?'

I glance up at him again.

'You look frozen,' he says. 'Here.' He takes off his jacket and pushes it across the table.

I should tell him where to shove it but I'm too cold to stand on whatever may be left of my dignity. I put it round my shoulders and nod but don't bother saying thank you. After all, it's his fault that I'm heading towards hypothermia.

'Why can't you trust me?' he pleads again. 'I don't want

Marc's death on my conscience.' He tries one of his wry smiles. 'Do you really think I'm that much of a bastard?'

But it's neither the time nor the place to go into that. I've two voices warring in my head: the first is shouting, 'Kick him out! Don't listen!' while the second whispers, 'What if he *is* Marc's only chance?' And I'm back in that same old circle of indecision.

He sits, waiting, tapping his knuckles softly against the table. Wisely, he keeps his mouth shut. He lets me work the odds out for myself.

If I weren't so exhausted, I might be able to concentrate. I listen to the clock: tick-tock, tick-tock. Have I any ideas at all? Perhaps I've got one. And before I can change my mind, I just come out and say it.

'Okay, let me ask you something. If our situations were reversed, if you were in my position and it was Sarah who was being held to ransom, how would you deal with it?'

His eyes narrow, the way they always do when her name is mentioned. His forehead furrows into creases. But he doesn't hesitate in his reply, not even for a moment. 'Well, for starters, I wouldn't be sitting here talking about it.'

'Exactly,' I agree, rising quickly to my feet.

Surprised, he looks up at me.

I force a smile. 'So what are we waiting for?'

Chapter Twenty

Johnny

So much for a quick escape: I knew I was fucked as soon as I clocked that flashing red light but I didn't realize how badly until I turned around and saw her. That flimsy shirt, those long legs, that whole semi-naked business didn't do much for my resolve. It's hard to stay focused when there's only a thin layer of cotton between you and your imagination. Even in the dark, in the moonlit shadows of the kitchen, I spent more time searching the outline of her curves than in listening to what she had to say.

Which is probably why I've ended up doing the exact opposite of what I intended.

We've barely talked since we left. She went upstairs to get dressed, retrieved her bag, came down and got into the car. And ever since we've been driving towards the dawn. The radio's on low, some doleful tune to match the early-morning mood.

How much of what I told her was for real? Some,

certainly. I don't want the filth on my back. I don't need that kind of grief. Of course, once I've disappeared even Dee will give in and agree to call them but I'm gambling on the fact that when this happens she'll have the sense – bearing in mind what I know about Carl – to keep my name out of it. But will she? And what about Simone? How will *she* be persuaded to keep her mouth shut?

I glance across at her. Grim-faced and determined, she's staring straight ahead at the road. All in all, as she's driving, this is probably a good thing, but I get the impression she's got as many crazy thoughts running through her mind as I have.

And I'm cursing, yet again, that I didn't clear off when I heard about Eddie. I should have let go, cut my losses and run. What was I thinking? Prison must have mashed my brains. Now, to add to all my other problems, I've developed this shitty guilt complex, this insane notion that I might *owe* her something. But I don't. I *don't*. No, I got all that sorted hours ago.

So why has it crept back inside my head again?

Because she gets under my skin. There's no denying it. She always has. From the moment we met, I knew she'd be a thorn in my flesh, a fucking pain. Everything was going fine that first day at the Buckleys' until she walked in. I only had to look across the room to see the scrutiny in her eyes, the coolness, to know that she'd be trouble.

Just like Sarah.

Jesus, what makes me keep thinking that? She's really nothing like Sarah, nothing at all. Well, superficially perhaps, same colour hair and eyes – but so have ten million other women. And yeah, I always liked sparky brunettes, but it was only ever a preference. When it came to opportunity, I never let prejudice stand in my way.

So I guess the only thing they have in common is their ability to make me feel guilty.

I get out my tobacco and start to roll a cigarette. Okay, fine, I'll make a private deal, something to salve my whimpering conscience: I'll pick up the diamonds this morning and spend the afternoon pulling in some favours. I'll ask around, look up those old faces again, and see if anyone can come up with a name, any lead, any hint as to who could be holding Marc. I'll give her a fighting chance before I leave. You can't say fairer than that.

A weird persistent squeak interrupts my train of thought. It takes a second to realize it's the sound of the wipers scraping across the windscreen. I glance up at the glass. A storm of white flakes are floating down from the sky.

It's snowing!

And I can't help smiling. I wind down the window and put out my hand. The flakes fall and melt against my fingers.

Simone gives an exaggerated shiver. 'What's the matter,' she snaps, 'you never seen snow before?'

For a second I feel almost embarrassed. What am I doing, acting like a wide-eyed kid? It was just an instinct, a step back into the past. Quickly I withdraw my hand. And then, to restore some pride, I retort softly, 'Yeah, I've seen it before – it's just been a few years since I actually touched it.'

She gets the message, and her cheeks go that satisfying shade of pink. What's she thinking about – my eighteen years, my eighteen years of fucking nothing? I hope so but I doubt it. My world's a thousand miles away from hers.

Before she's fully recovered her self-possession I go back on the attack and ask, 'So, when you called the cops, what exactly were you going to tell them?'

She frowns. 'The truth, of course. What else?'

'Well, it would have been a bit awkward trying to explain away the ransom note without landing Jim and Dee right in it. There'd be some probing questions about those diamonds. It wouldn't have looked too good for them.'

A tiny growl emerges from the back of her throat. 'You mean, it wouldn't have looked too good for *you*. They didn't have anything to do with the actual robbery.'

This is the opening I've been waiting for. 'Ah,' I say softly, producing a nicely timed wince.

I can feel her eyes on me, a series of quick assessing glances. Then she barks out a laugh. 'Oh come on, you can't expect me to believe that!'

'I'm not saying he was actually on the job – God, Jim couldn't nick his own socks – but these things take planning, information, investment. You don't just roll along in a van one night and help yourself.'

Still she's insistent. 'No way!'

'Okay.' I shrug, watching the whitening road for a few seconds. Then I deliver the master blow. 'So if he wasn't involved what do you think I gave him five grand for – two weeks' bed and breakfast?'

That clearly rattles her. I can hear the sharp intake of her breath.

'Because I owed him,' I continue calmly. 'I didn't like him, I never have, but I'm not the type of man who forgets to pay his debts.'

'Or because he was going to help you,' she argues, but the confidence is drifting from her voice. 'He was going to help you get the diamonds back.'

'And why on earth would I pick a stupid bloody drunk to do that?' I shake my head. 'No, I didn't *choose* Jim, I *owed* him. There's a difference. He came to see me a few weeks before I got out and – how does it go? – he made me an offer I couldn't refuse. He's been waiting eighteen years to get his share. I'd have done the same thing in his shoes.'

Even if I say so myself this whole story, virtually off the cuff, is inspired, a pure stroke of genius. She's been searching for an explanation as to why I ever went to stay with the Buckleys – that whole loyalty shit never quite rang true – and I've just come up with a top-grade Class A reason. Now, when she calls the cops, she's going to have to think twice about how much she tells them. If she drags me into it, she'll be running the risk of exposing Jim too.

But Simone's no pushover. After pondering this news for a street and a half, she asks, 'So you're claiming that Jim came to the prison and threatened you.'

Now put like that it clearly sounds ridiculous. So I counter the statement with an amused semi-laugh. 'Threatened me? Of course not. He's hardly Mr Mafia. No, let's just say that he reminded me of where my obligations lay. And offered me a fair and reasonable deal. It didn't seem too bad a proposition: I got somewhere to stay, a few home comforts, a chance to get my head together – and he got to keep an eye on his investment. Not ideal, maybe, but an acceptable compromise.'

The snow's coming down harder now, blanketing the pavement and the bonnets of cars. Does she believe me? I know she doesn't want to but it all adds up in the way that wrong things often do. And it helps that Jim and Dee have already lied to her – she can no more trust them than she can me.

'I still don't get it,' she says, annoyingly.

I try not to sigh. 'What don't you get?'

She purses her lips. 'I don't *get* why Jim was ever involved in the first place. I mean with the job or with you. You've already told me that you and Dee had ...' She hesitates, maybe looking for a respectable description. 'Had a relationship, so why would he even consider—'

'Because he didn't know,' I interrupt, attempting a slightly shame-faced expression, 'not then and not now. Oh, he knew there'd been someone, he knew she'd been playing around, and I may well have been one of his major suspects, but he was never *sure*.'

She throws me a look of undisguised contempt.

I take it on the chin. 'Hey, I'm not proud of it. It was just something that happened. We've all done things we regret.'

She gives me another filthy glance. Shit, I hope they haven't had one of those heart-to-hearts that women love to indulge in, one of those drunken, intimate, sharing caring sessions where Dee told her everything.

But it would appear not. Unless she's the actress of the century, Simone appears genuinely bemused. Her teeth are biting down, chewing on her lower lip. I try to objectively assess the evidence she has, to put myself in her position, and yeah, the 'facts' I've given her add up. It all makes a distorted kind of sense.

Well, apart from one obvious anomaly. And she picks up on that. 'But Jim wasn't like you. He was never a . . .'

I stare at her. Thief, robber and gangster are probably the words she's trying to avoid. Perhaps she thinks I'll take offence. And quite right too. I like to think I approached my career with a certain degree of professionalism. I was a villain, yes, but never some sordid piece of low-life.

She swallows hard and draws another breath. 'I know he's no angel but he doesn't go looking for trouble.'

'No,' I agree, 'but he was always up for business – Jim knew a good deal when he saw it.' I smile. 'We can all be tempted, love. Just look at Marc.'

There's not much she can say to that.

She takes a fast right-hand turn, cutting across the oncoming traffic with the minimum of care. The tyres slide a little on the ice. 'So you're saying Jim was owed?'

I nod encouragingly. She finally seems to be getting the gist.

'Okay.' She pauses. 'So does that mean that Eddie Tate was owed as well?'

Fuck, I didn't see that one coming. Still, at least I don't need to lie. 'No, Eddie wasn't owed anything. He was paid fair and square on the night of the job.'

'But Jim wasn't?'

'Obviously.'

'Why not?'

'Because . . . because it was complicated.'

She gives me one of her sneering smiles. 'I can do complicated,' she says. 'Try me.'

'It's better that you don't know.'

'What I don't know can't hurt me, right?'

'No,' I reply swiftly, 'what you don't know can't hurt *me*.'

Which shuts her up for a moment.

But not for long enough. She's off again a few seconds later. 'So, let's get this clear. Without going into incriminating detail, Eddie was paid but he still thought he was owed – why exactly was that?'

Christ, it's like facing the Gestapo.

I could refuse to answer but that would just mean prolonging the interrogation. She isn't going to give up in a hurry. 'Because he was a greedy little bastard.'

As if bad-mouthing the dead offends her, she flinches.

'Just like Foster,' I add bitterly.

Simone quickly turns. 'Roy Foster was on the job too?'

There's shock in her voice, and alarm. I presumed she was already aware of that although, come to think of it, there's no reason why she should be. Perhaps I imagined that Dee had told her or that she'd simply put the pieces together.

I should have kept my stupid mouth shut.

Now she's gone ominously quiet. And I suddenly understand where her logic is taking her: three thieves on a major diamond heist and now two of them are dead. Which leaves me, the sole survivor, as convenient heir to a fortune. I can see how it's all adding up: first I kill Foster, then Eddie, then ...

God, if it wasn't so mad it might almost be funny. And if she knew there was a fourth, if she knew about Dixie, she'd really be crapping herself!

'What's the matter?' I ask as if I haven't got a clue what's going through her mind.

She shakes her head, trying not to frown.

And I know it's bad, bloody sick, but I can't resist the temptation of playing on her fears. Most of it's down to indignation – she's already got me pegged as some fucking self-serving serial killer – and the rest is just an excuse to regain some control. I've been on the back foot ever since she caught me creeping out of the house.

I take a long slow drag of my cigarette. 'Some people just push their luck too far.'

I watch her hands tighten round the wheel. She doesn't reply. Of course she doesn't. She's too busy wondering what the hell to do next. It's no great shakes being trapped in a car with a possible psychopath.

I avert my face to grin furtively out of the window.

But then, as she puts her foot down and rapidly picks up speed, I can't help acknowledging that it's no great shakes either to be trapped in a car with a woman who *thinks* she's with a psychopath. I can almost smell her dread. Her mouth twists and falls. And maybe I've pushed her too far because we're definitely going quicker than we should. It's early morning but that isn't to say the roads are empty. Far from it.

She's suddenly swinging in and out, indicating late, if at all, skidding round corners and driving like a nutter. And as the road flashes by, faster and faster, there seems every chance that we'll end up wrapped securely round a lamp post.

I try not to look scared. I mean, shit, I'm a man, not some bloody girl. So I hang on to the side of my seat and grit my teeth. I'm not even sure where we are – an anonymous back street with nothing to recommend it, just two rows of neglected shabby houses with flaking paint and mean front gardens. A sad and ignominious place to die. Before my life dissolves in a flurry of snow and squealing brakes, I reach out to try to repair the damage.

I touch her on the arm and force a laugh. 'Hey, come on, you know me better than that.'

She slows but only a fraction.

And for the second time today, I find myself almost begging. 'Simone? Come on, you've got it wrong. I can explain.'

Now she's finally communing with the brakes, thank God. We're slowing, and turning left on to the forecourt of an overpriced twenty-four-hour chain restaurant. She pulls in by the entrance.

'Okay,' she says, glaring at me, 'you want to explain, you can do it over breakfast.'

'Sure,' I agree, mentally counting the notes that are left in my wallet.

She gets out, slamming the door behind her.

That's the trouble with women like Simone – they never come cheap.

*

She smiles sweetly at the waitress, ordering scrambled eggs, toast and coffee for two, before turning to scowl at me again. 'So?'

So where to start? It would help if I wasn't so goddamn tired, if I'd managed even a few hours' sleep last night. I started this stupid game but I'm too exhausted to play it out. Now I just want to put things back on an even keel.

Through habit, I glance around, seeing if anyone's close enough to hear. Considering it's barely dawn, this place is busy, a yawning mass of salesmen and early-morning travellers, but apart from the scrape of knives against plates and the thin rustle of newspapers, there's not much else to break the silence. I lean forward and lower my voice.

'Look, I know what you're thinking but why would I do anything to Eddie? Shit, I've just spent half my life inside. You think I want to go back? I didn't even want to talk to him, never mind ...'

She raises her brows and stares at me.

'I *didn't* kill him.'

'So what did you mean when you—'

I lift my hand in a dismissive flap. 'It was just a comment. I wasn't suggesting that *I'd* done it, just that he probably stepped on someone's toes, pushed them too far. He was like that – sly, greedy, always on the lookout for the main chance.'

Do I feel bad about rubbishing Eddie when I know what actually happened? Not really. None of what I'm saying is a lie. Although he didn't deserve to die the way he did. And I do feel uncomfortable, even faintly guilty, about keeping her in the dark over Carl. She'll be going back to that house, living with him, seeing him every day . . .

She says very softly, 'But you *did* kill Roy Foster.' Pausing, she takes a breath. 'Was that something to do with the diamonds? Is that why you argued with him?'

As if the suggestion is preposterous, I shake my head and laugh. 'God no, it wasn't anything to do with that.'

And thankfully, as I haven't yet thought of what exactly it might have been to do with, the waitress arrives with our breakfast. She's a skinny kid with long brown hair, pretty in an angular sort of way. Dumping the tray on the table, she gives us both a glance before she starts to unload it: plates, cups and saucers, cutlery. A few seconds later her gaze flickers back, lingering on my face for a good while longer than is conventionally polite. It could be my stunning good looks but I suspect it's more connected to my ugly if glorious array of bruises.

'Thank you,' I say, smiling broadly.

She turns away, saving the full force of *her* smile for Simone. I try not to take it to heart.

There's a silence after she leaves. We both stare down at our plates. Then, although I'm not especially hungry, I pick up my knife and fork and start to eat. For the next five minutes, as I plough through my overcooked scrambled eggs and toast, chewing with exaggerated enthusiasm, I'm temporarily free from uncomfortable questions.

It's only when I finish that the danger levels start to rise again. It would help if I could have a cigarette but we're stuck in another of those no-smoking joints. There are big red signs all over the walls. Since I've been away the world has apparently turned into a tyrannical health zone.

As she reaches for her cup, I watch her lips open. And she's not just planning on drinking her coffee. She's about to start again, to pick up the threads, to launch yet another attack on my dubious integrity.

Time to get in there quick.

'Whatever you want to know,' I say smoothly, 'just ask.'

She gives me one of her interrogative glares.

'Anything,' I insist.

She takes a sip of her coffee and then lays the cup back on its saucer without even a tremble. And there's something about that steady movement that sets my nerves on edge. She should be worried, more worried than I am – but she isn't. She's aware that I'm on the defensive.

'Anything?' she repeats.

I nod, trying to look blasé.

'Okay.' She pauses again, pushing her plate aside. 'So who knows about the robbery, about the diamonds?'

'I can't tell you that.'

As if I'm being deliberately obstructive, she leans forward, folds her arms and sighs.

I lean forward too and meet her face to face. 'I don't mean I won't, I mean I *can't*. I've got no idea who Eddie may have talked to – and even if he didn't, if he kept it buttoned, there are still plenty of others who could have taken an educated guess.'

'Not to mention all the people you've been meeting recently.'

Now probably isn't the time to tell her that all my 'meetings', bar one, have had nothing to do with the ice. So I just shrug. 'Those guys are safe.'

It's clear that she isn't convinced but she lets it go. Instead she asks, 'So how much exactly are these pink diamonds worth?'

'Hard to say.' My shoulders lift into a shrug again. 'A lot. Although they obviously can't be sold on the open market.'

'Obviously,' she repeats, drily.

Hoping to forestall any more awkward questions, I flick out my wrist and stare with deliberation at my watch. 'We should be getting off.'

Although where the hell we can go at this ungodly hour is anyone's guess.

In the end we head out towards West India Docks. I'm thinking of Billingsgate Fish Market, not the most romantic location in the world but then we're hardly on a date. At least she can cruise the cod and haddock while I make small talk with strangers and pretend to be busy. It'll kill some time until I meet Patrick.

A silvery dawn has broken over the City. The snow's still falling, a swirling haze of white that's begun to settle, giving an almost luminous quality to the streets. Simone has put her cross-examination on hold. The traffic's beginning to build and she's staring straight ahead with that fixed expression; it might be concentration or, more likely, she's quietly gathering ammunition for a later round of questions.

We pass through East Smithfield and Limehouse. Have

they changed? Perhaps, but it's hard to tell how much. I'm gazing through the windscreen, between the swishing wipers, trying to spot familiar landmarks. In the end it's an unfamiliar one that grabs my attention.

She clocks me peering up. 'Canary Wharf Tower,' she reveals like a tourist guide. 'What do you think?'

I think it's pig-ugly – but impressive too, at least in the way that anything's impressive when it towers above everything else. I search for the perfect critical response. 'Well, it's certainly ... *big*.'

It seems to take a moment for the full impact of my words to sink in. 'Big?' she eventually repeats, incredulously.

I widen my eyes in an imitation of hers. 'Hey, whatever you've heard, love – size *does* matter.'

I hear the sharp exasperated intake of her breath. She glares at me, then turns her attention back to the road.

Grinning, I stare up towards the building again. It's got a flashing light on top. And just as I'm thinking of how flashing lights are haunting me this morning, I suddenly realize – shit – that it's Monday, *bloody* Monday. And unless things have changed since I was last here, the market's only open from Tuesday to Saturday. I'm going to look pretty stupid when we roll up at the gates and find them firmly locked.

Time for a quick change of plan. Digging in my pocket, I get out my phone and pretend to check the messages. Melanie taught me the rudimentary details: how to ring out, take a call, how to send text messages and receive them; other than that, the menu's a complete mystery. I scroll through it, ignoring the bleeps, pretending to know what I'm doing. 'Jesus,' I mutter, shaking my head.

'What?' she asks.

I give a long groan. 'I'm sorry, we've got to turn around.'

It takes over an hour to get to Camden. The roads are blocked, the commuter traffic crawling slowly through the snow and ice. And, to top it all, there's a nasty one-way system guaranteed to fray the most patient of tempers. We're going round in circles, on our third lap, when she asks: 'Do you know anywhere we can park?' Almost instantly she frowns. Of course I bloody don't; the only route I've been negotiating for the past eighteen years has been from my cell to the fucking landing.

Twisting round the backstreets, she eventually finds a space near a pub. She pulls up, parks and turns the engine off. I look at my watch again. It feels like we've been travelling for ever but there's still half an hour to go before I meet Patrick.

'So where next?' Simone asks, releasing her seatbelt.

I gaze out at the snow. 'From here we walk,' I reply, 'unless you'd rather not. You can stay here if you want. We can always meet up later.'

Not surprisingly she pulls a face, flounces out of the car and slams the door. Then stands outside, shivering, while I deliberately delay getting out. I carefully fasten the buttons on my coat and wrap a scarf around my neck, and glance out of the window. Shifting from foot to foot, she's doing the dance of the truly freezing. If I had an ounce of decency,

I'd move a little faster, hurry things up – but I haven't and I don't. We might not be at war but we're not allies either.

A few minutes later we're walking side by side in silence.

Dodging the traffic, we finally cross the road and pass through Gloucester Gate into Regent's Park. If we'd arrived a bit later we could have had a meander round the zoo – seen the spiders and snakes – but I doubt, at this early hour, if the inmates have even raised their heads.

We pass an empty kiddies' playground and then turn left along the Broad Walk. To our right the grass, already carpeted in white, stretches into the distance. If we stroll slowly enough the cafe may be open by the time we reach it. I stop for a moment, gazing aimlessly towards the horizon, but Simone, unsurprisingly, shows no inclination to loiter. Her breath comes in short steamy bursts as she stamps her feet impatiently against the ground.

However, she has the good grace not to chivvy me along. Or perhaps she doesn't dare. Maybe she's worried that, like an escapee from the cages behind us, I might suddenly take fright and bolt. It's a reasonable analogy. I suspect she often thinks of me as more animal than human, as something base and uncivilized, a creature without morals.

I lift my head and audibly sniff the air.

Simone glances over. 'Any danger lurking?' she asks drily.

I don't answer straight away. Instead I gaze beyond her, peering intently between the trees, until she gradually becomes uncomfortable and, tracing my line of vision, begins to stare too.

'What is it?'

I shrug. 'Nothing.' And in fact there is nothing – I've made damn sure that we're not being followed – but I say it in that careless, over-reassuring tone, as if I could simply be trying to protect her.

'What is it?' she asks again. Now her voice has dropped, slipping almost into a whisper. She hunkers down, her chin sinking into her collar. 'Johnny?' A slight shiver makes her shoulders tremble.

I pause for a few seconds more and then grin. 'You know, I could have sworn I saw a squirrel.'

She instantly pulls herself up straight and glares, a full hard-on Simone special. 'I suppose you think that's funny,' she snaps, and without waiting for a reply, she turns her back and waltzes off.

'C'mon,' I say, after I've run a few paces to catch up, 'lighten up. Don't be so touchy. Things are bad enough without us falling out.'

She sighs.

I'm sure I'm about to get the 'You think this is all one big joke' lecture, and gird my loins accordingly. But in the event she saves her breath and gives me the silent treatment until we swing right on to Chester Road. Unable to resist any longer, she finally says, 'You ever heard of the boy who cried wolf?'

I turn to grin at her again. 'Yeah, but there's always two sides to every story. I mean, it can't have been much fun for him, stuck alone on that hillside, day in, day out, with only a flock of bleating sheep for company. Isolation can do terrible things to the human psyche. You know, he might just have been lonely, searching for a little attention.'

As if the idea of giving *me* any attention is complete anathema, she lowers her eyes to the ground.

Eventually, I laugh. 'You're right. I spent *way* too long with those psychiatrists.'

We pass into the more formal area of the park, the gardens that during summer are always filled with roses. The snow is still falling. She walks beside me, not too close, not too far, a resolute if reluctant escort.

It's a relief to see that the lights in the cafe are on. I step up the pace, hoping the doors are open too. They are. A few people are queuing for drinks but there's no sign of Patrick. I look at my watch – there's still ten minutes before we're due to meet.

'You go on in,' she says. 'I'll follow you.'

This time she doesn't stick to my heels but wanders off round the gardens. Either she's finally starting to trust me or she just can't stand another second of my company.

I buy a pot of coffee and choose a table away from the window and the other customers. It's warm inside, too warm, and as I sit and wait I get that weird creeping sensation again: agoraphobia, claustrophobia, some fucking phobia anyway, something that fills my mouth with cotton wool and makes my heart race. My body's starting to sweat, to run hot and cold; I can feel the perspiration pricking my temples.

Just as I'm thinking of going in search of fresh air, Patrick's hand descends on my shoulder making me start.

'Jumpy,' he laughs, settling into the chair opposite. But his smile quickly fades as he sees the bruises on my face. 'What the . . . ?'

'It's nothing.'

'Don't give me that shit.' He stares at me with those rheumy blue eyes, weaker than they used to be but still as penetrating. 'What's going on?'

I shake my head.

'You're in trouble,' he says.

'No. No, I'm not,' I insist. 'It's over, finished. Just a little welcome-home present.'

Patrick's in his seventies, maybe even pushing eighty now, but his brain's still revving on full power. He doesn't hesitate. 'Christ,' he murmurs, 'the Fosters?'

I don't confirm or deny it but instead lift up the pot. 'Here, have some coffee before it goes cold.'

'You should have stayed with me when you came out. You're always welcome. You know that.'

But we both also know that it wouldn't have made a difference. They would have tracked me down eventually. Best it's over and done with. And anyway, apart from the fact I had plans of my own, I couldn't have stood it in that house. Surrounded by pictures of Sarah, her eyes following me from room to room, there'd have only been grief and regret.

In the past ten years I've come to terms – as much as I can. But I only have to look at Patrick to see the enduring pain in every crease and line of his face. It fucks me up. He lost a daughter and I lost a wife. Well, *ex*-wife if we're going to be pedantic, although the ink was barely dry on the papers when she ...

As if listening to my thoughts, he frowns. 'You have to forget it all, Johnny, get on with your life.'

'Move on,' I say, with audible bitterness.

His eyes rise solemnly to meet mine. He knows me too well, can read me like a book. 'No, it isn't that easy. I'm not saying ... ' He hesitates, his gnarled fingers drumming a silent beat against the side of his cup. 'But do you really think Sarah would have wanted you to—'

'Of course not,' I agree too quickly, abruptly terminating whatever platitude he's about to deliver next. Shit, I don't want to get into this conversation. I understand that he means well, that he likes to talk about her, that it maybe even brings him comfort just to speak her name – but I can't bear to hear it. *Sarah, Sarah.* Those two syllables are already doing a waltz around my head.

He takes a brief sip of his coffee and winces. I'm not sure if it's the temperature, the taste, or my apparent lack of sympathy that makes the corners of his mouth curl down. Whatever the cause, I feel instantly remorseful. It's consideration and respect he deserves, not dismissal.

He puts his cup down with a clatter.

I think, for a moment, that he's making a point. And who can blame him? I was far from the perfect son-in-law – and an even worse husband: a villain, a cheat, a man who ineptly managed to get himself locked up for eighteen fucking years. The last thing I expect is a round of applause.

But as I stare at his hands, I realize the tremor isn't due to anger or blame but to something that he can't control. The years have taken their toll. I didn't notice it when we met a few days ago but then I was so self-absorbed, so intent on playing out the game, I wouldn't have noticed if the Angel

Gabriel had spread his wings and popped down to grab a cappuccino. All I wanted was to make the arrangements to get my diamonds back.

'Sorry, Patrick, I didn't . . .'

He sees me looking and with a wave of his hand flaps my words away, along with their implicit pity. Reaching into his jacket, he pulls out a small black pouch and slips it across the table. 'She kept them safe for you.'

Although this isn't strictly true – *he's* the one who has kept them hidden for the past decade – I don't argue the point. 'I know. I appreciate it. And look, thanks for getting that cash to the Buckleys too.' In one easy practised motion, I slide my palm over the package, draw it back and drop it discreetly into my pocket. 'Thanks.'

Sternly he says, 'There's something you can do in return – if it isn't too much trouble.'

I lift an eyebrow, wondering what's coming next.

Leaning forward a fraction, he lays his hand briefly over mine. 'It's a lot to ask, I know, but . . .' He pauses and gradually his mouth breaks into a smile. 'Try not to fuck up the rest of your life.'

Relieved, I smile back. I'm about to laugh, to reply, when he pushes out his chair and rises to his feet. I try to stop him. 'Hey, you're not going, are you? Come on, you've only just arrived. Stay and finish your coffee.' And I'm not just asking out of courtesy, out of affection, but out of something far more desperate. I'm developing an irrational fear that this is the end, that I might never see him again.

He shakes his head. 'Things to do. We'll keep in touch.'

Anxiously, I stare up at him. It's not as though I can afford to lose one of my few remaining allies. Of all the people I've cared for, and it's hardly an extensive list, Patrick has always figured large. Was his last comment sincere or was it just one of those empty phrases that we all occasionally fall back on? I'm worried that he feels he's discharged his duty, that there's nothing left to link us any more. If that's the case then ...

Except there always will be a connection. Sarah. And perhaps I was wrong earlier, perhaps I do want to talk about her, perhaps I do need to say: Hold on, let's talk, let's talk about *her*.

But I can't. I can't go there.

Patrick hovers, looking down. 'One last thing,' he says, as he prepares to leave. He leans in and lowers his voice. 'I take it you know that girl in the corner?'

Surprised, I glance quickly over my shoulder. Simone's sitting with her face in her coffee, trying to appear unobtrusive. As our eyes meet, she abruptly looks away – fast, but not fast enough; she hasn't quite mastered the art of surveillance.

'Yes,' I reluctantly admit, 'but she's not ... She's just a friend. She's not ...'

Damn, I don't want him to think that I've taken up with some other woman, that I've been crass enough to bring her here, that I've forgotten Sarah.

But Patrick just bows his head and laughs. 'Shame,' he murmurs, 'I was kind of hoping she was looking at *me*.'

Chapter Twenty-One

Simone

The tall white-haired guy didn't stay for long. He detoured past my table as he left, murmuring, 'Good morning' with a wink. So much for being undercover; perhaps I need to work on my technique.

Now I'm not sure whether I should stay here or go over to join Johnny. Probably best to stay put, to let him make the first move. I sip my coffee and wait. I light a cigarette and wait. The minutes crawl by but still he doesn't turn. Sitting forward with his chin in his hands, he's either gazing through the window or into empty space. Unable to view his face, I can't read his expression but almost certainly know what it is; I don't need to see those hard grey eyes to feel their coldness. I stare at his back. His shoulders are stiff and hunched, the posture of a less than joyous man.

It doesn't bode well.

It bodes even worse when he finally gets up. Barely sparing a glance, he jerks his head with a cursory nod in the direction of the door. I feel like a dog being summoned by its master. Angry as this makes me, I have the sense, for once, to glue my lips together. I've seen him in this kind of mood before.

While he strides silently and purposefully forward, I trot obediently at his heel. We're going away from the car but I don't mention it. Taking deep calming breaths I try to hold on to my temper. Patience is what is called for here, not to mention tolerance. Whatever the temptation, I have to bite my tongue, to look at the bigger picture. Johnny's clearly upset – it doesn't take a genius to work that one out – but the worst thing I could do is to open my big mouth.

After a bit he leaves the path and heads towards the banks of the lake. Following dutifully in his wake, I remain docility personified, the perfect pet. I can only hope he doesn't throw a stick and expect me to retrieve it.

When we reach the edge, I stand beside him and wait. I'm getting used to waiting. He's staring out across the water. It's quiet here. People have more sense than to hang around in the freezing cold. I look at Johnny. He doesn't look back. So I raise my eyes and gaze up at the heavens instead. The sky, close as a ceiling, is a sheer metallic grey. The snow has almost stopped, just a few faint flakes drifting down, but the air is still stinging. Shivering, I drop my head and bury my chin back into my scarf.

'What's the time?' he asks abruptly.

He's got a watch of his own but as it's clearly too much effort for him to take his hands out of his pockets, I glance down at my wrist. 'Ten past ten.'

He nods, grunts, and then instantly forgets my existence. Returning his attention to the lake, he frowns. For the next ten minutes he's silent again, motionless, his blank eyes narrowing to some distant horizon. He doesn't speak but his anger, his frustration, whatever it is that's tormenting him, almost physically spills out around us.

It's at moments like this that I'm truly scared. I've hardly come to terms with his presence, never mind the complexities of his character – and there's some serious grief there, not just anger but real vitriol, bitterness, a vicious resentment that I can't begin to understand.

Who the hell is Johnny Frank?

I don't get any clues from looking at his profile, at least no more than I've already garnered. All I know for certain is that something's eating at his soul. It's partly the obvious – prison, Sarah, the years he has lost and can never get back – but I'm sure there's a missing piece, a frightening piece, a part of the equation that he's keeping firmly hidden.

I stand by the lake and shiver. I'm in the middle of Regent's Park, in daylight, in a public place that should feel safe. But it doesn't. I don't. I'm scared of being with him. And I'm terrified of *not* being with him, of what might happen if he takes off, if he leaves me again. He's done it once before – almost twice, if you count this morning.

I should have let him go. God, that would have been so much easier. I should have stayed in the warm cocoon of the flat. I should never have walked down those stairs and confronted him. He'd have found a way out eventually, through one of the windows perhaps. And by now the fear, the agony, the responsibility, would be shared with Dee and Jim ... and the police.

I close my eyes.

The Canada geese gather squawking at our feet and I begin to feel vaguely normal again. A man with a briefcase strides smartly along the path behind us, followed by another, and then by a couple walking a spaniel. Gradually Johnny seems to relax and as if nothing has happened he turns to look at me.

'We should make a move,' he insists brusquely, as if *I'm* the one who's been palely loitering.

We stroll back through the gate, past the cafe, and through the gardens.

Although his mood has lifted he's still frowning.

'Problem?' I ask softly.

'Nothing you need worry about.'

Which makes me bristle again. I don't like being treated like a child. 'You know, it's been my experience that the moment someone tells you not to worry is precisely the time that you *should*.'

As if my comment doesn't warrant even the briefest of replies, he shrugs.

We turn left on to the Broad Walk and I can't stop thinking about the man in the cafe. I recognized him, of course, from our last excursion into London and the question escapes from my lips before I can prevent it. 'Who is he, the man you just met?'

'Nobody.'

'Everybody's somebody,' I reply. 'He must have a name at least.'

Johnny's upper lip curls. He doesn't want to tell. He doesn't want to talk. He wants me to stop pestering him, to shut up and leave him alone. But why should I? He's not the only one with troubles. Marc's out there somewhere, alone, afraid, relying on me to get him out of this horrific mess. I haven't got time to tiptoe round Johnny's finer feelings.

As if he can outwalk my questions he's moving faster now, tramping through the snow. Every few steps I have to run a little to catch up with him. 'Who is he?' I ask again. 'Does he have the diamonds? Is he getting them for you?'

Suddenly Johnny stops dead and whirls around to glare at me. His eyes fix on mine angrily. 'Okay,' he spits out, 'if you have to know, if it's *that* important to you, his name's Patrick, Patrick Croft – and no, he doesn't have anything to do with the diamonds.' He pauses briefly. 'He's Sarah's father. He's my dead wife's father.'

'Oh,' I reply, quickly lowering my gaze. There are some questions you always regret asking and this is one of them. I try to think of something adequate to say. The word emerges as a whisper. 'Sorry.'

He turns away, resuming his military march towards the gate.

The next few hours are an almost identical re-run of our first London trip. Trudging from street to street, sitting in smoky cafes and noisy pubs, I keep my distance as he huddles in corners with his dubious mates. To no avail, I try to read their lips as they talk. With me, Johnny has remained distinctly taciturn but in the company of others his mouth doesn't stop moving. Each man he meets I study discreetly – could this be the one with the diamonds, the one who has what Johnny wants? I watch their hands, waiting for the tiniest of movements. How big or small will the package be? I've got no idea.

By half past three I'm growing tired and hungry. And I'm getting suspicious too. It isn't possible that *all* these people, or even most of them, are connected to the diamonds – so what is he actually discussing? An escape route perhaps – a plane or train, a private boat moored in some isolated spot. Is he making arrangements for a new passport, a new identity? Or is that just the stuff of make-believe?

It's getting dark, the leaden sky descending like a lid on a box, when I wearily follow him out of one pub and we cross the road towards another. By the door I hang back, unwilling to spend yet another fifteen minutes pretending to read a newspaper that I've already scoured from cover to cover. What's the point of me following him around? I've learned precisely zero. And it's not as though my presence will prevent him clearing off. He could take to his heels right now and lose me in a minute.

'How much longer?' I ask.

The thin unfriendly smile appears again. He's clearly been saving it for me. 'Twenty minutes.' He shrugs. 'Half an hour.'

My heart sinks. I've drunk enough orange juice to drown everything but my sorrows. I stare at the grimy uninviting windows. From inside the sounds of a jukebox vie with the even more raucous boom of a crowd of drunken men. No, I can't bear the thought of sitting on my own in yet another seedy pub whilst fending off the advances of every half-cut male who thinks a woman on her own must be desperate for his company.

Glancing along the street, I see the bright lights of an internet cafe. Now that could be useful. Nodding towards the building, I say, 'Look, I'll leave you to it. I'm going to get a coffee.'

Johnny looks bemused, as if *I'm* the one who might be planning an escape. Before he can speak I raise my hand and walk away. 'See you later.'

I stride along the pavement and swing through the entrance into a warm and bustling room. Why I should feel safe here, I've no idea – but I do. There's something comforting about the place. It might be the pervasive scent of coffee, of hot chocolate, or the gentle click, click, click of agile fingers on keyboards. There's activity without too much noise, a feeling of communication, a sense of things being quietly and efficiently achieved.

I buy a latte and thirty minutes of computer time. I sit down, sip my drink and stare blankly at the screen. Then slowly, in the enquiry box of the search engine, I type in two words: *pink diamonds*.

The results appear in a matter of seconds. I click on a site that seems promising and start to read. As I scan down the page, the word that appears most frequently is *rarity*. Pink diamonds, especially the larger ones, are apparently scarce. What appears to be important is cut, carat, clarity and colour. And according to the experts, their extreme scarcity means that they are highly valued. Nothing too surprising there until my eyes fall on the prices. Jesus! The best specimens have been sold for over six million dollars at auction. What? Still peering at the screen, I slide slowly down in my seat. Even if Johnny's aren't the best, even if they're far from the best, they must still be worth a fortune. No wonder he's reluctant to give them up. And no wonder there's someone out there prepared to kill ...

I try to focus, to concentrate on the information, on the 'free passage of light', the purity, the brilliance, the lack of inclusions, but it all just swims in front of me. Of course I always knew that good diamonds were very valuable, but these numbers, these millions of dollars, are beyond my comprehension.

I take a deep breath, shut my eyes and open them again. Going back to the search engine, I type in *diamond robberies* and wait. Just as I'm scrolling through the most famous – Amsterdam 2005, Antwerp 2003, the Millennium Dome 2000, Cannes 1994 – Johnny walks through the door. Damn! Still years adrift from the date I'm looking for, I quickly close the window. So much for half an hour, he's barely been ten minutes.

He walks swiftly through the banks of computers and nods towards the screen. 'Anything interesting?'

'I was just checking my e-mail.'

He smiles. 'Any news?'

I smile back. 'Nothing much. How about you?'

He shakes his head. Our smiles are false. We're both

avoiding the truth, prevaricating. He's playing his game and I'm playing mine. The rules, if they exist, are utterly obscure. I've given him opportunities to walk away but he just keeps coming back. Why? If those diamonds are as valuable as I think they are, he isn't going to exchange them for Marc.

'So how does it work?' he asks. He leans over my shoulder to stare intently at the screen. He's close, too close. I can smell the damp wool of his coat and the very faint scent of aftershave. Funny how I didn't notice the latter in the car – but then I wasn't this near to him. It makes me uncomfortable. I want to shift away but that would look too obvious.

He frowns at the information in front of him. 'What do you have to do?'

I forget sometimes that he's been adrift for eighteen years.

'What do you want to know?' I point to the empty box of the search engine. 'All you have to do is type in what you're looking for, click on the button, and the computer will – well, should – come up with suitable matches.'

My fingers hover on the keys while Johnny continues to frown. He does this so often that even when he stops the lines persist as shallow indentations. Probably the sites he'd like to see, the type he's undoubtedly heard about, are not the kind he'd want to view in my company. Perhaps I should type in *sex* and give him a thrill ... on the other hand, best not. He might keel over with excitement.

Tired of waiting, I say, 'Look, I'll show you.' I enter *Canary Wharf* and a few seconds later, the first ten of thousands of hits appear on the screen. 'Then you can click on any of these headlines and go directly into the site.'

'What about people, names?' he asks.

I point the mouse back towards the search engine. 'It depends. Who do you want?'

He hesitates.

'Why don't you sit down and have a go,' I say, glad of the opportunity to move.

But as if the computer might bite, he puts his hand briefly on my shoulder to stop me getting up, and shifts back a fraction. 'Ted Ainsworth,' he announces, spelling out the surname.

It doesn't mean anything to me. 'Anything else – you know, like what he does, anything to narrow the field a bit?'

Johnny chews on his lower lip while he thinks about it.

I can understand the difficulty. Beyond the word *shady*, there's little else to define most of his associates.

'Lawyer,' he eventually replies, surprisingly.

'Yours?'

He snorts. 'If he was mine, sweetheart, I'd already know his address.'

I let the endearment float over my head. Perhaps I'm getting used to it. Typing in *lawyer* after the name, I ask, 'Is he likely to be in London?'

He nods so I add that too.

There are over six hundred hits and I slowly scroll down the screen. 'Any of these seem likely?'

Johnny leans forward again. Now he's so close I can even hear him breathing. 'Try that one,' he says, pointing at a site for a firm called Ainsworth, Jolly & Co.

As soon it comes up, he smiles. 'That's it. That's the one.' Taking a small black notebook from his pocket, he copies down the address. It's a street not so far away in Euston and I know, as he glances at his watch, that we've got yet another visit to make.

I'd like to take a moment to peruse the information in front of me – all I've gathered is that they are, unsurprisingly, a firm of lawyers – but Johnny's already walking away. Without even a thank you.

Outside, the snow has turned to a thin drizzly rain. The white paradise of earlier has melted to slush beneath our feet.

'Why do you want to see him?' I enquire as we make our way back to the car. 'This Ted Ainsworth guy, what's he got to do with anything?'

He doesn't answer.

'Johnny?'

But it's pointless. I might as well be talking to myself. I could throw a tantrum, refuse to move until he tells me what's going on – but I'm just too tired to bother. He'd only lie to me anyway, make up some cock-and-bull story. No, I'm better off keeping my head down and my eyes and ears open. Perhaps I'll learn something useful in Euston.

By the time we get back to my trusty Fiat, thankfully still parked where we left it – not that anyone would choose to steal the poor old thing, they'd have to be desperate – the evening rush hour has started. We make slow progress through the snarled-up traffic, inching along the streets. Johnny looks at his watch so often he starts to make me nervous.

'They won't close before five,' I tell him. But I go ahead and jump the lights, infected by his air of urgency.

It's a quarter to by the time we pull into the forecourt. With the help of my *A–Z*, Johnny's done a reasonable job of navigating. Only a single wrong turn when I narrowly missed hurtling down a one-way street. The glare of oncoming headlights lingers unpleasantly in my brain. I'm still holding my breath as I find a space, pull in and switch off the engine.

He's out of the door before I've even removed the keys.

I quickly jump out after him.

'It's okay, you can wait here,' he says.

I slam the door and sigh. 'God, we're not going to have this conversation again are we? Don't you ever get bored?'

He glares at me across the top of the car. 'Shit,' he says, raising his eyes to the rain-filled heavens. 'Simone, love, has anyone ever told you what a pain in the arse you can be?'

'Frequently.' I turn to look up at the building. It's a modern, flashy-looking piece of architecture with lots of glass. I can see a jungle of greenery through the tall transparent frontage, a selection of flora dominated by the ubiquitous palm. I glance back at Johnny. After his initial enthusiasm, his eagerness to get inside seems to have diminished. He's standing, staring up, shifting from foot to foot. I wave a hand. 'So, what are we doing? Are we going in or are we just here to admire the view?'

It's the first time I've seen him look – well, not afraid exactly, but definitely uneasy. Maybe walking into a building full of lawyers reminds him of times he'd prefer to forget ...

or perhaps he's got another reason to feel anxious. For a second, as he stares up at the windows, I have the impression he's about to change his mind, to get back in the car again, to order me to drive away from here as quickly as we can.

'What's the matter?'

I don't expect a response – I'm getting used to being ignored – but amazingly, after the briefest of hesitations, he actually replies, though it's not an answer as such. 'You know what I really hate?'

It's tempting to make a few suggestions – aggravating women, lawyers, cops, and any member of the Buckley family spring instantly to mind – but I keep them to myself.

'Favours,' he says with a long bitter sigh. 'I really hate asking for fucking favours.'

'What favours?'

But he's not listening any more. His eyes are fixed firmly on the doors he's about to walk through, his thoughts a million miles away.

'What favours?' I gently prompt.

But the moment has passed. He shakes his head, puts his hands in his pockets and walks towards the building. I fall in behind him.

It's abnormally warm, virtually tropical, in the reception area. My boots sink into deep-pile carpet. Everything about the place stinks of money. From the pristine decor and the leather sofas to the pretentious display of modern art on the walls, there's a surfeit of luxury, an almost obscene exhibition of wealth. I glance down at my jeans spattered with mud. But let's be honest, even garbed in the very latest of fashions, some snazzy little number by Versace, I'd still feel completely out of place.

My inferiority complex hurtles into overdrive as my gaze settles on the receptionist. A cool, tall, blue-eyed blonde, she's every woman's nightmare: the Antichrist with breasts.

Johnny, however, strolls over to the desk as if he has every right, and more, to be there. If he didn't annoy me so much I might almost admire him. 'Mr Ainsworth,' he demands. 'I need to see him.'

The Ice Queen glances down at the open book on her desk. 'Do you have an appointment?'

'No.'

'Oh,' she says. Her scarlet mouth puckers into disapproval. 'Well, in that case I'm sorry, but Mr Ainsworth is busy. If you'd like to—'

He doesn't wait for the rest of the brush-off. 'Tell him Johnny Frank's here.'

Her expression, if it's possible, slides into something even less friendly. A touch of frost enters her tone. 'I'm sorry but I'm afraid—'

'Johnny Frank,' he repeats. He nods towards the nearest sofa. 'There's no rush. I can wait.'

She gives him a hard stare but it's wasted. He's already turned his back. She watches, unsure, as he strolls confidently away. He's either important or a chancer – she can't make up her mind which. Eventually she turns her belligerent attention to me. In five seconds flat her gaze has rolled from my head to my toes, making an assessment so dismissive that it would rock even the most confident of females. Following Johnny's lead, I do the only thing I can – retreat.

It's only as I'm walking away that I realize the place is full of mirrors. From every angle, I'm faced with a multitude of less than gratifying images. My hair, a victim of the snow and rain, looks like it hasn't been combed for a year. There are definite bags under my eyes, a pair of dull mauve shadows. Even my skin looks grey. I shudder and slump down beside Johnny on the plush velvet cushions.

There's a pile of magazines on the coffee table in front of us, all the latest editions. *GQ*, *Esquire*, *Golfing Weekly*, even *Playboy*. Ted Ainsworth clearly isn't intent on attracting a female clientele. I look at Johnny. He glances back, shrugs, almost smiles. I look at the receptionist. She's on the phone, whispering furtively into the receiver. I get the feeling we're about to be thrown out.

But I'm wrong. Within a couple of minutes the lift doors open and a suave thirty-something male sweeps into the foyer. He's so good-looking, so dazzlingly handsome, that my jaw drops. Is everyone who works here obliged to be beautiful?

Perhaps it's in the job description. He walks in a straight line, as if he's heading for the exit, but just as I think he's about to pass by he stops and turns to face us.

'Johnny Frank?'

Johnny, with a lifetime of never voluntarily admitting to anything he doesn't need to, gazes silently back. Whoever this man is, he clearly isn't Ted Ainsworth.

The Adonis pauses for a moment and then smiles, his

mouth opening to reveal two rows of perfect white teeth. 'You don't remember me.'

Now Johnny's eyes narrow, his head tilting up a little to examine the stranger. His frown makes its customary appearance. But he still doesn't speak.

The wonderful mouth gives a low harmonious laugh. 'Well, *you* haven't changed much, mate. Still as talkative as ever. I take it you wanted to see my old man?'

Johnny finally shifts off his seat and stands up. 'Dean?'

'You've got it.'

'My God,' he says, staring at him. And a look I haven't seen before spreads over his face, a mixture of incredulity and what might almost be pain. As if the ghost of Christmas Past has just entered his line of vision, a reminder of all the years he has lost, he slowly shakes his head.

Dean laughs again. 'I guess it has been a while. How are you doing? I heard you were out.' He extends a hand, grinning. 'It's good to see you again. I hope you're not after a brief already.'

'Not yet,' Johnny replies, in what I hope is a joke.

'Thing is,' Dean continues, 'you obviously haven't heard but ... well, Dad's not around any more.'

I hear the sharp intake of Johnny's breath. 'I'm sorry, I didn't—'

Seeing his expression, Dean quickly jumps in again. 'Hell no, I didn't mean ... No, the old bugger's still alive and kicking. Even the devil isn't clamouring for *his* soul. He just doesn't work here now. He's retired – or so he claims. Although that doesn't stop him constantly interfering. You should give him a call.'

'I was hoping to see him.'

'Not today,' Dean replies, emphatically. 'Well, not unless you've brought your passport with you. He's living in Spain.'

And just the mention of that country reminds me of Marc again. Spain, bloody Spain – what is it with that place?

A despondent sigh escapes from Johnny's throat.

'Maybe I can help,' Dean says.

Johnny doesn't look convinced. 'It's complicated.'

'Complicated is what I do.' He glances around the opulent foyer. 'Complicated is what I get paid for.' Putting a hand on Johnny's shoulder he insists, 'Come on, come upstairs. We'll talk about it there.'

For the first time, Dean's gaze shifts over to me. His eyes are a strong clear blue, his lashes almost too prettily dark. I try not to swoon.

'Oh, this is Simone,' Johnny admits reluctantly. He utters my name as he might describe some minor ailment, an embarrassing rash or irritation.

Dean's perfectly manicured hand is already reaching out for mine.

'Nice to meet you,' he says.

I'd like to reply 'likewise' but as his warm fingers fold around mine, I have the ominous feeling that any response might emerge as an embarrassing squeak. I smile and nod.

We go up in the lift, a miniature reproduction of the luxury foyer. There's something that feels distinctly like velvet on the walls. Everything metallic shines. Even the rows of floor buttons are bright as silver. No fingerprints here. For the brief time it takes to ascend, everyone is silent.

The doors swish open into the cool sea-blue of Dean's spacious office. It's dark outside and the windows, floor to ceiling, reveal an illuminated view across the city. It's panoramic, amazing. I try not to gawp. This, of course, is only the next reception area.

Dean turns his blue gaze on me. 'Would you like a drink?'

I nod again. I'm beginning to feel like a silent witness. Clearing my throat, I open my mouth and finally manage to say, 'Thank you. Coffee would be nice.'

He glances towards the blonde behind the desk. 'Alison. Three coffees, please.'

As he and Johnny disappear into the inner sanctum, I'm left to my own devices again. The blonde, this one a touch less frosty than the last, smiles at me. I wonder how she feels, being treated like a waitress. When she emerges from her prison, click-clacking across the wooden floor, I catch a glimpse of her Jimmy Choo shoes. No, if she's paid enough to be able to afford those particular high heels, I'm sure it doesn't bother her at all.

In her absence, I gaze around the room. Who says crime doesn't pay? This space alone must have cost more than a few high-profile trials to decorate. It's only as I glance down at the coffee table, as I start to idly peruse the glossy brochures, that I realize Ainsworth, Jolly & Co. are more involved with the corporate side of law than the criminal. Business takeovers, sales and mergers are clearly more in their line of work than the shady misdemeanours of the underworld.

So what the hell is Johnny doing here?

It would make sense that a lawyer, or at least a certain

kind of lawyer, might be holding the diamonds. But Johnny didn't even know this address until half an hour ago. And if the gems were here all along then why have we been trudging all over London? No, I don't think Dean Ainsworth, or his father, has any connection to Johnny's diamonds – well, not unless they used them to buy the building. And why am I calling them *Johnny's* diamonds? Whoever they belong to, it certainly isn't him.

Alison deposits a china cup and saucer on the table. The aroma of freshly ground coffee beans rises up. 'Thank you.'

She bestows another small smile.

'Busy?' I ask sweetly. The smartest detectives always engage the staff in conversation.

'Very,' she replies bluntly, before returning to the computer. Her fingers fly swiftly, expertly across the keys, with a touch so soft it's barely audible. The smartest detectives, I recall too late, never ask questions that can be answered with a single word.

The minutes tick by. I wonder which of his many 'complications' Johnny is sharing with Dean – his lost property, the unfortunate death of Eddie Tate, or perhaps his recent and unwelcome encounter with the Fosters. Maybe Mr Ainsworth Jnr runs a lucrative sideline in one-way tickets to Bolivia.

At regular intervals, Alison peers at me over the rims of her designer glasses. She's clearly worried that I might purloin the silver teaspoons. It's hardly surprising. Neither Johnny nor I look exactly reputable, he with his bruised face and I with my mud-spattered clothes. To say we lower the tone is an understatement.

Exhaustion is catching up. It's warm in the room and the sofa, soft as a bed, is enticingly comfortable. I can feel my eyes beginning to close. I've been without sleep for too many hours, driven purely by adrenaline and coffee. Just forty winks perhaps, a catnap, something to refresh the brain.

I'm sliding into that blessed state of oblivion, limbs relaxing, all thoughts dissolving, when the door to the inner office suddenly clicks open. In the silence of my head it sounds like a gunshot. Startled, I spring back to reality.

Johnny's the first to emerge, looking – what? Certainly not pleased but not unhappy either. More puzzled than anything. Dean glides out behind him, his expression entirely neutral. I stand up to join them as they stroll towards the lift.

'Don't be a stranger,' Dean says, shaking his hand. 'And if there's anything else – you know where I am.'

Johnny nods. 'I appreciate it.'

Finally registering my presence, Dean turns and graciously extends his hand again. I expect him to repeat the courtesies of earlier, 'Nice to meet you,' or something of the like. Instead, he smiles enigmatically and says, 'Good luck.'

'You too,' I reply automatically.

It's only as I step into the lift that the inanity of my response begins to register. Judging from the evidence to date, luck's the last thing Mr Ainsworth is in need of. I stare down at my boots until the doors have closed. Whatever happened to my confidence and charm? I swear I had some once.

Johnny doesn't seem eager to share whatever news he may have. When we reach the ground floor he walks swiftly through the foyer. I follow in his wake. The Ice Queen raises her head and stares after us. She's probably memorizing our descriptions in case she needs to call the cops.

'Damn it,' Johnny mutters, as he climbs into the passenger seat. And that isn't encouraging. I've got no idea what particular aspect of the whole God-awful mess he's referring to. I get in, fasten my seatbelt, start the engine, reverse out and manoeuvre the car towards the exit.

'Where to?'

'I need a drink,' he says. 'That hotel, the one we stayed in before. Take a right. It's only down the road.'

I slide back into the traffic. For the next five minutes, we don't speak. From one set of lights to the next, we edge slowly forward. I glance at my watch: five thirty, the time I'd usually be starting to shut up shop, to bring in the flowers. I wonder what Kerry Anne's doing now. Does she wonder where I am? God, I wish I was there, that I had nothing more to worry about than cashing up and sorting out the roses. Is Dee with her? Perhaps she is, trying to occupy the time, to lose herself. I miss her. I even miss the aimless bickering. That was preferable to this. Although, let's face it, almost *anything* would be better than this.

'Simone.'

What now?

'The lights,' he says.

I look up. They're on green. And he's not the only one complaining. There's a queue behind me getting ever more restless. Someone starts hooting. I take off more quickly than I should, stopping only inches from the car in front as the queue grinds suddenly to a halt again. What's the point in rushing? No one's going anywhere.

'Are you okay?' he asks.

It's Monday evening. The deadline runs out on Thursday, the deadline on my husband's life, and there's still no evidence, not even a hint, that Johnny has either got the diamonds or would be willing to hand them over if he had. Just how okay, how perfectly calm, does he expect me to feel?

Ignoring his question, I stare straight ahead.

'Simone?'

'I can't do this any more. You've got to talk to me, I need to know what's going on.'

'I'm not sure.'

'For God's sake, don't I have the *right* to know?'

He hesitates. 'I mean I'm not sure what's going on.'

'What?' I feel a chill slide down my spine. If Johnny's in the dark, if things aren't working out, then what chance has Marc got? 'You can't get the diamonds. Is that what you're saying?' I lower my face over the steering wheel. 'Jesus!'

'Fuck it, Simone, keep your eyes on the road! We're no use to him dead.'

'Or alive either, the way things are looking.'

'Don't be so hysterical. Did I say I couldn't get the diamonds?' He leans back in the seat, expelling one of his anti-female sighs.

I take a second to absorb the information. Then I ask quietly, 'So what's the problem then?'

'The problem is that I don't know who we're dealing with.'

'And that matters *because*?'

He looks at me like I'm an imbecile. 'That matters, sweetheart, because if we don't know who they are, then we don't know whether we can trust them or not.'

And now he's introduced a whole new element of fear into the equation. 'You mean, we could give them the diamonds and they could still . . .' I don't need to finish the sentence. I don't think I could even if I wanted to. A vice has started to tighten in my chest, squeezing at my heart and lungs.

Johnny turns his grey face to the window.

It takes me a moment to get my breath back. 'So why would Dean Ainsworth know anything?'

'He wouldn't . . . but his old man might. *He* moves in rather less desirable circles. Ted always has his ear to the ground.'

'Very useful,' I say caustically, 'if he wasn't sunning himself on a beach in Spain.'

'They do have phones in the Mediterranean.'

Perhaps I shouldn't have been so dismissive. A brief surge of optimism quells the shaking in my hands. 'You managed to talk to him?'

'Briefly.'

'And?'

'And he'll get back to me.'

I bite my lip in disappointment. This is another dead end, I'm sure of it, nothing worth getting excited about. 'Is he a friend of yours?'

'More of an associate.'

'A villain then,' I say, with a certain edge.

Johnny grins. 'Takes one to catch one.'

I swing a left and then a right, slipping into the forecourt of the hotel. I want to park near the entrance but there are no free slots so I do a further circuit and choose the first available space. I stand shivering in the rain while he gets the bags out of the boot. I'm relieved we're staying here; I couldn't take another night of Dee's terror. It's all right for him – he just yawns and clears off to bed – but I'm left with all the questions, the tears, the trauma. It tears me apart. And although I know it must be worse for her, at least I'm out here *doing* something, I can't cope with all that endless grief. She may crave comfort but I'm suffering too.

It's dark where I've parked. The overhead lamp isn't working. If I hadn't been so preoccupied, I'd have noticed it. Perhaps I should move the car to somewhere more visible, but I can't be bothered. I'm tired and hungry and I need a hot shower.

Johnny slams the boot shut and comes to join me. He doesn't speak. His face has assumed that familiar blank expression. I can't tell if he's angry or thoughtful – or neither. Perhaps all he's contemplating is a hot meal and a chance to get his head down.

We've only taken a few steps when I hear the noise behind me, a faint sound like the scuff of a shoe against concrete. I glance over my shoulder, nervously, but there's no one there. Just my over-active imagination playing tricks. Still, there's safety in numbers. I edge a little closer to him. But we've barely covered another yard when it comes again, more distinct this time. The hairs on the back of my neck stand on end. And now I know, I know for certain that we're not alone. 'Johnny,' I whisper urgently, but it's already too late.

I turn, horrified, as someone emerges from the shadows, a black-clad figure. I want to scream but I can't; fright has paralysed my throat. He lunges towards us. I can hear his ragged breath, can almost smell his malice, and then I see it – the deadly flash of metal as he raises his hand ...

And suddenly instinct takes over. *I'm too bloody young to die*. With a desperate leap, I hurl myself at him, my shoulder making heavy contact with his upper arm. He gives a small muffled grunt of surprise, and there's a reassuring clatter as the weapon slips from his fingers and falls to the ground. Still standing sideways, I lift my boot, run it the length of his shin and stamp down with all my strength on the top of his foot. This time he squeals like a pig and doubles over. I raise my knee to try and catch his chin but he topples sideways, grabbing my coat and dragging me with him.

The next few seconds are a blur of grasping hands and curses. I scratch and kick. He tries to punch. Then we're rolling together, a mass of thrashing limbs. I reach out and grab his hair – he grunts. He hits my ribs – I moan. My heart's pumping, my brain in a fever ... but somewhere, distantly, in the back of my mind, I'm aware of Johnny's absence. I'm aware of him doing precisely nothing.

Then suddenly his arms are around me, too strong to resist, wrenching me off, pulling me away. What? What the hell is he doing now? He's got it wrong. It's not me he should be—

'Simone! Leave it, leave him!'

He drags me unceremoniously across the concrete. I struggle, confused, but he doesn't let go until my body goes limp and I finally stop fighting.

At first there only seems to be silence but I gradually become aware of a panting, whimpering sound. It takes a moment to realize this is coming from me. A faint stinging pain drifts into my consciousness. I lift my bleeding palms and stare at them.

Johnny says, 'It's okay, you're okay. You're safe.'

I turn and gaze into his eyes. I want to believe him but it isn't true. We're not safe at all. Can't he see? The attacker is only a few feet away from us, groaning, swearing, a rich tirade of abuse spilling from his mouth. And he's getting to his feet again, standing up, another minute and he'll be ... Pushing aside Johnny's hands, I try to raise myself too. He takes hold of my elbows and pulls me back down.

'Simone!'

Why doesn't he understand? 'He had a knife,' I whisper, grabbing hold of his arm.

But now our assailant is making a retreat. He staggers back a step, still cursing.

'It's okay,' Johnny repeats. But he isn't talking to me. He's talking to *him*.

The man in black turns his head.

'It's okay, mate, it's just a misunderstanding.' Johnny sounds reassuring.

What's going on? I dig my nails into his flesh. 'He had a *knife*,' I insist.

Johnny flinches, reaches behind and picks up an object

from the ground. He drops it into my lap. It's not a knife, nothing like a knife. It's only a lightweight torch with a thin metallic ring around the lens. I stare at it, confounded. A slow sick feeling rises up from my guts.

'I don't understand. I don't . . .'

He pulls me slowly to my feet. Although I couldn't stand without him, I resent his help. As soon as I'm upright, I struggle out of his grasp, shrugging free. I glance from him, to the torch and back again. Now he's starting to smile – and his expression is so smug, so utterly unbearable, that I know I've done something irretrievably stupid . . .

I glance towards the man in black. He's still limping, nursing his injury. As he sees me looking, he raises a shaky hand and points.

'Just keep that crazy bitch away from me!'

Chapter Twenty-Two

Johnny

So now I've got two head cases to deal with. Jesus, and I thought I was in need of therapy. Simone looks like she's about to be sick and he's still whining like a bloody kid. And okay, now probably isn't the most propitious time for introductions, but I suppose they have to be made before they try to kill each other again.

'Simone,' I say, holding on to her elbow. 'This is Brian Quigley, a friend of Eddie Tate's. I arranged to meet him here tonight.'

I feel her slowly deflate as if someone has stuck a pin in her. 'What?' she asks in a tiny voice.

Quigley's still brushing himself down. He glances up anxiously as if she might be about to launch another attack. 'Arranged to *meet*,' he repeats resentfully, 'not get mauled by some fucking witch.'

'Arranged to meet in the bar,' I retort. 'What do you expect if you creep up on women in deserted car parks?'

'Why didn't you tell me?' Simone asks. 'For God's sake, if I'd known you were meeting someone then . . .'

I pick up the bags and start towards the entrance to the hotel. If I don't go now we'll be arguing the toss all night and I've got more important things to do, a strong drink being top of the list. They stare after me, annoyed, bemused, but after a moment, unwilling to be left in each other's company, they reluctantly follow.

But it doesn't stop the recriminations.

Quigley mutters under his breath. ' . . . fucking liability. You should keep her on a leash.'

'Bloody idiot!'

'Psycho!'

Shit, I've had enough of this. I stop under a lamp and put the bags down again. Turning to Simone, I ask, 'Are you hurt?'

She rubs at her elbows, glances down at her grazed palms. Eventually she shrugs. 'Not really.'

'And you?'

Quigley gazes resentfully down at his foot but isn't about to admit to being damaged by a girl. 'I'll live,' he replies sulkily, 'no thanks to her.'

'Well then. No harm done. So perhaps we can drop the sweet talk and get on.'

Simone gives me a look. I think she's starting to suspect – quite rightly as it happens – that I could have been a little faster in my intervention. But it's not every day you get to see a panting wildcat rolling on the ground with a piece of low-life. Some moments have to be savoured.

But before she can set the whole damn argument off again, I say, 'You'd better get cleaned up before we go inside. There's mud on your face.'

She dabs at it, ineffectually, with a piece of tissue. 'What's the problem,' she asks bitterly, glancing from Quigley to me, 'scared I'll lower the tone?'

I don't bother responding. Instead, taking her chin in my hand I lift her head up towards the light. She resists but only for a second. She's too tired for another fight. I remove the tissue from her fingers and place it in front of her mouth. 'Here, spit on this.'

As if I've just asked her for a blow-job, rather than a sample of saliva, her face creases into disgust.

I shrug. 'Suit yourself.' I spit on the tissue, and with a few quick swipes clean away the dirt. 'That's better.'

She doesn't say thank you. Instead, she instantly wipes the palm of her hand across her face. Some people have no manners.

The bar has just the right level of activity, not so quiet that we might be overheard but not too busy either. A selection of swing tunes, easy listening for sales reps, bounces through the speakers. We find a table in a corner and squeeze round it. I've bought three large whiskies, enough alcohol, hopefully, to set us on the road to appeasement.

I'd rather Simone wasn't here but I don't have a choice. After everything that's happened, I'm not prepared to leave her on her own. She might get to thinking – especially about the cops – and fuck knows what she might do then. No, best to keep her occupied. And close.

Quigley, acting the hard man, empties half his glass and narrows his eyes. 'So?'

This is as much for Simone's benefit as mine. I understand that he's got his pride to restore – it's hardly macho, scrapping with a girl – but I haven't got all night. I lift an eyebrow and stare silently back.

It doesn't take him long to lose his cool. 'So what do you want?' he asks defensively. 'Why d'you ask me here? I don't know nothing about Eddie.'

'Sure you do. You were his mate, weren't you?'

As if it might be a trick question, he lifts his skinny shoulders and shrugs. He glances evasively around the bar.

'And you want to know who killed him.'

That gets his attention. Like a vengeful little goblin, his ears prick up. He puts his elbows on the table and shifts forward.

I pause. Then, leaning towards him, I whisper softly, 'Well, so do I.'

He sits back, disappointment curling the corners of his mouth. He was hoping for a revelation, an opportunity for revenge, but I've provided him with neither. 'And why the fuck should you care?'

'Let's just say, it's getting in the way of business.'

Now he's suddenly interested again. 'Business?'

Money. That's what he's smelling, a chance to grab an earner. 'So you tell me what you know, who he was seeing, what he was involved in – and I'll make sure you haven't had a wasted journey.'

His sleazy eyes roll from me to Simone.

'Don't worry about her, she's very discreet.'

His gaze slips from her face to her tits but doesn't get any further. 'Yeah, I bet she is.'

Simone opens her mouth to protest. I give her a kick under the table. She flinches, glares, but draws her lips back together in a sulky pout. I wonder why that turns me on so much.

'But don't provoke her,' I say to him, 'she's not what you'd call exactly *stable*.'

Now it's her turn to kick and she doesn't hold back. Her boot slams hard into the side of my calf – and I've some idea of what Quigley just experienced. I grunt. I twist my head and stare at her.

'You okay?' she asks, all sweetness and light.

I rub my hand down my leg. There'll be a bruise the size of the Bahamas there tomorrow.

Quigley peers at us both. 'What's going on?'

'Nothing.' I throw him a packet of fags. 'Help yourself.'

He does. He takes three out, lights one and slips the other two into his pocket. All the time he's watching us, wary, suspicious. For a second I wonder if he might do a runner but no, he's too wily for that.

'So what can you tell me?'

'Depends,' he replies cautiously. He's still trying to figure out what his information may be worth. 'You saw more of him than me. He was camped outside your fucking house for a fortnight.'

I ask softly, 'You think *I* killed him, Brian?'

He snorts into his whisky. 'You think I'd be here if I did?'

Good. I wanted him to say it, for Simone to hear. I shrug. 'I don't know what to think.' I stare at him; it's a cold, expressionless stare. 'For all I know, you may have come to try and shake me down.'

He laughs but only for a second. 'What?' A gleam of fear enters his eyes. He takes another gulp of whisky and licks his cracked lips. He squirms in his seat, drawing deeply on his fag as if it's some kind of inhaler. The ash drops down the front of his shirt. He's getting worried now, scared that I'm accusing him of something that he hasn't done. His voice rises a fraction. 'I never said . . . I never . . . What would *you* kill him for?

You never had nothing against Eddie. You go way back.'

'We had our differences.'

'Yeah,' he agrees nervously, 'but everyone knew that was just Eddie. No one ever thought, I never thought . . . '

Now I've got him on the defensive, it's time to put the knife in. 'And there was Mr Ainsworth claiming you were just the guy to help us out.' I stand up as if I'm about to leave. 'Looks like he was wrong.'

At the mention of the name, Quigley starts. The blood drains from his face. He leans forward, grabbing hold of my arm. 'I am,' he says almost pleadingly. 'I want to help.'

Funny how Ted has that effect on people.

I hesitate. 'You sure?'

Like one of those nodding dogs, his head starts to bounce. He may have temporarily lost the power of speech but his will to live is unimpaired.

'Good.' I shake off his hand, sit down again and smile.

He tries to return the gesture but his mouth seems caught in a rictus of dismay. Still, I won't take it personally. When it comes to the humble art of courtesy, he's not had much practice.

Eventually he finds his voice again and now he's desperate to tell me everything. 'You know what he was like about them diamonds, Johnny. They was all he thought about. He couldn't let go, couldn't stop himself. Talking about them, that's all he ever did, always—'

I slam my fist down on the table. 'Christ!'

He instantly shuts up, his scared eyes darting from my hand to my face.

I raise my own eyes towards the ceiling before lowering them, slowly, to meet his again. 'I need *names*, for fuck's sake, people he was talking to, leads – not some bloody history lesson.' I expel my breath in a long despairing sigh. 'We all know about Eddie's obsessions. We don't need a fucking inquest on them.' I wait a moment before leaning forward again and pushing my face invasively into his. 'You see, we're looking for someone, Brian, someone else who's disappeared. Marc Buckley. He's in trouble and we need to

find him – fast.'

He shrinks back. 'You think he's been snuffed too?'

I feel Simone flinch beside me.

'No,' I insist. I'm about to add *not yet* but think better of it. An edgy Simone is one thing, a hysterical one quite another. 'No ... just tell me who Eddie was seeing, who he was talking to. Just tell me that and we can all go home.'

I'm not even sure if I'm on the right track. Quigley may

have been close to him, a mate, but that doesn't mean anything. Criminals and confidences rarely go together. Lies and secrets are wrapped around a villain's life like clingfilm. I don't press him. He needs time to think about the best course of action. And that, of course, is self-preservation.

I sit back and sip my drink.

Quigley gazes silently into his.

Another few seconds and . . .

'Marc Buckley?' he eventually repeats.

And I'm just beginning to think that we might be getting somewhere, might finally be making some progress, when Simone goes and fucks it all up.

'Yes,' she responds too eagerly. She sits forward, almost sending her glass flying. 'Do you know anything? Do you know where he is?'

He scowls. 'What's it to you?'

'I'm his wife,' she says, before I can stop her. '*That's* what it is to me.'

It's obvious what's going to happen next. The likes of Quigley, no matter what the circumstances, won't resist a chance to get their own back. It's not been the best day of his life. He's been taken by surprise, attacked and humiliated. Add a little intimidation to the mix and he's hardly likely to be in the mood for holy forgiveness.

'His wife, eh?' he sneers. 'Well, maybe he ain't gone missing at all, love. Maybe he just found someone new to play with.'

Simone looks as if she's about to launch herself across the table. She half rises and leans forward, her eyes blazing. 'If you've got nothing useful to say,' she hisses, 'then just shut your stupid mouth. We haven't got time for wasters. It's information we need, not a bloody agony aunt.'

Quigley shifts smartly back. He may be a man but he's way past his prime, slight, skinny, almost old enough to be her father — no match at all for a woman on a mission. Although it's been my experience that the small guys are the ones to watch, quick to take offence, over-sensitive, he doesn't seem too keen to pursue the confrontation.

He gives her a bitter look but doesn't retaliate.

She sits back, folds her arms and glares at him.

Eventually Quigley, outstared, turns his attention towards me. As if he's finally had enough, he mumbles, 'I don't know nothing about this Marc, okay. I ain't heard nothing. But you may want to talk to them Fosters.'

'You think they're involved?'

'I told you,' he says, frustration raising his voice a tone or two, 'I don't know *nothing* about that. All I know about is Eddie.'

'Eddie was seeing the Fosters?'

'That's what I said, weren't it? That Paul, Roy Foster's son, and his nephew, Micky. I saw them down The Eagle.'

'Once, twice, how often?'

He shrugs. 'Couple of times.'

So maybe there is a connection between them and the ice. Perhaps Eddie decided he needed some younger blood, some muscle, to help him get what he wanted. But then why would the Fosters jump me in Norfolk? It doesn't make sense.

'Did he say why?'

'You know Eddie,' he replies, as if he's still alive. He frowns. 'Kept things close to his chest, didn't he? Went his own way most of the time.'

He hesitates again and I wait, patiently, certain there's something more.

Even Simone has the sense, for once, to keep it zipped.

After a few seconds he continues, 'They was paying him though, I know that much. Flashing the cash he was. But don't ask me for what. I dunno, okay?'

'Okay.'

'Or nothing else,' he insists. He gathers his coat around him, preparing to leave.

I write down my mobile number on a piece of paper and hand it to him, along with three closely folded notes. Without looking, he palms them neatly into his pocket.

'There's plenty more where that came from. Ask around. You hear anything else, even a whisper, you give me a call.'

He stands up, takes a step, and then glances back. He looks me straight in the eye. 'And when you find out who did Eddie – you give *me* a call.' I nod. Perhaps one day I will. I watch him as he walks stealthily out of the bar, head bowed, his gaze fixed firmly on the carpet. He looks like what he is, a small-time grubby villain, a liar and a thief. But even scumbags have feelings and loyalties ... and the occasional friend.

'So what do you think?' Simone says. She tugs at my elbow.

I turn. Her eyes are shining, excited, ludicrously optimistic. She's already got the Fosters in the frame. They've been tried, convicted and sentenced without even so much as a nod towards the evidence. If she had a piece of string, she'd probably hang Quigley by his scrawny neck too.

'What do you think?' she asks again. I knock back my last inch of whisky. 'Odds on? Well, another twenty seconds – and some work on that right hook – and I reckon you could have taken him.'

The room's the same as the last one we had. Different floor but still identical. Same magnolia walls, same beige curtains, same kettle – and same happy atmosphere. Simone's still pissed off by my flippancy. In fact she bloody hates me for it. But I don't give a damn.

We've both had a shower, got clean, got changed, and now she's sitting on her bed in a pair of pale blue pyjamas. Rosy-cheeked and fragrant, she'd be irresistible if it wasn't for that vitriolic glint in her eye.

'I don't understand. You heard what he said. What's the matter with you?'

'What's the matter with *you*?' I retort, rubbing a towel through my hair. Shit, it's almost like being married again, being accountable for every action, every single thought that runs through my head. 'So Eddie saw the Fosters, so what? You think they'd have met him in a public place, talked to him, given him money, if they were planning on—'

'No one's saying they planned it,' she interrupts. 'Maybe it just . . . just got out of hand.'

'No,' I insist. 'They didn't kill Eddie. They couldn't have. They wouldn't.'

'What makes you so certain?'

And it would be easier if I could tell her but I can't. I'm stuck in this mess, this maze that I can't find my way out of. Carl's got a lot to answer for. I lift my shoulders. 'Because it's not their style, not their way. Okay, they're not saints but they're not . . .'

'Not killers?' she asks. 'What, not even for a million quid? A couple of million?' She wraps her arms around her knees. 'Haven't you heard? People will do anything for money.'

I shake my head. 'Some things, not *everything*.'

'It's obvious. It's staring you straight in the face.'

'It's crap.'

She glares at me. 'Oh yeah?'

I throw the towel down on the bed. 'They wouldn't have been so careless. The Fosters are old school, professional; they'd have covered their tracks. Fifty people, more, must have seen them talking to Eddie. They didn't even try to keep it quiet. Whatever they were paying for, they were doing it openly.'

'So maybe they were careless,' she says, 'or arrogant.'

'But they're not. They're not stupid and they didn't kill Eddie. We have to disconnect the two — I'm not convinced his murder is anything to do with what's happening to Marc.'

She looks up at me, astounded. 'And you really believe that?'

'Quigley doesn't think the Fosters killed Eddie. If he did, he wouldn't have said what he did tonight.'

'And you trust him?'

I shrug. 'As much as I trust you.'

Simone turns and swings her long legs over the side of the bed. I can see the contours of her breasts through the thin cotton. She focuses her cynical eyes on me. 'And just how much, exactly, is that?'

I take a moment. I'd like to be generous but there's no point going overboard. 'Enough,' I eventually say.

She gives me a long hard look before standing up. 'You want a coffee?'

'Sure.'

Switching on the kettle, she clatters a couple of cups down on the counter. 'So if you're right, then what was Eddie being paid for?'

'I'm still trying to figure that,' I tell her honestly. 'Maybe they were paying him to keep an eye on the house, to follow me if I came out, to see where I went. Maybe all *they* were after was the lowdown on my movements.' The more I think about this possibility the more probable it becomes. I try to work through the idea. 'I mean, if Eddie was already hanging round, there wasn't much point in them being there too. All they had to do was drop him a few quid and Eddie would keep them up to date. As soon as I showed my face he'd be straight on the blower.'

'It's just a hypothesis,' she says.

'A reasonable one,' I reply, 'if all they wanted was the opportunity to beat the shit out of me.'

She adds the water, gives the coffee a stir, and passes me one of the cups. 'Which leaves us where?'

'Looking somewhere else.' I stare down into the dense brown liquid. 'Jeez, is this coffee or mud?'

'You don't like it, make it yourself,' she retorts, climbing back on her bed and pulling the duvet round her knees.

'You ever thought of the diplomatic service?'

'You ever thought of saving your wisecracks for someone who's listening?'

I lean back, stretch out my legs and cross them at the ankles. Maybe I should cut her some slack. Like Quigley, she hasn't had the best of days. And if she doesn't feel those bruises now, she'll certainly feel them in the morning. 'Sorry. Just trying to take your mind off things.'

'Well, don't. I'm not in the mood.' Holding her cup with both hands, she sinks her face into the steam and takes a few tentative sips. 'Two days,' she says, as if I might have forgotten. 'Two days. That's all we've got left.'

Well, strictly speaking, it's all *she's* got left, but now might not be the moment to share that unpalatable truth. By this time tomorrow, I intend to be a hundred miles away. I've done my bit, asked around, made the calls; it's not my fault if no one's talking.

Suddenly my mobile goes off, an irritating scale of notes that makes me wince. 'Yes?' The voice is a familiar one. I keep my answers monosyllabic and the conversation lasts less than a minute. For the duration, Simone sits bolt upright, her eyes fixed expectantly on me.

'What?' she asks, as soon as I've hung up. 'Who was it?'

I throw the phone down on the bed. 'Ted Ainsworth.'

'And?'

I shake my head. 'Nothing yet.'

She sinks back into the duvet. 'So we're no better off,' she says, despondently. 'We don't know any more than we did before. What if we don't find out, what if—'

I have to interrupt before she sinks into a pit of despair. And that, as experience has taught me, will inevitably be followed by tears. 'Sure we're better off. It's a matter of elimination, isn't it? There's no point chasing down blind alleys.'

'Brilliant,' she replies, 'and now you've eliminated the Fosters, who *exactly* is next on your extensive list of suspects?'

She's got a point. Maybe I have been too fast to dismiss them. But whatever way I look at it, it just doesn't feel right, doesn't fit. 'Come on, even Ted doesn't think they're responsible for this.'

'And who's Ted Ainsworth – the bloody Oracle?'

I lean over the side of the bed. Reaching into my bag, I pull out a bottle of whisky. 'I need a drink.'

'For God's sake.' She looks at me with contempt. 'Is that your answer to everything?'

Ignoring her, I go to fetch some glasses. To be honest, it's a welcome opportunity to turn my back. I'm skilled at lying, expert, but that doesn't mean I always like it. Ted's done the rounds and there's not even a whisper. Silence. That's all there is out there. And that's not good news. Whoever's holding Marc, they're tight, professional and smart. They've brought the lid down on this kidnap, sealed it like some fucking coffin.

I need to think. I need some whisky. I need some whisky to think.

Without bothering to ask, I pour two generous measures and place one glass on her bedside table. She can drink it or not. It makes no odds to me. I leave the bottle on the floor and then slide back on to my bed and stare up at the ceiling.

I close my eyes. Whatever's going on, there must be something to grab hold of, a name, a place, a piece of string that winds back into the past. There's a loose end somewhere, I'm sure of it. I slide through the roll call of names, everyone who was on the job – Dixie, Roy Foster, Eddie Tate . . .

All dead, except for me.

Which isn't encouraging.

Back to the Fosters. Maybe that whole assault routine was just a cover to put me off the scent, some kind of clever double bluff? Then there's Quigley – do I really trust that piece of shit? And who else might Eddie have been in league with? I'm so paranoid that even Melanie springs into my mind. Quickly, I shake her out again. Then there's Patrick and Alan. Even Dean's inscrutable brows lifted when I mentioned the ice. He could know more than he's letting on.

A few minutes pass before Simone speaks to me again. Her voice is smaller now, almost apologetic. 'So what next?'

I open my eyes and look at her. She's curled up in a ball. I have the impression that if she could, she'd transform herself into something tiny, a marble or a coin, and roll away into the night. I need to keep her occupied, distracted.

'We wait. Plenty can happen in forty-eight hours.'

'But you're sure you'll get the diamonds?'

I nod. I even manage a reassuring smile. 'Hey, don't worry. It's under control.'

She sips her whisky, unconvinced but unwilling to press me. When push comes to shove I'm still her only realistic option. Slowly, she uncoils and stretches out. I wonder what she'd do if I made a pass at her? It's a sordid thought but then I've never been renowned for my gentlemanly qualities.

For a while I let my thoughts wander into places they shouldn't. If anything's going to happen between us then it has to happen tonight. A farewell shag for all the good times we've had together? Maybe she just needs a bit of encouragement, an opportunity to let me know how grateful she is . . .

Then, out of the blue, she suddenly says something guaranteed to cool my ardour. 'Who was Dixie?'

'Who told you about Dixie?'

I must have snapped because a frown gathers on her forehead. 'Alan mentioned him. He just mentioned him, that's all.'

I wonder what else Alan told her. He's got a gob on him the size of the Blackwall Tunnel. I knew it was a mistake to leave them together. I gaze into my whisky. Best to keep it short and sweet. 'He was a friend. Someone in the past.'

As if I might elaborate, she waits.

But I'm not falling for that old trick. Silence doesn't bother me. I can hold *my* tongue until the fucking cows come home.

'Was Dixie with you on the Hatton Garden job?'

Jesus, is she guessing or did Alan tell her that too? Perhaps she got my whole bleeding biography while I was standing at the bar. I say abruptly, 'He's dead, okay? He died in prison. Can we drop it now?'

But in a way I've already answered her question.

'Alan seemed nice,' she says. 'I suppose you two go way back.'

I'm not sure if she's still digging or just making general conversation. 'Far enough. He used to work at the club. His wife was a friend of Sarah's.'

'Really? She must have been upset when—' '*Everyone* was upset.'

There's a short silence.

'Those diamonds,' she murmurs, 'don't you ever wish that you'd never set eyes on them?'

The diamonds are in my pocket. I reach down, automatically, to touch them. Perhaps I should have got rid, hidden them, posted them, shifted them somewhere safe, but I couldn't bear to let them out of my sight. They're my future now. The only prospect I've got left.

She sighs into her glass. 'There's a curse on those things.'

'Yeah, right.' I give a short brusque laugh. 'You really believe in all that garbage?'

Simone swings round to face me, her eyes bright. 'So how many people have died because of them already?' She counts them off on her fingers: 'Roy Foster, Eddie Tate, Dixie . . .' but then her voice starts to crack and she suddenly stops.

And we both know what she isn't able to say, that there might yet be a fourth.

I hear her take a deep breath. 'Are they really worth it?' she continues softly. 'Do you really imagine those diamonds will make anyone happy?'

But nothing she says is going to change my mind. I understand what she's trying to do. If she can't appeal to my conscience, can't *guilt* me into handing them over, her only alternative is to spook me into it. Villains are big on superstition, on signs – they've got more fucking rituals than the witches in *Macbeth*. But not me. I don't believe in all that shit. You make your own luck, face your own fate.

I take a moment, as if I'm inwardly debating the mighty forces of karma. I sip earnestly on my whisky. Eventually, I turn to her and smile. 'Maybe you're right.'

She smiles back with a gratitude I don't deserve.

Which sets me back to thinking about the night's possibilities. It would be a shame to waste our last evening together. It's good to talk but there are plenty more enjoyable things we could be doing. 'Here's to happier times,' I declare, leaning forward and refilling her glass.

She chinks it lightly against mine.

I'm not trying to get her drunk. Well, not exactly. Okay, I'm kind of hoping that the whisky might lower her resistance, cloud her judgement a little, remind her of how much she owes me, but that's all. I'm not the type to take advantage but if she should decide to show her appreciation then who am I to deny her?

I lean back and put my hands behind my head. 'Do you remember the first time we met? You were soaked, drenched. God, you looked so miserable.'

'I was.'

'And not overly pleased to see me.'

'I was tired,' she says.

'You hated my guts.'

She turns, insistent. 'I didn't *hate* you. I didn't even know you.'

'Enough to realize that you didn't want me there.'

She shrugs. 'Maybe. But it wasn't personal. There are only so many problems you can deal with in a day.' Then she quickly adds, 'Not that I thought you were—'

I start to laugh. 'It's okay,' I say, holding up my hands, 'I get it.'

Slowly her lips widen into a tentative smile.

She's not beautiful. Not perfect. But it's her flaws that turn me on. I like her sulky mouth, the way it naturally turns down at the corners. I like her wary eyes. I like the way she doesn't always think before she speaks; there's something impulsive, challenging, about her. At another time, in a different place, perhaps we might have ...

'Anyway,' she says, 'as I recall, you weren't all that impressed with me either.'

'Ah, first impressions. They can't always be trusted, can they? I'd like to think we've moved on since then.'

I'm hoping she might throw me a compliment, a scrap of hope, but instead she replies, 'So tell me about Sarah.'

Christ, she certainly knows how to kill a mood. What is it about women – always wanting to resurrect the past, to drag your traumas into the light? They can't let things lie. All I was after was a quiet drink, a little flirtation, but all *she* wants to do is conduct a fucking post-mortem. Why did she have to go and mention Sarah?

'I've got a better idea. Why don't we talk about you?'

Hearing the sudden change in my tone, she sits back a fraction. 'What's there to talk about?'

'Oh, I don't know.' I shrug. 'Why don't you tell me your

plans for the future? I mean, you're getting on a bit – are you really going to spend the rest of your life playing flower-girl?'

Women don't like it when you mention their age; it's one of those taboo subjects like their weight, the size of their arse or how much they spend on their shoes. They don't take kindly to their career choices being mocked either.

She makes an angry exasperated sound in the back of her throat. 'And are you going to spend the rest of *your* life breaking the law?'

'God, have you ever listened to yourself?' I shake my head. 'Sanctimonious isn't the word for it. You're married to a fraudster. He's hardly the Angel bloody Gabriel.'

Simone glares at me. Then, with more self-restraint than I've given her credit for, she turns her back and switches off the bedside lamp. 'I need some sleep.'

So much for a night of passion.

She may be able to sleep but I can't. Four hours later I'm still lying supine, wakeful, gazing up at the ceiling. The curtains are open and my eyes have adjusted to the dark. We've got a room at the back, overlooking the car park, and occasionally I hear the sound of a vehicle pulling in, of an engine being cut, then the hurry of footsteps on the concrete. Some late-night traveller looking for shelter. Someone with nothing more to worry about than a shower and a bed with clean sheets.

I'm still dressed, wearing jeans and a T-shirt. All I have to do is pull on my jacket, pick up my bag and leave.

The time has come, hasn't it?

A few feet away, Simone breathes softly. I try not to think of how she'll feel when she finds me gone. That's her problem, not mine. Serves her right for giving me so much grief. I won't miss her, not for a second. Why should I? I'm better off on my own. Still, it's a shame it had to end like this, with scowls and bitter words. But there's no point hanging around. There are three stations down the road, Euston, King's Cross and St Pancras; surely I can get a train to somewhere.

'So long, sweetheart,' I whisper.

Simone stirs slightly but doesn't wake.

I mean to get up, to make a move, but instead I light another cigarette.

It's cold outside. I can see the frost on the window. Maybe I should wait a while. What's the point of freezing my bollocks off on an icy platform when it's warm in here, safe and comfortable?

And unable to stop myself, I start going through the facts again, rolling through events, trying to piece the fragments of this ransom mess together. Somewhere, in an obscure corner of my brain, there's a clue I've overlooked. I'm sure of it. I'm certain. If I delve hard enough, root around, I can find that loose thread, give it a yank and ...

After all, it's a matter of pride. There's some bastard out there, some scumbag who thinks he has the right to steal my diamonds. I need to keep searching. Dig deep enough, turn over enough stones, and something nasty will eventually crawl out. That's reason enough to keep on digging. Although, truth is, I've got another reason too. Just call me sentimental but I would like to leave Simone with *something* – even if it's only a glimmer of hope.

I begin with Ted Ainsworth. Okay, we go way back but we were never bosom buddies; contemporaries rather than friends. He might owe me a favour but he's shown an unusual interest, an unexpected enthusiasm, in helping me out. Twice today – or rather, yesterday – he got off his fat arse, picked up the phone, and talked to me. Was that down to respect, to history or something else? Perhaps he and Dean both know more than they're letting on.

Then there's Eddie Tate. What secrets has *he* taken to the grave? Perhaps if I hadn't been so determined to avoid him, he might have told me something useful. He never got the chance because I never gave him the chance. And then Carl stepped in. What did he say to him, do to him? I close my eyes. Jesus. I *know* what he did. I don't want to think about it.

And of course there are the Fosters – angry and resentful. Instinctively, I place a hand over my ribs; they're still sore, bruised and tender, an uncomfortable reminder of just how far they were prepared to go.

And finally there are the people I trust – Melanie and Patrick. I shiver. Could either of them hate me enough, despise me enough, to do this? It's not an easy question to answer. If it hadn't been for me, Dixie would never have ended up in jail – and Melanie would not have lost her father. That's motive enough. And Patrick's got good reason too. I made his daughter's life a misery, condemning her to a life of empty hope and prison visits. But would he have handed over the diamonds if he . . .

Shit, what's the point? I've been through this a hundred times before. They've all got reasons, motives, but none of it makes the kind of sense it needs to. I stub out my cigarette and instantly light another. I reach down and retrieve the bottle of whisky.

Okay, one last drink. I pour a large one, a very large one, and stare back up at the ceiling. Let's go back to the beginning and start again. The only flaw, as far as I can see it, is their decision to take Marc. He wouldn't have been my first choice. Why not Dee? A woman would have been easier, less of a risk, less danger of a struggle. Especially in broad daylight. Unless...

And then it suddenly comes to me. There's a cracking in my head, like boiling water flowing over ice. I sit up, leap off the bed and stagger over to the window. Shuddering, I wipe the sweat off my forehead. What's happening? Jesus, I don't need to ask. I know what's happening.

I'm having a bloody revelation.

With my hands against the window, I stare out into the night. Like a madman, I beat my palms against the glass. Fuck. How stupid have I been? How fucking, fucking stupid?

Chapter Twenty-Three

Simone

I think it's the rain at first, pounding against the glass. A storm. I turn over, wanting to go to sleep again. It's only as I open my eyes that I see him standing there, a bleak silhouette against the window, his hands raised in a frenzy of rage.

'Johnny?'

He doesn't turn, doesn't even acknowledge me.

I sit up, still half-asleep, not sure if this is real. I put on the lamp and say, more forcibly, 'What's wrong? What are you doing?'

He stops. As if exhausted, his hands fall down by his sides. 'We need to talk.'

And suddenly I'm wide awake. Fear runs through me like a blade. 'What's happened?' I leap out of bed. 'It's Marc, isn't it? You've heard something. Oh God! Tell me, tell me!'

And now, in a blind panic, I'm grabbing his shoulders and shaking them. 'Please!' My heart's jumping. I can hear my voice edged with hysteria.

He takes hold of my arms and lowers me back on to the bed. 'It's not Marc. He's safe. I swear.' And his voice sounds different too, tight and restrained, as if he's fighting to keep control. 'Stay there,' he says. 'I'll make some coffee.'

I put my hand to my chest. *It's not Marc. Marc's safe.* I keep repeating it to myself. I sit shivering, swaying back and forth, on the bed. I want to force him to tell me what he knows but first I need to clear my head.

He glances over his shoulder. 'Why don't you get dressed while I make a drink?'

'Why? Where are we going?'

Again he doesn't answer but starts messing with the cups and saucers, picking them up and putting them down as if he needs to keep occupied. I can hear a faint hissing from the kettle as it starts to boil.

I gather up my clothes and take them to the bathroom. Now the immediate fear has dissipated, it's been replaced by an oddly surreal sensation, as if this might just be part of some complicated dream. I feel slightly sick too, the way you do when you've been abruptly woken up. Quickly, I pull on jumper and jeans. I wash my face, brush my teeth, and stare at my reflection in the mirror.

Johnny knows something, something important, and he's about to share it. I want him to tell me and I don't – because there's something in his eyes that looks like pity. So why should he feel sorry for me? There's only one reason. Marc may still be alive but time's running out . . .

I can't bear to think further.

I stumble anxiously back into the room and perch on

the edge of the bed. There's a cup of black coffee on the table and I take two fast gulps that scald my throat and make me cough.

Johnny's standing by the window. He comes over and sits down beside me. 'Now you have to listen and you have to stay calm, okay?' Then immediately he gets up again, pours whisky into a glass and passes it to me. 'You may need this.'

Now the panic's beginning to resurface. 'But you said he was fine, you said—'

'He is. I give you my word.'

I take a sip of the whisky. Maybe it will help calm my nerves.

Then Johnny starts to pace, raking his fingers through his hair. He walks from one side of the room to the other.

He turns by the window. 'Look, Simone ... I haven't always been straight with you. I'm the first to admit that. But do you trust me? Do you trust me at all?'

In an echo of his own answer to that question, only hours ago, I smile faintly and shrug. 'Enough.'

'Enough to believe that I wouldn't lie about *this* – about Marc?'

I force myself to nod.

He picks up his glass of whisky and knocks it back in one. If I didn't know better I'd think his hand was shaking. 'Okay.' He sits down beside me again. Hearing him take a deep breath, I prepare for the worst. But still he doesn't speak.

'Johnny?'

He can't look me in the eye. Instead he stares down at the carpet. Eventually, he clears his throat and says, 'Okay. I'm not sure where Marc is exactly but I *am* sure that he's safe, that he's not in any danger.'

'What do you mean?'

He repeats, 'Marc's safe.'

'You're not making any sense.' I wonder how much whisky he's drunk tonight, if he's had any sleep at all. Perhaps these are just the ramblings of a drunken insomniac. 'You've seen the ransom note. You know what happened to Eddie. How can he be?'

He shakes his head. 'Simone ...' Then he gives a long sigh. 'Fuck, I can't believe it. I'm such a bloody fool.'

'For God's sake,' I almost shout, 'look at me, can't you?' I grab hold of his arm. 'And tell me what's going on. I can't take any more. You wake me up in the middle of the night, you say you *have* to talk to me and then ...'

He does look at me now and then, oddly, he laughs. It's not an amused kind of laugh but the very opposite: bitter, harsh and nasty. It makes my flesh crawl.

'Marc isn't in any danger,' he repeats. 'He never has been.'

I stare at him, alarmed, the first stirrings of a different kind of fear blossoming in my gut. I'm in a room, alone, with a man who's served eighteen years for murder. If anyone's the bloody fool, it's me.

He leans in closer. I can smell the whisky on his breath. When he speaks again there's a coldness to his voice, a clearly suppressed rage. 'There was *never* any threat, *never* any kidnap, never any bloody *anything*. We've both been taken for a ride, sweetheart. We've both been sold up the fucking river.'

Jesus, now I know he's drunk. Or mad. He's finally lost the plot.

'No,' he says, seeing the expression on my face. 'You're the one who's got it wrong.' He stands up and goes to pour himself another drink. '*You're* the one clinging to a fantasy.'

My heart starts thumping as he sits down beside me again. I make an effort not to flinch. Best to keep calm, to try and humour him. What's the time? I glance at my watch. Twenty to four – the bleakest and loneliest time of the night.

If I screamed, would anybody hear me?

'I know what you're thinking,' he says. 'But I'm not lying. I promise.'

Why is he saying this stuff? I've watched all the cop shows, seen all the hostage scenarios. All I have to do is stay completely calm. Softly, I try to reason with him. I even attempt a rather shaky smile. 'But that can't be true, Johnny. How can it? You were there, you saw the note, you know about Eddie, and you know how worried Marc was – he was frightened, desperate—'

'Marc wasn't afraid of Eddie's killer.'

And he says it with such firmness, such authority, that a sliver of ice runs down my spine. And with it my first terrifying doubt.

But still I attempt to refute it. 'We were together,' I insist, 'don't try and tell me that he wasn't scared.'

He laughs again. 'Oh yeah, he was scared all right – but it wasn't about being next on the list. That was the one thing he *didn't* have to worry about.'

My fingers clench around the glass. I draw it carefully

towards my mouth and take a drink. 'And what's that supposed to mean?' It's intended as an accusation but emerges as more of a whisper. And even as it sneaks out through my lips, I get the terrible feeling that I don't really want to hear the answer.

And Johnny, despite his anger, seems equally reluctant to provide it. He hesitates, his forehead creasing up into that familiar frown. 'Because he knew,' he eventually says softly, 'he *knew* who'd killed Eddie.'

He's waiting for me to ask but I won't. I can't. My lips can't even begin to form the question.

He draws in his breath again. 'It was Carl.'

Now I'm the one to laugh.

'What?' he snaps. 'You think he's not capable?'

And that brings me up short. If there's a memory that will never leave my head, it's the one of Carl and Gena outside the house last Christmas. I saw what he did to her. I witnessed his brutality and the pleasure he took in it. But there's a difference isn't there, between . . .

'Carl killed Eddie Tate,' he repeats slowly, 'and Dee helped cover it up.'

No, that can't be true. It's madness. I can feel the dampness under my arms, the gathering sweat of fear. I turn to him, incredulous, confused. 'I don't believe you.'

'She told me herself. She even gave me the details but I'll spare you those, they're not recommended on an empty stomach. It's all to do with the diamonds, of course. Carl thought Eddie was standing in the way so he decided to remove the obstacle. And that's why Marc was so eager to get to Spain. Like me, he didn't fancy being implicated in a murder.'

I shake my head. 'No.'

But Johnny continues regardless. 'Quite when they hatched their inventive little plan, I'm not sure. But they had to act quickly. They knew I wouldn't hang around after Eddie's killing – I wasn't going to wait for the knock on the door – and that meant they were going to lose the diamonds too. So they had to come up with something – and fast.'

I stare at him, open-mouthed. None of this is true. It can't be. Because if it is, then I know what's coming next and it's going to tear my bloody heart out.

'There was only one person left who might be able to persuade me to pass those diamonds over: Someone who had nothing to lose, someone who'd do *anything* to help save her husband—'

'No,' I shout, 'you're wrong, you're twisted. You're bloody lying!'

Johnny drops down on to the floor. He kneels at my feet and takes hold of my hands. 'I'm sorry, sweetheart, but they used us both. There was never any kidnap. While we've been running round in circles, chasing our tails, your husband has been holed up in some hotel, ordering room service and living the life of fucking Riley.'

I pull my fingers away and cover my eyes. Suddenly it seems so viciously clear that all I can do is think of reasons to deny it. 'No, they wouldn't, they couldn't. They're my *family*.' But even as I speak the word, I know it's meaningless. I'm an outsider. I always have been. I've never really belonged.

'I'm sorry,' he says again.

But still I can't bring myself to accept it. Carl couldn't do that to Eddie. And Marc couldn't do this to me, couldn't let me suffer, couldn't put me through all this hell. I'm his wife, for God's sake. He loves me. 'No, you're only saying it because... because you want to keep the diamonds. You don't want to hand them over. You want to keep them for yourself.'

I'm grasping at straws but who cares? Anything's better than facing the truth.

Patiently, he replies, 'So why haven't I just walked away? I don't need to be here, telling you any of this. The minute I worked it out, I could have packed my bag and gone, conscience clear, nothing left to worry about.'

He stands up and walks across the room. Picking up his jacket, he removes a small black pouch from one of the pockets. He brings it back and throws it down on the bed.

'Open it,' he says.

I do as he asks. I turn it upside down and empty the contents over the duvet. A handful of gems spill out. Small, pretty, perfect, they catch the light from the lamp and sparkle. I stare at them.

Johnny's still standing over me. It's as if he's waiting for something, a reaction, a response, but I'm not sure exactly what he wants.

They're diamonds. I've seen diamonds before, although not loose like this. I pick one up and hold it in the palm of my hand. So this is what greed and misery look like. It's for these tiny pieces of sparkling carbon that three men have already died.

'You want them,' he says abruptly, 'you keep them. If you really believe that Marc's in danger, you take them home and give them to Dee.'

I look up at him, bewildered. 'What?'

He shrugs. 'You've got a life to save, haven't you? Go on. Gather them up. Put them in your handbag. Why not?'

'Because . . .'

'Go on,' he urges. 'What's stopping you?'

But he already knows what. Just like I do. There's a dammed-up river of grief inside me, waiting to burst, and it's getting fiercer and stronger by the minute. I'm not sure how much longer I can hold it in. My husband's betrayed me, my so-called family has deceived me, and sometime soon I'm going to have to face up to it. With one fast angry movement, I swipe the gems off the bed. 'You can keep your fucking diamonds!'

A few seconds later – and I can't remember how I even got here – I'm standing in the bathroom, leaning over the basin. The water's running. I want to be sick. It would be better to vomit, to get rid of all the bile, but all that comes out of my mouth is empty retching. Any pain would be better than this, any *physical* pain. I smash my fist against the wall. It hurts – but not enough. I want to cry but I can't. Instead, I lean forward, rest my forehead against the cool white tiles, and silently pray: *Please God, please God, help me!*

I turn the water off and listen to my own uneasy breathing.

I stare into the mirror. A ghost returns my gaze, wide-eyed, haunted. I'm still waiting for the full force to hit me, to sweep me off my feet, but all I feel is . . . emptiness.

Walking back into the room, I find Johnny sitting on the bed with the diamonds in his hand. He must have crawled around the floor to retrieve them. Not very dignified – but who the hell am I to talk? I'm the woman whose husband has used her, abused her, and left her hanging out to dry. You can't get more undignified than that.

He holds them out to me and smiles. 'Do you know how much they're worth?'

What does he want to do – rub my nose in it?

'Go on,' he says. 'Take a guess.'

Jesus, has he no sensitivity at all? But as he's clearly not going to give up, I think back to the internet cafe, to the website, the facts and figures on the screen. Although I'm not sure how much they weigh, I do know that pink diamonds are rare and precious, I know they're valued for their weight and clarity and colour and ...

He smiles. 'About thirty grand,' he declares, 'on a good day.'

That's not even close to the figures I was reading about. They should be worth more than that. They have to be. I mean, no one's going to ... but slowly it registers: these are diamonds all right, but they're not pink, not even remotely pink – they're a clear bright white. I glance up at him, frowning. 'I don't understand.'

'It's ironic, isn't it? All this mess, all this shit, over something that never actually existed.'

'I don't understand,' I say again. It's like I'm caught in a loop that I can't escape from. 'I don't ... '

Johnny pours the gems from one hand to another. 'There

never were any pink diamonds,' he says. 'Plenty of these but that's all.' He stops and holds them up towards the light. 'Not that I'm complaining.'

And now I'm even more confused.

He looks at me. 'You don't get it, do you?'

I don't get anything. A white mist has fallen over my brain. Nothing makes sense. Nothing has even *approached* sense in the past twenty minutes.

'It's not that complicated,' he explains. 'We went in, did the job, and came out. It ran like a dream, no problem. We got what we wanted. It was only later that ...' He stops and stares down at the diamonds. Then he reaches for his glass and drops another inch of whisky down his throat. 'It was only later that the papers claimed we'd got away with a damn sight more than we had.'

'Why would they say that?'

Johnny shrugs. 'My guess? Probably an insurance scam. The pink diamonds could have been on the premises – perhaps we just missed them – but more likely they were stashed at home in some lucky jeweller's safe. Come the robbery, he saw the perfect opportunity to cash in twice – to claim the insurance and then sell the ice on privately.' He laughs. 'Jesus, we did that guy such a favour.'

I laugh too. The response is involuntary. And almost instantly I want to scream. What the hell am I doing? My life's just been smashed to pieces. I shouldn't even be listening to him but I am. I shouldn't be able to concentrate, to take in a word, but it's currently all I'm capable of doing. As if all my hopes, my emotions, have been cut away, I feel like

I'm floating, drifting, clinging to any small chance of rescue. And if that means contributing to this crazy conversation then I'll do just that.

'But if Roy Foster and Eddie were with you then why did they think ...'

'Only Roy was in the building. Eddie was the driver; he was waiting outside. And Roy saw what we took but later he began to have doubts, to question his own eyes, to imagine that one of us – Dixie or me – had managed to hide them.' He rakes his fingers through his hair again and glances up. 'The power of the press,' he says, wryly.

'And that was what the fight was about?'

He nods. 'And of course after the ... accident ... Eddie started believing it too. It became one of those myths, you know, a rumour that just fed off itself.'

'So everything's that happened, everything that ...'

'For nothing,' he says. Carefully, he pours the diamonds back into the pouch. 'These are all that's left. Sarah kept them for me.' He pauses. 'Patrick kept them for me.'

I feel like I've been holding my breath – for an hour, for a week, for a whole bloody lifetime – and as I finally let go, as my lungs deflate, grief and rage merge together in a torrent of resentment. 'But you let Jim and Dee believe in that myth. You lied to them. You *encouraged* them. What were you doing?' Gradually my voice is rising. 'This is all your bloody fault!'

Before I can stop myself, I'm beating on his arms with my fists. 'This is your fault!' And the tears are starting to flow, to stream down my face. '*You* made them do this!'

Johnny doesn't even try to defend himself.

'I hate you!'

He flinches but still doesn't back away.

I know I'm wrong, that it's Marc I want to shout at, to bite and scratch and hurt, but blind rage urges me on. I need someone to damage right now, someone to blame. Inside my head, anger and humiliation are conducting their own battle. I feel lost, destroyed, *abandoned*. How could Marc do this to me? To let me think that his life was in danger, that someone was holding a gun to his head. Christ, all that fear, that dread . . .

My fists continue to take revenge on Johnny's arms. 'Why did he do it?'

'I'm sorry,' he murmurs.

'You're sorry? You're bloody sorry? You don't even know what that means.' Sobbing, I hit and shout until I'm all burned out. Gradually my hands grow heavier and my head sinks down. 'Why?' I keep asking, over and over. 'How could he do this to me?' And eventually, exhausted, I can't protest any more. I can barely move either.

Johnny pulls me towards him.

'Why?' I whisper. I'm trying to stop the tears, to stop being such a victim. I fold against his shoulder and he wraps his arms around me. And even as he's doing it, I'm thinking how wrong it is, how twisted – of all the people in the world, he's the last I should be taking comfort from.

'It's okay,' he says.

And I should pull away, I know, but just for a while I need him there. Just for a while I want to feel safe. It's easier to close my eyes, to cling to him, than it is to face the truth.

'It's okay,' he whispers again, although we both know it isn't.

I've got my face against his shirt, against his chest. I can smell him, that distinctive soap and tobacco smell, overlain now with whisky. But I've never *felt* him before. Not like this. I want to keep my eyes closed, to fall into an endless sleep. I'm not sure how long it is, five minutes, maybe ten, before I finally stop crying. I want to pull away but haven't got the strength. As if he's holding me by force, I murmur, 'Let me go.'

But his arms have already set me free. I'm fighting against nothing.

'You know why I stayed?' Johnny asks softly. 'You know why I didn't just walk away?'

I make a vague snuffling noise, the closest I can get to an answer.

'Simone?'

And now pride finally finds its voice. I lift my head and stare at him. 'I've no idea. Because it amused you? Because you felt *sorry* for me?'

'No,' he retorts smartly. 'Jesus, you're the only one who thinks that.'

'I've got a bloody right,' I wail.

Johnny sighs. He reaches out and wraps his hand around my wrist. 'I stayed for the reason Dee hoped I would.'

Dee. As if I ever want to hear that bloody name again. And I can hear her voice in my head saying, *He likes you. Be nice to him*. She was prepared to let me do anything, *anything*, to get those diamonds for her. And I almost did. There were times when I came recklessly close to . . .

Well, if that's what Dee wanted, then maybe I shouldn't disappoint her. I take his hand in mine and turn it over. I stare at his wrist, at those deep violent scars. I never did ask but I don't need to. I know what they signify: that he understands pain, that he's been somewhere terrible, somewhere far worse even than this.

And we're alone now, aren't we, the two of us? Both betrayed. What difference would it make?

Chapter Twenty-Four

Johnny

Simone looks up. She pauses for a second, those stricken hazel eyes examining my face, before her lips close over mine. There's an urgency about it, a need, but it's more punishing than passionate, a kiss rooted firmly in despair. But I don't try to fight it. Why should I? This is what I've been waiting for.

Together, in a clumsy embrace, we fall back on the bed. She's under me and then beside me.

Her mouth briefly searches for mine again, before she jerks away, almost pushes me away ... and then instantly draws me closer again. Her hands move restlessly over my body, across my shoulders, down my spine. She doesn't speak, doesn't murmur a word. The only sound is our own uneven breathing. Through my clothes I can feel the sharp roaming edge of her fingernails, a sensation midway between pain and pleasure.

How long since I've been touched like this?

Now she's taking off my shirt. She undoes the buttons and reaches inside. Her hands are caressing, gliding gently over the bruises. I lean in towards her. I run the flat of my palm along her belly; the skin's soft and warm, inviting. Sliding quickly north, too fast perhaps, I pull up her jumper and grope for her breasts, cupping one in each hand, feeling for the curves, for the flesh beneath the lace, for a new place to put my mouth. Her body arches towards me. For the first time, she makes a noise, a softly whispered moan.

There are worse places to lose yourself than between a woman's breasts. And this wouldn't be a bad place to linger if we weren't both so fucking crazy. There's no time for idle contemplation. My fingers move quickly down. She lifts her hips and I wrench off her jeans, over her thighs, her ankles, and throw them on the floor. She's still wearing her bra, her red jumper, but all that remains on her lower half is a pair of cream silk panties.

I stare down at her.

She sees me looking. Her hands reach out again, stroking my thighs, moving up and down, skimming, tantalizing. As she hears me gasp she pulls me in against her. She moves against my groin, her hips rising.

I groan, closing my eyes. Jesus!

I put my legs between hers and push them apart. There's no finesse here, not on either side, no honeyed words or sweet seduction. There's only need and desperation. Quickly, I fumble with the zip on my own jeans.

And then, just as I know that I'm going to take her, to finally have her, I raise my head and see her face. She's leaning back against the pillow, staring at the ceiling. Her eyes are open but blank, and she's crying, silently crying . . .

I stop dead, my lust instantly dissolving. I don't mind a few grateful tears *after* the event, but seeing them before tends to cool the ardour.

What the hell am I doing? With a sigh, I regretfully roll off her.

'Don't,' she whispers. She reaches out, wraps her arms around my neck, but her heart's not really in it.

I prop my head up on an elbow and stare down. 'This isn't a good idea.'

Silently, she gazes back.

This is probably the time when I'm supposed to say *Hey, it's not you, sweetheart, it's me* but even I can't bear to come out with something that crass. Instead I stand up, pull the duvet over her legs and go in search of a whisky anaesthetic.

I take the two glasses back to the bed. Simone's already struggling back into her jeans. She looks offended, as if I'm the cause of yet another major rejection. She glances up at me with those mournful eyes. I'd like to offer some comfort but I've never been big in that department; lying, scheming, manipulating, yes, but not compassion, not sympathy.

'I'm sorry, I shouldn't have—'

But even as I start to speak she waves my words away as if she knows they'll do more harm than good. 'It doesn't matter.'

I perch uneasily on the edge of the other bed. Slowly, I do up the buttons on my shirt. If tonight is the night of exposure then I've barely started yet. 'There's something else I need to tell you.' I pause. 'Why I came to the Buckleys' in the first place.'

She doesn't seem especially interested. Sitting with her arms wrapped around her knees, she's studying the floor.

'Simone?'

'You already told me why.'

'Not all of it. Not the whole truth.'

As if she's had enough truth to last her a lifetime, she sighs despairingly. 'Why should I care?'

Which is a reasonable question. I guess she's got enough to deal with without adding my sordid confessions to the mix. Still, I've never let anything as superficial as consideration stand in my way so I open my mouth and eventually, when I'm partway through, she unwinds and picks up her whisky and finally begins to listen. Some of it she knows and some of it she doesn't but I let it all spill out, the whole damn story, from beginning to end.

There's a long silence after I've finished. I get the impression, unsurprisingly, that I haven't exactly gone up in her estimation.

'How do you know it was Jim?' she asks. 'How can you be sure he made that call?'

'Believe me, I *know*.'

It's not the most convincing evidence but she lets it pass. 'And you and Melanie,' she continues, 'if all this hadn't happened, if Carl hadn't . . . ' She stumbles over the mention of his name, a shiver running through her body. 'What would you have done to Jim?'

I don't reply for a moment. I'm far from sure of the answer. Shrugging, I say, 'I wanted to kill him.'

'You could have done that on the first day you got there.'

'I wanted him to suffer first. I wanted him to lose everything I'd lost – his home, his wife, his family. I wanted him to *hurt*.'

'And then?'

I shrug again. 'I don't know.'

Another gloomy silence falls across the room.

Then she asks, in a small voice, 'Do you think Marc had second thoughts about using me? Do you think that's why he wanted to go to Spain?'

'Yeah, maybe.' Personally, I think he panicked, that he bottled it, but that's a sentiment best not shared.

'It's okay. I'm not trying to make excuses for him.' She smiles, a glimmer of the old Simone returning. 'He's weak. I've always known that.'

'You're better off without him.'

'Thanks,' she replies, caustically.

I sit back on the bed and stare out of the window. It's still dark but on the distant horizon there's a faint streak of light, the precursor to dawn. There's a lot of weird stuff going through my mind – rage and frustration being only a part – and I'm trying to get it in order, to make some sense of it. It doesn't do a lot for a man's pride, or his reputation, to be duped by a bunch of fucking amateurs. Then again, compared to Simone, I've probably got off lightly. I may have a dent in my ego but she's got a bloody big knife sticking out of her back.

'Perhaps you were right. When you said it was my fault.'

She shakes her head. 'I was angry.'

'No. If I hadn't been so busy trying to screw up their lives, I might have noticed what was going on. I should have *seen* it. I should have realized.'

'They took us both for fools.'

I don't need reminding. 'Fuckers,' I murmur.

Suddenly she gets up and starts moving round the room, picking up her things and throwing them into her bag.

'What are you doing?'

'Getting out of here. There's nothing to stay for any more.'

'Are you going home?'

'Of course not,' she says, with exasperation. 'What the hell would I want to do that for? I never want to see them again, not *any* of them, for as long as I live.'

'So you're going to let them win.'

She rounds on me. 'I don't see any winners here, do you? They haven't got their diamonds, I haven't got a husband, and Eddie Tate's still very dead.'

Simone carries on with her packing but I'm not giving up yet. 'You can't let them get away with it.'

It's only a second before she looks up and it isn't with affection. 'No, you mean that *you* can't. You know what your problem is, Johnny? Everything's about *your* past, *your* pain, *your* bloody mess. You've just jumped from one prison to another and you can't even see it. You're so wrapped up in your own vengeful little world—'

Quickly, I snap back at her. 'I've got a phone. If I want a shrink, I'll call one up.'

'You see? You won't even listen unless it's something you want to hear.'

I stick my face in the whisky glass again.

'And that's not going to help,' she says.

We glare at each other. But suddenly the corners of her mouth curl up.

'God, how ridiculous is this?'

'Truce?' I suggest.

She nods. 'No point parting on bad terms.'

'You can't leave yet.'

As if to challenge that assertion she zips up her bag and reaches for her coat.

'You can't drive, Simone. You've been drinking.'

'*You've* been drinking,' she replies, 'I've only been sipping.'

I glance at her glass, at the inch of whisky remaining. Truth is, I can't remember how much she's had. 'Okay, but you're still upset, you've had a shock. Just sit down for half an hour. Stay and have some breakfast at least. What's the rush? Come on, let me make you a coffee.' She hesitates. 'Come on,' I plead again, this time throwing in a shameless grin, 'be a pity to smash up that ritzy car of yours.'

Which almost raises a smile. 'All right,' she agrees, '*one* coffee but then I'm definitely out of here.'

Once again I mess around with sachets and spoons while she sits on the edge of the bed, her bag at her feet. She looks like someone waiting for a train. She looks like what she is – a traveller passing through. It's strange to think this may be my last memory of her.

'So where are you planning on going?'

'I'll stay with friends for a while.' She pauses. 'And you?'

I take over the coffees and sit down opposite to her. 'I know where I *want* to go. Trouble is, my driver's just resigned. It kind of leaves me stranded.'

'Oh.' She smiles over the rim of her cup. 'Well, if it's not too far, I suppose she might be persuaded to give you a lift. Somewhere local?'

I wait for a second before I drop the bombshell. 'Big house, pleasant garden, Essex way.'

Her jaw falls open. 'What? You want to go *back*?'

'Christ, Simone, isn't there one little bone in your body that wants revenge?' I see the expression on her face and quickly revise the comment. 'Okay, let's not even call it revenge – tit for tat, payback, or hey, how about *squaring the account*? That's kind of apt, isn't it?'

She shakes her head, staring at me like I'm mad. 'I'm moving on. That's what you should do too. I'm letting go.'

'You're running away.'

Knowing that I'm trying to provoke her, she simply shrugs. 'Call it what you like.'

But I haven't finished yet. 'Don't you want the chance to prove, just for once, that they can't walk all over you?'

There's a small hesitation, the tiniest, before she says, 'No.'

It's enough. The window may not be open but it's no longer firmly locked. 'Don't you see? We've got the perfect opportunity. We've got it all worked out but *they* don't have a clue. One day, that's all I'm asking. Just one more day. What difference will that make?'

'I'm not going back.'

I change tack a little. 'There must be things you need there – papers, clothes, passport.'

'I'll get someone else to pick them up.'

'If Dee doesn't trash them first.'

Simone starts, her hand jumping. The cup clatters in its saucer. She puts it shakily down on the table. 'She wouldn't . . . '

'Oh, what? Because she's not that kind of woman, not vindictive, not the type to commit some petty act of vengeance?'

'Let her,' she says, not very convincingly. 'It's only . . . stuff.'

'Your stuff.'

'I'm not going back,' she repeats. 'I can't.'

I lean forward and take her hands. 'Look, all I'm asking is that you come with me, that you pretend, just for a few hours, that you don't know what they've done. God, you'll hardly even need to speak to them. If we get there late enough, you can take a shower, say you're tired, go up to bed. You can get all your things packed and we'll be out again before you know it.'

'And I can leave the rest to you?'

'Yes,' I say, too eagerly to register the disgust in her voice.

I feel her fingers move to extricate themselves. She almost slaps me away. Then she glares at me intensely, her eyes dark and cold. 'And you think I want any part in this?'

It takes a moment before the full impact of her question, and the implication behind it, begins to sink in. To say I haven't made myself clear is an understatement. 'What are you saying, that you think I'm going back to . . .'

Her gaze falters, uncertainty creeping over her face. She bites down on her lower lip.

'Simone?'

She doesn't reply.

I groan, and then I laugh out loud. 'Fuck, Simone, what goes on in that head of yours? You think I'm going back to kill him, don't you? What, to shoot him, to stab him, to strangle him in his sleep?'

She winces but still refuses to answer.

'Or maybe just to bore him to death with an endless stream of questions.'

That jolts her head back up. 'Well, I'm glad you find it so amusing.'

'I'm glad you find it so credible.' I take a deep breath. 'Look, I know you're hardly my greatest fan but do you really think I'd ask you to do that – to drive me to a house where I planned to kill someone?' And in case that sounded too concerned, I quickly add, 'I wouldn't want *you* as a fucking witness.'

'So why? What's the point?'

The whisky's all finished. I light a cigarette and look at her. She's sitting like a statue, motionless, waiting.

'It's all about love, sweetheart.'

Chapter Twenty-Five

Simone

How did he manage to talk me into this? If I had any sense I'd be high-tailing it in the opposite direction by now, going in search of Katie and a shoulder to cry on. Instead I'm driving back towards the place I least want to be – and the people I least want to see again.

But maybe Johnny's right, maybe this isn't something I should run away from. Demons should be faced. Isn't that what they say? But then the people who say it have probably never met my in-laws.

We've managed to kill all of the morning and most of the afternoon by tramping aimlessly through the streets. Outside is where he's most comfortable, no matter how cold or wet. So, like a couple of reluctant tourists, we've done Covent Garden, Oxford Street and Bloomsbury. I wanted to have a scout around the British Museum but Johnny seems to have an aversion to antiquities. Actually, apart from whisky, women and tobacco, he seems to have an aversion to most things.

Now it's already growing dark again. The rain's hammering down against the windscreen, a rain that's been falling perpetually since last night. My feet are soaked, all my clothes faintly damp, but I'm not bothered. I've more on my mind than smelling of roses.

'What if I say something I shouldn't? What if I let something slip?'

Johnny glances at me. 'Best keep your mouth shut then,' he says, with his usual diplomacy.

The one advantage to driving is that I don't have to look at him. In fact, this is what I've been specifically trying to avoid for most of the day. This is the man, after all, who I suddenly decided to kiss, who's seen me half-naked, who's had his hands around my breasts. I'm not exactly in a comfort zone.

'So where do you think Marc might be staying?'

He shrugs. 'You know him better than me.'

It's clear Johnny doesn't really want to talk but I can't stand the silence. I need some sound, some basic communication, just to keep the nerves at bay.

Perhaps he senses my anxiety because after a moment he says, 'Somewhere close to home, I bet.'

'You think a hotel, a bed and breakfast?'

He starts to roll a cigarette, his fingers moving deftly. 'I did but I'm not so sure now. I don't think he'd chance it. If he stayed in his room, especially for a whole week, he'd draw attention to himself, and if he left it he'd run the risk of being seen. He could bump into someone you knew.'

'So maybe he's out of town.'

Licking the paper, he stares straight ahead out of the

window. 'Yeah, but how did he get there? I was only gone an hour and Jim, Dee and Carl were all there when I got back – so were the cars, yours *and* hers. The only other way he could have got that far was to use public transport or a cab – and that doesn't seem likely – or if he hired a car ... but again, that's a risk. Most places won't take cash these days, only credit cards, and that leaves a trail.'

For someone who's been out of circulation for eighteen years, Johnny seems to have a solid grasp on current business practices. 'So you've looked into it then – hiring cars?'

He gives me one of his wry smiles. 'It's important, don't you think, to keep abreast of current developments?'

And maybe it's my imagination, or my paranoia, but I get the feeling he just placed an unnecessary emphasis on the word *abreast*. Thankfully, it's dark so he doesn't have the pleasure of seeing the flush rising into my cheeks. 'Perhaps the club, then,' I say too quickly.

Of course he chooses this moment to light his cigarette, the flame flaring briefly but just long enough to read the expression on my face. Keeping my eyes on the road, I refuse to look back at him. I know he's wearing a grin that any Cheshire cat would be proud of.

He takes a drag and shakes his head. 'What, down in a cold damp basement, sleeping on the floor, on some battered sofa, roughing it? No decent washing facilities, no TV, no home comforts? I don't see that as Marc's style, do you? He's hardly Mr Camper.'

'He's roughed it before. He's been inside.'

'That's what I mean,' Johnny replies. 'He's hardly likely to voluntarily repeat the experience. I may be wrong but I've got this gut instinct that he won't have strayed too far. If it all went tits up he'd want to be able to get back in a hurry.'

I try not to wince at the phrase. 'So where?'

'There must be someone he can trust. A relative, a friend?'

I rack my brains but can't think of anyone. 'He's not exactly big on friends. After ... well, after the last time he went down, it cut something of a swathe through that particular front.'

'*Cut a swathe*, eh?' he mimics, grinning.

We're coming up to red traffic lights. Quickly checking the rear view mirror, and finding no one close, I slam my foot abruptly on the brake. He shoots forward with the force I was intending and then slams back against his seat.

'What the ...'

I turn to glare at him. 'Please don't laugh at me.'

Johnny frowns but his mouth slowly breaks into a smile. 'Christ,' he says, rubbing his neck, 'remind me never to cross you over anything *really* serious.'

The lights move on to green and we shift forward. I swing a left, keeping my eyes on the road. The traffic's getting busier now, the commuters spilling out from their offices. I'm stuck behind a row of tank-like 4×4s. As our speed gradually decreases, I drum my fingers on the wheel.

'You still mad at me?' he asks.

'What do *you* think?' I don't even give him space to reply. 'Oh, don't bother answering that. I know what you think – that I'm some stuck-up prissy bitch who doesn't know her arse from her elbow.'

He laughs. Then he winds down the window and throws his cigarette out. The rain sprays inside, showering his face and hair. 'I didn't mean to take the piss,' he says, with about as much sincerity as he's capable of. 'If it's any consolation, I'm on edge too.'

Except he isn't. He's loving every minute of it. He can't wait to get back, to start working on that devious revenge plan of his. Still, it isn't going to help my anxiety levels if this escalates into a row so I nod and let it pass.

Johnny switches the subject back to Marc. 'Look, the day he went missing, is there anything you can think of, anything different, odd?'

'I didn't even speak to him. He was still asleep when I left.' I've been over it time and time again. The only unusual fact about that morning was that we'd made love the night before, a pretty rare occurrence over recent weeks. But that's a fact I'm *not* prepared to share with Johnny – there's such a thing as too much information. 'I came downstairs. Jim was in the kitchen, drunk. You remember?'

He nods. 'No surprise there.'

'Then I gave you a lift into town. I parked, you went off to see your parole officer, I went inside and . . .' Suddenly, I stop. Something *has* occurred to me. I peer through the windscreen, between the wipers, while a memory slowly unravels.

'Simone?'

I glance at him, frowning. 'I'm not sure. It might be nothing but . . . well, Kerry Anne – she's the girl who works in the shop – she was in a right strop. It wasn't like her; she's more the placid type, easy-going. That's why it was so weird. She said it wasn't anything to do with me but it was. I'm sure it was.' I can visualize her face, her cross little mouth and angry eyes. 'And she asked about you.'

Johnny's brows shoot up. 'Asked what?' 'Who you were, your name.' 'Idle curiosity?'

I shake my head. 'No, it was more than that. She was really interested. She'd been watching you. It was like . . .' I struggle to find the right description. 'It was like she was almost *accusing* me of something.'

We hit the next set of lights and grind to a halt again.

Johnny grins. 'Maybe she was jealous, seeing you with such a good-looking guy. Maybe all she wanted was my number.'

Now it's my turn to laugh. 'You reckon?'

'Thanks.' He pretends to be offended. 'You really know how to boost a man's ego.'

'Sorry, I never realized it needed encouragement.'

He grins again. 'So is she pretty, this Kerry Anne?'

'She's certainly young.'

'Got a boyfriend?'

I glance at him. 'Why? Are you thinking of applying for the post?'

'Do you think I should?'

But this time I don't reply. Gradually the trivial exchange has been sparking off an entirely different, and thoroughly unwelcome, chain of thought. I've got that sick feeling in my stomach again. Christ, I hope I'm wrong. I hope I'm just jumping to some manic, sleep-deprived conclusion.

Johnny's quick to pick up on the change of atmosphere. He stops the banter and asks, 'What are you thinking?'

'Marc and Kerry Anne,' I murmur. I don't need to elaborate. It's not a complicated equation – he can do the maths as well as I can. Shit, all those times I saw them together, chatting, flirting, and not once did I ever imagine . . .

As the lights change, I jam my foot on the accelerator and lurch forward, but I have to brake again almost as quickly. The traffic's too dense to argue with. 'For fuck's sake.'

'Hey, take it easy.' He reaches out and touches my arm.

I'm not sure what he's more worried about – my erratic driving or my state of mind. Although I guess either might be a threat to his immediate survival. I shake his hand off. It's not restraint I need – it's space to think. I've got a stream of images sliding through my head, a running sequence of the past few months: Marc coming to the shop, Marc flirting with Kerry Anne, all her questions, her smiles, her endless queries about the state of our marriage, all those glances that I took for some kind of puppy love.

Now suddenly, dismally, all the pieces are falling into place.

'I'm sorry,' he says.

The last thing I need is his pity. I snap, 'What are *you* sorry for?'

Wisely, he doesn't attempt to answer.

The traffic's finally moving again and I'm able to slip into a side road. It's a longer route but, with the rush-hour congestion, probably a faster one. I wish I could stop thinking but I can't. I keep seeing her, hearing her, reliving every time we've stood together in that shop with her asking me about Marc, looking away, blushing. God, just how blind have I been?

Travelling up the hill, I crunch the gears and swear again.

But it's not just her I'm mad at. It's Marc I'm saving my real rage for. As if it isn't bad enough, knowing that he's set me up, used me – and Jesus, I'm barely getting used to *that* idea – I now have to face the probability that he's being having an affair as well. And not just any bloody affair but one with my coy nineteen-year-old assistant.

Johnny, sensibly, has continued to keep his mouth shut. It's only when we rejoin the main road that he speaks again. 'Why are you going this way?'

'I'm going to the shop.'

He jerks forward, alarmed. 'What?'

'You heard me.'

'Shit! You can't. You know you can't. If you go in there and . . .'

'And what? Confront her?'

'You'll blow it all to fuck,' he says. 'You know you will.'

I let him sweat while I try to find a parking space. We do a couple of turns around the block. There's nothing legal so eventually I just pull in across the road and cut the engine. It's five twenty and the lights in the shop are still on.

'Don't,' he says.

But I've already undone my seatbelt.

'Please.' He puts his hand on my arm again.

I know it's not me he cares about, only his own sacred revenge. I say, 'I'm not going to blow it. I promise. I just have to be sure.' I get out of the car and then lean back in. 'I'll only be ten minutes. Why don't you call Dee, tell her we're almost home.'

'What, give her time to start crying again?'

I give him a tight smile. 'Sure, why not? We may as well have the full performance.'

Dodging the traffic, I jaywalk across the road. I pause outside the shop to examine the rows of winter pansies, the hyacinth bulbs, the green shoots of the narcissi in their pots. It feels like a thousand years since I was here last. This was somewhere I felt safe once. How did it all go so horribly wrong?

I take a few deep breaths and arrange a smile before I step inside. Kerry Anne glances up and almost jumps out of her skin. Her eyes widen in surprise and alarm. I can almost see the blood drain out of her rosy cheeks.

'Simone!'

One look at that guilty little face is enough. I'd like to slap it very hard but it's a pleasure I'll have to forgo. 'Hi, how are you doing?'

'W-what are you doing here?' She stumbles over her words. 'I mean . . . I mean, I thought you were away.'

'I was,' I reply simply. I dump my coat on the counter and glance around. 'So, how's it been – busy?'

She's terrified that I might know, that I've found out about the two of them. Her throat's making tiny gulping motions while she tries to smile and speak at the same time. 'Not bad. Okay,' she murmurs faintly.

I wonder how long they've been at it and what Marc

originally told her – probably that clichéd old line about his wife not understanding him. Not that she'd have needed much persuading; she'd have run naked round the daffodils if Marc had asked her to.

'Coffee?' I say brightly, going through to the back. Best to leave her for a minute before I act on the impulse to pull that newly blonde hair out by its roots.

I put the kettle on and pick up two mugs off the drainer. I'm pretty sure I know where he is now – all snug and comfortable in Kerry Anne's flat. She'll be cooking his meals, ironing his shirts and catering to all his other needs too. Of course neither he nor Dee will have mentioned anything about the ransom or the diamonds.

But now I come to think of it, he'll probably have told her that I was having an affair – which would explain her exaggerated interest in Johnny last week and why she spent the morning looking daggers at me. Yes, that would be just like him. Anything for the sympathy vote.

I take the coffee through and pass a mug to her. 'Are you okay?' I ask, all concern. 'You look kind of pale.'

As if playing an invisible piano, her fingers dance nervously over the counter. 'No,' she squeaks, 'I'm fine, I'm fine.'

'Long day, huh?'

She makes a valiant attempt at a smile. 'So, did you, er . . . did you have a nice time?'

She'll be straight on the phone to Marc as soon as I've gone, giving him every detail, so I suppose I'd better make the effort to appear anxious. I rearrange my features into an approximation of worry. 'It wasn't so much a holiday,' I reply evasively, 'more of a ... well, just a break really, a chance to think things over.'

Kerry Anne nods her head so hard I think it may fall off.

Poor little cow! To be honest, I'm starting to feel sorry for her. She's got no idea of the bigger picture, of the game the Buckleys are actually playing. She'll be under strict instruction not to divulge Marc's whereabouts or, more importantly, even to admit having seen him. She thinks she's protecting him from his unfaithful wicked wife, but I know that as soon as this is over Marc will dump her.

Still, that doesn't excuse the fact that she's slept with him. And so long as I'm here, I may as well turn the screws. I might never get another opportunity.

'Can I ask you something, Kerry Anne – do you believe in fresh starts?' I pause, thoughtfully. 'You know, that terrible, really *awful* things can happen, but that you can maybe put them right again?'

She hesitates. She thinks I'm talking about my marriage but I've kept it ambivalent enough that when she repeats it to Marc, he won't get suspicious. He'll have a minor heart attack, of course, when he hears I've been in the shop – and boy, I'd love to be a fly on the wall at that point – but then he'll be smugly confident that I was actually referring to the kidnap.

'I'm not sure,' she replies, her eyes growing wide again.

'It's not always easy to recognize what's right or wrong, is it?' I sip my coffee and gaze pensively into space. 'Everything gets so complicated, so confused. I mean, sometimes you don't know what you've got until you've almost lost it.'

She stares despondently down at the counter.

I suppose I should take consolation from her discomfort – at least she's got some semblance of a conscience. But, on the other hand, that hasn't stopped her from doing what she's done. And God knows for how long.

I put the knife in and twist it. 'So, do you think me and Marc make a good couple?'

She visibly flinches. 'Of course,' she mumbles.

'Really,' I say, over-brightly. 'Why's that?'

Now she looks like I feel – as if she wants to throw up. She makes a vague shrugging motion with her shoulders. 'Well, you know, you're ... you're ... '

And I'm just beginning to enjoy myself when the door swings open and Johnny strolls in.

Frustrated, I glare at him. 'What do *you* want?'

'There's a meter bitch on the prowl,' he replies, with his usual surfeit of charm. 'Are you ready to go, sweetheart, or do you want a ticket?'

'I'm not finished here, yet.'

Kerry Anne glances from him to me, her eyes growing hard. But there's a flash of relief in them too. 'It's okay,' she says quickly, 'I can finish up here. I can lock up.'

Great. So she's not only got my husband, it appears she has my job as well.

He picks my coat up from the counter. 'And you must be Kerry Anne,' he says, turning towards her and smiling broadly. He puts out his hand. 'Nice to meet you.'

As if he's offered her a poisoned chalice, she withdraws a step, but hasn't quite got the courage to refuse. I watch her gaze sweep his face, silently absorbing the cuts and bruises. She's not sure how to react but reluctantly places her fingers in his. 'Hi.'

And there's something about her being forced to shake hands with my so-called lover that makes me want to snigger. Suddenly I'm not so sorry that he's here, that he's making her feel awkward, that he's making her squirm. She deserves it – and more. I'm almost tempted to grab him and kiss him in front of her. That would give Marc food for thought.

But of course I don't.

There's barely time for a backward glance as he takes my arm and manoeuvres me through the door. 'Come on. We've got to go.'

I let myself be bundled out.

I give her one last faint smile. I hope she'll pass it on to Marc. It's the nearest I'll get to any kind of goodbye.

'So?' he asks as we scoot across the road.

'So?' I snap back. 'What did you think – that I needed saving before I scratched her eyes out?'

He grins. 'Didn't you?'

I get in the car and slam the door shut. I dig in my pocket, find the pack of cigarettes, take one out and light it. My hands are shaking. 'The bastard's probably been shagging her for weeks.'

It's another fifteen minutes, a slow crawl through the evening traffic, before we reach the house. Up until now, anger has kept the butterflies away but my nerves are starting to flutter again. I can feel the dampness gathering on my palms.

'Are you sure we're doing the right thing?'

'Just think of what *they've* done,' he replies.

Which is all very well if you follow the 'an eye for an eye' school of thought. And I'm not denying that I want to pay them back — I'd like to kick Marc in the teeth just for starters — but I'm still not convinced this is the right way of going about it.

Turning anxiously into the drive, I wait for the gates to open and then lurch forward so carelessly that I scrape a wing against one of the pillars. It makes a nasty tearing sound. Although on this occasion he'd be perfectly justified, Johnny doesn't comment.

'Relax,' he says instead, 'it'll all be over in a few hours.'

More like eight or nine. I glance at my watch. It's barely six o'clock. Ahead the lights from the house are visible, four golden squares spilling out across the gravel. I do a three-point turn so the car's facing back in the right direction. Then I switch off the engine and try to catch my breath.

Johnny gives me a thin reassuring smile. 'Don't worry.'

For him this is all so simple, black and white, a matter of principle. Of *honour*. But he hasn't spent the past few years living with the Buckleys, eating, talking, laughing, arguing with them. I hate what they've done but we still have history.

As if he can read my mind, he murmurs, 'You don't owe them anything.'

Sometimes he can be so glib. 'What's the matter?' I snarl. 'Scared I'm going to change my mind?'

'Are you?'

'No,' I say quickly.

The seconds tick by. We sit quietly together, partners — albeit reluctant ones — in crime. I'm only here because he can't do this without me. He needs my help and if I don't go through with it, then God knows what he might do instead. Perhaps it's what's referred to as the lesser of two evils.

Or am I just using that as an excuse to make me feel better about my own part in it all?

Surprisingly, no one has come out to greet us yet. They can't have heard the car. Maybe they've got the TV or radio on. I take the opportunity to ask the question that's been nagging at my brain since this morning.

'So what about Carl?'

'What about him?'

'He killed Eddie Tate.' I grind my fists into my thighs. The thought of it still turns my blood to ice. 'He tortured him, he ... Christ, you know what he did. What are we going to do?'

Johnny frowns. 'What do you want to do?'

'He's sick, he's dangerous. He should be locked up.'

'So what do you suggest? You want me to call the cops, grass him up? If I do that, I'll be implicating myself. It won't take them long to find out I was living here and they're hardly going to believe I had nothing to do with it.' He pauses. 'And much as I respect your admirable desire for justice, sweetheart, I'd really rather it wasn't at my expense.'

I search for my cigarettes again, find one and light it. I throw the pack into his lap. 'So he just gets away with it? He just walks free?'

'There's a saying, isn't there – *what goes around comes around*?'

I wind down the window and lean out. The garden smells of rain. I turn to look at him again. Through the shadows, I search the profile of his face. Occasionally I think I know what's going on in his head, but at other times – like now for instance – I don't have a clue.

'Do you really believe that?'

'Why not?' He lights his own cigarette and smiles. 'Although there *is* another option.' He digs in his pocket, gets out his mobile, and starts searching through the address menu. 'I could always ring Quigley . . .'

I start. 'What? You can't do that. You heard what he said – he'll kill him!'

'Carl killed Eddie,' Johnny replies impassively.

I reach out, grab his phone and turn it off.

He shrugs. 'I thought you wanted justice.'

I glare at him. 'Not that kind.'

'Ah,' he repeats, softly, 'not *that* kind.' He lifts his cigarette and takes a drag. 'I get it. You don't mind him dying slowly, you don't mind him rotting in jail for twenty years, every day a relentless fucking misery, but when it comes to execution . . .'

I snort, rolling the phone between my fingers. 'Is that what you'd have preferred?' But even as the words leave my mouth, I'm regretting them. Those scars on his wrist are coming back to haunt me. I close my eyes and bite down on my lip. 'No, I'm sorry. I didn't mean . . .'

But now the back door has suddenly opened and Dee is descending on us. There's no time left to explain – even if I could.

If I ever had doubts that I could actually do this, it only takes a glance at Dee's contrived woebegone face to know the answer. I get out of the car and try not to flinch as she wraps her Judas arms around me.

'You poor love. You look exhausted.'

Trapped against her ample bosom, I make a vague mumbling sound. Before I can utter anything more articulate – or more damning – Johnny rapidly propels us inside.

'Come on, girls, let's not hang about.'

The kitchen is just as it always was – the big oak table, the pans hanging on the walls, the stained wood floor. It's the same but different. Or maybe I'm the one that's changed. I feel like a stranger now, a visitor. There's a pot of coffee on the go but instead of helping myself, I pull out a chair, sit down and wait.

Dee goes straight for the cupboard and the alcohol. She takes out a couple of bottles, whisky and gin. 'What you both need is a drink.' Which, roughly translated, means that what *she* needs is a drink – a large one.

I can't say I blame her. Maintaining a farce like this must be damned hard work. I'd like to get blasted myself, out-of-my-head, drunk, but I can't. I'm going to have to drive later. Still, I don't refuse the offer – one won't do any harm.

Jim lumbers into the kitchen, smiling faintly. He clearly wasn't expecting us back today and is still in a state of semi-sobriety. Unlike Dee, he's not a natural liar and his eyes move furtively between us, not sure where to settle.

As if he can't resist the urge, Johnny goes over and slaps him on the back. 'Jim! It's good to see you again.'

He makes a vague nodding motion, glancing anxiously towards Dee.

'Sit down,' she says, impatiently.

Jim does as he's told and she slams a large glass of whisky in front of him.

Johnny, grinning, takes the chair opposite to mine.

So now we're all seated round the table, a nice little foursome. There's no sign of Carl, thank God. If she's got any sense, Dee will have packed him off for the night. She wouldn't risk a repeat of the last fiasco ... especially now she's so close to getting what she wants.

There's a moment of silence as we all raise our glasses and drink. Dee can barely contain herself. She's hyper, excited. There are pink diamonds dancing in front of her eyes. She wants to ask, she's desperate to ask, but she's trying to control herself.

Johnny momentarily looks down, leaves a brief pause, and then slowly lifts his head again. 'Don't worry,' he says. 'Everything's fine. The diamonds are safe. They'll be here tomorrow.'

'Tomorrow?' Her face falls in disappointment. She was hoping we had them already. She was thinking that's why we were back. She was hoping she could take them, hold them, feel a million dollars slide coolly through her fingers.

I look away, disgusted.

'They'll be here,' Johnny repeats.

His foot finds my ankle under the table.

Quickly, I glance up. 'Yes, tomorrow. For sure. Definitely.' I force myself to meet her eyes. And then, perhaps with an excess of drama, I reach forward and grasp her hand. I expect her fingers to be cold, as nervous and clammy as mine, but they're not – they're soft and warm. Somehow that revolts me even more. 'Marc's going to be all right, Dee. I promise. I swear he will. We're going to save him.'

Johnny kicks me again. I can almost hear the intake of his breath. He's worried. He thinks my response is over the top, too obvious, but I know better. She's so wrapped up in her own game, she won't take a second to think about ours.

But he's not leaving anything to chance. 'Twelve o'clock,' he says. 'That should give us plenty of time.'

Dee's not overjoyed but it could be worse. She squeezes out a smile. 'You're sure?'

'I'm sure.'

For the next couple of hours, like an aspiring actress, she goes through the motions. We get treated to the fearful mother, the agony, the full array of desolate gestures. She moans. She weeps silently into her gin. And there's no denying that her trembling lips and smudged mascara are an art form in themselves. If ever anyone deserved an Oscar, it's Dee Buckley.

Eventually, with a flourish, she produces the latest ransom note and drops it on the table. 'Here,' she mutters hoarsely, 'this arrived yesterday.'

Johnny solemnly picks it up, reads it and slides it across to me.

The typewritten note gives instructions of where and when the ransom should be handed over. Ironically, they've chosen the recreation ground – the place where I first read the details of Eddie Tate's death. Thursday at 5 p.m. Practically speaking, it's not a bad choice. With three approach roads and the woods behind, there are plenty of routes for a quick escape.

I glance up. Jim frowns and sinks his face into his whisky. Dee plays with the bracelet on her wrist. There's a kind of hysteria rising inside me, a mixture of rage and laughter. It all seems so clear now, so bloody obvious. How did I ever fall for it?

Johnny's the only one who'll meet my gaze. He gives a slight shake of his head, a warning perhaps or just a reminder to hold my tongue.

I know if I stay here any longer, I'm likely to lose my cool. And I'm thinking that it's time to make my excuses and leave, when the front door opens and slams shut. If I'd made the move just a minute ago I could have avoided him. It's too late now. Carl's strolling into the kitchen.

'Oh, back already?' he says with feigned surprise.

Dee glares at him. 'I thought you were out for the night.'

He helps himself to a drink, shrugging off the comment. Then he pulls out a chair and sits down next to me. 'How are you doing, Simone? You look kind of . . . tired.'

Has he seen the fear in my eyes? There's something about that pause, or maybe simply his proximity, that makes the hairs on the back of my neck stand on end. He's sitting so close his elbow is almost touching mine. He smells of beer and sweat and an unpleasant sweet aftershave.

'Fine,' I mutter.

'That's good.' He nods, glancing around at his audience.

'That's good, isn't it?' Slyly, he adds, 'Marc's a lucky guy, having a wife like you.'

And just for a second it flashes through my mind that he knows what we're going to do. *He knows*. Quickly, before he can spot the trembling in my hands, I hide them under the table. Of course he doesn't. He can't. It's just my paranoia slipping into overdrive.

'I mean, it's not every woman who'd—'

'Are you hungry?' Dee interrupts, 'I can make you something to eat.' She may be tipsy but her antennae are on red alert. Trouble is the last thing she needs this evening.

'I'm not staying. I've got to meet someone.'

I glance at Johnny – there's a curious smile playing round his lips – but he's only got eyes for Carl.

'Meeting up with the lovely Melanie?' he suddenly asks. 'How is she? I haven't seen her for a while.'

My heart plummets. God, what's he playing at?

I feel Carl bristle beside me. 'No, I dumped the little tart.'

My sharp intake of breath must be clearly audible but Johnny, with surprising restraint, simply lifts his brows a fraction.

'And she seemed such a nice girl.' He leans back, his cool grey eyes narrowing to ice. 'Although maybe too high maintenance. Women like Melanie can be very ... demanding. They tend to go elsewhere when their needs aren't adequately provided for.'

Carl opens his mouth and bares his teeth. 'And what the fuck is that supposed to mean?'

Although he knows – along with everyone else – exactly

what it means. The implication is hardly subtle. And no man, no matter how confident, can tolerate *that* kind of slur.

Dee tries to interject again but Johnny talks over her. 'First Gena,' he goads, 'and now Melanie . . .'

'And who was catering to *your* wife's needs when you were banged up?' Carl spits out venomously. 'What makes you such a fucking expert?'

Christ! I flinch, ready for the shit to hit the fan. Any reference to Sarah's fidelity and Johnny's liable to explode. But incredibly he doesn't. Instead, with studied calculation, he turns and stares lasciviously at Dee.

'Oh, I'd never claim to be an expert but – well, I've had my moments.'

As if a bomb has dropped, an ominous silence falls over the room.

Even Jim can't pretend it hasn't happened. His rheumy eyes become bulbous. Understanding that a response is expected, positively demanded, he takes a deep breath and tries to stand up. The attempt is doomed before it's begun. Impeded as he is by his weight and the booze, he gets securely lodged between the chair and the table.

I look away, embarrassed.

Dee grabs his arm and pulls him back down. 'Jim!' And with that single word a message passes between them: *tomorrow we'll have our revenge.*

Carl understands it too. He barks out a laugh, swings his jacket over his shoulder and, with one last evil look at Johnny, stalks out of the room and down the hall.

As the front door bangs, relief shudders through my body.

He's gone. Quickly, I get to my feet and Johnny stands up too. Our eyes meet across the table. What does he think I'm about to do – name and shame, reveal the guilty parties?

'I'm tired. I'm going to have an early night.'

Relieved, he sinks back into his chair.

'Oh, don't go yet. Stay and have a nightcap,' Dee insists, acting as if the scene we just witnessed has never taken place. What she really wants is an opportunity to get me on my own, to find out for certain if Johnny's going to deliver – and how I managed to persuade him.

I give her a smile. 'We'll catch up tomorrow.'

Upstairs, I drag a holdall out of the wardrobe and start packing. Most of my clothes, my computer, my books and CDs, will have to be abandoned. It's a matter of priorities; I can't take everything. In fact, I can hardly take anything. Bouncing a heavy suitcase down the stairs in the middle of the night doesn't even border on the feasible.

While I go through the motions, I try to switch off. As if I'm embarking on a short holiday, I choose only the bare essentials. But I feel almost apologetic towards the articles I reject. I pick them up, hold them once last time, and put them down again. I try to tell myself that one day I'll retrieve them but in my heart I know it isn't true. What I'm leaving now, I'll never see again.

Perhaps it's easier to concentrate on inanimate objects than on real people. If I start thinking about Marc, our marriage, the end of our life together, there's no telling where it may lead. There's already a nasty little lump in my throat. I swallow hard. I have to hang on to the fact that whatever has happened, it would eventually have come to this anyway – in a month, in a year. I could never have stayed with him.

But will I ever be able to forgive him?

I gaze around the living room. I want to let go. More than anything, I want to let go – but surrounding me are too many memories. It's the little things that hurt the most: his mug still sitting on the coffee table, one of his jackets hanging on the peg behind the door, the paper he was reading. Tears prick my eyes. Angrily, I swipe them away. *This is your life*, a tiny voice whispers in my ear. For a moment, I think my knees are going to buckle. The voice comes again, taunting me, tormenting me. I wince but then silence it with a deliberately licentious image of Marc and Kerry Anne. It's enough to halt any further slide into sentimentality.

Zipping up the bag, I slide it behind the sofa. Hopefully Dee won't make a late-night visit but I can't afford to be careless. And that's something, or rather *someone*, else to focus attention on – my conniving, double-dealing bitch of a mother-in-law. If Johnny's doing his job, she'll already be well on her way to drunken oblivion, but that won't stop her crawling up the stairs if she thinks she might extract one last piece of useful information.

I guess that's where Johnny and I differ. *His* hatred's focused directly on Jim, straightforward, simple and absolute, whereas mine keeps shifting, rolling through the family, laying blame wherever it might stick. And that doesn't exclude myself. If I'd been smarter, if I'd done things differently, then maybe . . .

I sink down on the sofa and bury my face in my hands.

Can I really go through with it?

For a moment I think about retrieving my bag, sneaking out through the front door, and taking off. I could jump in the car and turn my back on the whole damn mess. I could be miles away before anyone even notices I'm gone. Why not?

But I know why not: because I'd be taking the easy option, because I'd be landing Johnny right in it. And for all our differences, I'm not prepared to do that. A promise is a promise.

And anyway, he's not the only one with a score to settle. I've been trying to pretend that I'm not the same as him, that I don't have the same instincts – but it's not true. I'm angry too, bitter and resentful. I want to beat my fists against the wall. I've been hurt and I want some retribution.

And Johnny was right – it *is* all to do with love. What Marc loves most, what he's always loved most and valued even above our marriage, is the thrill of the forbidden. On that golden altar he's been prepared to sacrifice everything.

Slowly, I take off my wedding ring and place it on the table.

Chapter Twenty-Six

Johnny

The clock's chiming three when I creep softly down the stairs and slip into the Buckleys' living room. The curtains are still drawn. It's pitch black. And shit, she almost gives me a heart attack as I flash the torch around. Sitting perfectly still, curled in a chair in the corner, she emerges from the shadows like an enemy sniper.

'Simone?'

Slowly, she uncoils.

We agreed to meet at three thirty. I'm early — and she's even earlier. How long has she been waiting here?

Tilting my head, I listen for any sound from the room above. Hopefully, they're both so blitzed they won't wake before morning, but it pays to be cautious. We won't get a second chance. Should I leave the door open or close it? Perhaps best left open, just ajar, in case one of them stirs and wanders down for a glass of water.

She rises and comes to stand beside me. In one hand she

has an empty bag, in the other a scrap of paper. She silently points towards one of the paintings on the wall. Excellent. A couple of minutes and we should be out of here.

I swing back the picture to reveal the safe behind.

'I'm not sure about this,' she whispers.

'What?' Fuck, this is all I need. Her and her bloody conscience.

She's grasping the piece of paper even tighter now. 'It's stealing, though, isn't it?'

'You think it's theft?' I try to keep my voice low and steady. 'Personally, I view it more as compensation. How much do you reckon eighteen years is worth – ten grand, fifty, a hundred? What kind of price would *you* put on it?'

'They haven't got that kind of money.'

'Well, you don't have to worry then, do you?' If we carry on like this we'll be here all night, still debating the issue when Jim and Dee wake up.

She takes another moment to think about it and then, somewhat reluctantly, passes over the numbers. It's a good thing Marc writes everything down – and even better that Simone knows exactly where.

Before she can change her mind again I pass her the torch and get stuck in. The light wavers a little as she shines it on the dial. It doesn't take long. And there's nothing so gratifying as that tiny click of success. Well, perhaps one thing – the sight of a healthy pile of cash.

Bingo!

There must be a hundred grand at least, neatly stacked in bundles of fifties.

Simone gasps. 'Where did that come from?'

I start pouring it into the bag. Still whispering, I reply, 'I believe they've been liquidizing their assets.'

'I don't understand.'

'For that quick getaway to Spain.'

She glares at me. 'You knew this was here, didn't you?'

I shrug. 'Let's call it inspired guesswork.'

Simone's getting cold feet again. She wasn't expecting me to find more than a couple of thousand. She could just about square that with her conscience but this ... this is robbery on a grander scale.

'We can't take all that,' she hisses.

'*We're* not taking it, sweetheart – *I* am. Did I say I was offering to share it?'

Which shuts her up for a couple of seconds. She hops nervously from one foot to another. 'I'm still helping you,' she retorts. 'I've given you the bloody number. What if they call the police?'

I throw the last of the cash into the bag, close the safe, and replace the picture. 'That's not very likely. They've got Carl to think about, remember?'

The mention of his name makes her shiver.

Playing on her fears, I quickly add, 'So, come on. Let's get out of here before the little shit crawls home.'

That gets her moving. We walk on our toes, quickly through to the kitchen. While she sorts out the alarm, I hold the bag to my chest. Lying against my heart, it creates a pleasantly warm sensation. It's hardly a fortune but it'll do. At least for starters. Jim hasn't paid his dues, not by any means, but the rest can wait . . . he won't be going anywhere in a hurry.

In the silence of the night, the low bleep from the alarm sounds as fierce as a siren. I cross my fingers that even if it does penetrate their semi-comatose brains, they'll imagine it's just Carl returning. Straining my ears, I try to discern any hint of movement from above. Was that a creak of floorboards?

I hold my breath.

No, it's just one of those noises that all sleeping houses make, a bricks and mortar equivalent of a snore or a groan.

We slip outside. Simone closes the door with a resounding rattle. Shit! Standing back a step I gaze up at their unlit bedroom window.

All quiet, thank God. No sign of life.

'Sorry,' she whispers.

I put a finger to my lips.

The car's unlocked. I open it on the driver's side, throw the bag on the back seat, release the handbrake, and start to roll it gently along the drive. It's too risky to switch the engine on. Even through deep sleep, that's likely to rouse them. Although, God, the crunch of the tyres against the gravel is hardly peaceful.

Would it be a complete disaster if they discovered us now? Not really. I've already got what I want. We could jump in and be away before they could stop us. But being a few hours ahead of the game is always useful. And anyway, I like the idea of them waking up in the morning, smugly self-confident – and finding us gone. It kind of adds to the magic. She leans against the passenger door and pushes too.

We're making pretty good progress, almost halfway to the gates, when something suddenly springs to mind. I stop and peer across the roof. 'Simone, where's your stuff?' She's either travelling light or she's forgotten it.

She looks up, startled.

'Your things,' I remind her.

And I'm just thinking *Hell, no, we'll have to go back*, when she shakes her head. 'It's okay,' she whispers, 'it's in the boot. I put it there earlier.'

Christ, why is it that women never listen to a word you say? How many times did I tell her – five, ten? Specific instructions not to take any unnecessary risks, not to take any chances, and especially *not* to go hauling suspicious amounts of luggage round the house. We had an arrangement, an agreement. It wasn't that bloody complex was it, not too hard to understand?

'What?' I snap at her. 'What if you'd been caught?'

She snorts. 'Well, I wasn't, was I? You were all so pissed, you wouldn't have noticed if the 10.23 from Liverpool Street had come crashing through the house.'

Which might be true but I'm not about to admit it. 'That's not the point,' I say weakly.

She makes one of those derisive female noises.

Scowling, we put our heads down and start pushing again. Now our silence is dictated more by irritation than necessity. We're far enough from the house to talk freely but we don't exchange a word.

At the end of the drive, we change places. She walks round the bonnet to the driver's seat, and I stroll round the boot to the passenger's. As the electric gates open, she takes one last lingering look in the mirror. What's she thinking? I don't know. Hopefully, that she's well rid, but there's no accounting for the female psyche.

She starts the engine and we exit on to the street. There's not another car in sight. Turning right, she takes our usual route towards the City. I can tell she's itching to put her foot down, to make a quick escape, but instead she stares stolidly at the speedometer, keeping to the requisite 30 mph.

She doesn't ask where I want to go.

And I don't tell her.

We're at the first junction before I realize I've been holding my breath again. God knows what I've been anticipating – perhaps for Dee to run screaming, naked, after us. That's not a pretty thought. But then nor is the prospect of a fleet of flashing blue lights. Although if it came to a confrontation between Dee or the cops, I'd opt for the latter – at least I might stand *some* chance of survival.

I dig out my cigarettes. In a spirit of reconciliation – and relief – I light one and pass it over to her.

'Thanks,' she murmurs.

It's another mile or so before she opens her mouth again. 'I still don't understand where all the money came from.'

'Jim's sold The Palace.' That was one piece of useful information that I picked up on my aimless jaunts around the City. 'Some of it's in the bank but ... well, you know what your husband's like when it comes to creative accounting. Let's just say this was a nest egg the taxman wasn't going to get his hands on.'

'So they won't be completely bankrupt then?'

I sit back and smile. Jim's got a serious load of debt and the house is mortgaged up to the hilt. Hoping he'd soon be on his way to Spain, he's sold the club for a damn sight less than it was worth – and now he's about to find out that he isn't a diamond millionaire after all. Still, no point disturbing Ms Morality's conscience with the details. 'Course not.'

She nods. 'Can I ask you something else?'

'Sure.'

'Speaking hypothetically,' she says, 'what would you have done if the kidnap had been for real?' She pauses. 'I mean, if it had *all* been for real, if you'd actually had the pink diamonds and Marc had really been in danger and . . .'

She stops short, her fingers gripping the wheel.

Now's probably a good time, maybe the smartest time, to lie – especially if I don't want to end spread-eagled on the pavement with a bagful of notes drifting in the wind. But then again, what's the point? I could lie through my teeth but she'd still know it was bullshit.

'Speaking hypothetically,' I reply, 'what do *you* think?'

She frowns while she considers the answer. Her eyes narrow and her mouth slides into that familiar sulky pout. I suspect she's going to produce one of her smart-arse comments – but she doesn't. Instead, she just sighs.

I count my blessings. She asks, 'Can you wind down your window?'

I glance outside. It's the middle of the night. It's freezing and the rain's just started to pour again. 'It's pissing down.'

'Just do it,' she insists.

'What for?'

Simone turns to look at me. 'Because you stink of bloody whisky.' Fuck, sometimes she really gets on my nerves.

Meet Lolly Bruce

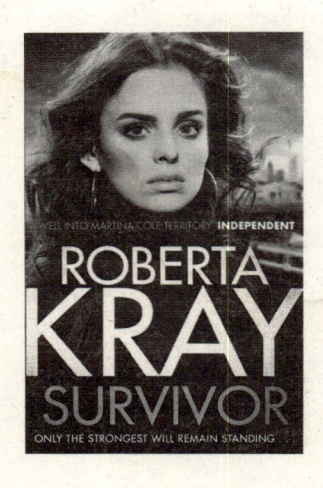

Lolly has always known her mum was different. Sometimes Angela Bruce was ill in a quiet sort of way, but other times she roamed the Mansfield estate shouting about whatever had wormed its way into her head that day. Either way, Lolly was on her own so she learned how to look after herself pretty quickly.

Mal Fury has never got over the disappearance of his daughter all those years ago, but there's still hope because the police never found Kay's body. So when his private investigator turns up a lead that connects Kay to Lolly, Mal needs to find out more. But in doing so, he's delving into a decades-old mystery that could throw Lolly's entire world into chaos and she'll need every ounce of her survival instinct if she's to make it out the other side ...

The Next Instalment

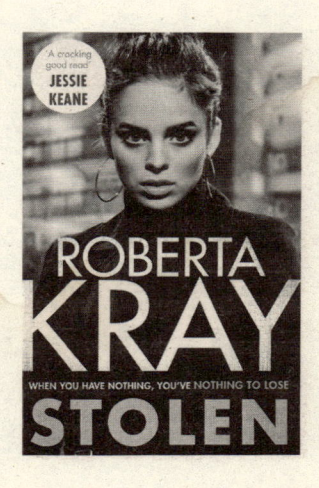

Lolly Bruce spent several years in the lap of luxury, but now she's back in a world she knows: London's East End. Her guardian Mal Fury is doing time, so Lolly is working on the wrong side of the law to get by. She'll need to use all her street smarts to keep her safe in Kellston.

Then one day the Old Bill turn up on her doorstep. Mal is on the run, but why when he has only months left to serve?

Private Investigator Nick Trent knows better than to get involved with the Furys, but his better judgement doesn't count for much when it comes to Lolly. Before he knows it he's agreed to help her track down Mal, and take on whatever the East End underworld throws at them ...

Out November 2019

Meet the Quinns

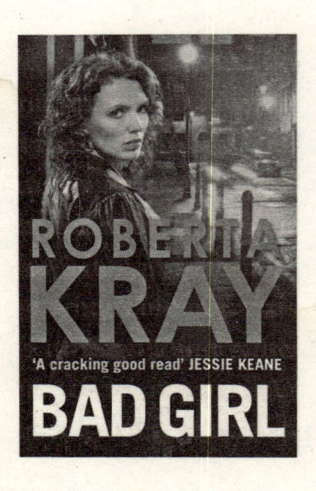

The Quinns are one of the most feared criminal gangs in London's East End.

So the reaction of Joe Quinn to the news that his daughter Lynsey is involved with a policeman is predictable and swift, and a pregnant Lynsey finds herself out on the street, bruised and alone.

At the age of eleven, Lynsey's daughter Helen is returned to the clan. Hated by her grandfather, loved only by her uncle, she struggles to fit into a world she doesn't understand. As warring factions battle for control of the East End, tragedy is about to strike again.

How can Helen survive? And who can she trust when the Quinn family's criminal past comes back to haunt her?

Meet Ava Gold

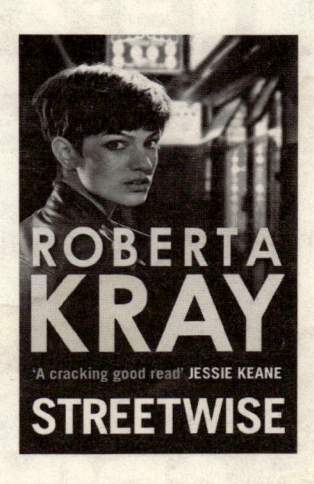

Ava Gold's employment options are rapidly shrinking and, not wanting to go back to driving minicabs, she lands herself a trial run at being nightclub owner Chris Street's personal driver. Chris is one of the men about town in Kellston, East London, and is initially suspicious of having a female driver, but Ava soon proves her worth, and beyond.

Still, working for one of the notorious Streets – who have a past history of violence reaching back to the boom time of the sixties – is never going to be easy. Chris' ex-wife is newly involved with his worst enemy and his younger brother Danny and his crazy girlfriend are up to something that will pull Ava into a world of blackmail, murder, sex and greed …

CRIME AND THRILLER FAN?

CHECK OUT **THECRIMEVAULT.COM**

The online home of exceptional crime fiction

KEEP YOURSELF IN SUSPENSE

Sign up to our newsletter for regular recommendations, competitions and exclusives at **www.thecrimevault.com/conne**

Follow us

@TheCrimeVault

/TheCrimeVault

for all the latest news